# TALES OF THE
# SHADOWMEN
## Volume 12: Carte Blanche

## *also from Black Coat Press*

# TALES OF THE SHADOWMEN

## Volume 12: Carte Blanche

edited by
Jean-Marc & Randy Lofficier

stories by
**Jason Scott Aiken, Matthew Baugh, Adam Mudman Bezecny,
Nicholas Boving, Nathan Cabaniss, Christophe Colin,
Matthew Dennion, Peter Gabbani, Brian Gallagher,
Martin Gately, Travis Hiltz, Rick Lai, Nigel Malcolm,
Jean-Marc Mouiller, Cristofer Nigro, Pierrick Rival,
Frank Schildiner, Sam Shook, Michel Stephan,
Artikel Unbekannt, David L. Vineyard** and **Jared Welch**

translations by
**Michael Shreve**

cover by
**Mike Hoffman**

A Black Coat Press Book

Visit our website at www.blackcoatpress.com

ISBN 978-1-61227-447-8. First Printing. December 2015. Published by Black Coat Press, an imprint of Hollywood Comics.com, LLC, P.O. Box 17270, Encino, CA 91416. All rights reserved. Except for review purposes, no part of this book may be reproduced or transmitted in any form or by any means, electronic or mechanical, including photocopying, recording or by any information storage and retrieval system, without permission in writing from the publisher. The stories and characters depicted in this anthology are entirely fictional. Printed in the United States of America.

# Table of Contents

*As faithful readers of* Tales of the Shadowmen *know, Doctor Francis Ardan is a proto-Doc Savage character created by French author Guy d'Armen in 1928. A new book featuring two more of his exploits is scheduled to be published by Black Coat Press in early 2016:* The Troglodytes of Mount Everest & The Giants of Black Lake. *As for* The People of the Pole, *it is a remarkable 1907 proto-*Lost World *novel by Charles Derennes, translated by Brian Stableford, also available from Black Coat Press, ISBN 978-1-934543-39-9. In the story that follows, one of our newest contributors, Jason Aiken, decides to send Doc Ardan looking for that mysterious race of intelligent reptiles...*

## Jason Scott Aiken: *Ardan at the Pole*

*January 3, 1928, Baltimore, MD*

This afternoon, I had lunch at the Baltimore Gun Club in the company of Mr. Hareton Ironcastle. A naturalist and renowned explorer, he had sponsored my membership into the club several years ago. Although, Michel Ardan (a distant relative of mine) has his picture placed prominently on the wall of the establishment, this connection didn't guarantee my admission to this selective group. Ironcastle's heartfelt recommendation, along with my military record and scientific background were vital in acquiring membership.

Ironcastle, a good friend of my father, related tales from some of their adventures to me. He was able to fill in some gaps about my father's life that I hadn't been aware of. Mr. Ironcastle was also interested in my days as a pilot in the Great War. He seemed fascinated with aviation in particular.

When he asked about the possibility of Arctic flight, I raised my eyebrows. Knowing I was onto his leading questions, he produced a rugged, well-traveled satchel from beneath his chair. The veteran explorer reached in and withdrew a manuscript, then placed it on the table for me to examine. I judged it to be an older document, close to 20 years old. The text was in French, but for the sake of ease, I will list the English translation here.

*The People of the Pole*
*Written by Jean-Louis de Venasque*
*Transcribed by Charles Derennes*
*Completed November 25, 1906*

I looked at Ironcastle inquisitively. Over the years, I had heard rumblings of the de Venasque manuscript, but up to this point, I had never met anyone who had seen it, let alone owned an actual copy of the document. I inquired if this was in fact the original document. Ironcastle stated it wasn't the original, but the one and only copy of Derennes' transcription of de Venasque's original document. This was Derennes' own copy, and he never produced another.

According to Ironcastle, the original de Venasque manuscript was in the private collection of the anthropologist who discovered it, Louis Valenton. He is a professor at the College de France. The manuscript was found in a petrol canister by Valenton while on the Yalmal Peninsula, near the mouth of the Ob. It was Valenton who allowed Derennes to make a copy.

Valenton and Ironcastle were old acquaintances. At some point, three years ago, Derennes sent the copy to Valenton unexpectedly, instructing him to find a proper home for the document. Valenton had no need to have the original manuscript and the copy. He also wanted to follow through on friend's wishes. This led to him sending the manuscript to Ironcastle.

Ironcastle asked if I would read it and provide an opinion on the veracity of Jean-Louis de Venasque's account. He didn't have to ask me twice, for my curiosity was piqued. He excused himself from the table to allow me time to read the document.

Although the account was quite lengthy, my skill at speed reading allows me to read, and comprehend, written documents in a quarter of the time as the average person. The contents were engrossing, and I found myself rapidly turning the pages. I will summarize the account of de Venasque below for a frame of reference.

On April 26, 1905, Jean-Louis de Venasque, a French nobleman, and his acquaintance, Jacques Ceintras, an engineer, departed in their dirigible from Franz-Josef Land in an attempt to reach the North Pole. The pair piloted the vessel across the frozen plain until they reached a violet-lit area that is the North Pole, complete with flora and fauna. They found miniature pterodactyls and a race of intelligent humanoid iguanodons that lived in a subterranean realm beneath the pole.

The mental state of both men seems to deteriorate over time. Ceintras went mad and eventually killed a number of the iguanodons after they prevented the pair from leaving in their dirigible. This was thanks to a type of magnetic locking mechanism the creatures employed, which anchored the aircraft to the ground. Eventually, Ceintras and Venasque parted company. Ceintras chose to walk across the frozen plain to certain death. Venasque stayed at the pole and chronicled what transpired. He placed his manuscript in a petrol canister and threw it into the nearby river, hoping it would make its way out to sea.

Once I finished reading the manuscript, I sat at the table in silence for fifteen minutes. There have been a handful of explorers who have claimed to reach the North Pole since de Venasque and Ceintras attempted the feat. The claims of these explorers remain questionable to this day, but none claimed to have seen the fantastic sights de Venasque described. The situation with the de Venasque account was quite unusual. I had to admit to being a bit skeptical of the source,

Valenton. If the claims were true about the iguanodons, the manuscript would support Valenton's own theories, which weren't widely accepted by the scientific community.

In 1906, after returning from an expedition in northern Asia, Valenton brought back the bones of a previously undiscovered creature. He dubbed it the *anthroposaurus*. He postulated it was an amphibious reptile that possessed both intelligence and reason. Valenton believed the anthroposaurus to be a contemporary of the first humans. He conceded the species was now extinct, but perhaps some had survived and evolved. If true, the iguanadons mentioned in de Venasque's manuscript could be the descendants of Valenton's anthroposaurus.

I can't say my doubts ended at Valenton. The writings of de Venasque himself were also a bit troubling. Even when taking into account that he was writing these documents in complete human isolation, expecting to perish in the coming days, there was something not quite right regarding his demeanor. This account might very well have been an elaborate fantasy written by a psychotic who murdered his friend, and attempted to justify it by creating his own warped reality. The violet light, iguanadons, the miniature pterodactyls, and underground realm may all have been fictitious. The two explorers didn't have the friendliest of relationships to begin with. Perhaps their dirigible suffered a catastrophic failure and they became stranded at the North Pole. The animosity between them may have risen to the surface, and a life was taken as a result.

Yet, if this was the work of a madman, it was very well constructed and full of some interesting concepts. Especially when one considered when it was written. It was too bad de Venasque hadn't made it back to civilization. Had he returned to France, he would have had a future as a fiction writer.

When Ironcastle returned I related the above conclusions to him. He listened intently, but didn't show any emotion until I stated my final thought on the matter. The only way to verify the account would be if someone journeyed to the North Pole to investigate. Ironcastle smiled and nodded in approval. He asked me if that was my way of volunteering. I paused for a moment, and stated that it was. Ironcastle was pleased; he proclaimed he had reason to believe portions of de Venasque's account. I asked him to enlighten me, but he looked around the room and shook his head. He then told me it wasn't the time or the place to discuss such things.

Ironcastle and I left the Gun Club together. He wished me luck and instructed me to reach out to him should I need anything. I began planning once I got back to my lodgings, which my cousin and his bride have allowed me to use while in Baltimore. I'll be leaving tomorrow morning to gather resources and begin planning the expedition.

*March 12, 1928, Kabarova, Russia*

I have spent the last two weeks in this small Samoyed village situated south of the Jugor Straight, near the entrance to the Kara Sea. This is the same village where de Venasque and Ceintras prepared for their voyage in their dirigible. All inquiries made around the village support their presence here in 1905. Some of the villagers who were children, or young adults, remembered the pair very well. From the descriptions of the villagers, I was able to sketch the appearances of the two and have the townsfolk confirm my accuracy.

Tracking down the lover of Ceintras proved to be quite easy. I spoke with her... and her son who is now 23 years-old. She accepted the fate of Ceintras long ago, but in private, she asked me to bring back his body, if there was one to be found. I made no inquiries on the parentage of her son, as it was simple to deduce.

My means of travel will be a Boeing Model 40 A. It's one of only twenty-five built. I'm making some customizations to the engines and frame to allow for better performance in cold temperatures. The craft must also be modified to allow for additional fuel. Luckily, compartment space is plenty. If need be, I can easily fit a passenger in the cargo hold with my equipment.

Preparations are going splendidly. I hope to have the modifications completed in the next few days, followed by a test flight by the end of the week. If successful, the aircraft will then be transported by ship to the southern tip of Franz Josef Land, just as de Venasque and Ceintras transported their dirigible. My cousin has graciously lent me the use of his ship, the *Faucon Occidental* for transportation.

### March 16, 1928, Franz Josef Land, Russia

The test flight was a success. I arrived this morning in Franz Josef Land aboard the *Faucon Occidental*. Camp was set up. All preparations are set for a sunrise flight tomorrow morning. My plan is to spend the rest of the night in my mind palace in preparation. If all goes according to plan, my next journal entry will be from the North Pole. For purposes of record-keeping, I will use a chronometer of my own design to keep track of the time, and day while at the pole.

### March 17, 1928, The North Pole

Although the area surrounding the pole is in total darkness this time of year (with the sun due to rise in the next few days), I was guided to this spot by an orange light on the surface. Upon landing, I observed the obvious lack of violet light, as well as any plant or animal. The ground was a solid sheet of ice, with no sign of any river or stream. The source of the orange light I observed from above was a small signal fire. I quickly unpacked my supplies and set up a tent for shelter. I plan to use this as my base of operations while investigating the surrounding area. I'm going to take refuge from the cold and attempt to get some rest before exploring the area further.

*March 18, 1928, The North Pole*

I woke feeling refreshed and eager to begin my investigation. After eating my morning rations, I returned to the fire. Utilizing the flames, I ignited a torch. Around the blaze I observed a path of well defined footprints that led to the fire. The footprints then circled around the fire, and disappeared back into the darkness. The tracks made a large horseshoe shape. Judging by the depth and rendering, the same person must have been walking over their own footprints for some time.

The below zero temperatures at the pole required me to bring some prototypes I recently completed. I'm particularly proud of the undergarments that prevent my body heat from escaping. Pair these with the heat packets I inserted in my boots and gloves, and I was able to stay out in the open for hours at a time. I've been letting my hair and facial hair grow since leaving for Russia, and it has come in very thick. Every little bit helps. I donned a pair of pilot goggles as well. After checking my handset to ensure the tracking device on the plane was functioning, I pursued my investigation of the footprints.

I walked parallel to the trail for ten minutes before my vision started to blur. After approximately two more minutes, I began to lose my equilibrium. My knees buckled, forcing me to stop my trek. I closed my eyes and concentrated on my breathing, taking an internal diagnostic. Before I could complete a hypothesis, the sensation faded. My vision cleared and I was no longer off balance. I decided to continue following the trail, when I noticed the footprints were no longer visible. After circling the area, I was unable to find any sign of the tracks. The only footprints I could locate were my own. Not only that, but I noticed I felt a bit winded, as though I was at a higher altitude than before.

An examination of the horizon revealed I was on a plateau between two mountain peaks. This shouldn't have been possible. I posited that I may have blacked out during my trek and somehow ended up there, thanks to my prodigious physical abilities. Even for me, that situation seemed remote. I consulted my hand-held tracking device, but the screen gave no indication of my aircraft's presence. The device was functioning, as the dot indicating my position was active, but there was no sign of my plane.

When modern technology fails me, I'm always open to more archaic methods. So I looked to the stars. I had studied the arctic sky upon landing the night before. Gifted with an eidetic memory, I can assure you the sky I was observing was no longer the same sky. Even the Pole Star, Polaris, proved difficult to identify, as it was out of position.

With both technological and archaic means of navigation failing me, I chose to attempt to retrace my footsteps. I turned around and began trekking back in the opposite direction. Continuing on the same course away from my shelter and means of egress would have been most unwise, regardless of how far away I actually was.

As I turned back, I noticed movements in my peripheral vision. I was being flanked on both sides.

I had just enough time to pivot and execute a *baritsu* technique on the assailant on my right, which flung him into the attacker on my left. Both fell to the ground on impact. The two tripped over each other trying to get back their footing.

They growled at each other in their disorientation. Clearly, these beings had never encountered the martial arts before. Their confusion was to my benefit, as it provided me time to study their appearance. I also gave some ground to put some distance between us, as to better observe them.

They weren't human. Well, they weren't *homo sapiens*, that much was obvious. Their faces resembled Neanderthals'. They snarled and made gestures at me. I would describe their skin pigment as yellow, and they had thick black manes. The beings wore white animal skins, presumably of the polar bear. They were squat, approximately 5'4" in height, but they were stocky. They were especially broad in the shoulders. These were powerful-looking creatures. Judging by their heads and hands, they had large skeletal structures as well.

As I prepared for their attack, two more creatures appeared behind them. Then two more behind those. The initial two creatures I encountered had their blood up and this worked up the other four into a frenzy as well. It's my belief that they were verbally communicating with each other. They kept staring at me with what I can only describe as murderous intent. Finally, they reached beneath their cloaks and produced daggers made of bone.

It was my estimation that I was capable of snapping their necks or backs with my bare hands on an individual basis. However, this would be a difficult task when fighting them simultaneously. It was evident if all six were to rush me at once, there would be little I could do. Even a smoke pellet from my vest would only delay the inevitable. I was outnumbered six to one on an icy plateau with no escape. Coming to the conclusion that I was faced with a fatal outcome, no matter the situation in hand to hand combat, I decided to engage them with a weapon.

I reached into my belt and drew my dagger, the God Slayer. This is an ancient blade I discovered on an archaeological expedition in the Caspian Sea. The name is derived from the scrolls found cached with the blade, which claimed it once slew a deity. The blade was razor sharp and made of an alloy that I haven't been able to identify. I had little doubt in its capabilities to sever the thick muscle and bone of these creatures.

If the creatures had attacked first, I wouldn't have been able to defeat their superior numbers, so I took the initiative and launched myself at the first two creatures. Gripping the blade with a backhanded grip, I made a single arching cut across the throat of one creature, severing his jugular. I grabbed the second creature by his mane and drove the blade through his forehead and twisted for good measure.

Two others came at me, but they attacked head-on and I had the advantage of a longer reach. I kicked one squarely in the face to buy some time. Then I spun behind his partner and attempted to sever his spinal cord at the base of the neck. I did cut him, but evidently not deep enough. The creature attempted to get back to his feet, but I stabbed down and embedded the dagger in the top of his skull. Expecting attacks from the final two, I spun around and prepared to defend or attack. But the final two weren't attacking. As a matter of fact, they were giving me some ground. I was about to back away and go about my business when I discovered the reason for their hesitation.

Out of the darkness walked even more creatures. A quick count put their numbers at roughly a hundred. These creatures were garbed in thicker animal hides, and all carried spears. It was apparent I had only met the forward scouts of this larger army. The remaining two scouts eyed me with sinister intent. The joy was apparent on their cruel faces. The situation looked grim until the scout closest to me looked puzzled and began sniffing the air. He looked to his right, pointed and yelled in alarm.

In the direction he pointed was a large group of warriors, their bronze armor and swords gleaming in the moonlight. I counted their number to be at sixty. They didn't have the superior numbers, but this didn't seem to faze them. Their leader shouted: "*Lomar rus!*" as he led the charge into the fray.

It was an epic and savage battle, with both sides rending flesh and bone all around them. As much of a spectacle as it was, I didn't think it would be wise to be around to answer to whomever the victors might be. I retreated and took the opportunity to quickly rehydrate and consume some rations. Then I made my ultimate exit from the scene.

I approximated the direction where my aircraft was supposed to be to the best of my ability, and began running in that direction. I needed to get away quickly, but didn't want to burn excess calories due to my situation. My rations were limited. So I jogged lightly, and went into a wolf trot once I felt I was far enough away from the battle. According to my chronometer, I wolf-trotted for a half hour. The peak I was running toward didn't seem to be getting any closer. I continued my pace until I became overcome with disorientation once again. Closing my eyes and focusing on my breathing got me through the episode once more.

When I opened my eyes, it was to a violet-lit sky. I wasn't standing on ice any longer, but grass. A feeling of warmth came over me. Twenty yards in front of me was a flowing stream. I was now at the very place described by de Venasque. Seeing the stream, I knew the dirigible and entrance to the underground tunnels must be nearby. I crossed the stream and made my way over a small hill. On the other side was the dirigible, still anchored to the surface. I crouched down and produced a pair of binoculars, then scanned the area.

I saw no signs of movement at first, but I did spot the door to the tunnels described by de Venasque. I remained in a crouched position at this location for several minutes before venturing down to the dirigible.

On my way down, I observed footprints both human and non-human. The human footprints were consistent and appeared to belong to the same person. While the non-human footprints were inconsistent and seemed to belong to different individuals. Before approaching the dirigible, I buried the God Slayer. If the magnetic clamps were still active beneath the vessel, I didn't want to have my dagger pinned to the surface as well. As I rounded the base of the dirigible, I noticed a small campfire that was still burning. The remains of a small fowl-like creature were still on the spit roast.

I proceeded to enter the dirigible by knocking on the cabin door, but no answer was given. I entered and saw the reason why: there was a man on the floor curled into the fetal position. I crouched down and examined him. He was a little bit older, but it was without a doubt de Venasque. However, he didn't look nearly as aged as I expected him to. My diagnosis was he was suffering from malnutrition from a lack of a balanced diet. From the scraps around the room, it appeared his only source of nourishment was from meat of the fowl-like creatures. I felt his abdomen and it was rock hard as well. I deduced he must be having difficulty passing stool, causing him added discomfort.

I undressed out of my heavy arctic garb and unpacked the supplies. My first order of business was to get some nutrients in his system. I administered an IV solution mixed with ingredients from my first-aid kit. I also performed an enema to help him with his abdominal discomfort. While he didn't awaken for nearly three hours, his bowels did vacate multiple times. I observed the look of discomfort on his face disappear. The man was a bit confused when he first woke up, but this was eclipsed by his joy at how much better he was feeling. He thanked me for my help and introduced himself as Jean-Louis de Venasque. I shook his hand and introduced myself, before he drifted back off to sleep.

To say this has been a busy day for me is an understatement. According to my chronometer, it's now 22:00. I can't begin to understand the events of today, but hopefully tomorrow will bring some answers. I'm going to refill Venasque's IV bag and get some rest myself.

*March 19, 1928, The North Pole*

After awakening at 07:00, I checked on de Venasque. Upon measuring his pulse, he jolted upright. Not used to having anyone touch him for quite some time, this startled him out of a dead sleep. He then remembered the situation and my name. I explained to him how I came to be there and what I had discovered since arriving at the North Pole. I explained the periods of disorientation to de Venasque and he stated it started happening to him as well. De Venasque proved to be quite sound of mind despite my earlier conclusions drawn from his manuscript. He appeared to have overcome the mental stress inflicted upon him.

De Venasque indicated he has been the one lighting the signal fire, and if I had followed his footprints exactly, I would have reached his location much sooner. Apparently, the North Pole is in a state of flux due to the Earth's magnetic field surrounding it. This has caused a strange phenomenon to develop. De Venasque calls them "invisible doors," but I believe they are rifts in space and time.

When one travels through them, they visit the North Pole, but not necessarily the native North Pole of their own time or dimension. It's just a theory and I have no way to prove it, but, "once you eliminate the impossible, whatever remains, no matter how improbable, must be the truth".

The Great Detective's logic is ever sound, and proved quite reassuring. Especially in the face of what could be considered a supernatural event.

I indicated to de Venasque, that if he could lead me back to the signal fire, I had an aircraft ready. I told him I was willingly to fly him and Ceintras back to Russia, or anywhere else they would like to go. The mention of Ceintras' name caused a frown on de Venasque's face. He relayed that he hadn't seen Ceintras since he left the camp of his own will. De Venasque told me he kept track of the days by when he fell asleep. However, once he became ill, his sleeping habits became too erratic to be accurate. By his estimation, five years had passed, possibly more (which again tells me there is a peculiar distortion surrounding the North Pole). De Venasque stated Ceintras was surely dead by now. He explained he had only managed to survive by consuming the miniature pterodactyls and their eggs. His only source of water came from the stream.

When I asked him about the iguanadons, a look of fear washed over his face. According to him, when Ceintras committed his act of murder, it was like a ripple in a pond. Ceintras introduced the concept of murder into their culture, and they haven't been the same since. Although they still allowed de Venasque to live on the surface, the iguanodons would attack him if he entered or approached the tunnel. I asked him if he had had any luck with the magnetic clamps, but he said he gave up finding a solution some time back. He told me the door to this dimension he and Ceintras accessed in the air would be very difficult to find now anyway. He suggested we both leave on foot via the ground "door" which he used to keep the signal fire lit.

I agreed, but didn't wish to leave right away. After traveling all this way, I intended to visit the underground tunnels and observe the iguanodons. We left the dirigible, and I retrieved the God Slayer. De Venasque walked me to the rift he used to return to our native pole, and I instructed him to wait there for my return. I couldn't enter the tunnels without a disguise, so I made use of iguanodon skins de Venasque had in his possession, as well as a fresh iguanodon corpse found near the stream. The corpse had its throat torn out, but it could still be made into a suitable mask. De Venasque indicated this type of martial combat was becoming more and more common among the People of the Pole.

Once completed and donned, I asked de Venasque for his opinion. He gave me high marks, but stated I would most likely be the largest iguanodon in the tunnels, and would be sure to stick out. This was especially true if they happened to look down at my legs and feet. I decided to go forward with my plan despite the dangers. My examinations of the iguanodon corpse led me to believe the creatures didn't seem to be very physically imposing. But clearly their teeth and claws could be deadly. Before leaving, I had de Venasque sketch me a map of the tunnels so I could better navigate them.

I parted ways from de Venasque and trekked back towards the dirigible. The entrance to the subterranean realm was an iron door nearby. Although the door was heavy, I opened it with relative ease. I shut it behind me, and made sure to test it still opened before descending into the tunnel. Feeling no danger of being trapped from within, I allowed my eyes to adjust to the darkness and followed the tunnel down into the earth.

I can confirm everything de Venasque reported in his account as accurate. While cautiously making my way through the underground labyrinth, I observed the machine which supplied the violet light, as well as the rookery. The map de Venasque provided proved to be no longer complete, as the iguanadons have continued tunneling deeper into the earth since his last visit. I cautiously proceeded, deeper than de Venasque ever ventured.

The People of the Pole have been busy. I traveled for nearly ten minutes before discovering a side cavern they had hollowed out. I entered and lit a small torch. A hideous figure met my gaze in the form of an idol resting on an altar in the middle of the room. It was a grotesque toad-like figure with a rounded belly and a haunting smile. De Venasque's original account made no mention of any deities worshiped by the iguanodons. However, judging by the craftsmanship, it couldn't have been made at the hands of the iguanodons. I have to conclude that they found the statue while tunneling. What ancient civilization worshiped this creature as their deity I don't know, but I intend to look into it.

I attempted to move closer for a better look, but I was interrupted when one of the iguanodons entered. I did my best to avoid conflict, but I was unsuccessful. As I tried to slip out past him, the creature noticed my lower body and began to scream. It then snapped at me with its teeth. I swayed back to avoid the bite, then clasped its jaws in my hands. It was unable to open its mouth further, but it was already successful in raising an alarm. The sounds of more creatures approaching could be heard echoing from further down the tunnel. It was apparent I needed to make an expedient exit. I snapped the neck of the creature, and removed my disguise so I could run at full speed. Not having the disguise on also let me use the God Slayer freely.

The creatures never caught me from behind. I had a large enough head start on their pursuit, but I did run into many creatures (literally) on my way through their community. Most I knocked over without incident, but I did have to use the knife on a few who aggressively charged me. I made short work of them, and I escaped back to the surface without any trouble. Once on the surface, I ran to where de Venasque was waiting for me and we entered the rift back to our native dimension.

De Venasque said we shouldn't worry about being followed, as the iguanadons never venture anywhere close to the rift.

Tonight, we will spend the night in my tent before embarking on our return flight to Franz-Josef Land in the morning.

*March 21, 1928, Kabarova, Russia*

It's been an interesting two days. De Venasque and myself have returned to Kabarova for the time being. I plan on returning to New York City tomorrow morning, but I have much to do before my departure. I have written a private account detailing the expedition that I will personally deliver to Hareton Ironcastle once I reach the United States. I have asked for him to keep all of my findings confidential for the time being, and I'm sure he'll agree.

Also, I have decided to keep the personnel I contracted for this expedition in my private employ, and I've hired de Venasque to oversee them. The North Pole is a mysterious place (one must wonder if the South Pole has similar phenomena surrounding it, but that's a question for another day). As unusual as it may be, I believe the pole would make a great location for private reflection. I plan to have de Venasque and the workers construct a base of operations for me near the pole, outside of the area of the anomaly.

I will spend my final night in Kabarova sketching out the design of the base in solitude.

*Dedicated to the late, great Philip José Farmer and the members of The New Wold Newton Meteoritics Society who paved the way.* **The author would like to give special recognition to Rick Lai. Rick first postulated that Doc constructed his retreat after saving arctic explorers several years prior to the author independently conceiving this story.**

*Matthew Baugh plucked the two rogues, the Duke and the King, from Mark Twain's* Huckleberry Finn *and wondered what might have happened if they had ever met a bunch of characters with even more incredible stories to share. Enter Doctor Omega, and the West will never be the same again...*

## Matthew Baugh: *The Lament of the Duke and the King*

*Alabama, May 26, 1846*

"Hurry!" the Duke of Bridgewater shouted, holding out his hand.

The King of France was breathing too hard to reply. His arms and legs pumped as he struggled to catch the slowly-moving train.

"They're going to catch you," the Duke yelled, as the mob of angry towns-people surged after his friend.

His words seemed to prompt the King to greater speed. The older man gained ground, then gave one great lunge. The Duke caught his hand and hauled him up until his feet were safely on the train coupling. As the King huffed and wheezed, the Duke leaned out again.

As the train picked up speed, their pursuers we're left behind. Only a few of the younger men still struggled to keep pace.

"You rubes!" the Duke yelled, waving his fist. "You dumb yokels!"

As even the most determined runners gave up, the King recovered his breath enough to start laughing. The Duke joined him, and the two threw their arms around each other. After a while, they stopped. The King leaned back against the car, and stroked his long white whiskers, while the Duke studied the train cars they were in-between.

"Ungrateful wretches," the King said. "Still, it's like the good book says, *when a town don't receive the blessings you offer, you need to wipe the dust off your feet, and head out.*"

"Maybe the next town will be more appreciative," the Duke said.

"Maybe," the King replied. "In the meantime, I'd like to find a spot on this train where I could sit down and relax. My old bones are sore after the chase them folks give us." He thumped a knuckle against the car he was leaning against. "Reckon we can get inside here?"

"I'm thinking that's the mail car," the Duke said. "It'll be locked up tighter than anything else on this train."

"Mail car?" The King's eyes lit up. "They sometimes carry a fair piece of money on those."

"Are you crazy?" the Duke said. "It ain't possible to rob a moving train. Least of ways, nobody's ever figured out how."

18

"How about the other car, then?" the King asked.

The Duke tried the door, which proved to be unlocked. The car was empty, except for a number of suitcases and trunks. The King's eyes lit again as he looked them over.

"This is perfect," he said, grinning and stroking his beard.

"What are you talking about?" the Duke asked. "We can't stay here. The porter will see us when he makes his rounds."

"Ah, Bilgewater," the King replied. "That lack of imagination is probably why you ain't higher in the aristocracy. Come on and help me open some of these.

A short time later, the Duke and the King, dressed in more respectable, but poor-fitting clothing, sauntered into the dining-car. The tables were full, except one at the far end, where two empty chairs sat next to an elderly man and a dark-haired young woman.

The pair sauntered to them with an air of perfect confidence.

"Your pardon, sir," the King said. "Could my friend and I join you?"

"Of course, of course," the man said. "I am Doctor Omega, and this is my companion, Miki."

"A pleasure," the Duke said, taking a chair. "I am..." He stopped abruptly as the King trod on his toe.

"I apologize for the rudeness, but my friend and I are traveling incognitiously."

"Ah!" The Doctor's eyes sparkled with curiosity. "Well, I have had to go incognito a few times myself. We shall respect your privacy, gentlemen."

The Duke studied the pair for a moment. The white-haired gentleman was well past sixty, though he had the erect posture of a school-master. He was dressed in a black frock-coat. His companion was petite, in her late teens, and pretty, in an exotic way.

"I perceive you must have been a missionary, Doctor," the Duke said. "I assume this girl must be one of your converts from among the heathen Chinee?"

"My friend and I have also made it a part of our work to spread the good word in our travels," added the King.

"Heavens, no!" the Doctor exclaimed. "I am a man of science, not a preacher."

"And I am not Chinese, or a convert," the girl said. "I am the Doctor's assistant, and I am from Japan."

"Ah," the Duke said, trying to sound thoughtful. "Then you're still a heathen? No offense meant, of course."

"Doctor!" Miki complained.

"Tut, tut, my dear," replied the older man. "Remember where we are. We must make allowances."

"What do you... ow!"

The Duke glanced over at the King, who had stamped on his toe. Standing over them was a stern-looking conductor.

"Your tickets, gentlemen," he asked.

"Our tickets?" the Duke said, forcing indignation into his voice.

"They've already been checked," the King added. "Don't you people even talk to each other?"

"Our tickets are in our car!" the Duke said. "It's very inconvenient of you to interrupt us during our dinner for this."

"You know what I think?" the conductor asked. "I think you and your friend are a pair of no-good tramps with no tickets at all and that you're trying to bum a meal off a paying passenger."

"Excuse me," Doctor Omega said, taking a wallet out of his coat. "If it's a matter of tickets, it should be simple to resolve. How much for these two gentlemen?"

"That's not good idea, sir. I don't think..."

"Yes?" The Doctor's tone was that of a stern teacher to a particularly backwards student. "Young man, I suspect I have at least one academic degree for every year you have been alive. I can assure you that, if I feel the need to have someone do my thinking for me, I will let you know. Ah!" He pulled a coin from his wallet. "I don't seem to have any local currency, but I trust this will do."

The conductor's eyes widened. He raised the coin and bit it, then his mouth fell open. "Solid gold!" he whispered.

"It's a sixteen harzmo piece," the Doctor said. "Odd denomination, I know, but the Hynerians use a base four counting system. They have only four digits on each hand, you see. I trust that's sufficient for two tickets."

"Yes, sir," the conductor said. "Um...gentlemen, I hope you enjoy the trip."

As the conductor hurried away, the Duke exchanged a glance with the King. He could tell that his companion had had the same thought he did. This odd doctor was an opportunity made in Heaven!

"Gentlemen, please have a seat," Doctor Omega said. "It may be a little tight when our other companion rejoins us, but you are welcome."

"We are deeply grateful for your kindness," the King said as the little group took their seats on two comfortable benches, facing each other.

"Deeply grateful," the Duke echoed.

"Indeed, it is good to find friends—let alone friends of quality—seeing how far our fortunes have fallen," continued the King.

"Fortunes?" Miki inquired, her eyes wide.

"Indeed," the King replied. "The two of us should be at the very pinochle of society, but we has fallen on hard times."

"It is a sorrowful affair," the Duke agreed.

"You wouldn't know it to look at him," said the King, "but my friend here is the hare to one of the most exempted titles of England. He is the rightful Duke of Bilgewater!"

"Is that right?" the Doctor said, raising his eyebrows and smiling.

"It is," the Duke replied, "though it should be pernounced Bridgewater."

"Ah!" the Doctor said.

"And my friend's perigee is even higher than mine," the Duke continued. "He is the long-lost Dolphin of France."

"Excuse me," Miki said. "I thought the Dauphin was executed in Paris during the Reign of Terror."

"That is the common story the Revolutionists spread, but it ain't the truth," the King said. "The truth is that I was rescued by..."

At that moment, the door opened and a tall man stood framed in the opening. He wore a long, military-style coat and a wide-brimmed officer's hat that obscured his features. He kept his hands in his pockets, but the Duke could see his feet, which were clad in some sort of articulated metal boots, like a knight's armor. His face, or at least what the Duke could see of it, was partly covered by a metal mask with a gleaming, red glass eye. Every now and then, a puff of steam would emerge from his coat, along with the smell of oil.

"Come in, General," the Doctor said, smiling. "Allow me to present our guests, the Duke of Bridgewater and the Dauphin of France."

The General closed the door behind him but continued to stand.

"The Dauphin?" he repeated.

"I am indeed Looey the Seventeen," the King said.

"But the Dauphin died in 1795."

"That's what *I* said," Miki said.

"One should be careful what one reads in history books, they're always changing," interjected the Doctor, his eyes twinkling with amusement.

"But I was there," the General said. "In France, I mean. I had come to help the people who were being oppressed by the aristocrats, and stayed to help the aristocrats when the people began to execute them."

The Duke raised his eyebrows at this, for the General—what could be seen of him—didn't look old enough to have been there. The King, in the meanwhile, continued as if no one else had spoken.

"Well, as you might know, I'd been cooped up in the Temple Tower with my Mam, but, after they kilt my Pap, Looey the Sixteen, they decided to take me out of there. It weren't all bad, though. They stuck me with a shoemaker named Simon and his wife, and they was decent enough folks. There was also a nice lady, name of LaFreeze, or LaForce, or something like that, who used to visit."

"Madame LaFarge?" Omega asked, his eyebrows raised very high.

"That was it! She was always knitting—said it was sumthin' special, just for me. Alas, sumthin' happened to her afore she could finish. Anyways, whilst

Simon and his wife was giving me a 'publican education, the Knight of Moulin-Rouge came and tried to rescue my Mam."

"Maison-Rouge," the Doctor said.

"Pardon?"

"I believe you're referring to the Chevalier de Maison-Rouge."

"I am indeedy!" the King said. "Anyways, old Mason-Rouge's scheme failed and they caught him and chopped off his head, along with the heads of his whole gang. They kilt my Mam, too, and then stuck me back in the Temple.

"I was alone and bereft of family and friends. Fortunately, there was a man named La Salle what had been hired to paint a portrait of me. Turned out he was really an agent of the Baron of Bats, and had been sent to rescue me and replace me with a lookalike."

"Mmmm," the Doctor said. "I do remember the Baron de Batz. He was a cunning and ruthless plotter."

The Duke was surprised to hear that the Doctor too, claimed to have been a witness to the Revolution, but the King seemed to take no notice.

"La Salle did a nice job sneaking me out," he continued, "but I fell into the Seine and he thought I'd drowned. Fortunately, another of Baron of Bats's pals was on hand to jump in and fish me out. He was an athletic feller, name of Moreau."

"Moreau!" the General exclaimed. "The Doctor and I have met him. It was I who incited his animal people to revolt."

"It's a different Moreau, General," the Doctor said. "André-Louis Moreau was a jack of all trades: swordsman, legislator, playwright, and actor. He is best known for his portrayal of Scaramouche."

"Of course!" Miki said, clapping her hands. "He was in that play we saw in Paris in 1791, wasn't he, Doctor?"

"Indeed, my dear; *Don Juan Triumphant.*"

"He was excellent, and Marguerite St. Just was so lovely," she said. "But the play wasn't very well written, I'm afraid."

The Duke shook his head. Surely this girl—who looked no more than seventeen—wasn't claiming she had been alive back then too, was she?

"It is better as an opera," the Doctor replied. "That is, it will be better as an opera; but we are getting off the track. Please continue, your majesty."

"Where was I?" the King said. "Ah! Well, Bats was working with the Moron-Rouge, or the Scarlet Pimpernel, as the English called him..."

"A great man!" the General said. "Though I believe it is *Mouron Rouge.* I wish I could have worked with him, or even known who he was."

"We Bridgewaters were a part of the Pimpernel's circle," the Duke said. "I suppose, after all this time, it's all right to tell you that he was really the Prince-Regent's butler, Mr. Edmund Blackadder."

"I would not have guessed that," the General said. "I'd have guessed he was Sir Per—"

"Tut, tut," the Doctor said. "We're getting off-topic again. Please tell us, did the Pimpernel get you out of France?"

"Sort of," the King said. "Bats and the Pimpernel had a falling out and Bats turned him in to the police. Fortunately for me, the Pimpernel had already arranged for his folks to get me onto a smuggling ship. The captain was a wild man, dressed like a scarecrow, mask and everything. He outrun the French ships and got me safe to England. From there, I was handed off to a tall American frontiersman named Bumppo, who brought me safely to this country. Alas, since then, my fortunes has taken a turn for the worse."

"Doctor, these men are liars," Miki said.

"My dear, I have told you about invading the privacy of others," the Doctor replied. "Please forgive my young friend, gentlemen. She sometimes uses her telepathic powers injudiciously."

"Of course," the King said. "What kind of powers did you say she had again?"

"She is a mind-reader," the General said. "She must be probing your thoughts as we speak."

"Is that all?" the King said. "Well, me and the Duke here is in that line ourselves. I learnt that trick from Joseph Balsamic, hisself. Also reading fortunes and creating rain."

"That's right," the Duke said, "and I learned the power of clouding men's minds from Dr. Mesmer. I can read someone's thoughts as clear as pages in a book."

"Is that right?" Miki demanded standing to her full height. "If that's so, what am I thinking of right now?"

"Um…you're thinking of someone with an 's' in his name," the Duke said.

"Nope, she's thinking of a dragon," the King countered.

Miki's eyes went wide. "That was just a lucky guess!"

Doctor Omega had closed his eyes as the volume of the conversation increased. Now he spoke with a tone of impatience. "That is quite enough bickering, thank you! I see I shall have to explain you to each other."

He fixed his eyes intently on Miki.

"You are correct of course, my dear. These two rogues are confidence men, tricksters, much like their supposed teachers, Anton Mesmer and Joseph Balsamo. Though, unlike those two, they lack even the rudimentary psychic abilities needed to give their claims any verisimilitude. The Dauphin's guess was startlingly good, but I suspect that was your doing. In your irritation, you accidentally projected an image of your colossal, radioactive, reptilian friend into his mind."

He shifted his gaze to the King and the Duke, who squirmed. "You are liars, gentlemen, but you are very talented and audacious liars, and I have a need for someone with your skills.

23

"As I'm certain you know, the United States declared war on Mexico earlier this month. What you may not know, is that General Antonio López de Santa Anna has been named commander of the Mexican forces and plans to use this opportunity to become a dictator of an expanded Republic of Mexico. His ambitions would be doomed to failure, of course, but he has the services of an evil scientist named Dr. Campos. This criminal madman has uncovered a mind control device left on earth centuries ago by Kukulcan, a benign alien from a distant world. My companions and I are pledged to stop Santa Anna and Campos, and we could use your help."

"Actually," said the Steel General, "I have not yet decided where my loyalties lie. The Americans are the clear aggressors in this war, and I must always fight on the side of the oppressed."

"Yes," the Doctor replied. "The General's complicated ethics makes the whole proposition rather unpredictable. He is an immortal of sorts, a perennial rebel who has camped with Washington at Valley Forge, assisted Toussaint L'Ouverture in Haiti, and fought for Greek independence with Lord Byron. He never dies, but loses bits of himself in each conflict, and has been mostly replaced by mechanical parts.

"I am a traveler as well as a man of science, and have been to many places and many times. I met Miki in Tokyo in the year 1996, and we came across the General in 1831, Virginia. He had been badly damaged during Nat Turner's Revolt, so I helped to patch him up. I'm sure this all sounds peculiar to you..."

"Not a bit," said the King. "As it happens, me and Bilgewater has done her own share of time travel. I am from hunnert zillion years in the future, and he come from the distant past, before Atlanta sunk into the ocean. I can speak for him when I say, we'll be happy to join in your noble quest."

The conversation became more casual after that, with the Doctor telling stories of some of his experiences, and the King vying to top him at each turn. After a while, the General produced a banjo and entertained the others until, one by one, they dropped off to sleep.

It was full dark when the Duke found himself nudged awake by the point of his companion's shoe.

"Bilgewater," he whispered, "we gotta get off this train."

The Duke nodded and glanced around. Miki and Doctor Omega had fallen asleep and there was no sign of the General. The Duke breathed a sigh of relief at that. He found the mechanical man frightening, and doubted he ever slept.

The two left the room and headed to a junction between cars. After a few moments, the train slowed for a curve and the pair jumped off. The two rose as the train passed and massaged their bruises.

"Good riddance!" the King said.

"Them folks were some kind of crazy!" The Duke said.

24

"They wasn't crazy; they was playing us along. I dunno what they was up to, but you can be sure they was aiming to skin us out of every cent we have."

"But we ain't got any money."

"They didn't know that, did they?" The King shook his head disdainfully. "Nope, I don't know how their scam works, but you can bet it's a big one. I pity the suckers they falls upon with their stories."

"It's a damned shame," the Duke said as the caboose passed them by. "You can't trust nobody no mores."

"That's the God's truth, Bilgewater," the King replied. "But it ain't a total loss. That time-travel angle—I can see some ways we could use that to net us a pretty penny..."

*For the uninitiated, "Barton Werper" is the name of the fictitious author of five unauthorized Tarzan novels published in 1964-65. Adam "Mudman" Bezecny, a new contributor to our anthologies, decided to use him, along with another Jungle Lord, Nora the Ape-Woman from the eponymous novel by Félicien Champsaur (Black Coat Press, ISBN 978-1-61227-403-4) and the ever-amazing Doctor Omega, for a fanciful African yarn with cosmic consequences in...*

## Adam Mudman Bezecny: *The Revelation of the Yeti*

*Africa, 1966*

The dusty Ugandan road was creating a plume of ash-white smoke as the car bounced along it. Barton Werper looked at his aged companion, whose face flashed quickly back and forth between bemused joy and bitter discomfort

"First time in the African heat, eh, Doctor?" Werper asked.

Doctor Omega raised his head haughtily and sniffed.

"Hardly," he replied. "I've been to worlds much warmer than this, my boy. Tell me, have you ever basked in a summer afternoon on Vulcan?"

"Vulcan! You mean the one from that new sci-fi show?"

Werper was still a young man. He resembled his father, though he was trying to grow one of the stylish mustaches of the time, and his hair was a bit longer. The show in question was a fun past-time for him. (He wasn't quite cool enough to yet say "groovy.")

"No, no, of course not. I meant another planet entirely, in another time— you couldn't possibly have heard of it. Tell me again, Warter—er, Barter—what is the name of the man we're about to meet?"

Werper's arms strained to get the old jalopy around the dawning curve.

"Our guide's name is Robert John Kilgore. In his correspondence, though, he said he preferred to be called Ki-Gor."

"Ha! What a ridiculous name. Truly ridiculous! Like your biographical subject, that Jungle Lord. One of many, I've heard. But the original was yours, I believe?"

"His Lordship is certainly the most famous, but some in India did start out earlier. Someone called Mowgli, for example."

"Yes, that's right, I remember Mowgli... Well, how long until we reach the estate of this, uh, John-Gor?"

"Wrong continent, Doctor! It's Ki-Gor, remember? As for that, we've just arrived!"

Doctor Omega squinted at the small and humble house that sat hunched below the tall and ancient trees. Already, the chipped front door was opening to reveal a handsome muscled man, his hair lightened and flesh tanned by the merciless sun. He was clad only in a loincloth and a leather belt, which carried on it several weapons. His tempered face broke into a smile as he waved to the arrivals.

Werper waved back, then parked the car and stepped out.

Doctor Omega listed after him, taking time to examine the now-tarnished paintwork of the car. It was hardly a *Cosmos*, but there was something appealing about a simple yellow automobile. Maybe someday he'd have to look into finding one like it for himself. But for now Ki-Gor was talking.

"Gentlemen!" Ki-Gor exclaimed. "Hail and welcome. I hope the drive from Kampala was not too much of a hassle."

"I've had worse, Mr. Ki-Gor," Werper said. "And my blood, for all its infamy, is strong. My father, Lieutenant Werper of the Belgian Army, was tough as nails, even if he became sort of a villain in his final days."

"Yes, I have heard of him. Almost as poor of an abuser of the native peoples of this continent as that ivory trader in the Congo. But you've done good work despite him, son. You told some stories that may not have been told before. Getting an audience with his Lordship is a privilege rarely granted."

"I doubt my skill was enough to accurately convey what he told me about what we're seeking on this expedition," Werper said. "Maybe, if I can keep my line of books going, I can do a sequel to follow up the mystery of the Abominable Snowmen that my subject fought."

Doctor Omega seemed distracted as he looked up at the sky. There was nothing in particular to look at, but, in that moment, it was more entertaining than his companions' discussion. Then, Ki-Gor looked at him and raised an eyebrow.

"And why did you volunteer to leave your fabulous ship to journey into the heart of Africa, Doctor?"

"It has been a long time since I have been on safari," the Doctor said with a cheeky grin. "And in any case, I would be very curious to know if the Yeti exists in this part of the world as well. I heard stories about these creatures when I was a guest at a monastery in Tibet. They believed that some varieties of these animals had origins on another world."

"It's still hard for me to imagine other worlds, Doctor," Werper said simply. He turned to Ki-Gor. "Are we ready, Mr. Ki-Gor? I am eager to start as soon as possible."

"Of course. We'll leave in a minute. I just would like to introduce you to the female member of our company."

Doctor Omega's face lit up.

"It's good to have some manner of diversity in our little expedition, hm? I'm eager to meet this woman."

"Here she comes, Doctor. This is Nora, sometimes called the Ape-Woman—the daughter of such, actually, by a purely human man."

Another figure emerged, wearing similar garments to those of Ki-Gor, although much more conservative. From what Werper and the Doctor observed, her body was lined with the same hard muscles that marked Ki-Gor as a product of a world far from their own lives. She was a captivating and beautiful woman in terms of conventional beauty, and seemingly ageless.

Doctor Omega had met Nora, who was the child of an orangutan and a human—or maybe a great ape turned into a human—a long time ago. He also remembered meeting another like her, one Paula Dupree. In each case, the simian parent was something closer to human, rather like the Yeti he sought.

Of course, he also recalled meeting another human-animal hybrid, named Felifax, who was the laboratory-created son of a human and a tiger. Primitive though it may seem to him, he had to admit a certain degree of admiration for the 19th century of this world, for having the means to create such miracles. If indeed this sort of glorified bestiality was something to be admired...

"*Bonjour, Docteur,*" Nora said.

Her voice had retained her French accent, but otherwise did not betray her origins at all—humanity was still clearly dominant in her; it was a compassionate humanity, but also one backed up by that quiet potential for animal brutality.

"Along with Ki-Gor, I'll be your guide into this territory, in search of these man-apes," she continued. "Perhaps then we can find the source of the material the Jungle Lord talked about in the interview he gave you, Mr. Werper. I look forward to working with all of you."

Doctor Omega and Ki-Gor were satisfied with her statement and walked into Ki-Gor's home. As Nora and Werper followed them, the Ape-Woman leaned towards the writer and whispered:

"Even if you did do something of an injustice to his Lordship. Plagiarism and clichés are no way to get through life when dealing with people worthy of respect."

Werper looked down in guilt, remembering that there was a reason why he was here. Personal redemption.

Nora and Ki-Gor had already drawn up maps that would take them to another site, distinct from the lost Egyptian city that Werper had heard about in his interviews, where the Yeti were forced to fight for sport in a savage and blood-soaked arena.

Ki-Gor had found a lost Egyptian civilization, called Memphre. Some said this city was, like many of other "lost" cities found throughout Africa, such as Opar and Kor, one of the colonies of Karkosa (subject to variant spellings). Some said there were even stranger things in the Americas, his wife Helene had told him. It seemed any number of nameless civilizations had left behind lost cities in Mexico.

At the mention of that country, Doctor Omega smiled broadly.

"I don't visit Mexico all too often," he mused, "but when I do, it's always with a great spirit of adventure. It's a place plentiful with vampires, werewolves, robots and mummies. Mr. Werper, you should write about it someday!"

"I just have to worry about satisfying my own curiosity about these Abominable Snowmen before going any further," Werper said. "I couldn't find much more on the winged men of my novels, nor of the silver globe, the serpent-men, and any of that. But getting a lead for this will help me rest assured."

"We're happy to help, if it means another break from boredom," Nora said, with apparent sincerity. "Ki-Gor and I are in an evaporating age for our kind. Soon we'll have to find some sort of retirement."

"Ages rise and fall like waves, my dear child," said the Doctor. "You will always have something to keep you occupied."

"We must still be careful," Nora said. "Our source said that this land is prone to... strangeness."

"Strangeness?" asked the Doctor. "Of what kind?"

"Shifting dimensions. A sense of displacement. It is said to be one of the places of the world that is... soft."

"And some," Ki-Gor added, "claim that vile cults still thrive there, of a kind unseen since the days of Solomon Kane. They worship elder demons."

His voice had such an ominous tone that it troubled Werper and Doctor Omega, who had heard more than a handful of stories about his various adventures, and the terrible places and monsters he'd braved.

Barton Werper was nervous. Ki-Gor and Nora were fighters in their own right, and Doctor Omega could defend himself with his keen mind, but he was just a writer from the Midwest... words wouldn't do anything to stop a fiendish gorilla-man from tearing him to shreds, or a hooded cultist from stepping out and gutting him in the name of some foul, squirming thing from the stars.

He remembered some of the names of the beings Ki-Gor was presumably talking about... Cthulhu, Azathoth, Dagon... Writers far more articulate than he had written about these unknowable deities. His thoughts were so troubling to him that he murmured aloud:

"What does a glorified Sasquatch have to do with the Great Old Ones?"

"Consider another name I heard in Tibet, my boy," said the Doctor. "That of the Tcho-Tcho. They are hairy dwarves, similar to Africa's own *agogwe*... er, I hope I'm pronouncing that correctly... They worship some of those nameless and ghastly things, in their own strange manner."

Then he smiled, almost paternally, in a way that mildly unsettled Werper, who thought he enjoyed showing off his many fields of knowledge way too much.

"There was a family I heard about during a brief time in the Congo, when I was looking into my mother's ancestors," Nora added. "The Jermyns. They, too, worshipped the Great Old Ones and... wait!"

She held her hand up, and, at once she seemed authoritative. She suddenly appeared to take on inhuman features as she sensed danger around them. Even Ki-Gor looked civilized by comparison.

"Where did this fog come from?" Ki-Gor and Nora said, almost at the same time.

The jungle man tried in vain at sniffing the air to pick up olfactory clues.

"It's the wrong temperature for a mist like this," he said.

Werper was regretting Doctor Omega's decision to bar guns from the expedition—there *was* something wrong going on here, and that possibly meant they were close to their quarry, or else something that was viewing *them* as prey.

His eyes flashed to the daggers on Ki-Gor's belt. Nora likewise had a blade. That made him feel a little more comfortable, but that was lost as the Doctor gave a cry of distress.

"Doctor?" Werper said.

As he put his hands on the Doctor's shoulders, the old man shrugged them away.

"I'm quite alright, my boy. Just a mild shock. I had a brief impression of traveling in space—like on my ship."

"Perhaps we *have* moved in space," Ki-Gor murmured. "This fog may be the evidence of some sort of... gateway. It has no reason to be here."

Evidently, he, too, had felt the physical impression of traveling.

"I'd hate to question the map, but maybe we should go back and find another way around?" Nora suggested.

Ki-Gor nodded, and began to lead the way back through the trees.

Werper felt a flinch of disappointment—perhaps walking deeper into the jungle would help expose the source of what was causing the others—though not himself—to experience that sensation of having left Earth. But before he could think it through, Ki-Gor raised his hand.

"I don't think we *can* turn around," he mused grimly.

Doctor Omega gave a small cry as he saw what spread before them. Nora and Barton, however, were stunned into silence.

What had once been a path through the jungle was now a cliff-side. The jungle was far, far below them, stretching out endlessly in a landscape that indicated they were many miles farther from Ki-Gor's residence than they had traveled over the last several hours.

Not even the Doctor knew the name of the place they had found—one of these shifting places that rotates through space, connecting at random sticking points around the globe. Some had once referred to it as the Plateau of Leng.

Nora ran a hand through her coarse black hair.

"Dimensional shifts, then," she sighed. "This is my first."

"Scarcely mine, my dear girl," the Doctor said gleefully.

But despite his paternalism and confident experience, his face was a portrait of seriousness.

"We must be very careful from here on... Perhaps we will find our bounty sooner than expected, but we must also keep our wits about us. We will need to get *out*, eventually."

"So you're used to getting lost, then?" Werper said in an exasperated tone. "Maybe you *can* get us out, then, Doctor."

"I'm all too familiar with being called a hopeless navigator, Mr. Werper. And I must say, I am rather tired of it! Hm! In any case, it is Nora and Mr. Ki-Gor who appear to have gotten us lost..."

A flash of anger went across the Ape-Woman's face, but Ki-Gor raised his hand defensively.

"Bickering amongst ourselves like children isn't going to help us. Let's head deeper into this plateau—we *are* stuck on it, for better or worse. But as a last resort—there may yet be resources for us to climb down its face."

Wordlessly, the other three agreed. They retraced their steps once again, and descended into the mist-shrouded alien jungle.

Despite the temperature being so bizarrely mild, Werper was sweating. The same phenomenon that had caused that sensation of displacement was now upon him, pouncing rather than slowly creeping in, like it had done with the others. Occasionally, he would glance to the side and have the fleeting impression of seeing shapes moving around him through the trees, or hearing whispers from the darkness. He couldn't make out what they were saying, but knew that listening to them would only lead to madness.

Eventually, Nora squinted and scurried ahead. Doctor Omega noticed she was studying something.

"Well, now—are those runes on those chipped stones?"

"I believe so, Doctor," Nora said. "It's been awhile since I've read Aklo."

"Aklo, it is, eh?" the Doctor wheezed. "Oh, that cannot be good, that cannot be good at all. Where I come from, that is a language used only by the worshippers of the beings we discussed earlier."

"Then, there is a cult here," Ki-Gor concluded. "And its patron god must be the one known as Yog-Sothoth."

The Doctor's already-pale face drained of its remaining color.

"The Yeti, or Abominable Snowmen," he whispered, "are not just any variety of ape-men. True, some instances are mere hominid gorillas, but others are distinctly less... animal. On Pluto, they are called the Mi-Go. They are the servitors of the one you know as Yog-Sothoth."

Werper then looked up and realized that none of them had noticed how dark it had suddenly become.

Then, they came, chittering from the darkness. Their mushroom-crustacean bodies, scuttling, cheeping, and murmuring in the jungle.

Ki-Gor and Nora drew their knives, while the Doctor raised his hands in what Werper assumed was a gesture of protection. He tried to maneuver so that

31

he was in the center of the triangle they formed, but the ensuing battle was chaos.

Even twelve years past his retirement, Ki-Gor was as spry as any young warrior, and his dagger cut the Mi-Go savagely. Nora had a knife, too, and was screaming in rage, which shook Werper to his very core. Her ancestry was coming out, and she wrestled the Mi-Go despite the slippery ichor that covered their bodies. Some of the creatures were pulped in her grip, while others, she tore chitinous chunks from until they stopped moving.

Doctor Omega calmly approached one of the creatures, which loomed over him, and in a swift movement unbecoming his appearance, lunged forward with a strike at one of the Mi-Go's soft points, shouting "Hai!" This single strike was enough to knock the creature unconscious—if they were conscious to begin with.

The writer's vision began to blur. He felt his legs go weak under him, and he squeezed his eyes shut tight. When he opened them, he was on his knees, but the others had defeated the Fungi from Yuggoth.

Doctor Omega smiled—or Werper thought he smiled—as he offered him a hand up. He then experienced another jarring sensation of being pulled through space as his three companions led him even deeper in the jungle—perhaps assuming he would emerge soon from his altered state. But everything stayed foggy, and Werper was now having trouble remembering if there really was mist, or if this was all just his eyes...

In no time at all, they were deep amongst the high stones of a Cyclopean city, which they could see extended as far as the eye could see.

As Werper slouched against a tree, Doctor Omega took a pair of opera glasses from his jacket and looked out into the city.

"I can see something. It looks like a door. Perhaps it is a spatial portal of some kind. An artifact of the Ancients, no doubt—the same Ancients who built this city."

"It could be our way home," Ki-Gor suggested.

"Yes, but I can see that there is some kind of gathering near the gate. A flock of Mi-Go, led by people. Humans."

"The cult, no doubt," Nora said.

In that moment, they knew what they had to do.


The four sorcerers stood at the gateway that divided the world. Here, in Leng, they could capitalize on the shift in space to complete their quest.

At the head of the trio, grinning at the three others, was Doctor Karswell. Even he didn't remember how he had come by his extended life, especially as the demons he served had become increasingly strange. He had faked death countless times since his days at Lufford Abbey in Warwickshire.

Alongside him were three other masters of the dark arts, who, like him, had had their lives greatly enhanced by the powers of the Outer Gods. They were

Madame Palmyre, who worshipped the entity known as Baal; Cristaldi the Mexican warlock, who had once fought Dracula; and an American simply called the Master, who worshipped an unknown god called Manos, until earlier that year, when incidents led to him to join the others.

"Will it be soon, Palmyre?" Karswell asked. "The gate is now charged from our years of work here. The Great Old Ones have treated us well. Now, we may bring forth the presence of Yog-Sothoth."

"His release into this dimension will shatter time itself," the French sorceress replied, her voice smooth and cunning. "Perhaps then I will find my lover again."

"I, for one, do not seek or need redemption," the Master said authoritatively. "What Yog-Sothoth has decreed, so have I done. His limbs of fate will doom this world." The Master spoke often that he believed the Outer Gods were firm believers in the propagation of torture and violence.

"I *do* seek it," Cristaldi interjected. "It may rid me of this insanity that drives my life beyond my control. I do not want to kill the people of the world, but there is a tiny voice in me who makes it sound wonderful." And then he immediately burst into laughter.

Karswell was glad to know they were so close. His eternal life in a timeless world would be spent learning all of the secrets that had been hidden from him by the universe. But suddenly, he remembered something very important.

"The Mi-Go patrol has not yet returned!"

"Yes..." Cristaldi hissed. "I sensed... interlopers. But I forgot they were here until now..."

Karswell slapped the centuries-old man across the face angrily.

"You old dullard! Who are these interlopers?" '

Behind them, the Master and Palmyre gestured at each other to move closer to the gate. They would need to protect it if the Mexican warlock's predictions came true.

But as they did so, all Cristaldi needed to do was point.

"Doctor Karswell—you can ask them yourself."

Karswell whirled around. *No!* he thought. *It's too soon!* But there was nothing that could be done. The athletic woman and the nearly-nude man were already lunging towards them.

"Destroy the invaders!" the British occultist screeched.

Nora was going after Palmyre, having sprinted ahead to the gate. The sorceress's eyes closed though her eyelids still fluttered, and she began to chant an incantation. The Ape-Woman was ready to knock her to the ground.

Karswell and Ki-Gor were at each other's throat. Using a spell, Karswell set his hands blazing with fire, ready to consume the jungle man.

Doctor Omega calmly approached the hunched Cristaldi. Their eyes began to glitter at the prospect of a mutual battle of wits.

And at last, Werper staggered, weaving between Karswell and Cristaldi, across the plaza. He was trying to avoid everyone, but he was suddenly standing toe to toe with the Master.

The Master stared deep into Werper's eyes, but they were blurry as the writer's head continued spinning. The Master then realized that he was not connecting with the man's mind—something was wrong with it, and it was getting worse the closer he got to the gate.

And he *was* getting closer as he approached the Master. He was about to *attack* him...

That's when the Master experienced his first punch to the face. Bullets were nothing to him, because he would just send them into a parallel world as they traveled towards him. A fist, though, was attached a larger mass, and it was simply harder for the person on the end of it to be pulled into another dimension. He went flying backward and his head slammed against the gate.

Werper, sweating heavily, screamed from fear.

That scream caused Karswell to look up, as he was in the process of being pinned to the ground by Ki-Gor. The Jungle Man was about to pinch his neck in a way that would render him unconscious, but before he went down, Karswell was able to cry out:

"That boy is beating the Master!"

The Doctor had been attempting to hypnotize Cristaldi, just as the Master had tried to enslave Werper. When he heard Karswell's statement, he looked up to examine Werper's target. During this time, Cristaldi cackled and waved the heavy gnarled stick he leaned on. Energy suddenly swirled around Doctor Omega, forming bars, and soon solidifying into metal.

The Doctor was now sealed in an iron cage, and the others could hear his loud protestations.

Nora looked up as her twisting pull had thrown down one of the Mi-Go that Palmyre had called up. She saw that the sorceress was bolting, but even with her bestial strength, she could not get the fungoid creatures away from her in time to stop her. She was running towards the gate. As she went through it, Nora observed that the image flickered and became that of another world. The gate was randomly changing its destination across various planes of reality. How this would aid Yog-Sothoth, she did not know. She couldn't think hard about it while tearing apart these "Abominable Snowmen."

Barton Werper was lunging towards the Master again, and grabbed him by the hair. Before anyone noticed, he shoved the cultist's head through the portal. He had no idea what he was doing—the world was just a bunch of churning colors to him, set to the music of endless Aklo chanting.

The gate flashed again. Doctor Omega flinched as the man in the black robe was suddenly *sans* his head—his neck sheared by the shift in dimensions.

"Oh, Werper, my boy..." the Doctor whispered.

Karswell was unconscious. At last Ki-Gor stood up, even as Cristaldi assessed the situation.

"The woman's animal state has scared away Palmyre," the Mexican Warlock said. "The young man has murdered the Son of the God of Primal Darkness. The English Doctor is unconscious. I do not wish to pursue this conflict anymore. I surrender, and will aid you in a return from this place..."

Ki-Gor and Doctor Omega seemed satisfied with this.

"You will no longer attempt to call forth the Outer Gods, and torment the people of this country?" Ki-Gor asked.

"I swear it. I... have toiled too long in the service of darkness, to rebel against the hateful evil of a monster I once fought. I deserve only exile, trapped forever in these far lands."

In good faith, he dissolved the Doctor's cage. Nora could read souls and had felt a repulsive evil in the other three cultists, but there was no such thing in the aged Cristaldi. She was about to voice this as Werper stood and charged the Warlock.

"Werper, stop! Stop this foolishness at once!" Doctor Omega cried.

He was about to seize Werper himself when Ki-Gor restrained the writer with great efficiency.

"This place has been bad for his mind," the Jungle Man said grimly. "I'm not sure he'll be able to recall the facts of this adventure, much less write about them."

"So he didn't get the closure he sought," Doctor Omega sighed. "Perhaps in time he will recover. But meanwhile, what a waste. What a terrible waste!"

Cristaldi stood as the others approached this portal.

"Go, and take the wicked Karswell with you," he said. "I will use what power I have left to open a gate to return you to the Africa of Earth. Then I can begin my path of relearning the ways of virtuous magic."

Nora nodded in response, and wished the man the luck of his gods.

Using gestures of his hands, Cristaldi slowly pulled an image of the African jungle into view in the oval gateway.

"Go quickly!"

Doctor Omega held Barton Werper by the shoulder, as one last time, Nora led them, with Ki-Gor in between. The Jungle Lord was carrying Doctor Karswell. He turned around and took a last look around him. It had been good to be in a place so close to home, yet still as alien as Memphre. He felt—young again, despite everything.

They rested upon landing. Werper was already calming down, now that he was free from the madness of the Plateau of Leng. The Doctor was silent; Nora and Ki-Gor were exhausted.

The Doctor wondered if Werper's sanity had been forever destroyed, as the young man's mouth stopped foaming, and he slipped into dreams about unfathomable titans of the void. These creatures also dreamed in the darkness of Africa, sleeping but not dead.

The true nature of the Yeti who, in Tibet, were merely abominable creatures of the snows, now stood revealed in that most terrible of their many aspects.

Doctor Omega did not sleep as Nora and the others did—his kin did not need to sleep as often. And he thought about these Yeti, and how he still had just as many questions as young Werper did.

He hoped he never encountered them again. Not even the *Cosmos* could outrun the tendrils of something like Yog-Sothoth.

*From darkest Africa to the foreboding woods of the Ardennes in Northern France, near the Belgian border... This clever murder mystery with supernatural elements by Canadian contributor Nicholas Boving brings together three very different investigators, as well as two charismatic suspects, and a fearsome threat...*

## Nicholas Boving: *The Evil Among Us*

*The Ardennes, 1929*

Doctor John H. Watson wiped the lather from his face, slipped his straight razor into its case and went back into his room. There he tied his tie, slipped on a Norfolk Jacket and went down the stairs to the dining room, whistling with pleasure and with nothing more on his mind than a good breakfast and a day of investigation. He was staying in the Ardennes, the dark, forested area in Northern France that, at that time, suited his need to get away from the slush and noise of London as it approached the Festive Season.

Having disposed of a plate of ham and eggs, he was half way through a rack of toast and comfiture and was looking forward to a cup of coffee when the dining room door burst open and a large man wearing a heavy dark cloak and trilby entered. He stopped; saw Watson and a look of surprise crossed his face.

"*Mon Dieu, Docteur Watson, n'est-ce pas?* What the Devil brings you to these benighted parts?

Watson looked up from his coffee.

"Good God! Inspector Maigret! I thought Paris was your beat."

Maigret frowned. "Actually it's *Commissaire* now."

"My apologies. But at last someone has seen fit to reward your true worth. Nevertheless, why this lonely part of France?"

"My wife has relations nearby..." He spread his hands. "Also, I was in Reims organizing Flying Squads and a matter came to my attention..."

"But this is not Reims."

"A welcome diversion," Maigret said, smiling thinly,

Watson indicated the other chair at his table and offered coffee. Maigret accepted gratefully.

"Perhaps a little something else. The morning appears to be a bit chilly."

Watson signaled the waiter for a brandy. He dabbed his lips with his napkin, leaned back and lit a cheroot. "And what may I do for you?"

Maigret smiled.

"There is a problem..." he began.

"Which you can no doubt solve most capably without my help."

"A locked room—or rather, chapel," Maigret said, leaning forward. "An impossibility, and, murder most foul."

Watson pushed his plate away and filled his battered pipe. Maigret smiled again. He knew his bait had been taken.

Maigret swallowed his brandy at a gulp.

"A member of our local aristocracy, the Comte d'Ingraville, has been most foully murdered."

"I fail to understand why this should concern me, Commissioner," said Watson, frowning.

Maigret cut in.

"It is the manner of the killing, Docteur. I confess I was on the point of telegraphing Paris when someone mentioned your name, and I realized here was the perfect man to aid me in solving this dastardly crime."

"Look, I'm very sorry, but I am not a young man: seventy-five is a shade old to be running around the countryside after murderers."

Maigret chuckled.

"Then this will no doubt stir the blood." And his look was a shade wicked. "Besides, Doctor, there is a rumor that this d'Ingraville was, in fact, not what he professed to be, but was indeed the notorious Comte de Saint-Germain."

Watson stared.

"Good God, the man is a myth, and besides, even if he were not, he is supposed to be an immortal, and hence..." Watson spread his hands as if to state the obvious.

"True," replied Maigret, nodding, "but cannot immortals be dispatched by beheading? So goes the story."

Watson was intrigued despite his earlier protestations.

"And this d'Ingraville, or Saint-Germain, has been beheaded?" he asked.

Maigret nodded, satisfied that he had his fish hooked. Watson shrugged.

"Very well. I suppose there is no harm in looking."

He got up, went to his room, and returned a few minutes later wearing an Inverness cape and a thick tweed cap. He carried a stout cane.

"You have a car?" he asked.

Maigret laughed.

"On these country roads, we should be in a ditch before a half kilometer. No, the old-fashioned modes are still the best."

The drive was cold. Maigret's pony trap rattled along the track that led to the back of the chateau, splashing through muddy puddles and jarring bone-shakingly through the ruts. The day had deteriorated rapidly from merely uninviting to downright unpleasant as the darkening clouds hurried, driven by a chill north east wind, and there was a hint of rain.

"I think there will be snow by tomorrow morning," Maigret said, gloomily.

"Then we must be quick. The evidence, if there is any, will be obliterated."

There was little enthusiasm in Watson's voice as his thoughts strayed back to the inn and a roaring fire.

The towers of the chateau showed briefly through a gap in the chestnuts. Maigret nodded.

"There is a chapel on the far side near the lake. It is new."

"How far?"

"Five minutes' walk, no more."

The building was a small Gothic mistake, no more than fifty feet by thirty in dimensions. There was a mock bell tower at one end. Its chief claim to anything was that it failed to fit into the older landscaping with startling success.

Watson stopped to take it in from a distance as he believed in getting a wide picture before looking for details.

What was remarkable at once was the complete absence of windows and the one double door centered in the wall facing them. Apart from being out of proportion, it was massively constructed, or what was left of it must have been. He walked quickly towards it, then stopped twenty yards short.

The door, which had been made of three inch thick oak planks with iron bands at two-foot intervals and heavy studs driven in for added impregnability, had been ripped off its massive iron hinges, and even from that distance, Watson saw what appeared to be great, bright scratches in the weather darkened timbers, bigger than any he had ever seen, and he had hunted both the Bengal and Snow Tigers. He turned to Maigret.

"May one ask what...?"

"I cannot conceive of anything that could possess such strength," replied Maigret, spreading his hands.

He jabbed a finger at the doorway from which the lintel and even some stones had been dislodged.

"The Comte is in there."

Watson moved forward and stopped at the entrance. At close quarters, the devastating violence was even more startling. The door had been held closed by heavy bolts on the inside, the desire for privacy further enhanced by a key and lock of heroic proportions.

"The key is still on the inside," Maigret pointed, "and it is in the locked position. Similarly with the bolts."

Watson nodded.

"And the hinges have been ripped from their bedding, taking the stonework with them. There is a force at play here that I have only seen with explosives."

"And yet, it cannot be that."

"Indeed. There is no mark of flame and no smell of gunpowder or dynamite. Besides which, an explosion of this magnitude would have been plainly heard."

Maigret cleared his throat in the manner of someone about to do something unpleasant. Watson smiled grimly, stepped over the debris and went inside.

Quite what he was expecting, he had no idea, but certainly not the charnel house he found. It was like stepping into the bloodiest of slaughterhouses.

The Comte d'Ingraville—or Saint-Germain—was inside, or at least, the various parts of his body were. At a glance, Watson could see none missing. He had a strong stomach and had experienced some unpleasantness in his time in Afghanistan, but nothing had prepared him for the sight of a human body basically dismembered, eviscerated, the limbs not cut away, but literally torn from the body, the sinews whitely exposed, the bones shattered.

He took a deep breath, and then realized the torso had no head. He found it in a corner, beneath a shattered table, the eyes still wide and staring, as if gripped in death by some appalling horror. His feet crunched on broken glass, the remains of wine bottles; food was trampled into the floor. The mess was indescribable.

"Great God in Heaven," he murmured. "What can have done this?"

There was the scratch of a match and the smell of tobacco smoke disguised some of the already cloying smell of death.

"Have you perhaps in your travels...?"

Maigret left the question hanging without much hope of a positive answer.

Watson shook his head.

"Nothing. But perhaps there are more things in Heaven and Earth than we imagine."

"The door alone would have kept out anything of which I am aware. Look at it: it has been smashed almost to matchwood."

Watson filled and lit his pipe.

"The thing one notices is that it has been broken outwards, which presupposes there was something inside. At any rate, I doubt a team of cart horses or even an elephant could have pulled it open like that."

He whipped around and went outside. Maigret followed.

"See," Watson said, jabbing his cane. "There are no marks of large animals; merely our footprints, your gendarme's, and presumably those of the Comte."

The puzzle deepened in Watson's mind. It would take a team of oxen yoked to the door to even force it open it as it was meant to keep people out, all bolts and locks being on the inside. But it has literally been ripped off its hinges.

He went back inside, frustration mounting. His foot hit a pewter mug, sending it rolling across the floor into a darkened corner. He was about to ask Maigret to take him to the chateau to interview the staff, when he heard a whimpering sound from the corner.

Watson peered into the gloom, saw movement and hurried over. To his horror, he saw a girl, blood-spattered and cowering like a terrified animal.

As he approached, she screamed, an eldritch sound of pure terror and scrabbled wildly in a vain attempt to burrow into the stone.

It took the combined efforts of the two men, gentling her like a spooked horse, to bring her to some semblance of calm before they could get her out of the corner and wrap her shivering body in a blanket from the pony trap.

Maigret shouted to the gendarme. The man hurried in and gave a gasp of shock when he saw the girl.

"Do you know her?" Maigret asked the policeman.

"Certainly, Commissaire," replied the gendarme. "She is the daughter of a farmer on the estate of Monsieur le Comte."

Maigret eased the whimpering girl out into the light, where she stood, eyes darting from side to side and wild as a trapped rabbit.

"What has happened to her?" he asked Watson.

The Englishman shrugged.

"You know as much as I. May I suggest she is taken home. She needs warmth and her mother's love. Then, maybe..."

He let the question of her return to sanity hang unanswered.

As the gendarme took the girl away, Maigret's face was a study in cold anger.

"She must have been d'Ingraville's latest toy. The devil of it is, she is otherwise unharmed, but something has unhinged her mind."

Watson smacked angrily with his cane at an inoffensive weed. The seed head flew off, reminding him unpleasantly of what lay inside the chapel.

"Let us hope she will recover."

"Maybe she can offer an explanation."

"I doubt you will get any sense from her," Watson shrugged. "I have seen fear like that. It unbalances the mind."

The sky was turning darker and the wind rising further with the spatters of rain turning to stinging sleet. It seemed Maigret's earlier forecast would be proven correct.

"Come," Watson said firmly. "Let us see what the Comte's servants have to say, and then we will return to the inn where lunch and hot drinks will be the order of the day."

Maigret posted gendarmes at the chapel with strict instructions to allow no one inside but himself or Watson.


Watson turned to look at the man who had let them in after what had seemed an eternity of knocking against the heavy front doors.

"You are the Comte's butler?" he asked.

"Steward, Monsieur. I am the steward."

There was a pathetic hint of pride in the man's voice.

"Ah. Just so." Watson laid his stick and hat on a small table. "And how long have you served the Comte d'Ingraville?"

"All his life, Monsieur, and his father before him for twenty years."

"So there is little about the family with which you are not familiar?"

"I was honored with their confidence, Monsieur."

"And so," Watson nodded, forcing a thin smile, "tell me, when did you last see your master?"

"At sunset yesterday."

"What was he doing?"

"Preparing to go to the chapel, Monsieur."

"Was this something he did often?" Maigret cut in.

"At least once a week, Monsieur."

"And what did he do at the chapel?"

The man's face closed.

"It was not my place to inquire of the Comte's business."

"And yet you knew." Maigret snapped his fingers. "Come, man. You have said you had the family's confidence, so it is useless to pretend ignorance now."

"There are punishments for abetting a crime," Watson said, in an icy voice.

"And this crime is murder of the foulest kind," Maigret added.

"I but carried out orders," replied the Steward, cringing.

"Which were?" The snap in Watson's voice would have stiffened a guardsman.

"To prepare the chapel with food and drink."

"What else?" Watson already knew.

"To escort the young ladies to the chapel."

"Like the miserable child we have just seen?"

The Steward nodded.

"There were others, but they usually came from towns hereabouts. They were paid, you understand..."

"This girl had no choice," sneered Maigret. "This is already a crime. I warn you. Speak the truth."

The man was visibly shaking.

"Her father—you understand—he farms the Comte's land..."

Watson gave a throaty sound of disgust.

"Blackmail. If your master were still alive I would thrash the skin from his back."

"What happened with this girl?" continued Maigret.

The man swallowed hard.

"I took her to the chapel. The Comte let her in. The doors were locked and barred as always. I had strict orders never to disturb him, for any reason."

"And how did he seem? What was his demeanor?" asked Watson.

It took a little pushing on the Englishman's part to get the Steward to admit that the Comte had not been his usual self. Ordinarily, he went to the chapel with considerable eagerness, but on this occasion, he had seemed anxious.

Maigret tried to bully the man into an explanation, but achieved only dumb insolence and an utter lack of cooperation, as if the Steward no longer understood what was being asked.

"There was no one else with him?" Watson inquired.

"No one, Monsieur," replied the man, shaking his head. "I swear on my mother's grave."

Watson turned to Maigret.

"We shall get nothing more from this one. Let us interview the rest of the servants before we leave."

Back at the inn, Maigret told Watson what little he had learned of the Comte, that is, that he had mysteriously returned to take up residence some years after his father had apparently died, rather suddenly. The young Comte, who bore a startling resemblance to that father, had assumed the title and claimed his birthright. It wasn't long before he was regarded by all with circumspection that bordered on fear.

Then, the accursed chapel had been built, the chateau staff fled, and those who remained were dregs who neither cared, nor had any place to go.

As they waited for lunch to be served, Maigret nursed a brandy and leaned towards Watson.

"What I need, Doctor, is for this affair to be closed before the newspapers get wind of the scandal."

Watson stretched his bad leg to the fire, letting the heat ease the ache caused by the cold.

"I'm not sure what use I can be, except perhaps as a second pair of eyes."

Maigret's smile said he thought otherwise, and he said so.

"You have something of a reputation, and of being a man who finds a mystery irresistible. Does this not catch your imagination?"

Watson smiled back.

"Damn you Maigret. I came here for peace and to write."

As they ate Maigret continued the biography of D'Ingraville.

It seemed the Comte was at odds with everyone. He loudly professed to be an atheist and went out of his way to antagonize a local theologian and religious historian, Monsieur Mocata, who was well known for his immense knowledge of the arcane and esoteric. D'Ingraville mocked him publicly and called him fool for believing in the supernatural. There was bad blood and, on more than one occasion, Mocata, had tried to attack his tormentor.

The local priest, *Abbé* Dervelle, Père Jules, was equally disgusted by the Comte's behavior and came in for much ridicule.

Watson had looked up sharply at this new information, but Maigret had disabused him.

"That man, Mocata, is of a studious and sedentary nature. I can imagine him struggling to lift one of his tomes, let alone tear an oak door from its hinges. And Abbé Jules is in his seventies."

Maigret pushed his plate away and proceeded to fill his pipe from a battered pouch.

"We are presented with an insoluble mystery, Doctor; an impossibility. We have a room without possibility of access due to its construction, a door too strong to force, and yet it happened, and a man is horribly dead."

"Not impossible, Maigret. We have a great puzzle and, as yet, no solution, but be assured, a solution there will be."

"Iron bars slotted into place. Why, even a circus strongman could not so much as make a small bend in those. And yet they are twisted like corkscrews."

Watson took out a cheroot, lit it and signaled the waiter for brandy. The sounds of the storm were increasing.

"It's a good thing we inspected the chapel surrounds this morning," he said. "By tomorrow, the storm will have obliterated every sign." Sleet rattled against the windows like bird shot. "I have sympathy for your gendarmes."

"They will doubtless have disobeyed me and found shelter," said Maigret shrugging.

As he smoked, Watson pondered the little they knew. He ticked the items off on his fingers.

"The key is still in the lock, and the inside bolts are padlocked. No one is going to disturb the Comte. For a man to have got in is patently impossible, and even if there is some monstrous deformed creature at large, it would have been seen and nothing could have had that strength."

He paused and took a deep draw on his cheroot.

"There is also the small matter of the great gouges in the wood. I cannot get it from my mind that they are claw marks; yet, they are like no claws I have ever seen."

Watson felt a chill that had nothing to do with the weather.

"We are missing something, Maigret. Either it is something so obvious as to be overlooked, or else so bizarre it does not even enter our minds."

They retired to the smoking room for more brandy and coffee. For a while, there was no sound but the storm and the comforting crackle of the log fire. Then, Maigret coughed and cleared his throat.

"With regard to claws, there are many legends of werewolves in these parts."

"Werewolves are just scary stories dreamed up by superstitious peasants," Watson said, chuckling.

Maigret sighed noisily.

"Then how do you explain this terrible death, *mon ami?*"

"I don't, not yet," replied Watson, smiling. "But I will. Which reminds me. Who else knows about this?"

"No one except you and the local *gendarmes.*" Maigret's eyes twinkled. "They are, after all, superstitious peasants, too."

"*Touché.* But they'll keep quiet?"

"If they want their pensions, certainly."

"Yes, I'm told a good threat works wonders." Watson got up. "I am going to send a telegram to a good friend of mine who may be able to help."

"What friend?"

"Father Brown. He has a great deal of experience with the inexplicable."

"All religion is inexplicable," said Maigret, amused. "At least, to me."

Watson kept his opinions to himself.

"Brown's expertise goes rather beyond dogma and formula."

He returned a few minutes later to announce that the telegram had gone out and that he was going to bed.

"I think tomorrow we should pay a visit to this historian of yours," he suggested. "If there was friction between him and d'Ingraville, then he may shed some light on the mystery."

"What about Abbé Jules?"

Watson was ambivalent.

"Disapproval of such behavior as the Comte's is part of his job. I think we will mine a better lode from Monsieur Mocata—at least, for the moment."

"The Abbé's house is on the way. It would be worth a short stop."

"I am in your hands Maigret," replied Watson, yawning.

The foul weather had passed by the time they set out after breakfast, and the world had been magicked from its autumnal colors to a pristine white. They paid another quick visit to the d'Ingraville chapel to check on and replace Maigret's gendarmes.

Maigret remarked that at least the cold weather would preserve the body until Watson's friend arrived. They then got back in the pony trap and within fifteen minutes were being welcomed into Abbé Jules' parlor.

The priest made it plain that he had been disgusted by the Comte and his evil ways and openly admitted that he had always foretold the man would come to a bad end. But he showed no sorrow, just a quiet triumph.

"You do not appear surprised," Maigret said.

"How could I be?" replied the Abbé, shrugging. "The Lord is forgiving, but even He can tolerate only so much."

Watson suppressed a smile.

"So d'Ingraville's death can be attributed to God's wrathful hand?"

Abbé Jules' eyebrows rose.

"Can you believe anything else?"

Watson got up. He knew they would get no further in this interview.

"I thank you, Monsieur l'Abbé. And I regret having troubled you."

"It is no trouble, Monsieur. Perhaps I shall overcome my repugnance of d'Ingraville's way of life and say a prayer for his soul. The chateau is not far."

"Charitable," Maigret said, "but unnecessary. In any case, the crime scene is forbidden to any but those authorized."

"But surely..." the Abbé protested.

"I regret, but it must apply to all," Maigret responded, shaking his head.

Abbé Jules inclined his head in mute acquiescence, and Watson was a little surprised to see what he thought to be a flash of anger in the watery eyes behind the spectacles.

As they trotted down his drive and turned onto the road, Watson saw the priest still standing, watching them.

Mocata stood silhouetted against the tall window of his study, his back to Watson and Maigret.

"The fool did not believe," he sneered. "See where it has got him."

Watson's eyes narrowed.

"And what was the form of this disbelief?"

Mocata swung around and angrily demanded:

"Are you a policeman that you question me?"

"No, but Commissioner Maigret is, and it would be in your interests to answer my questions."

"The Comte believed in nothing. He publicly disparaged all possibility of the great powers."

"By powers, I assume you mean God?"

"Assume nothing, Englishman. Do you believe in God?"

"As a good Christian, of course."

"Then indeed, you must also believe in the Devil—the powers of darkness."

"The Devil is a boggle to scare the less educated," replied Watson, shrugging.

"How so? If you believe in good, you must also believe in evil. The universe must have balance, or it will fly apart."

"But good will prevail."

"Is that what you believe? Then you are naïve. Like a pendulum, the forces sway, first one prevailing, and then the other." Mocata made a sound of disgust. "That damned fool denied the possibility, and look where it has got him."

Maigret was quick to snatch what might have been a slip.

"What do you know of his death?"

"That he brought it upon himself, perhaps," replied Mocata.

As they left to return to the inn, Maigret growled his disbelief.

"The man knows more than he is saying."

He shook the reins and the pony started moving.

"Maybe," said Watson. "But there still remains the small matter of a door ripped from its hinges by something with the strength of an enraged bull elephant."

Maigret confessed himself at an impasse. He checked again on the gendarmes at the chapel, reiterating that no one was to enter.

As they left, dark clouds were pulling across the blue morning sky like a blanket. A thin wind sprang up and Watson pulled his cape tighter around his neck. It was most puzzling. The motives for killing—at least the apparent ones—were debatable at best, and yet, nothing else had presented itself as a possibility. He shelved idle speculation as an unprofitable exercise and turned his mind to thoughts of Father Brown.

Brown was a man who had taken a side path from his chosen way that few would care to follow. The specialty of exorcism was not for the faint-hearted, but it didn't take up all of his time, and neither did his normal priestly duties. Father Brown was also an accomplished detective. However, his path had steered his studies into the esoteric and the arcane.

That was why Watson had asked him to come. There was something nagging at the back of his mind, but for the life of him, he couldn't put a finger on it. He only knew that he wanted his old friend's advice.

The fact of d'Ingraville's death was of little concern to him as, from what he had learned from Maigret, it was only a matter of time before he would have found himself on the receiving end of a bullet or a blade. Likewise, the sight of a bloody death was not uncommon where he had spent his army years. What bothered Watson was the extraordinary violence of the slaughter. He had seen the results of a man killed by a tiger, and it had in no way approached what had occurred in the chapel. And there were the matters of the lack of footprints, and the claw marks on the door, made by something outside his experience...

At the inn there was a telegram from Father Brown saying he would arrive on the late afternoon train.

Watson and Maigret had lunch, then spent the afternoon back at the chapel. Watson carefully searched a circle about a hundred yards in diameter outside the chapel for clues. There was nothing. No footprints other than the almost snow-covered ones of Maigret's boots, his own stout shoes, the gendarmes' and the Comte's elegant shoes, walking in tandem with those of the unfortunate girl. Certainly no animal prints other than the usual: a fox, a deer and what looked like a wolf. He was puzzled, however, by a slash of bark torn from a pine, as if some great body had brushed against it.

In the end, it began to get dark and he gave up the fruitless exercise, left Maigret to his own investigations, and drove to the station to wait for Father Brown.

The priest bustled along the platform dressed in his worn soutane and black hat. The grey tweed overcoat thrown over his portly frame made for an almost comical sight.

Watson took his friend's valise and a satchel containing books, and guided him to the pony trap just as the clouds kept their promise and the weather began to turn for the worse again.

The Englishman started to make for the inn, where he had booked a room for his old friend, but Father Brown insisted they drive directly to the chapel.

By the time they arrived the first snowflakes were falling and the weather threatened another stormy night, a fact seemingly unnoticed by the priest.

On entering the charnel house and seeing d'Ingraville's headless corpse, Father Brown made the sign of the cross.

"You would pray for a man like that?" Maigret asked.

"Every soul deserves the chance of Paradise. And God forgives all sins."

Then with the aid of Maigret's bull's eye lantern, he examined everything in the chapel with the thoroughness of a customs officer looking for smuggled goods.

Finally, he stood in the middle of the destruction and stroked his chin.

"One thing is a near certainty, my friends: whatever he may have called himself, these are the remains of the Comte de Saint-Germain."

"What? You are sure?" said Watson, stunned.

"As near as I can be," replied Brown. "He matches the descriptions too well for it to be a coincidence. It seems the Immortal Man has met his match." He shrugged. "As to the what, and why, I confess to being at a loss for the moment, but..."

He gave a sharp exclamation and hurried to where a table had been overturned, scattering bottles and food. He bent down, scrabbling through the detritus and then rose stiffly to his feet, holding a blood-spattered book.

Watson and Maigret looked over his shoulder. It appeared to be quite old, being bound with embossed leather with gold writing. The priest held it somewhat gingerly.

"What is it?" Watson asked.

"Why would Saint-Germain need a Bible?" Maigret inquired.

Brown wiped off some of the blood with a table cloth and replied:

"It is not a Bible. But if my fears are right..." He let the rest of the sentence fade, then stuffed the book into his robe. "Let us return to the inn. There is nothing more to be done here." He indicated the corpse. "He can be removed. The fellow can tell us no more."

Maigret gave instructions for the gendarmes to take the Comte's remains to the local morgue, drove Watson and Brown back to the inn and said he would join them next morning. As they got down from the trap, he called out to the priest:

"The book. Will you have deciphered it by then?"

"Deciphered, I doubt it," said the priest. "But certainly, I will have determined what it is."

He turned and hurried into the inn and Watson knew it was not the weather that caused his haste.

Watson did not see Father Brown again until dinner when he came into the smoking room where the Doctor sat with his feet on the fender, enjoying a cheroot and a pre-dinner whisky. He signaled the waiter for a drink for the priest, then said:

"Do you not find it somewhat fortuitous that we three should be available. Maigret, who had official business nearby; you, who are studying esoteric manuscripts at the Bibliothèque Nationale; and myself, well, just being at this place and time at all?"

Father Brown said something about there being no such things as coincidences, and then sat staring into the flames, silent until his drink came. He held the amber liquid to the lamp, letting the light play through the colors.

"Man has created some splendid things," he said, "and Scotch whisky is one of them; but he has also created great evil, such as this." He took the book from his robe. "The original of this it is supposedly written in blood on human skin."

He drank whisky and put the glass down carefully.

"That is not the original I take it?" asked Watson.

"Thankfully, no," replied the priest, shaking his head.

"What is it? It appears to have a profound effect on you."

"It is called *Kitab el Khaouf,* The Book of Terror, and sometimes *Kitab al Dunya al Aswad,* The Book of the Black Earth, supposedly written in the late seventh or early eighth century by an Arab named Abdul el Hazid, also known as The Mad Arab, though he also got it from a much earlier source. But whichever way you look at it, the results could be very unpleasant."

"Such as?"

"It is said that if certain words or phrases in the book are spoken aloud, or even written, dangerous, evil powers can be let loose, and horrible things happen. The book is written in an ancient alphabet, like runes."

Watson, who had come across some eerily evil things in his time, found himself staring at the book with a sense of foreboding.

Brown finished his drink at a gulp. Watson signaled the waiter for a refill.

"Lucifer will walk the Earth," muttered Father Brown.

"I beg your pardon?"

"If the original exists, it could unleash great evil."

"You say *if?*"

"It is by no means certain." Father Brown laid his hand on the book. "As I said, this is not original, being no more than a hundred years old at best. There has always been much controversy as to whether there ever was an original..."

"Then, why create a forgery of a myth?"

"One assumes for the usual reasons, money." Brown smiled crookedly. "There are many gullible people who will believe because they wish, or need to."

Watson threw his cheroot stub into the fire.

"I get the feeling that you, however, do believe in its existence."

The waiter came with another whisky. The priest smiled gratefully.

"My research has led me to that conclusion," he said.

"One wonders who has the original," Watson mused.

"Some Satanist no doubt," Brown shrugged.

"Oh, come now!" said Watson, laughing. "Such people are fiction, or at worst, have unhinged minds."

Father Brown showed a flash of impatience.

"Indeed, they are not, Doctor. But also they do not advertize themselves." He laid a hand on Watson's sleeve. "But be very certain that they exist and are powerful. A book such as this would be priceless to such people."

Watson got up.

"I shall look on the bright side and assume it does not exist. And now, I suggest dinner or another very great evil will occur."

His friend looked puzzled. Watson laughed again.

"I shall be hungry. Come, old friend. Sufficient unto the day."

The following morning found Watson and Father Brown at their breakfast when Maigret strode into the dining room, dusting snow from his coat. He called loudly for coffee and sat down at the table.

"Well, Father, what of the book?" inquired the Commissioner.

Watson spread comfiture on his toast.

"And a good morning to you too, Maigret," he said.

Maigret wasn't to be put off. He threw a telegraph on the table.

"It appears Paris is becoming disenchanted with our, or should I say my, progress."

"Remind them you're busy," said Watson, rather unsympathetically.

"Then they would no doubt tell me to mind my own business and not interfere in a local inquiry, and send some smart young *flic* to take over."

Watson took a bite of toast.

"Considering the lack of evidence, and the apparent impossibility of the crime, perhaps they should get off their comfortable chairs and lend a hand."

Maigret was still not amused. He sat down heavily, almost with an air of defeat.

"Have we nothing?"

"Father Brown has some interesting information about the book," said Watson.

Maigret visibly brightened. He leaned forward.

"You've solved it?"

"Not solved," said the priest, shaking his head. "But I now know what the book is and what it might be used for."

Maigret appeared not to know whether to be pleased or disappointed.

"So are we any nearer to discovering the perpetrator of this butchery?"

Again, the priest shook his head. Maigret could barely contain his impatience.

"This book... What can it tell us? What might it be used for? Father, I am consumed with urgency."

Brown glanced at Watson, who barely hid a smile. His old friend had an impish sense of humor and he knew he was teasing the Commissioner.

Father Brown placed the book on the table.

"This is a copy of a volume called the *Kitab el Khaouf,* or the Book of Terror. It was supposedly written in the late seventh or early eighth century by a man called Abdul el Hazid, also known as The Mad Arab. As I have told John, it is supposed to allow whoever owns it to call down violent curses on his enemies."

The silence that followed was broken only by the sound of a log settling in the hearth. Then Maigret sat back, his disbelief painted across his lined face.

"Surely, Father, you do not expect a hard-headed policeman such as myself to accept such fairy tale."

"Maigret," Watson cut on, "Father Brown has made it his life's work to become an expert on exactly this kind of thing. If he says it is possible, then I for one believe him."

Maigret looked from one to the other. He saw nothing but the truth. He threw his hands up.

"Very well." He slapped the book. "You say this is a copy. Can it work the same... miracles?"

The slight hesitation told Watson the policeman still found it hard to accept.

"No," replied Father Brown, shaking his head. "For that, you would need the original."

"And you believe it exists?"

"I know it does." The priest's voice was very soft. "And from what I have seen at the chapel, I do not believe it can be far."

"But why would d'Ingraville have a copy?" Watson asked.

"I, too, am puzzled. From what you say, he would have no interest in it," Brown replied. "However, we should refer to him as Saint-Germain from now on."

Maigret jabbed his finger at the book.

"What if his dismissive attitude was a facade to hide his true purpose? What if the orgies in the chapel were black magic rituals?"

"No, Commissaire," said the priest, shaking his head firmly. "I searched the chapel thoroughly. There was no evidence to suggest anything but behavior of the basest sort. We shall have to look elsewhere for the answer to that. But one wonders how such a man came to have the copy in his possession."

"It seems to me there is only one man to answer these questions," said Maigret, his voice firm."

"And who might that be?" Watson inquired.

"The antiquarian, Mocata."

"Your reasoning?"

"The man said that Saint-Germain had brought it upon himself."

"It is somewhat thin evidence with which to confront a man and accuse him murder," Father Brown demurred. "And anyway, from what Watson has told me, Abbé Jules, too, had little cause to love the Comte."

"A man of the cloth?" said Maigret, appalled. "A man of God?"

"Am I not a man of God, too?" said Brown, smiling. "And yet I know of these things."

"As a student, Father, not a practitioner," Maigret protested.

He got quickly to his feet.

"I propose to pay this Mocata another visit," he said.

"And do what?" Watson asked.

"Confront him. Show him the evidence. I have often found that the cleverest criminal will succumb to direct questioning when presented with such."

Father Brown, however, was not to be hurried into action.

"Commissioner, suppose that what you suggest is right, that Mocata is responsible, I doubt he would, as you say, *succumb*. He would not be an ordinary criminal, but one who could call on the powers of darkness."

"And I have the powers of the law. We will see which trumps which."

The priest threw an imploring look at Watson.

"Make him see sense, John. Mocata may or may not be responsible. He may have the book. But if we charge in, he will in all likelihood show us the door."

"Maigret, you cannot barge in without some kind of solid reason," tried the Englishman. "Do you not require a warrant in France? And what are you planning to charge him with?"

Maigret pulled a revolver from his pocket.

"This is my warrant."

"It won't wash, Maigret."

"Then, I shall simply pay him a visit."

The bit was between the policeman's teeth and he was going to run. Watson saw there was no way out of it but to go with him and try to keep the damage to a minimum. Watson knew it was an act of desperation on his part to keep his masters in Paris off his back.

The snow was falling heavily as they got into the pony trap and set out for Mocata's house. Both Watson and Father Brown had tried again to deter Maigret from what they considered a rash action, but without success.

The priest had begged for more time. There were others whose opinions he needed before he could feel sure of his ground. Watson had tried to point out that without evidence, all they would achieve would be to warn him.

It was to no avail. Maigret had slapped the reins and the pony had taken off at a smart trot despite the poor visibility. Twice they nearly slid off the road into the ditch, and once the poor pony had become confused and run them into a snow bank, from which it took the better part of half an hour to extricate themselves, and considerably unnerved the already high strung animal.

As the weather worsened, Watson again tried to persuade Maigret to abandon his efforts for the day, or at least until the snow ceased, but he was up against a brick wall. Maigret's tenacity in a case was legendary, but his companions felt he was carrying that legend to extremes.

Then, they came upon Mocata's gate so suddenly it nearly resulted in a spill as Maigret sawed the reins and brought both whinnying pony and trap to a skidding halt. Watson grabbed Father Brown to prevent him being thrown out and turned on Maigret, his anger rising.

"Enough, Maigret," he shouted. "We are with you in this, but you are now behaving like a man possessed. Have a care, or I, for one, will call it quits and you may confront Mocata alone and do as you wish."

The Commissioner turned on Watson with a snarl, one fist raised. And then he dropped his arm, eyes wide at the realization that he had indeed been behaving irrationally.

"My God. Watson, please forgive me. I am behaving like a fool. I have had the *grippe*... Not at all like myself. What is happening to me...?" He laid his hand on Father Brown's sleeve. "You are right. This must be done with circumspection. Will you please take the lead in this questioning? This is your area of expertise."

The priest tossed the blood-spattered copy of the *Kitab el Khaouf* onto Mocata's desk.

"What do you say to that, Monsieur Mocata?"

"That it is a forgery. The book does not exist. It is a myth."

"And yet it does," Father Brown said, softly. "And I believe you know it. Is it possible you even know where it is?"

Mocata picked up the book, turned it over in his hands, flipped through it and put it back on the desk.

"Where was this found?" he asked.

"I believe you know," Brown replied.

"Humor me, Father. Oh yes, I know of you. A man whose life's work has been the mysteries and arcane of this world is likely to know of those who share his interests."

"As I have heard of you," said Brown, nodding slightly.

Watson was surprised. His old friend had said nothing about knowing Mocata. The Antiquarian repeated his request. Brown raised an eyebrow before answering:

"In the Comte d'Ingraville's private chapel."

"Chapel." Mocata spat the word. "More likely, his obscenity." He looked sharply at Father Brown. "What makes you think I would know that?"

"The book's reputation and your public displays of antipathy for each other."

Mocata made a dismissive gesture.

"Bah. I admit I did not wish him well, and his reputation was unsavory, but to kill him for it?" He faced Maigret. "One does not kill a man for such a thing."

Maigret pointed at the book.

"What of that? Father Brown says it has great powers for evil."

"The original has many things said about it, that among them," said Mocata, shrugging. "But that thing is a forgery, put about by God knows who, and for God knows what purpose. But it was not me, and, as I have said, it is a myth."

"And if I say it isn't?" said Father Brown.

Mocata smiled, but the smile did not reach his eyes.

"Then it isn't, and I am wrong."

He went to a side table, took up a decanter of brandy and offered it. There were no takers. He poured a small amount into a cut crystal glass and drank it.

"Anyway, Commissioner, just what is the purpose of your visit? It must be pressing to bring you out in such weather."

"This is in connection with the murder inquiry in the death of Comte d'Ingraville."

"You dare burst into my house to accuse me of God knows what?" said Mocata, angrily.

"You invited us in," Watson said calmly.

"Common humanity would not allow otherwise. I would not send a dog out in such weather."

"But you might a demon," replied the Englishman.

Mocata's eyes widened with amazement. Then he laughed with what seemed to be genuine amusement.

"Is that what this is about: some hare-brained idea concerning that book?"

Watson though the man was either innocent as he protested, or a damned fine actor.

At that moment, Maigret forgot his promise and let his control slip. He took a step towards Mocata and jabbed an angry finger at the man's face.

"I could at least respect a man who has the courage to face his enemy, even a murderer. But someone who summons a fiend from Hell to do his dirty work is beneath contempt."

Mocata's laughter suddenly changed to anger. He slammed his fist on the desk, then picked up the book and tossed contemptuously at Maigret.

"Be damned to you, Monsieur. I have, with considerable restraint, listened to your ravings." He switched his attention to Brown. "And you Father, I am ashamed that a man of your standing could believe in this rubbish. The *Kitab el Khaouf* is a myth. The man who supposedly wrote it is a fiction."

There was a pause that was as near to embarrassment as it is possible to get and still maintain anger. Maigret tried to bluster. He was clearly frustrated. Then Mocata pointed a quivering finger at the door.

"I must ask you to leave my house, now, and never return."

Brown tried one more time, but he was on shaky ground. They had no proof.

"Abdul el Hazid was said to have been seized by an invisible monster in broad daylight and devoured horribly before a large number of fright-frozen witnesses. Does not that sound strangely like what happened to the Comte?"

Mocata barked his contempt.

"Said to? Invisible monsters? Father Brown, I had thought you a scholar, but you are naïve, even for a man of the cloth." He strode to the door and flung it open. "Now go before I call my servants and have you thrown out."

The pony, looking about as miserable as it was possible for a creature to look, stood forlornly between the shafts of the trap, its head hanging and its back covered with snow. Watson feeling a pang of guilt, went to the animal's head and gently brushed the snow away by way of apology. He then got into the trap and took the reins as he felt Maigret was in no fit mood to drive, particularly in such weather.

As they turned out of the drive onto the almost impassable road, Father Brown was the first to speak.

"The man's anger had the feel of righteous indignation. Perhaps we have made a grave error."

Watson clicked to encourage the pony.

"A legitimate reaction if he is innocent, but a brilliant dissimulation if he is not."

Maigret would have none of it.

"He is not, Watson. I feel it in my bones, and I am an experienced detective."

"We may know that Mocata is guilty, Commissioner, but of what?" he said. "That he caused Saint-Germain's death, most certainly. But charge him with murder by demon, and any court would laugh at you."

"Then what can we do?"

Watson's face was stern.

"Watch our backs, my friend. I feel Mocata is an evil man."

The journey was grim, the road worse, and Watson's attention was wholly occupied in staying out of the ditches. Then, just as he was about to get down and lead the pony by the head, the weather cleared and they broke free of the blinding conditions.

At that moment, the pony pricked its ears, whinnied and Watson saw it glance sideways, the whites of its eyes rolling. Something had spooked the animal badly. A moment later it got the bit between its teeth and panicked, and only the deep snow, acting as a brake, kept the trap from careering out of control.

"What the devil's going on, Watson?" Maigret shouted.

"Damned if I know. The animal's scared silly."

As he said it, the hairs on the back of his neck rose. He fought the runaway pony, but managed to get a look over his shoulder.

What he saw and felt made his blood run cold.

In the woods to their right, trees cracked and bent as if some great force was pushing its way through. Snow exploded from over-laden branches, and, to his utter horror, he saw great two-legged footprints throwing up great gouts of snow as if an unimaginable creature was inexorably pounding towards them.

The pony whinnied piteously and redoubled its efforts, bolting harder, threatening every second to send cart and passengers headlong into the ditch.

For a few moments, Watson's mind was blank, unable to comprehend what was going on. And then, with a shock that wrenched at the very core of his being, he realized what it was.

The demon, the myth, the thing that could not be and never was, was attacking them!

How? His mind screamed for an answer, a desperate way out. The answer came with a snap. The Policeman and Father Brown were both staring in open-mouthed horror, for they, too, had realized what was happening.

Watson roared at Maigret:

"The book! It's homing in on the book! Get rid of it as you value your immortal soul."

Maigret stared at him uncomprehendingly, but Father Brown understood. He reached into the detective's coat, also shouting for the book, echoing Watson's words.

Understanding dawned on the Commissioner's face. He frantically scrabbled in his coat pocket and, half standing, he hurled the book with all his strength.

Watson saw it arc, a black shape with leaves fluttering like a wounded bird, to land in the white virgin snow and disappear. Then he gave every atom of his attention to keeping the bucking and jumping trap under a semblance of control.

Behind them, he heard a roar so close it seemed almost as if the horror was upon them. The roar came again, and to his straining ears, it seemed like it expressed the frustration of a creature whose voice could only have been born in Hell. Again and again, the roar shattered the empty landscape, each time fainter and fainter, until it was no more.

Slowly Watson fought the panicked pony to a halt, then leaped out of the driver's seat and went to its head, cradling the poor thing as its chest heaved fit to burst. At last, with a great shudder, it seemed to understand what Watson was trying to do and its head drooped against him.

Finally, peace reigned. Watson looked up at the anxious face of Father Brown.

"What will happen?" he said.

The priest replied, and there was satisfaction in his voice:

"A curse that cannot find its home will return like a boomerang to the place from where it was sent."

"Then Mocata...?"

"...Is already dead and his soul in Hell."

The following morning, as Watson and Father Brown were again at breakfast, the pony trap rattled into the yard and, moments later, the coated figure of Maigret was silhouetted in the doorway.

"Well, Maigret," said Watson smiling. "You bring us news of Mocata, I assume?"

Maigret advanced slowly into the room.

"Abbé Jules was found by his curate this morning; dead. He had been eviscerated and decapitated and his body torn apart. It seems I shall have to apologize to Monsieur Mocata."

He asked for and got a brandy. He tossed it back at a gulp.

"Damn it, Watson. There's nothing a policeman hates worse than to have a crime, know who is responsible, and yet be cheated of bringing him to justice."

There was a long silence, then Watson asked:

"And what will you tell them in Paris?"

*A good monster story is always a welcome addition to the* Tales of the Shadowmen *roster, but what happens when the monsters are not real, but man-made... Nathan Cabaniss has dug deep into the world of B-movies to take us on a visit to...*

## Nathan Cabaniss: *The House of El Hombre Loco*

*West Germany, 1966*

Count Waldemar Daninsky pulled on the chain to test its strength, and the links held as tightly to the stone wall as they could. The strain of the pull got his heart beating, and already he felt the beast stirring in his chest. He checked his watch, and looked out to the veranda of the north tower he'd constructed onto his estate, where the sun was lowering itself towards the horizon like a circle of blood dropped into an orange sea. There was still time, despite the thudding pound of his heart.

Of course, there were other things the Count would rather be doing this evening. The Arabian Princess Dala was said to be in town, and the Count was not known to disappoint wealthy young heiresses when they came calling. But tonight would not be that night, as the cycle of the moon had come full circle and they were due for a night of its complete and rounded brilliance... along with everything that entailed. The Princess Dala would likely not be pleased to retire to his place after their dinner and find the Count transformed into a snarling bulk of fur and dripping fangs. Long ago, he considered it an abominable curse, but now it was little more than a nuisance.

He could barely remember the night it had happened—the night of his turning. At the time, it had seemed the defining event of his life, but now it was little more than a hazy recollection. Had it been a full-blooded alpha, or just some runt of the litter, who had given him the bite? Funny how the things that seem so important to us when we're young fade away in time, much like everything else.

He had searched for years to find a cure, and come close on several occasions. Of course, it would usually be a ruse staged by vampires looking for some werewolf blood, or aliens from outer space wanting to use mind control and have his other half wreak havoc across the planet... Daninsky supposed he wouldn't exactly be against a cure these days—otherwise he would be occupying himself with the Princess—but with the risks involved, what was the point? Besides, one rare benefit to his lycanthropy was his elongated lifespan, with which he could do whatever he pleased the other twenty-odd days of the month. Not a bad trade, in the grand scheme of things.

Dusk began to settle into night just outside the window, so the Count wasted no time. He finished off the glass of water he'd left by the door, preparing to affix the chains about his wrists and ankles and spend the night in the chilly, barren tower, but was halted by a sound emanating from the shadows: a low, mumbling groan, punctuated by a shuffling of feet. Already his keen wolf senses were sharpening, and Daninsky could smell another in the room with him.

He set the glass down carefully, committing every fiber of his being to hold the beast within back. Whoever it was, whatever they wanted, he had to try and talk sense into them before his other half tore them limb from limb.

"Listen to me, friend," he said loudly. "I don't know what you're after, but if you're trying to get at me, I'm afraid you've picked the absolute worst possible moment..."

A silhouette drug itself out from the shadows, and the dimming light outside revealed its true form. Its pale white skin shone brilliantly in the dark, with tattered and ragged clothes hanging off the thin but powerful form. But most striking where the eyes: yellow and thoroughly inhuman. Looking into them was like looking into the deepest recesses of one's own soul.

Daninsky knew his interloper immediately upon looking into those dull, yellow orbs. It was the creature known as Gouroull, the unholy "offspring" of Victor Frankenstein. He had crossed paths with him before, or at least a version of him. Dr. Frankenstein had left behind several such children; corpses reanimated through his arcane science.

The creature smiled at the look of recognition on the Count's face, flashing razor-sharp teeth as the moon's light crept through the tower window. Daninsky's heart pounded in his chest like a jackhammer, and the beads of sweat that broke out all over his body became trapped in his ever-growing hair.

The Count made no further attempt to control himself—if it was a fight Gouroull wanted, then it was a fight the creature was going to get.

Daninsky's vision went red, and the beast burst forth from its human shell in a manic howl. His wild eyes locked upon Gouroull, and, in an instant, he leapt across the room in a blur of fur and fangs.

Gouroull's demeanor changed as the beast charged at him, the lifeless yellow eyes widening in something that approached anguish. He raised his hands in an attempt at self-defense, but it was no use. The beast lashed out with a furred claw, knocking the creature off of his feet like a ragdoll.

In a blink, Daninsky was on top of him. Gouroull shrieked, but was cut off when the beast locked his jaw around his throat.

Blood splashed his mouth, and the Count had a sudden sense of disorientation. The red cloud faded from his vision, and the storm that welled in his chest calmed itself. In complete control of his actions once more, he looked down at his hands to see the blood covering not fur and claws, but normal, human appendages.

What was going on here?

The moon outside was full and bright, and yet his breathing was calm. His thoughts where unclouded by the pure, bestial rage of the other...

The sight of Gouroull on the floor snapped his mind back to the present, and Daninsky retched from the tangy taste of someone else's blood filling his mouth. He had killed before, of course—his other half had all but ensured such outcomes in his lifetime. But since he had taken to locking himself away in his tower, it had been so very long since it last happened, and he had never seen the results of a kill so suddenly with his human senses returned.

He sank to the floor on his knees, unable to take his eyes from his hands. Their human appearance, and the blood that stained them—a red unlike any other, far clearer than any one saw in the movies...

*Hold on*, Daninsky thought to himself, studying the color on his hands carefully. He followed the trail of red on the ground where Gouroull lay, the last of it seeping out of the wound from his neck. Gouroull was no longer a normal "human;" the blood that ran through his stitched-together veins was anything but red...

Upon closer inspection, Daninsky saw that something was amiss with the creature's pallid complexion. His skin looked... smeared. The Count placed his distinctly-human finger to Gouroull's brow, and it came back stained with the same chalk-white color, revealing a far more human shade of skin beneath. He pulled Gouroull's mouth open, found that the razor-sharp teeth were false as well. This was not Gouroull, but rather a human made up to look like the creature.

Daninsky's heart froze. The act of killing had left a bad enough taste in his mouth, but to have murdered an ordinary human in cold blood? Did the man even mean him harm? What was the purpose of all this?

He continued his study of the strange, dead man before him: up close, the furred vest and tattered pants also looked distinctly fabricated. Their dirtiness was intentional, as if they had been aged to look that way. Daninsky turned up the collar of the vest, and saw the label of a nearby rental house. The dead man had nothing in his pockets but a wad of petty cash. No hint of identification at all...

The Count rushed over to a basin of water he had prepared, and splashed it in his face to both clean off the blood and shake him out of his stupor. With his mind clearing off the last of its wolf-state, he looked once more to his hands, pink and soft and unquestionably human. His sudden change, the false Gouroull... None of it made any sense...

A storm rumbled outside, and a bolt of lightning briefly illuminated the window. In the flash, Daninsky saw his hands retake their furred appearance once more, only to become human again in the blink of an eye. The Count rubbed his eyes to make sure he wasn't seeing things, and felt icy fingers of doubt began to creep in at the edges of his mind. Was this what it felt like to go mad?

*What on Earth was going on?*

Pete Dumond made his move: queen to b8, putting black in check. Dr. Génessier put a hand to his chin, studying the board carefully. It was a reckless move, with the only option out of check being to capture the queen with his remaining knight. Why would his opponent throw away his most powerful piece?

"Are you sure that's the move you want to make?" Génessier asked as a courtesy.

"Quite," Dumond said, his eyes fixed on the board, waiting patiently for the doctor to make his move.

Génessier kept staring at the man, expecting him to look up and meet his gaze, but he didn't. That was one thing that could be said of his companion: once he had made up his mind, there was no changing it. Dumond was a man who kept to his ways with a dogged obsession.

Of course, the doctor himself had known obsession, known madness. There was the trail of bodies left in his wake in Paris. There was Christiane, his daughter, for whom he had done unspeakable things. All those pretty girls, all their pretty faces, and his daughter without a face of her own… Could anyone truly call such a thing madness? What father wouldn't do the same for his daughter?

He wondered where Christiane was now. He would forgive her, of course. The teeth of the dogs she'd let loose on him had left their mark, but not knowing where she was, whether or not she was okay—that hurt far worse. Dumond had promised to help Génessier the night he'd found him, his wounds hastily bandaged and sleeping in a pile of garbage—the celebrated surgeon thought to be dead to the world at large. He told the doctor that they would search for Christiane together, so long as Génessier agreed to help him. So far, Génessier had held up his end of the bargain, but Dumond had not.

Dumond was a man thought to be dead to the world at large, as well. He used to be a make-up artist in the movie business. A maker of monsters. When the studio where he was employed had him fired, Dumond decided to turn his monsters on the higher-ups, drugging and hypnotizing his young actors to murder the men responsible—a ploy that had quite literally gone up on flames. But Dumond lived on, continuing to hone his craft in the years since.

He was making his monsters now with the aid of Génessier's careful hand, ready to go out into the world and do their bidding. So far, it had been nothing more remarkable than robbing a few banks or scaring a handful of influential persons, but Dumond had designs on a greater plan. One that he didn't feel the need to share with his so-called "partner."

Seeing no better option, Génessier made his move, capturing the white queen with his knight.

"Sometimes, Dumond, I fear you are too reckless. It's like this business with the Count last night…"

"Reckless?" Dumond replied, finally taking his gaze from the board and meeting Génessier's. "We've been secretly feeding him the drugs for weeks now, applying the proper procedures for the hypnosis. Everything is moving according to plan."

Again with the "plan." Génessier wiped the corners of his scarred mouth with his handkerchief, whittling down all the possible options of reply. Asking straight questions always got him nowhere with Dumond. If he wanted to find out the details of whatever Dumond was planning, he would have to treat the conversation itself as a game of chess.

"You just seem to be showing your hand too early, that's all," the doctor finally replied. "The Count is not a man to take these displays of force lightly. Such tactics are likely to scare the prey away instead of luring it further into the trap."

"Or perhaps we're scaring the prey right to where we want it to be," Dumond said, pulling his rook from all the way across the board to black's side.

Génessier's mouth dropped. Dumond had secured the victory, placing him in checkmate. He was so wrapped up in capturing Dumond's queen he hadn't even seen the opening it left for his opponent to take.

"Daninsky will come to us, and then the plan will come full circle. All it takes is a proper manipulation of the pieces," Dumond said, picking up a pawn from the board.

In the blink of an eye, he made it disappear from his hand.

"I'm a showman, after all. Slight of hand is my forte."

Waldemar Daninsky paused at the gate, studying the warehouse carefully. The night of the false Gouroull's attack had led him on a trail of crisscrossing pathways. An old rental house for motion pictures, the address of an actor who had been out of work for years, and now this place: an old warehouse that belonged to no one, as far as Daninsky could determine.

The gate was nearly rusted shut, but unlocked. A strong push was all it took to break the rust away and swing the door open. He stepped within, and, with each step towards the warehouse, he could feel the hair rising on the back of his neck. It was the middle of the day, and the full moon had already come and gone, but once bitten, the wolf never truly left. The sharp animal senses that belonged to his other half were little more than a dull nerve, but still the warning alarms were sounding off all throughout Daninsky's body. Something was decidedly wrong with this place. He was walking into a trap...

He carefully made his way around the warehouse, and found only one entrance to be open—a small door located towards the back of the structure. It might as well have been cheese in a mouse-trap, but Daninsky had to know. Since killing the fake Gouroull, he had been trapped in a miasma of questions, without a single answer in sight. The full moon had brought out the wolf, just like it always did, but it retreated just as quickly as it had arrived. He could still taste the blood in his all-too-human mouth, still see the life pooling onto the floor from that out-of-work actor's neck. How had it happened? The Count had to know, and thus, he entered the warehouse unabated.

It was dark inside, and cool. He stood for a moment there at the entryway, listening for any warning signs: a shuffling of footsteps, perhaps, or labored, anticipatory breathing. But there was nothing—the entire place was silent.

He took another step forward, and, suddenly, floodlights switched on all around. A voice echoed from above via loudspeaker:

"Lights!"

Blinded at first, his eyes adjusted to the brightness and found themselves down a stretch of hallway with a bright red carpet and white walls on either side. At the end of the hall was a dead-end, where it split into two different directions.

"Camera!" the voice above continued.

Music then played, something out of a bad horror movie. A figure stepped out from one of the splintering hallways at the end: a pale, fair-haired woman nude beneath a flowing black cloak. In her hand, she carried a scythe that looked twice her size. She let her lower lip fall, opening her mouth to reveal a pair of elongated fangs.

"Action!"

The vampire girl ran down the hallway, the blade of her scythe catching the light's glint like a demon spreading its lips to grin over and over again.

Daninsky's pulse quickened, and he felt the change come over him. His muscles atrophied only to re-grow in powerful, bestial shapes. The hair on his arms thickened into a deep brown fur. The wolf was tearing itself out from deep within, all without the full moon's prompt. *How was any of this happening?*

He had no time for questions however, as the girl charged him at an alarming rate. Daninsky guessed she wasn't a real bloodsucker—just like "Gouroull," this was likely another starving actor. He feared his other half would tear her apart in an instant, and yet another innocent's blood would stain his hands. But then the realization hit him: the red hadn't overtaken his vision. His mind was as clear as it was while still human, even though his body had completed the wolf transformation.

Before he could ponder his current circumstances any further, the scythe ripped the air before him. His heightened reflexes allowed him to duck just in time, and Daninsky felt a sliver of hair clip itself from the top of his head.

He grabbed the scythe's handle, and threw the girl over his shoulder. She landed hard on the red carpeting behind him—hard enough to slam the false teeth from her mouth and knock her out cold.

His attacker subdued, the Count took a moment to gather his breath, and was amazed at the appearance of his furred hands. Despite the surge of activity, his heart wasn't pounding in his chest, and he wasn't consumed by blind rage. He had taken on the persona of the werewolf, and yet remained himself on the inside.

Footsteps echoed down the hall, and Daninsky was interrupted from his thoughts once more. He turned to face two new monstrosities. One was an enormous lump of rock and moss, covered in a strange fur from head to toe. With its black eyes and hooked claws, Daninsky thought it to be some kind of mutated sloth. The other was the strangest sight the Count had ever seen: some manner of extraterrestrial, with an enlarged brain jutting out from the top of its skull and elongated, insect-like arms that ended in sharp pincers.

The two lurched forward, and Daninsky wasted no time. He rushed down the length of the hallway at them, and could smell the very human fear underneath; more actors in suits.

Both attempted swipes with their claws, but their massive suits proved to be too restrictive in comparison to Daninsky's fierce speed. In an instant, he had the tops of their outfits torn off, and the quivering faces of the actors beneath froze in horror.

Daninsky let loose with a howl that shook the walls of the hallway, and the two men fainted in shock.

*I could definitely get used to this*, Daninsky thought, when more shuffling of feet sounded off from the hallway's corridor.

The Count almost grinned in satisfaction, eager to see what new "monsters" he could make soil themselves. He turned to face his new assailants, but was halted by the bizarre sight: a group of men in tatters, dressed like warrior monks readying themselves for a crusade. Except their armor was rusted, and their weapons carelessly dragged on the floor behind them. But worst of all were their faces, or lack thereof—the skin had been carved in horrid ways, and the eyes plucked right from their sockets. These were no actors playing dress-up; these poor devils had been mutilated to achieve their ghastly appearance.

They shambled towards Daninsky, moaning their suffering with each footfall. Daninsky did not feel it right to fight such creatures, but they shuffled on—whatever, whoever had put them up to the task must have had a hold on them like no other. As sad as it was to say, death would be a mercy for them.

Feeling his anger starting to rise once more, Daninsky bared his fangs, and let loose with tooth and claw…

"Oh, what a show!" Dumond exclaimed, cackling like a madman as he held his eye up to the camera's viewfinder.

Génessier sighed, and went back to loading the cameras that had run out of film with fresh reels. His companion took far too much joy in the suffering of others. It left a bitter taste in the doctor's mouth.

"You really are missing out, Génessier," Dumond continued, his eye still fixed to the viewfinder. "This is sensational. Absolutely, without question the finest images yet put to film!"

Having had enough, Génessier dropped the canisters of film in an angry clatter upon the floor. Dumond finally looked up from his damned camera, shocked at his partner's sudden outburst.

"Have a care, man! We're not getting any second takes after this…"

Génessier took a deep breath from his nose. He removed his glasses to clean them in an attempt to keep himself calm, but his thinly-veiled rage was still readily apparent when he spoke.

"I have helped you the whole time we have been together. You found me half-dead and nursed me back to health, and for that, I am eternally in your debt. But if I am to continue to aid you, you must hold up your end of the bargain and help me find my daughter."

Dumond fell silent for a time, before raising his hands in exasperation.

"My good doctor, I promise we will find your daughter. But at the moment? Our plans are finally bearing fruit. When I go back to Hollywood with this in my hands, they'll regret the day they let me go for the rest of their careers. I'll run them right out of town!"

"Hollywood?" Génessier said.

"Yes. Can you imagine how much money this'll make—footage of a real-life werewolf for the greatest film production known to man. I'll be bigger than David O. Selznick! I'll be the next DeMille!" He went to another of the cameras and put his eye to the viewfinder. "Now, keep loading that film into the cameras. I don't want to miss a frame…"

Génessier's hands began to tremble in anger. All the luring of out-of-work actors and young hopefuls, all the drugs and hypnosis, all the pain and suffering they inflicted over the course of their time together… It had all been in the service of making some damned film? So that Dumond could show up his old bosses in Tinseltown? No… nothing was worth this. He may have sold what little soul he had in his previous life, but that was for the love of his daughter—not for some cheap B-movie.

Génessier reached into his pocket and pulled out a thin scalpel. He slowly advanced for Dumond, raising it silently above his head as he approached…

Waldemar Daninsky let go the last of the scarred monks, and the battle was finally at an end. He looked behind him to survey the trail of bodies, monstrosities both real and fabricated, and felt sickened. Who would do such a thing, play with human lives so carelessly? Daninsky had a mind to give them a taste of their own medicine, and now that he was in complete control of his wolf form, he more than had the means to do just that.

The Count stalked the corridors, but there were no further entryways. At least, not to the naked eye… He caught the scent of blood through one of the walls, and discovered a hidden panel that opened by pushing on it. Inside was a man on his knees, multiple red wounds blossoming along his torso. Another man, one scarred beyond recognition, lay dead behind him with a bloody scalpel in hand, his neck broken.

The man on his knees looked at Daninsky absent-mindedly.

"Creative... differences..." he mumbled out, before falling over on his face.

Daninsky stood in the doorway for a moment, attempting to make sense of what he saw. There were several cameras lined up, each filming the corridor he was in previously through hidden windows. The Count went over to the dead men to search them, and found a rolled up document on the one with the stab wounds.

Unrolling it, he saw a title on the blood-stained cover: *How to Make a Werewolf*. He opened to the first page and quickly skimmed the words therein. It was a film script, the story of which eerily mirrored his life over the last few days. It told the story of two madmen, who drugged and secretly hypnotized a werewolf Count to where they could control his transformations for their own devious schemes.

Daninsky put the script down, and noticed that his hands were human again. He looked to the dead men on the floor... Was that what had happened here? Had these two unlocked the secrets only known previously to the full moon through drugs and hypnosis?

He concentrated hard upon his hand, reaching deep within to see if he could summon the wolf at will. His hand burst suddenly into a paw of fur and talons. Concentrating once more, Daninsky returned it to its pink, fleshy state.

Turning into a werewolf was now as easy as flexing a muscle.

*That's interesting*, he thought.

The girl made her way down the meadow through the chilly evening. She pulled her red hood more tightly about her shoulders, but it did nothing to stifle the chill running down her back. Something was watching her every move. She quickened her pace, eyes nervously at the ground in fear of what they might see.

A low growl sounded off from behind her, and the girl froze. She didn't want to turn around, didn't want to see the horror that crept silently at her heels, but still she was compelled.

She turned slowly, and saw the silhouette of two ears atop a mass of fur, with yellow eyes that burned in the shadows. She dropped her basket and put a hand over her mouth, a scream threatening to leap from her throat...

"Cut!"

The girl dropped her hand, annoyingly looked over at the camera crew to her left.

"Oh, what is it this time?"

The wolf in front of her transformed instantly into a human, revealing the face of Waldemar Daninsky.

"What's wrong, Guido?"

The director stepped out from behind the camera, berating his crew in Italian. He walked over apologetically to his actors.

"I'm sorry, it's not you two. You're beautiful, really… One of these imbeciles let the boom slip into picture. Tell you what, the two of you take five as we reset."

He went back to berating his crew in more Italian, and Waldemar lazily went over to the catering table to see what he could find. Wolfing out took a lot out of him, and they had been out in this meadow all night. He supposed he didn't have much of a right to complain, however, as these new werewolf movies had brought him no shortage of success and acclaim. Still, making pictures was a rough enterprise… especially at the budgets the studios gave him.

No matter. When he was younger he might have considered it a curse, but now it was just something he learned to live with.

*Felifax is the hybrid tiger-man created by Paul Féval, fils, in a 1929 novel available from Black Coat Press (ISBN 978-1-932983-88-3). Christophe Colin, a first time contributor to our sister French series* Les Compagnons de l'Ombre, *delves into the thin line separating Man from Beast, when he brings him in contact with the notorious Doctor Moreau in...*

## Christophe Colin: *Of Beasts and Men*

*Somewhere in the Pacific, 1931*

"What have you brought me, my children?" Dr. Moreau asked.

He was surprised by what he saw. As the sole owner of this new island, protected from prying eyes, he had resumed his experiments on animals, trying to evolve them into beast-men. In his small zoo, he had dog, monkey and lizard-men, but not this perfect human-tiger hybrid.

"Bring him to my laboratory and put him on the operating table," he ordered.

When Moreau arrived, all the beast-men gathered together into a noisy crowd and questioned him about the presence of this stranger on the island. Even Moreau could not answer their questions.

"My children, I need some peace and quiet to work. Get out of here!" he finally shouted.

All of them left, except for the leopard-man. Leaning casually against a shelf, he watched the doctor arrogantly. Moreau sighed. The leopard-man seemed to be making a point to disobey him just to provoke him.

"Once again, you leave me no choice," Moreau said. "M'ling, put the leopard outside!"

A bear-dog-horse hybrid possessed of superhuman strength, M'ling snatched up the leopard-man and carried him under his arm out of the laboratory. Just when he was about to disappear into the corridor, the leopard-man roared:

"Moreau, I hate you, you and your stupid laws! You make a fool out of me and I will get revenge!"

Ordinarily this kind of outburst would not affect Moreau, but, this time, a shiver ran down his spine. The leopard-man had always been rebellious, but not dangerous. However, an event as important as the arrival of this newcomer could help him sow the seeds of dissension among his peers and turn them off the course planned out by Moreau.

The doctor bandaged his patient's wounds and listened to him ramble. The stranger seemed to be speaking Bengali, a language that Moreau had learned as a youth. He was far from fluent, but he recognized many words. There was one that the patient repeated constantly, but that he did not understand: *Felifax!*

Was it this creature's name? Who had given it to him, and how could he speak so intelligently, even when mumbling?

Few of Moreau's experiments had the power of speech and, at best, their language was rudimentary, like a child's. But this animal was talking like a man and this ability filled Moreau with resentment because, in spite of his many attempts, he had never been able to achieve this feat.

Other questions haunted him: How could a tiger-man come into the world? Who had created him, and why? He also wondered from whence he had come? Maybe he had been sent by a foreign power, or by a rival scientist, like the mysterious Dr. Kramm, trying to steal and profit from the results of his experiments...

He shuddered at the idea that his children, even if some of them gave him a hard time, could be used someday as murderers, or cannon fodder in some deadly future war, like the world had seen fifteen years ago. To imagine them crouching in muddy trenches, blown to bits by artillery shells or, worse, gassed, was unbearable.

Moreau also knew that some of his subjects were not obeying his laws; they were rejecting them. He was especially distrustful of the leopard-man who spent his time provoking him and questioning his rules. Just by his presence, this Felifax could very easily sow discord among the beast-men and further the leopard's ambitions. Moreau could not allow this to happen.

The creature looked calm. He decided to leave it alone in his laboratory for a little while. After everything that had happened, he was exhausted. He needed to think about what to do next. Finally, he grabbed a rifle and returned to the lab to sleep. He put the bunk next to the operating table where Felifax was lying still.

Moreau fell asleep quickly, but, in the middle of the night, he was awakened by a roar. The leopard-man stood above him. He had broken the rifle and was threatening him with its butt.

"Moreau! I've always hated you. You and your wicked laws. A creature as weak as you can't call himself our master! I've made up my mind to kill you tonight and I'll blame your death on this mysterious visitor. Then I'll be the leader of the beast-men and we'll execute him. No one will dare to stand in my way!"

"Are sure about that?" a voice growled.

Felifax had just woken up and gotten between the leopard-man and the trembling Moreau. The two opponents watched each other as they performed a deadky dance of death.

Felifax and the leopard-man both roared at the same time. Their claws whirled around in the air. Each of them struck out to wound and harm the other. It was a tough fight for Felifax, because he was still not completely recovered from the injuries he had received in the shipwreck. It was hard for him to challenge the savagery and treachery of the other feline being. However, he did have one advantage over Moreau's hybrid: his keen senses and imposing size allowed him to keep a distance. But the leopard-man would not give up; he launched a volley of quick, accurate jabs that forced the Tiger-Man to step back.

Felifax was worn out. He fought as best he could, but the battle was not going well. He could not last much longer. He had to muster all his strength and attack as fast as possible. In a desperate move, he grabbed the leopard-man's throat and tried to strangle him, but the other fought with all his energy to survive. The leopard-man clawed at one of Felifax's wounds. In pain, the Tiger-Man loosened his grip. The sneaky feline then snatched up Moreau's rifle and used its butt to clobber Felifax, stunning him.

The Tiger-Man crumpled to the ground. His adversary tried to deliver a fatal blow; the rifle butt wheeled through the air, but, with amazing reflexes, Felifax caught it in his powerful grip. He pulled with all his strength and his enemy stumbled to the ground.

Forced to wrestle now, the two felines unsheathed their claws. No one could have predicted the outcome of this bloody battle because both creatures were fighting for their life. Felifax was pinned under his enemy, but matched him blow for blow, claw for claw. While the leopard-man was attacking without respite, trying to hit his enemy's pressure points, Felifax struggled to overpower and suffocate his adversary. All of a sudden, Felifax was hit in the stomach by his opponent's knee, and he had to release his vice-like grip.

Watching this savage spectacle, Moreau got back to his senses and frantically searched for something in his laboratory. He found it, at last, and approached the two combatants, shouting to the tiger-man:

"Felifax! Hold him steady!"

With the last of his strength the Tiger-Man threw his powerful arms around his enemy. Ignoring the claws that dug into his sides, he squeezed him hard against his chest. Moreau held up a syringe and plunged it into the leopard-man's neck.

The creature died almost immediately. He slumped in Felifax' arms. Exhausted, the Tiger-Man dropped the lifeless body and struggled to sit up.

Moreau squatted next to him and said:

"The animal world provides a great many poisons, and this syringe contained one of the most potent. He was a beast, and didn't deserve to die like this. However, had he lived, he would have killed both of us. That, my dear Felifax, I could not allow. Don't move... I'll dress these awful wounds of yours again."

While treating him, Moreau continued to converse:

"You were rambling and mumbling in Bengali. There was only one word I didn't understand: Felifax. I guess it was your name. Now that you're awake, maybe you can answer some questions. I would like to know the reason why you came to my island."

"To tell the truth," Felifax responded, "there isn't any. I was traveling on a ship that sunk in a storm, so it was pure chance that brought me here. I'm a castaway and would like to get back to India as soon as possible. Your name, however, is not unknown to me. Sir Eric Palmer told me about a Doctor Moreau who had once lived as a recluse on a mysterious island... Is this you? What are these beast-men? Animals or men?"

"My friend," Moreau said, "your interest in me is flattering. I am indeed this doctor you've heard about. Polite English society banished me because of my experiments, which they judged to be unnatural. But I am just a simple scientist, trying to unlock the secrets of our creator. After the failure of my first attempt, I decided to start from scratch again, and, thanks to my personal fortune, I was able to build a new laboratory on this nameless, undiscovered island. I believe civilization lies only on the surface, and men often behave like animals. I decided to prove that animals could be equal to men, even greater than them, by creating a perfect utopia that would be egalitarian and without violence. I'm glad to have met you because I was starting to lose hope. My hybrids always remain closer to animals than to men, and when I try to impose a moral code or strict conditioning on them, they quickly regress to their primitive state. Your presence proves to me that I can succeed and develop a creature like you.

"Also, you're in luck. A supply ship should be stopping by tomorrow. It is bound for India. For a fee, Captain Silver will have no problem accepting a passenger and, seeing that I am in your debt, I will pay for the voyage."

The next day, Captain Silver's ship, the *Silvermore*, arrived. Felifax and Moreau were waiting for it on the dock.

"The *Silvermore* should reach Chittagong in a week. My dear Felifax, your visit to my island was short and eventful. Still, I hope you won't harbor any bad memories of your stay. Naturally I have to ask you to keep my research an absolute secret. I wish you all the luck in the world and smooth sailing back home."

"It was a pleasure to make your acquaintance, Dr. Moreau. I miss India and I have many things to do there. I have to get back as quickly as possible."

Felifax boarded the ship and waved goodbye to Dr. Moreau.

*Journal of Dr. Moreau, July 17, 1931*

I'm thinking of asking Captain Silver to find me other felines for my future experiments. After Felifax's visit, I have made up my mind to use this species in my work. A Bengal tiger, or at least a puma, would fit the bill perfectly.

*Translation by Michael Shreve*

*Matthew Dennion brings the* Underworld *film series into the shared universe of the Shadowmen in this short, but important, tale that casts a new look at the events of the second film, and harks back to those of the third...*

# Matthew Dennion: *Turning Point*

*Paris, 1899*

The full moon was at its highest and, for the first time, Bertrand Caillet was glad to see the celestial body at its apex. His lycanthropic condition was now at the peak of its ferocity.

He had just completed his metamorphosis when the vampire kicked in his door. Her leather outfit clung to her lithe body like a second skin. She wore a long black trench coat that was open in the front and gave her the appearance of a cape draped around her shoulders. Her beautiful face was accentuated by her stunning blue eyes.

She was Selene the Death Dealer, and, as she leveled her gun at Caillet, he saw her as death personified.

The werewolf pounced on his attacker, forcing her to the floor, and forcing her pistol away from him. Caillet was stronger than his attacker, but the vampire was a warrior and an assassin trained specifically to slay werewolves. She grabbed Caillet's thumb and snapped it backwards, breaking the bone in two. Caillet howled in pain and grabbed his hand.

Selene moved like lighting, punching Caillet in the face, sliding out from under him, and delivering a kick to his temple. Caillet's face hit the floor. The vampire pointed her gun at the back of the werewolf's head.

In desperation, Caillet swiped his claw at Selene's thigh. He barely managed to graze her leg as she jumped out of the way. Seeing his opportunity, Caillet rushed across the room and jumped out of the window, falling several stories to the streets below.

He had no sooner hit the ground than a hail of silver bullets began raining around him. The werewolf ducked around a corner to avoid the deadly projectiles.

He took a moment to focus his mind as his master Lucian had taught him. He sniffed the air. His enhanced sense of smell was immediately able to locate the person he was looking for. If he could reach that person in time, he thought that he might even survive this encounter.

Caillet turned to run, but felt a searing pain in his shoulder.

He reached back and pulled a silver dagger from his flesh. He growled in pain and anger as he raced further down the alley.

Selene reloaded her pistol and continued her pursuit.

The scent of the man's house that Caillet sought was strong and far different than most other scents in Paris. The scent gave better directions than a detailed street map would have provided a normal man.

Suddenly a bullet grazed the back of Caillet's head. He turned to see Selene in midair, her knife drawn.

She landed next to the werewolf and slashed him across the midsection. The silver burned deep into the open wound which it had created. Caillet swiped his claw at the vampire, but managed only to tear her coat as she leapt backwards.

Snarling, the werewolf grabbed a lamppost and ripped it from the ground. He swung it like a massive club, hitting Selene with such force that she was sent flying back down the alley.

Caillet threw his weapon on top of her and raced out of the alley. He cleared the buildings and finally saw his destination, the Champs-Elysées mansion of the Great Psychagogue himself—Sâr Dubnotal!

As Caillet stared at the house, a silver throwing star buried itself into his calf. With the vampire right behind him, he limped into the house, whose front door was unlocked.

Selene followed him inside and saw Caillet crouched down in the middle of the entrance hall. The werewolf was injured and exhausted, making him an easy target. She walked in and drew her pistol from its holster.

Suddenly, Sâr Dubnotal appeared from a room to the left and rushed at her with one hand opened and the other balled into a fist. He was chanting a mystical incantation.

The vampire delivered a thrust kick to the Psychagogue's midsection, causing him to collapse onto the floor. She then refocused on the werewolf and emptied her pistol into him.

Caillet let out an ear-shattering howl as the last bullet pierced his heart. With her task completed, Selene turned and exited the house.

From the corner of the room, the Sâr and the injured Caillet watched as the vampire walked away.

"It worked," whispered the Psychagogue. "I was able to hypnotize her into thinking she killed you. Now, rest. We are masked from even her enhanced senses, for her mind believes that you have been slain."

Sâr Dubnotal helped Caillet to his feet.

"My part in your master's plan is complete," he continued. "The vampires believe that the werewolf is dead, just as the humans believe that Sergeant Bertrand Caillet is deceased. For all intents and purposes, you no longer exist."

Caillet winced as his body healed itself from the damage inflicted on it during the battle.

"My thanks for your help, Doctor," he said.

A flash of anger ran through the Sâr's eyes.

"Your gratitude is not nearly as valuable to me as your mission," the mystic said. "Long have I despised the senseless war that rages between the Lycans and the Vampires. Both species are being pushed toward extinction, while countless humans are being killed in the crossfire. I am only helping you to vanish because I feel that Lucian's plan is the only possible solution to this never ending conflict.

"Go, Bertrand Caillet, and use your abilities to find the descendents of the first immortal, unite the bloodlines, and put an end to this war."

Caillet nodded solemnly and departed.

*104 years later*

From the shadows, Caillet watched as Selene sank her fangs into Michael Corvin, the newly turned werewolf and descendent of the original immortal.

It seemed that whatever Sâr Dubnotal had done to Selene was still in effect, as she seemed totally unaware of his presence.

The vampire released Michael and ran to engage her sire. Caillet stared in awe as the first werewolf-vampire hybrid was born.

His mission had finally come to its successful conclusion.

*Maurice Leblanc initiated the theme of a duel of wits with twist upon twist by pitting his gentleman-burglar, Arsène Lupin, against the great detective himself, Sherlock Holmes. Peter Gabbani, a new contributor to our series, goes one better by pitting Lupin against another master burglar, A.J. Raffles. The pseudonym of "Rostat" in this story is mentioned by Leblanc himself as an identity used by Lupin when studying magic with stage magician Dickson (Harry's father) and Pickmann...*

## Peter Gabbani: *A Bond between Gentlemen*

*Paris & Vienna 1893*

Baroness Valentina started on the central figure. She hunted down the colors of the man's jacket: blue-black with brass buttons. Then she searched for hints of the red feather in his gold-encrusted black helmet, and then his red pants. Her gentleman worked on the wooden theater doorway. She had no initial attraction to the jigsaw puzzle. It wasn't her idea. Why would a Chenin blanc-drinking Parisian woman care about this picture, *Boulevard des Capucines & the Vaudeville Theater* by Jean Beraud, a four-year-old forgotten painting? This street scene, with its coated men in top hats and women in flouncy dresses, with its crisscrossing horses and backset row of trees covering the purpled buildings in the distance, was all alien landscape to her. These were mysterious people living lives to which she had no connection and no concern. But, still, she picked through the puzzle pieces, finding perhaps six fits per hour, which seemed to be the slowest possible advance to warrant continuing.

Evening after evening, with trays of supper installed on a side table, Baroness Valentina and her gentleman worked on the puzzle. The times were countless that she selected a piece from the scattered pile and tried to twist and angle it into place, only to eventually put it back in the pile. To witness her sighing and breathing frustrated puffs, it seemed a cruel task for her to master the assembly of this foreign world: the water-colored gravel in and out of the footsteps in the street was the same texture as the sidewalk. And these cardboard pieces, they were cut too near the dimensions of each other, and so when she built one of the central soldier's red pant-legs twice the size of the other and then claimed to be missing, for the other leg, the red pieces to make up the gaps in his missing left knee, the first examination supported her missing pieces claim. She was right. There were no other red pieces in the scattered pile, and his right leg, oddly segmented as it was, seemed to fit together without misspent tension on any of the pieces.

For three days, while they worked on other aspects, her gentleman on the gas lamps mounted to the theater walls and her on the eight pieces for the horse entering the scene from the left periphery, the central soldier stood mid-stride with an amputated left knee, though his right shin and foot were both completing the appropriate step.

Perhaps, her gentleman, Rostat, should have recalled when, earlier in the assembly, the outer boarder, upon first fitting, seemed to make a perfect trapezoid. And it was only by chance that he noticed the soldier's outlines weren't matching up correctly with the enclosing scene. So, finally, and with some mock exasperation, Rostat took two pieces from the right leg and constructed for the soldier the proper left knee. They had a laugh. For three days the soldier was like that, phantom-legged. Three days.

She went on to fit together the crowd while he organized the distancing purples according to shade. Slowly, very slowly, she put together the man holding the white-blue newspaper, then the wagon wheel, then the large refined lady with the collapsed umbrella and lorgnettes. Above them, the gilded chestnut trees sprang up in front of the facades. The men, proper, appeared on the wide sidewalk. A woman, stepping into the scene, looked in profile at the central soldier, who one now saw, as he passed a man doffing his hat, was heading straight for the viewer.

And like this the puzzle was put together. Occasionally, Rostat would lie back on the white tiger pelt that was stretched into a rug. Its fur would brush against his neck, and, retreating into reverie, he'd push his head back into the fur until white tufts came up on either side of his face, a not too disagreeable sensation, if only it gave time for the baroness to find a placement or two. Indeed, with the hiss of the fire in background, he would look over and wonder how Baroness Valentina could continue, struggling as she did. The puzzle, for her, seemed an exercise in overcoming frustration, and Rostat began to feel some uneasy pangs of sympathy.

But, slowly, all these characters found their existence as the result of innumerable failed trials amid the testing of mixed bodies and heads. This is how puzzles work. Perhaps a woman's dress was thought to be the theater awning, or the man's white-blue newspaper the glistening saddle sparkles, or the violet foreshortened glass of the lamps the paneled contours of the apartment buildings. And the trees, how many times did they attempt to graft them with their sidewalk mates, or scramble the golden letters on the building signs? And with each successful fit after an evolution of tries, overly painstaking as it was, they created the now-living world of Paris. Proper shadows were realized. Perspectives were maintained. The horse found its trot. And then, once finished, the glue was spread, it dried, and the puzzle-painting was framed.

"Where should we put it?" the baroness asked. "Let's put it someplace, oh shouldn't we?"

"I agree," Rostat said. "Well... you know... there is only one place that will do, only one place where this puzzle deserves to be."

"Where?"

"Above the orange sofa."

Baroness Valentina paused and looked at the painting, a real painting, a portrait, which currently hung above the orange sofa.

"Um... But I'll have to take that one down."

Rostat shrugged his shoulders, touched her on the arm, nodded, and the baroness slowly raised her eyebrows.

"For a little while, anyway," she said.

They were in the great room. The fire in the fireplace continued, a big fire, the kind that seemed to take up the entire wall. Rostat smiled. She took off her slippers and climbed up onto the orange sofa. Valentina had to reach behind the frame of the hanging portrait and unhook one of the wires that extended up to the ceiling. Then she twisted something on the back of the canvas itself, thereby releasing the whole painting from its mount. She brought it down and leaned it against the side of the sofa. Rostat continued to smile. Then she hoisted the puzzle-painting up and hung it in the vacated space.

"Oh, perfect," Rostat said.

Baroness Valentina stepped back and gazed at it as the firelight, flickering, altered the colors.

"You know," she said, "I used to not really like this picture as I had the devil of a time, as you could tell I'm sure. But now I do, and when I see it, I'm happy."

"I know," he said.

That night, the two of them fell asleep on the white tiger rug.

Morning came early for Rostat. There was a knock on the door, and Rostat slipped away without disturbing the baroness to find himself being handed a telegram from a Baroness Batka in Vienna.

*Too many baronesses*, he thought.

Before Baroness Valentina awoke, he excused himself from her apartment and glided down the icy front steps to the sidewalk. He had the old painting she had removed from the wall under his arm wrapped in a bed sheet—it was a Titian. Baroness Valentina found when she awoke, tucked into the puzzle frame, a small card with a name printed on it: *Arsène Lupin*.

A week ago, Lupin happened down this street and caught a glimpse of the Titian in the front window. A few passes by and he determined, yes, it was indeed a Titian. Some minor checking led to Baroness Valentina, unmarried, being the lone resident. Gaining an introduction and entrance was easy enough, but there was a small issue with how the Titian was mounted. It was attached to an alarm of some kind, something he hadn't seen before. So, the puzzle.

Her company was pleasant enough, and she was pretty enough. The food was delightful enough. Evenings out of the cold, lying on the white tiger rug, he didn't find that too disagreeable, and certainly not with the fire in the background. What he did feel at pains about, and would even qualify them as serious misgivings, was that the puzzle proved to be torturous to put together for Baroness Valentina.

He would watch her face and look into her eyes and see her brow wrinkle in frustration. He would do ten pieces for every one that she fitted, and she would notice the disparity and labor on with increased exasperation. But still, she persisted. And then her torture and hard-earned satisfaction was rewarded with, of all things, a betrayal.

But then, presently, as he was willfully slip-sliding down her icy front steps, he changed his perspective. Perhaps the puzzle will be appreciated as a symbol of her perseverance and as a manifestation of her will. It would be personal to her in a way that the Titian perhaps never was. After all, the Titian, despite it being prominently displayed, was not referred to once throughout the course of the week. Yes, Lupin thought, he had given her something much more valuable than a Titian. He had given her a trophy of personal achievement.

But now to Baroness Batka in Vienna: Lupin opened the letter:

*Dear Rostat,*

*You said to contact you if ever I was in a predicament of the most confounding nature. And this is it. My husband's business partner, Count Enzen, whom you warned us about all those years ago, is, I believe, conspiring to undo years of financial effort. But I am not sure what he is up to. He has contracted an Englishman, won't discuss it with my husband, and has adopted an air of suspicion and secrecy. Please help.*

*Grateful then and now,*

*Baroness Batka*

The lobby of the King of Hungary Hotel in Vienna had the benefit of high interior windows, which partitioned off a series of hallways and rooms overlooking the seating area. From a variety of vantage points, despite the natural light coming in through the glass-paneled ceiling, one could easily conceal oneself along the hallways behind these windows, and those below being watched would be at an awkward posture trying to monitor the angles.

Raffles took a seat with his back to the bar and widened his heavy eyes and smoothed out his coat. Count Enzen, taking a moment to settle the mass of his frame, joined him in the opposing chair, and two coffees were placed on the small table between them.

"The Austrian gentleman, indeed," Raffles said, gently tilting his head in appreciation.

Count Enzen moved his eyes away dismissively and surveyed the lobby.

The morning crowd at the hotel was mild, perhaps average, with luggage being moved across the room by uniformed bellboys the only signs of urgency. He saw a servant girl, solitary, tending to the plants in the center of the lobby, though she bent her arms slowly and carefully, with all the attention that was otherwise absent from Count Enzen's brutish appearance—the result of his hereditary wealth struggling to wield itself in modernizing Vienna.

"You seem out of place here, in the morning," the count said with a vague tone of superiority, still trying to hold onto some semblance of his ancient stature.

"Please, old boy. If only my English tailor could see me. A rumpled morning jacket...."

Count Enzen, with his unwithering gaze, further saw a man with an easel, painting in the corner. He saw patrons entering the hotel, brushing the winter snow from their lower garments and shirking off the abrasive chill. He saw a dozen other couples, willfully self-contained, seated in various chairs or crossing the room in various directions. That was all in the background.

"Why are we meeting here, of all places, and at this ungodly hour?" the count asked. "There are too many ears around. And the windows above, who knows who may be spying on us."

"Quite," Raffles said. "With all the ears here, friendly and otherwise, what better place to meet? Who would suspect us as being reckless enough to speak freely? Though not a *Pall Mall* in the place."

"Well, my time is being pressed. Do you have the analysis?"

Raffles placed two bond certificates from the Duxer Westbahn Railroad Company on the table beside the coffees.

"It's not good, I dare say."

Count Enzen leaned forward and twisted his blond mustache with his right thumb and forefinger. He then moved his hand to his brow and covered his eyes.

"Ah, counterfeit, as I suspected," the count said, clenching his fists.

On both certificates were detailed markings corresponding to particular features.

"Yes. You see the picot design in the corner on this bond, the original? It is blunted on your copy," Raffles explained.

"I see it."

"You see the bar delineating the signature line? And on yours?"

"Ah, I see it."

"You see the."

"Yes, my god, yes." The count raised his voice and pushed himself back in his seat, though his girth made such a movement mostly a matter of an exasperated grimace. "These bonds, the rest back in my safe, mark forty percent of my fortune. Forty percent!"

Raffles dragged his eyes around the room.

"Yes, there are ears here. So, please, if you would."

With Raffles' tone preforming the requisite deference, the count sat forward again, or rather he leaned his neck in Raffles' direction.

"Where did you get the proven authentic bond to match against mine?"

"I have my sources," Raffles said in a casual tone this time, as if the answer up to a certain point were obvious. "And you can see from the serial number that it's not one of yours."

The count looked to verify the statement, thought for a moment, and then spoke in his deep voice full of a bullish curtness.

"Raffles, you have a reputation," he puffed, "and I'm hoping your following answer lives up to it. What would you do if you were me?"

Raffles wasted no time in his reply in an effort to hasten the meeting. And though he was only beginning to become aware of his growing reputation as a cracksman, he didn't dwell on the idea for too long.

"As soon as I finished determining that the bonds were forged, I did two things. First, I did a little research and found out that, upon purchase of these bonds, you insured them with the Zinnsmeyer Insurance Company at eighty percent of face value. With your bonds being forgeries, how they passed the scrutiny of the insurance company, I'll never know. But I would hazard to say that eighty percent is better than zero percent. Second, if you check behind your wife's portrait in the library, you'll find that I did you the honor last night of removing the rest of the bonds from your safe."

Raffles took a sip of coffee, not out of a style for heightening the drama, but to moisten his voice.

"You stole from me?" the count asked, as if his ears had fooled him.

"Yes, of course."

"My bonds are gone?"

"Yes.

"Last night?"

"Yes, my god, yes," Raffles echoed, enjoying his morning coffee, this time for flavor.

Count Enzen, once more, curled his blond mustache. Certainly he was getting on in age, and the wrinkles on his forehead seemed to mark the years, but his shrewd faculties were still well with him.

"They are insured, you are correct," the count said, narrowing his eyes.

"Perhaps your maids have already come upon the open library window, left open for effect, certainly. And here, today, now, as I sit with you, I am pretending to ransom the bonds. Seeing us here, that's what others will think. Turn in a claim. Please, say it was me, as such an act would be well within my compass. I won't even deny it, old boy. I've been pursued by the Zinnsmeyer Insurance detectives before, even in England. It's hardly a bother."

"An insurance claim?" the count said into the air.

"Yes, please, hurry home and formalize the discovery of the theft."

Just then a short round man in a narrow-brimmed hat approached, holding a smaller man, almost a boy, by the collar.

"I found this one watching us from a window above. When I asked what he was doing, he tried to flee."

The count spoke calmly to Raffles:

"This is my driver, Gustav. I told him to search the halls above for anything suspicious. So, is *this* your man?"

Gustav jerked him forward.

"If I had a man, do you really think you'd catch him?"

The count paused, then gritted his teeth and shook his head.

"Gustav, please let the gentleman go and bring the coach around."

Gustav straightened the bewildered man's collar, and the two of them hurried away in opposite directions.

"Now," Raffles continued, "the claim and collection are yours. Your counterfeit bonds will be burned."

A look of pragmatism came over Count Enzen's face.

"Now," Raffles interjected, "for my fee..."

The count passed Raffles a small envelope full of banknotes.

*It's always strange when I am actually handed the money*, Raffles thought.

The count gave a courteous bow, a nod really, purely perfunctory, which was returned.

As the count started to take his leave, he turned back around.

"Herr Raffles, one more thing..." The count gave Raffles an additional envelope. "Please read this upon returning to your lodging. I think you will find it interesting."

"I will. And may I ask, have you read the *Tagblatt* recently?" Raffles said, as he was graciously tucking the second envelope into his breast pocket next to the bank notes.

"Please," the count said with an air of indignation. "I have people who read the papers for me."

With that, the count found his way to the exit, boarded his coach, and was off into the cold Tuesday morning.

As the King of Hungary Hotel continued with its morning commotion, however languidly, Raffles slowly finished his coffee and then rubbed his upper lip in contemplation. Glancing around, he picked up the count's coffee and carried it to the bar. He reached into the first envelope and took out a few crowns.

The man Gustav had collared sat alone. Raffles said some words, nodded, and placed a few banknotes and the coffee down in front of him. They had never seen each other before, but this was the proper gesture for such an imposition.

The painter, however, who all this time had been merely eyeing wisps of light around the perimeter of his canvas, peered around easel and then approached.

"Bunny," Raffles said. "I'm sorry I did not give you the proper credit for the bond research. You understand." And then, without waiting for Bunny to reply, "Did you want me to see your painting?"

"It may be a masterpiece," Bunny said, as Raffles rounded the easel.

"Why, not even a portrait; the canvas is still white, blank!"

"Yes, a masterpiece by... whoever... might... paint... something... on it."

Raffle and his companion, Bunny, made their way back to their hotel through the post-Christmas snow.

So far from British high society and the green cricket fields, Raffles was in Vienna because he had received a letter, an irresistibly flattering letter, the previous month from Count Enzen asking if he, Raffles, might come and authenticate a set of bonds issued by the Duxer Westbahn Railroad Company. The apparent mistake in attributing to him this field of expertise intrigued Raffles to the point of acquiescing to the invitation, however misguided it seemed.

Back at the Hotel Lippizan, at which he and Bunny had taken up temporary residence under the names of Karl Nuss and associate, Raffles lied down on the overly wide bed and pulled from his coat the count's second letter. He read it out loud to Bunny:

R,

*If you are reading this letter, then you have performed for me the service for which you were paid but which you unwittingly executed. My DW bonds, as you well know, are genuine, but your report that they were counterfeit was expected, for what thief wouldn't find a way to live up to his reputation? And so the theft of the bonds was also anticipated. And why would I willfully allow myself to be dispossessed of a small fortune by an amateur cracksman? Because the represented company, DW, as I discovered, will shortly be, how should I put it, folding its tent. And then the bonds would be worthless. So, thank you for the assistance, and the insurance matter, well, that was my plan from the beginning.*
*Unsigned, you understand.*

Raffles looked to the corner of the room, to his valise, which contained piles of Duxer Westbahn Railroad Company bonds. He smiled to himself and stretched out for his much anticipated Thursday slumber. Bunny joined him in relaxing on the overly wide bed, smiling.

When Count Enzen, on the other hand, returned to his building and checked his safe, the bonds were, of course, gone, but so were, to the count's complete bewilderment, all his jewels. And in the vacated space was an envelope.

Inside it were the *Tagblatt* headline Raffles had mentioned in passing, and a brief note. The headline said: "*Government to Nationalize Railroads.*" The note said:

*Count Enzen,*

*I do my homework. Nationalizing the railroads means the bonds will be honored, and thus this part of your fortune is now mine. The counterfeit bond, the example, was my own forgery. Your bonds are good, as you well know. And if, for any reason, these bonds were not honored, I would hate for our arrangement to be made public.*

*And sorry about the jewelry. How could I keep to our agreement when you attempted to deceive me?*

*Graciously signed,*

*Raffles*


Raffles, after sleep, and with Bunny still at his side, found his slumber disturbed by some excited voices across the way. After such a morning of supporting an unrefined appearance—still in his fist pair of morning clothes—and a late night and early morning of newspaper clipping, he was just then succeeding in recovering his condition, that is, until what seemed to be a flock of giggling women across the way pried open his eyes.

The two large ceiling-high windows in his and Bunny's room, four floors up, let on to a narrow but busy street, a street able to accommodate, by ample evidence, no more than two passing carriages. And as a set of generous forest-colored curtains adorned his windows, he was able to observe the day without being spied. Upon first glance, the disturbance was easily appraised.

Parallel to his room were the windows of the facing apartment building, and out of those windows leaned a collection of women. Attired in what seemed to be café dresses, full of floral flounce and frill, they occupied three separate open windows, each woman did, though all emerging from the same room.

Simply put, and to Raffles' amazement, they were dropping scoops of lime sorbet on unsuspecting sidewalk passers-by. Alternately, they would retreat in for new scoops, re-emerge, let the dessert slide off their spoons, giggle in anticipation, and then curl the curtains around their faces, while keeping their eyes free to see the gasps and shrieks. To Raffles, it was quite the spectacle. The sidewalk below was speckled in pale green, and the returning shouts were, well, less pale and less green.

Then he heard a shrill voice yell up from the street:

"Baroness Batka, I know it's you."

Raffles smiled. After putting on a tailored wickler of exceeding taste, he went downstairs to check the afternoon *Tagblatt*. No mention of the burgled bonds. The bar was quiet enough, and the winter light coming in through the windows was flattering enough, so Raffles sought to inquire about, according to his whim, the likelihood of obtaining a tray of finger sandwiches.

As Raffles turned, a man stooping in some harrowing preoccupation took the seat next to him.

"Something strong," the man said in English to the bartender.

"Something strong? I know these words," Raffles said, unable to keep to himself. "Why not something mild, but make it a double?"

"Please" the man said. "Your jokes..."

"Sorry, sir. Quite right you are... Tell me, if I may impose, women or money, what has you down?"

The man just looked at Raffles, dead in the eye, but didn't say a word.

"Ah, both," Raffles continued. A case of the devil's grip, I see."

A glass was delivered to the stooping gentleman.

"I see you are clutching that demmed glass rather tightly."

"Demmed? Certainly."

"So, demmed over business *and* women, you say?"

"Stranger, respectfully, don't take my attention away from my glass."

"Is there something I can do? A gentleman down on his luck is an injustice."

"Am I a gentleman?"

"I'm not without an eye for seeing such riding boots as yours as an emanation of your character. You don't, by chance, play cricket, do you?"

"Cricket?"

"No cricket, aye? But a gentleman, none the less."

"Would a gentleman... no, no, I can't. A gentleman's problems are his own."

"No, my good man. A gentleman's problems become the inherited accruement of all gentlemen." Raffles got up from his chair and gave an optimistic rap on the bar. "Perhaps an early supper, or a double light supper, so that we may exchange delightful impertinences? I would even go so far as to guarantee the evening?"

"Very well, we shall supper."

And with that, Raffles and the man went over and sat near the window, and very soon a tray of sandwiches was placed before them.

"Sandwiches as an aperitif? So be it."

"You were saying my problems are yours," the man said.

"Yes, indeed."

"Very well. Telling you this, I have nothing more to lose. My name is Baron Eugene. My wife is Baroness Batka." Raffles' ears blazed at the name. "And we live right across Strambergerstrasse, directly opposite this hotel. She thinks I am in the Far East, on an expedition to search for the necklace of Queen Myeongseong of Joseon."

"A necklace?" Raffles cocked is head toward Baron Eugene.

"Yes, with blazing sapphires arranged in an elaborate mesh of diamonds."

"Diamonds, too, you say?"

"Only, my guide, Sueyoung Yoo, failed me." The baron was lost in frustration. "Yoo was going to get the necklace for me. Yoo told me everything would work out. But more money was needed, always more money. For a new guide, new expedition permits, new this, new that. Soon, I was out of money—I even took my wife's jewelry to finance the effort…"

"You took her jewelry?"

"And now it's gone. And now everything is over, months ahead of schedule. I only had enough money to get back home. But home, that's where I can't go. I can't face my wife. She is expecting me to return with a fortune."

"But you don't have a fortune…."

"My wife… She…" Tears started to form in the baron's eyes. "Sueyoung Yoo!" he grunted under his breath. "Yoo said you could do it. We had a bond… I trusted Yoo." The baron reached out and touched Raffle's arm. "I thought our bond was good." His voice trailed off, almost in a trance. "I trusted Yoo…"

Raffles bowed his head. He thought to himself.

"Baron, you are staying here tonight?"

"I can't go home until I figure something out."

"Good. Good. Stay in your room, out of sight, and let's have dinner tomorrow night. I will work something out."

The baron's eye lit up.

"You'll help me?"

"I can do it. You can trust me. But we'll have to postpone our meal. We'll have two light suppers tomorrow night, at the same time as this."

The two men parted, and Raffles went back up to his room.

"Bunny, get us two train tickets for tomorrow night, if you will. The last train out. And then get yourself a hotel at the train station, the most beautiful train station hotel you can find," Raffles said with a wry smile, "as consolation, because you can't stay here."

"Why? What are you planning?"

"I don't have it fully worked out. But I think I am going to take an interest in the baron and baroness who live across the street."

Raffles said goodbye to Bunny after instructing him to remove all his, Bunny's, belongings from the hotel room, and then appeared in the lobby with, under his arm, a package that was very tightly wrapped. On the outside he wrote "*254 Strambergerstrasse*," and above this he wrote "*Karl Nuss, his own alias.*" Raffles motioned to a bellboy.

"Here, please deliver this across the street. Say it was delivered to the hotel by mistake. If they refuse delivery, just leave it with them and walk away. And tell them nothing about its origin."

From the lobby window, Raffles watched, as the evening lights of the hotel illuminated the street, the bellboy deliver the package. Perhaps a small verbal exchange was made, and when the bellboy returned, he gave the assurance that all was well.

Then, Raffles hurried up to his room, measured his windows, glanced across the street at the blackened windows, went back down to the lobby and, after words with the hotel manager, excused himself into the evening.

A few hours later, he returned, carrying a few wrapped packages, and hurried up to his room, 414. He suppered late in the hotel restaurant: lamb chops, assorted greens, and Ambertz wine.

After his meal, as evening passed into night, Raffles sat by his hotel room window, watching. As is well known, the exterior darkness has a way of amplifying lighted rooms so that they may be seen into from the outside. And since his lights were out, this effect did not encroach on his lodging. Thus, it was then easy to coordinate the extinguishing of Baroness Batka's lights followed by, a moment later, the departing of a carriage.

Once the streets quieted, well after midnight, he took from his bag a wired arrow, loaded it into a kind of hand cannon, and shot it into the opposing stone beneath the baroness' far left window, which was level with his present position. He detached the wire from his cannon and fastened it to a hook under his windowsill. Then, with the aid of a winch, he removed the slack from the wire, thereby securing a taut span connecting their two buildings. Once more, he fired, this time a second wire into the stone above her window frame and then fastened it to his outer wall, parallel to the first wire. Next, he pulled from a narrow canvas bag what turned out to be a banner, the top and bottom of which were affixed with brass ringlets. One by one, he clasped the ringlets to the wires, revealing, suspended over the street, a banner that read *"HAPPY NEW YEAR from the Hotel Lipizzan."* All was done, and the street remained quiet.

Earlier, he had persuaded the hotel management that he was in marketing, and had acquired permission to hang this banner, arguing that it was shrewd advertising, in return for a small reduction in the rate of his room, which did not really matter, except that the logic of a rate reduction served as proper false motivation.

Mid-morning the next day, with a light snow continuing to fall, there was a polite knock on the front door of the Baroness Batka residence, 254 Strambergerstrasse. When the door was answered, produced was a card from the visitor. It read: *"Police Detective-Inspector Walser."*

"May I speak with the baroness, please? This is urgent police business. The baroness speaks English, I hope."

The maid nodded slowly, somewhat confused, and withdrew. The baroness, who was a few feet away, dismissed the servant and stepped forward to meet the gentleman. Inspector-Detective Walser wore a broad blond mustache, which he toyed with between his fingers on his right hand.

"About yesterday," she began in steady English, as if the visit was about the raining sorbet, but the inspector-detective immediately stopped her.

"May I come in? This is about a package you received yesterday evening."

She led him into a small antechamber there on the ground floor. The inspector-detective hesitated for a moment.

"The ground floor is yours, as well? I was led to believe that you occupied the fourth floor."

"We have the whole building."

"*We*? Oh, is the baron at home, today?" the inspector-detective continued, looking around.

"He, incidentally, is in the Far East on a business trip. But you mentioned something about a package from yesterday?"

"I do not wish to alarm you," the inspector-detective said in the politest English possible, "but all indication is that you will be robbed tonight by Raffles, a cracksman from England, which is why I speak English, for I have tracked him here."

The baroness' back stiffened, and an awkward look of perplexity appeared on her face. Her mouth opened but no words sprang forth.

"Please listen," the inspector-detective continued. "True or false, a package arrived yesterday which was addressed to this building but intended for one Herr Karl Nuss?"

"True."

"Did you open the package?"

"No."

"Where is it?"

The baroness motioned toward a side console table, and the inspector-detective retrieved the package and placed it in her lap.

"Now, if you will open it, you will see that it contains a wealth of bonds for the Duxer Westbahn Railroad Company... Go on, open it, if you please."

When she did, the inspector-detective was proved correct.

"Now, leave the bonds and come with me."

The baroness placed the bonds back on the console table, and then she and Inspector-Detective Walser went across the street. As they were walking, the inspector-detective said:

"Look at that sign, *Happy New Year*. It's new, right?"

"Yes. New today, I think."

"And look where it is connected."

Into the Hotel Lipizzan they went, and up to the front desk. The inspector-detective, in the presence of the baroness, confirmed with the manager and the guest book that a man by the name of Karl Nuss was indeed staying in room 414. Then, quickly, he led her up to the door of the room and opened it with a key.

"This is his room. Look there in the corner, in the small valise."

The baroness peered over the rim of the suitcase. Inside were more bonds.

"And here... The Detective led her to the window. "First, I should tell you, Karl Nuss is Raffles."

"He is?"

"Do you know who Raffles is?"

"I… uh… no. Never heard of him. Only from you."

"Raffles, the amateur cracksman, really? He is very famous in England."

"And you said you have been sent here to catch him, yes?"

"If I can. He is going to, you see the wires of the sign, use this conveyance to negotiate the street between his room and yours."

The baroness sat down on the hotel room bed.

"Stand up, please!" The baroness jumped up, and the inspector-detective smoothed out the covers of the bed. "We can't let him know anyone was here."

"Oh, sorry."

"It's fine, please. Now we must secure things on your end."

They marched back to 254 Strambergerstrasse, and as she led him once more into the antechamber, the inspector-detective continued:

"Now, undoubtedly, Raffles knows this building inside and out. He knows where all the safes are and all the jewelry boxes and exactly what's in them. If your husband has business papers, he knows which ones are valuable and which confidences they keep. A locked drawer? It means nothing. A triple-jointed safe? That is his specialty. Matching earrings in one room and a necklace on the floor below? He'll find the set. So, Baroness Batka, there is only one way to stop Raffles." He took her by the elbow and directed her toward the inner rooms. "You must show me where you keep not your everyday pieces, but your heirlooms, what you would pass down. That is what he has a nose for."

"Certainly. There are two places."

She immediately led him to a small safe there on the ground floor, behind an innocuous picture of some farmland that was made to seem obscure beside other grand portraits of family members and distant properties.

"Here. My husband doesn't know about this."

From the safe she pulled out a black velvet pouch, and from it she revealed a necklace, but not just any necklace. The sheer brilliance of the sapphires was blinding. The interwoven diamonds formed a mesh into which the sapphires seemed suspended as though they were arranged fish in a net, the whole of which seemed would cradle a woman's head.

"What's…*this*?" he whispered in amazement.

"It is the royal necklace of the murdered Queen Myeongseong of Joseon, a kingdom in the Far East. My husband is there now, trying to find it, but I, through my channels, acquired the piece only last week. He will return empty-handed, and I wish to give it to him for our ten year anniversary."

"It's very exquisite, indeed," the inspector-detective said. He took the black pouch and extended the opening. "Here, let's put it back. This should be just fine."

She placed the necklace inside.

"You said there were two locations?" nodding toward the expanse of the rest of the house.

"Yes. There is one more safe, and it is up on the fourth floor. It contains everything else."

The inspector-detective put the black velvet pouch back in the safe and closed it, swinging the painting back into place.

"Very well. Let's proceed."

A small elevator was installed beside the staircase, and the two of them traveled slowly up floor by floor. The entire fourth floor, now that they had arrived and proceeded through a hall doorway, seemed to be the baroness' sleeping quarters: sitting area on the far side of the room, bed on the left, familiar curtains, the three infamous windows.

She quickly led him to a floor safe beneath the bed. As the bed sat high off the floor, she crawled under it, through the draping bed covers, and disappeared. A moment later her hand slid out a flat metal box. Recomposing herself, she stood and put the box on the bed. She opened it. It was empty.

"My jewels!" She scurried back under the bed, but nothing more was to be found in the safe. "They were here." She scratched at the box, as though trying to reveal a secret panel. Nothing. Then with a grunt, she heaved the box across the room and flopped on the bed. After a moment, she got up and took a deep breath.

"My jewelry was there, and now they're gone!"

The inspector-detective took a ponderous look out the window.

"Raffles, of course." Turning back around, "Baroness Batka, may I go under and search for clues?"

"Certainly."

"Out of courtesy I will ask: There is nothing of a sensitive nature that is not for my eyes, is there?"

"Other than envelopes and business papers, the safe is empty. Please."

The inspector-detective proceeded to lie on his stomach. Through the hanging bedclothes he disappeared. The baroness went to the window, and for the first time saw directly the banner that spanned the street. She opened the window and reached down for the lower wire. Indeed, it was firmly fastened and taut, perfectly sufficient to support the weight of a man. The inspector-detective quickly returned from under the bed and stood before the grieved woman, adjusting his rumpled clothes and patting down his blond mustache.

"My good woman, you are right. You have been robbed. And I saw you were analyzing the wires, his conveyance."

"Then, we are too late," she said, resigned, and slumped her shoulders. "Raffles has already been here."

"Let me go back to the station, get a few men for the investigation, ask some questions…"

"It's too late… And what will my husband say?"

"No, please. I'll go talk to the hotel, look again in his room, search for clues…"

"But Raffles can't be caught."

"I'll get leads and then follow those leads…"

The baroness flopped down on the bed once more, put her head in her hands, and started to cry. The inspector-detective, sensing that it was the right time to leave, affected a proper bow from the waist and let himself out.

As the day passed on and a heavier snow began to fall, giving the street lamps an extra glow at the onset of twilight, Raffles reclined in the lobby upon a plush settee and before a six-log fire outlined in brass fixtures, giving him a open view of the large double doors that gave passage to and from Strambergerstrasse.

Before him, slightly off to the side on an end table just in his periphery, was a small zucchini salad with strawberries and a honey balsamic, along with a miniature aperitif. The trim of the settee—was it sable?—tickled his wrist in the small gap between his white gloves and his satin dinner jacket. He almost smiled when he accentuated this contact.

*Ah*, he thought, *the indulgence of proper living.*

Outside, however, out of view beside the double door, beneath not the extra glow of the street lamps but the gray clouds of slate scraping across the darkening sky, was Baron Eugene, collar pulled tight with both hands. His breath was fogging up the golden windows of the hotel. He watched snow collect on his coat, waiting just a moment longer, and then nodded to the doorman, who, with the gathered heave that it took to budge the door, gave him passage into the hotel lobby with the six-log fire.

"Ah, my good baron," Raffles said, uncrossing his legs and hurrying to extend his arm to brush the snow off the baron's coat. "You were outside… in this weather?"

"I got restless, and…"

"Dinner, please. We have a table waiting, old boy."

Raffles let the events proceed naturally, though he saw a growing tenseness in his guest's face. Soon, after the first course of veal, certain words were uttered.

"I believe my wife has taken up a lover," the baron said.

This, Raffles had not expected. He put down his fork.

"You *believe*?"

"I saw her today, in this very hotel, go with a man upstairs."

Raffles thought for a moment.

"What did he look like, this man?"

"Blond mustache."

Raffles reached inside his breast pocket, pulled out a known item, and held it to his upper lip.

"Did the man look like this, like me?"

The baron gave a start and nearly knocked over his wine. Removing the prop, Raffles continued:

"Please excuse me. I was trying out a new character. I got the idea for a blond mustache from someone with whom I did business recently. Hear me out, if you please. There is no affair, of course. My name is Raffles, from England—my accent, you see—and I conspired to rob you and your wife this afternoon. Though, I did more than conspire, I carried it out. Now, your wife is perfectly fine, unharmed, and I even did so much as to take credit for the missing jewelry under your wife's bed—taking credit as Raffles, not as the man with the blonde mustache, naturally."

"How did you...? You were in my home?"

"Please, the compass of my abilities and all that... In your home I found your name on your business papers in the ground safe under the upstairs bed. Everything was just as you said. I took credit for the theft, because I at once grasped the situation. It was clear, and a gentleman's problems... And baron," Raffles continued, "you should know that *she* was able to successfully obtain the Queen's necklace, the one you were looking for in the Far East."

"She did?"

"Yes, your wife, for you!" Raffles took a deep breath. "There is more. That necklace, with the blazing sapphires..."

"You saw it?"

"Well, I did more than see it. I stole it."

"You stole it?"

"The necklace, yes. Please, be calm. I merely switched bags in the safe. The necklace is here, perfectly unmolested?"

Raffles reached into his pocket, produced a black velvet bag, and pushed it across the table. The baron seized it at once, stretched the opening, and gasped. Raffles continued:

"Now, you will go home to your wife and present to her the necklace, which you came into possession by the simple act of besting me in scuffle. I, as Raffles, took the necklace from your wife, and you took it from me. How did *you* know *I* had it? Simple. You were at this hotel the whole time watching me, as you were tipped off to my plans. It's a shame I can't use this hotel anymore. The beds are, well... if needs must be. So, go home to your wife."

"Raffles, I don't how to repay you," he said, getting up.

"Oh, and something else." Raffles signaled to a waiter, who walked over and presented a box to the gentleman. "Here inside are bonds to a railroad company. They are of no use to me."

"Bonds?"

"The rest of the bonds are in your home. Your wife has them. Keep them. Think of this as a gentlemanly gesture. These bonds will more than pay for the lost jewelry... And baron, one more thing." The same waiter approached and placed a small silver canister on the table. "Please give this to your wife. I assure you, it is perfectly benign."

91

While Raffles signaled for an Esterházy torta, Baron Eugene rushed home, bonds and necklace in hand, canister in his pocket, traversing the street with a magnificent stride, kicking up the snow in his path.

Turning to look back at the Hotel Lipizzan, he calmly let himself into 254 Strambergerstrasse. Baroness Batka stood there, expectantly, with almost an ecstatic expression, and beside her stood yet another gentleman, who reached out for a handshake.

"Herr Rostat, how can we ever repay you?" said the gentleman who was waiting inside and who was, in fact, the real Baron Eugene and had merely kept out of sight during this ordeal.

"Enough accounts have been settled. You counted the bonds that were here? You know what is left."

The box of bonds was presented, and Baron Eugene checked the serial numbers to ensure they were all there. They were.

"And the necklace, you go that back?" the baroness asked, almost doubting that such an act would be made.

"Queen Myeongseong of Joseon's necklace? Of course."

"That is not real, is it, those sapphires, the diamonds?"

"Yes, they are very real," Rostat said. "For only an authentic piece would cement our arrangement, as certainly Raffles would be able to detect a fake. And once we knew that gentlemen solidarity was the key to the plan, only an appeal to real human emotions would guarantee our success."

"But how did you bring the railroad bonds into play?" the baron questioned.

"A mere language game, using his English and the power of suggestion. By introducing a character by the name of Yoo, a name of the Far East, surely, and then by transitioning to the double meaning of 'you,' he took the sentence of trust and dependability to pertain to himself, Raffles."

"But the bonds, Rostat, the bonds?"

"Right. Same technique, a transition to the double meaning. The bonds between us and all that… Gentlemen solidarity, again, the guarantee of his participation. Oh, and Baroness Batka, I have something more," Rostat said.

He presented her with Raffles' silver canister, and when she opened it, she confusingly laughed. Inside was a scoop of melted lime sorbet.

And there is one more detail to add.

When Raffles had rejoined Bunny at the Westbahnhof, proud, for good reason, and ready to board the train to make their way back to England, Bunny was standing there with a large rectangular package wrapped in string and brown paper.

"My word, Bunny, a souvenir?"

"Hardly. It arrived at my hotel just before I left, addressed to you, no less."

"To me?" Upon checking the label and seeing his name, Raffles carefully undid the string, peeled away a portion of the paper, and saw, there, a brightly colored painting, a portrait it seemed.

"Is this a Titian?" Raffle said in amazement, breathless. "I believe it is."

"Then the portrait is complete," Bunny added.

A card was lodged in a gap in the frame. Raffles held it up to a nearby lamp and, amid the slow-falling snow, read:

*My dear Raffles,*
  *As a gentlemen's problems are, so too are a gentlemen's successes.*
  *Though, please stay off the continent in the future.*
                                                    *Arsène Lupin*

*Brian Gallagher has used Marie Nizet's Captain Liatoukine—from her ground-breaking 1879 novel* Captain Vampire, *available from Black Coat Press, ISBN 978-1-934543-01-6)—to introduce us to the complex and murky world of vampire politics, in "City of the Nosferatu (TOTS 10) and "The Trial of Van Helsing" (TOTS 11), moving forward in time. Here is his latest installment...*

## Brian Gallagher: *The Stake and the Sickle*

*Southern Russia, March 1920*

The Russian vampire Boris Liatoukine, it must be said, did not have a good war. He himself had been thinking this just prior to being shot at by some Bolshevik. Not only had the war concluded with his homeland going nowhere, but also the very country had been taken over by Bolsheviks—whom he was now fighting at that moment.

The Reds were fighting intensely, as well they might, given that the reward for retreat could well be death by order of the political commissar. However, Captain Liatoukine himself inspired terror in his own men, but also a certain respect. He knew his business and demonstrated it by raising his pistol and shooting a number of the Red soldiers dead with a few well-aimed shots. Such accurate shooting was attributed to his rumored supernatural powers. "Captain Vampire," his men called him—they believed he had inherited them from his father. His men were in fact wrong on just one count—he and his father were the same man. Certain difficulties due to the political changes meant that he had to rapidly become his "son"—losing his senior rank in the process.

A grenade landed near Liatoukine, killing one of his men and severely wounding another. Despite Liatoukine being the nearest to the explosion, his wounds were minor and he was thrown off balance only temporarily. Another couple of well-aimed shot dispatched two more red guards. His men were also doing well. They advanced forward, coming in close contact with their enemy. Bayonets were used. Liatoukine used his powers, speed and prowess—but not to the extent where it was obvious he was not human. He had made that mistake before.

Faced with such firm opposition from this unit of White Russian troops, the Red guards decided upon retreat. Liatoukine did not have enough resources to give chase.

A couple of survivors were left behind. One, an injured NCO, was taken captive. The other was an officer. Liatoukine ordered his men away whilst he dealt with him.

The Red officer was a young lieutenant. He was badly injured, but his situation was such that he could be saved. Liatoukine stood over him, and then kneeled next to him, pulling him up by his tunic, ignoring his pain.

"Brother officer... please... help me..." the man pleaded, looking straight at the vampire's cat-like eyes and pale, bearded face

Brother officer? Liatoukine swiftly understood that this meant the man was likely to have been a former Imperial officer, now working for the Reds. A traitor.

"I was in the Imperial Army," the man said. "I had no choice but to work for them. They had my family..."

"There is no excuse to work with these Bolshevik scum," Liatoukine hissed at him. "None."

The vampire glared at the prisoner, then started to drain him of his life. Liatoukine was a vampire that fed on the energy of human beings. He could take blood, but it was not enough to sustain him. Often, his victims would be found to have died of sheer terror or seemingly natural causes. The officer felt his life drain away.

Liatoukine would often take officers prisoner and interrogate them first, before eliminating them. Here, his anger got the better of him. His men had moved away and would see nothing. Liatoukine's fury meant that he turned the officer into a husk.

*Let the Bolsheviks see the corpse and be fearful*, he thought.

His men had captured an NCO—he would do for interrogation purposes. He took a last look at what remained of the officer.

"You should be grateful to me, 'brother officer.' As you are dead, it's likely your family will be left alone."

He went over to his men. Had they seen anything? They would only have seen a little. And a bit of fear in one's subordinates was no bad thing.

They started back to Novorossiysk, the town on the Black Sea where the anti-Bolshevik Armed Forces of South Russia under General Denikin had their headquarters. Theirs had been a reconnaissance mission, simply to see what was going on behind enemy lines. Their fight with the Bolshevik troops had not been part of the plan.

Suddenly, there was a sound—an aircraft. They all looked up. It was a Royal Air Force plane, heading towards the Reds. Part of the extensive British forces sent by Winston Churchill to help the White Russians' effort.

Back at Novorossiysk, Liatoukine returned to his quarters. At this moment, he was effectively an intelligence officer, spending time trying to find out what the Reds were up to. He also had duties as a liaison officer with the British forces.

He liked to go out and see firsthand what was going on. Hence the recent operation. Really, it was not a good thing to have been spotted and to have to fight his way out. However, he enjoyed combat. It stirred the blood—or whatever it was that ran in his veins. He wasn't sure himself. Regardless, at least the battle had resulted in the capture of an enemy NCO. The man spoke fast on the way back. He begged to join the White Army—but there was no way back for him, now. He feared the wrath of the political commissar, a certain Kostaki.

This Kostaki was ruthless in dealing with those who acted with insufficient zeal. Nothing unusual about that. Reds feared the commissars with good reason. No, what was odd—and the captured NCO confirmed it—was that it was known that this individual liked to rip apart the throats of those who didn't want to fight for the Revolution. Their bodies were found, drained of their blood. Again, nothing too outré by Cheka—the dreaded Bolshevik state security organization— standards. After all, their practices included throwing water over naked prisoners in sub-zero temperatures, turning them into frozen statues for all to see.

What interested Liatoukine was that the draining of blood was usually the mark of a vampire. Combined with the occasional sights of unaccountable green lights and reflections—some vampires caused this effect—that he himself had seen behind the lines, he was in little doubt that that Kostaki was a vampire. Furthermore, Kostaki was a name associated with a Moldovan vampire aristocrat— this was also rather suspicious.

Liatoukine was appalled that a vampire could lower himself to work for the Reds. He was all in favor of murdering and trampling on his lessers, but the Reds were too much. They were ill-bred certainly, but talking of power to the workers and so on, whilst lording over them, was too much hypocrisy, even for him. They also had little concept of the good things in life—although what little there was, they took for themselves.

Still, he did admire their use of terror. It amused him too—Lenin's man, Trotsky, the architect of Red Terror, might even have been considered too extreme by most vampires.

He was distracted from his thoughts by a commotion in the street. Some of the locals were crowding around, talking to each other excitedly and clearly somewhat fearfully. Liatoukine went outside.

He called out to an old woman whom he recognized; she always knew what the street gossip was. She came over quickly to him.

"What goes on, peasant?" he asked.

"It's the White Lady," she said. "She has struck again, attacking two young men. She crushed the throat of a tailor who was walking by the sea with his son yesterday evening—the son barely got away. The body was drained of blood when they found it."

Liatoukine waved her away. Ah yes. His other, more pressing vampire problem. A vampire aristocrat killing locals in and around Novorossiysk and even across the sea in Crimea. The "White Lady," they called her. Nothing wrong with killing a few of the locals for sustenance, but the rate of killing was much too high and providing the Reds with extremely damaging propaganda against the Whites. He would need to see this problem resolved—and swiftly.

At that very moment, behind Red lines, the people responsible for Liatoukine's problems were engaged in a conversation. Their location was a carriage in a stationary battle train of the Red Army. This carriage was a special one, off limits to the rest of the train's operatives, let alone anyone else.

The carriage was rather more comfortable than the rest of the train. A woman—tall, raven-haired and beautiful—was seated in a chair opposite a man with an aquiline face sitting behind at large desk. She wore an elaborate white wedding dress.

"I am so pleased your people have got me this lovely dress," said the woman. "The previous one was covered in blood. Where did you get it from, my dear Von Bork?" she then asked in a fake innocent manner.

"A bourgeois reactionary woman," Von Bork—the man opposite her—replied. "She had no further use for it."

The woman, who was called Polly Bird, knew what that meant. She was intrigued, however, to know more of his use of language and asked him about it.

"Your words...'bourgeois,' 'reactionary...' They do seem strange coming from you—the aristocratic master of espionage who once worked for the German Kaiser. How is it that you are now a Bolshevik?"

Von Bork seemed to bristle slightly.

"And how is it that you, a vampire, find yourself working for me, a mere human"

"I don't work for you. I work on behalf of the Sepulchre, in alliance with you," she replied with a smile.

Von Bork gave as good as he got, she thought. Still, it was good to remind him now and then that she worked for the City of Vampires, the Sepulchre, referred to as Selene by humans.

"Of course, you do," he said. "A little joke on my part. As to your question, I did much work in England, until I was caught by Sherlock Holmes. However, even then, I outwitted him as he rather obligingly informed me of the disinformation he had passed to me. I was handed over to Germany just prior to the British declaring war. But my own government saw me as a failure—the same government who sold Germany out at Versailles. As for the so-called patriots, they, too, saw me as a failure..."

His tone had become increasingly bitter.

"I was approached by German communists. They could see my skills. They were unconcerned that I had been apprehended by Holmes—indeed they were curious regarding my views of him. They were most impressed with my many espionage achievements..."

Von Bork did not say it, but they were also impressed by his critique of the Great Detective—had he been Holmes, he would not have exposed Von Bork but continued the deception, perhaps for many years. The Bolsheviks seemed to appreciate this form of thinking.

"You helped start the war," Polly Bird interrupted, "even working out the date of its start?"

Von Bork waved that away.

"Ludicrous British propaganda. You will find that it was a capitalist war against the working classes."

"And so the Bolsheviks offered you work?" asked Polly Bird.

"They did indeed," he responded. He then added "Naturally, I had begun to see the way in which the war had crushed the working class. They have had much use for my talents here."

His tone had turned from bitterness, to something rather less than convincing. For Polly Bird matters were perfectly clear; Von Bork—she noted he kept the noble "von" in his name—probably cared less for bolshevism than for power. The Bolsheviks gave him great power in return for his skills. Given the international network of the Reds, the Germans probably would come to rue the way they treated him so badly—if they had not already done so.

As if he had read her mind, Von Bork said:

"Germany will fall to revolution of course, and then my old capitalist friends will be dealt with. However, there is much to occupy us here. It appears that my plans are going well. Liatoukine is well aware of my operative Kostaki, including the fact that he, too, is a vampire. When he approaches him, he will be eliminated. The Whites cannot be permitted to have a vampire in their employ, even if they are not aware of it. I know there are rumors about him. It did occur to me to simply provide that information to the Whites and let them deal with Liatoukine—there is enough fear of God amongst them for that—but the possibility of them taking a pragmatic view of his services is too much of a risk. And I have no reason to believe that he would work for the revolution. His enmity to us is too well known, let alone his decadence."

Polly Bird smiled. There was quite a bit of "decadence" where they were, given some of the lavish items in Von Bork's carriage.

"Yes, I can assure you that Liatoukine would never countenance for one moment the notion of working for the, er, 'proletariat,' as you call it,"

Von Bork nodded with a frown.

These Reds took themselves so seriously, Polly Bird thought. She continued:

"I know him well. He was once on the Vampire Council of the Sepulchre. He was ambitious for the future. He did actually think that the Great War was going to be won very quickly by Russia, and that we would be controlling the Tsar thereafter. Well, that went wrong almost immediately, and his influence in our city has now vanished."

"Whilst yours has grown, I gather," said Von Bork, deciding to make a point. "You now are on the Vampire Council?"

"Indeed, I am," she replied. "Poor Boris is behind the times. He has picked the losing side. And we vampires are not losers."

Von Bork nodded. He had some knowledge of the politics of the Vampire City. During his time with the German Secret Service, he had had contacts with the Austrian Empire's organization that dealt with such matters—a Baron Vordenberg was in charge. And it was Vordenberg who had briefed him. The Baron would no doubt have been mortified as to such information being used to help the Reds. He wondered for a moment what had become of that organization. Had it survived the chaos of the war?

Whatever the case, Von Bork was quite happy to use these vampires to create terror and eliminate the formidable Liatoukine. He had a concern that the Whites may reward the Vampire Captain's skills with greater power. Whatever else Liatoukine was, he was good at being a military commander.

"I think it is likely that he will make a move against Kostaki soon," said Von Bork. "But he will find a team of Chekists waiting for him. They have been in place for a few days now."

"Are you sure that these operatives of yours can deal with Liatoukine? They are but human," Polly Bird said.

"They are elite Chekists. With Kostaki's help, they should be able to liquidate Liatoukine, whether he comes alone or with others," Von Bork replied. He then moved onto a related matter. "You are doing excellent work yourself for us as part of our alliance. Much terror has been caused amongst the ordinary people in White-controlled territory—with the aristocracy taking the blame."

Polly Bird smiled. She got up, resplendent in her appropriated dress.

"Thank you. Which reminds me—it is time for the 'White Lady' to go prowling again."

Also going out that night was Boris Liatoukine. It had only been less than a day since his contact with the Red forces. In that time, he and his men had extracted information from their captured NCO. The man had been most forthcoming—so much so in fact that they had spared his life, providing he now fought for the Whites.

His quarry, described to him vaguely as 'tall and bald,' was based in a small village held by the Reds. Kostaki was surrounded by troops, of course. However, he had his own quarters—this was crucial, as there would be no witnesses. Liatoukine knew that, like himself, Kostaki could survive during the daytime. He was still even more powerful at night, but at least the night afforded Liatoukine more cover in which to operate. Operating by himself, he was freer to use his abilities to move surreptitiously into enemy territory. He would deal swiftly with Kostaki; if possible, he would try to question him, but the priority was to neutralize him.

Whilst moving covertly through the village, Liatoukine was conscious of the Red soldiers in the gloom. None had spotted him—or so he thought. In actual fact, they had. They were just waiting for him to go into Kostaki's house, where they would corner him.

Liatoukine went into the house that was his target's headquarters. He went upstairs to the top floor and walked into what he knew to be Kostaki's office. He was completely confident of his ability to deal with his opponent.

Kostaki lounged behind a desk, his legs crossed on it. He, too, was confident, although this was not part of the plan. He was supposed to feign surprise, just to give the Cheka soldiers a second or two of extra time. He even had a line prepared and started it, something about expecting Liatoukine, but the Vampire Captain had begun whirling around.

Up the stairs came Cheka officers, in their distinctive black leather garb, One came down through a trap door in the roof.

How could he have missed all this? Overconfidence, thought Liatoukine.

All the Chekists had stakes in their hand. Some had guns—loaded with silver bullets perhaps?

Liatoukine had the advantage of superhuman strength and speed and used it. Those split seconds that Kostaki's arrogance had given him were put to good use. Using his own silver sword, he swiftly decapitated the Chekist who had come through the roof. The Vampire Captain could touch silver and thus used such a sword, but it was any breaking of the skin that could cause difficulty.

Other Chekists were coming in through the door. Liatoukine ran one through, then whirled around and killed another one coming through the window.

Meanwhile, Kostaki was not idle; he was attempting his own attack on Liatoukine. He fired his gun at the Vampire Captain, hitting his shoulder with a silver bullet. Energy fizzled out of the wound, but Liatoukine's body managed to expel the bullet before it could do further damage.

The Vampire Captain realized that matters were becoming a trifle desperate. He would have to call in a reinforcement.

Outside, the house a figure slowly materialized. It was another Liatoukine. It stood only a few foot from the nearest Cheka soldier. This second Liatoukine immediate raised a pistol and shot the soldier. The first Liatoukine had used a sword, as that was already in his hand. This second used his pistol, not only due to efficiency; but also to create a noise in order to distract his opponents.

All the Cheka troops heard the shot.

"Another one! He has an accomplice!" shouted one of them.

The second Liatoukine ran for the cover of the trees, with the troops in pursuit. He knew he would not be able to elude them all, not that that was his intention. As soon he got into the shadows, he faded away in much the same manner that he had appeared. The pursuing soldiers chased him anyway, simply believing that he was just ahead of them in the dark. This took away enough soldiers to improve the odds for the first Liatoukine.

However, it was still not enough.

In Kostaki's office, the gunshot had momentarily distracted the Chekists, giving the first Liatoukine enough time to dispatch two of them with his sword.

He still did not use his pistol, not wanting to take any attention away from his doppelganger.

Kostaki now had a stake in his hand, and had maneuvered himself behind Liatoukine. He rammed the stake in the centre of the Vampire Captain's back, straight through the heart.

Liatoukine looked down at the stake protruding from his chest. He looked bewildered. Then, he fell over sideways, crashing to the floor.

He lay there quite still, his eyes staring.

A Cheka soldier swiftly aimed his pistol at Liatoukine's head and fired a silver bullet. Parts of the Vampire Captain's brain splattered around.

"Dead," said the soldier.

"Stay here and keep an eye on him," Kostaki told the soldiers in the room.

He went downstairs and asked the Cheka troops what had happened outside.

"There was another one—somehow we had not spotted him. Some of the men are in pursuit," he was told.

This was not good news. Von Bork would not be pleased. Kostaki did not fear the German, but enjoyed his work as a Bolshevik commissar. It gave him a good cover to feed on humans and thus did not wish to jeopardize it.

"Get everyone onto finding him—at once," he ordered.

All the troops complied. Kostaki left a few men in the house, one directly guarding Liatoukine's body.

He then went into a nearby communications room to relay the news to Von Bork by a special field telephone.

The spymaster was not pleased with the apparent escape of what appeared to be an accomplice. However, he did seem satisfied with the elimination of Boris Liatoukine.

"Yes," the Chekist vampire said. "It went just as you said—the stake through the heart was the way to kill him. A silver bullet in the brain was also delivered."

"Very good," said Von Bork at the other end. "Keep watch on the corpse yourself. I shall arrive in due course to take it away."

Kostaki returned to his office. The first thing he saw was a body on the ground, with blood pouring out of a stake through its heart. But the body was not Liatoukine's! It was that of the soldier who was supposed to be guarding him!

Liatoukine stepped from behind him—very fast—grabbed him by the neck and held him mid-air.

"Not a word," Liatoukine said. "I am sure you know my abilities."

Kostaki kept quiet. He saw that Liatoukine's injuries appeared to be repairing themselves.

"Tell me what I need to know quickly, and I will let you live," Liatoukine continued. "You have my word as a nobleman of Selene. I will also permit you to come to the White side to work with me, should you wish it. I doubt your masters will be forgiving, but I offer you that way out, if you wish it."

The terrified vampire made a sound that Liatoukine took as assent. He put him down and loosened—but did not release—his grip on his throat.

Kostaki told him of how he had preyed on humans in Moscow. He told him of how Von Bork had captured him, and how he had offered him employment with the revolution—an offer he could not refuse, given that the alternative was a stake in the heart—the sure way of killing him. And, of course, such employment meant he was safe, providing he was discreet and followed the German spy's orders. Finishing his story, Kostaki said:

"We must go now. Any further details must come later."

Liatoukine simply re-tightened his grip and drained the vampire of energy. The body turned to dust, its fangs strangely surviving on the floor. The Vampire Captain crushed them contemptuously with his boots. Promises to vampires who worked for Bolsheviks had no validity whatsoever—besides, he needed Kostaki's energy.

Liatoukine proceeded downstairs and left by a back exit. The few Cheka who had remained behind did not spot him; they had no reason to believe anything was wrong. Liatoukine also moved very fast and ensured he headed in a different direction from the search parties looking for his "accomplice."

He moved though the dark countryside, helped by being able to see clearly in the dark. *That had been too damn close*, he thought. He had become too arrogant over the years. The wooden stake had been painful, but no more than that. The silver bullet had passed only through part of his brain, allowing for swift regeneration, his consciousness intact.

He very rarely used his doppelganger power, and only in the most serious of circumstances He barely understood it, for a start, seemingly being conscious in two places at once, something he found very strange. More importantly, he wished as few of his enemies to know of it as possible.

As soon as he realized it had been a trap, he knew there was more to Kostaki than just being a vampire who had opportunistically infiltrated the Bolsheviks. It seemed that Von Bork was after him after all.

No doubt when he worked for the Kaiser, he had gathered much valuable intelligence on vampires, either from within Germany or from the Austrians. The Bolsheviks were such hypocrites! They pointed out with relish the foreign help the Whites were receiving from the British, French, Americans and others, and yet, many in the Cheka were themselves foreign. His assailants had cursed in Chinese, and Von Bork was German. Of course, it was the Germans who had given Lenin safe passage into Russia in the first place...

Still, despite the close call, Liatoukine had succeeded in his mission of neutralizing Kostaki. Further, he now knew of the threat of Von Bork.

As a precaution, some years ago, Liatoukine had placed false information within a certain text in the Sepulchre. It stated that the only sure way to kill an energy vampire such as himself was by a wooden stake through the heart, much like other vampires. It had been a precaution against current and future enemies who would wish to destroy him. Von Bork clearly had great sources from within the Vampire City itself. The spymaster, it seems, was keen to use vampires in furtherance of the Red Terror.

These thoughts were most troubling for the Vampire Captain. Most troubling indeed...


Later, in Von Bork's rail carriage, Polly Bird, too, was troubled. She and Von Bork were engaged in conversation regarding the previous night's events.

"I knew the trap was too weak," she told him. "Liatoukine is not only a powerful vampire, but he has considerable military experience and skills. He is still alive, and who knows how much intelligence he gleaned from Kostaki before he killed him."

"*Alive*, is he?" replied Von Bork. "I thought your people referred to your condition as being *Undead?*"

"Do not mock me, German. You seem somewhat unconcerned as to events," she replied.

"Not at all! I am always concerned over events," Von Bork responded. "However, the reality is that the Whites are on the run. Even Churchill has started to tentatively talk to Moscow. The loss of Kostaki is unfortunate, as is those of a number of my troops; however, it is clear that victory is in our grasp. Liatoukine has nowhere to go. Soon, we will crush the Whites here in Southern Russia, and the war will be won. As for intelligence, well, Kostaki had no real link to Selene, let alone any knowledge of our little alliance. And even if he did, what could Liatoukine do with it? If we were promoted, yes, he could cause some trouble for us, but it is too late for that. Our victory is assured. The presence of his accomplice was certainly a surprise, but we will be ready for him next time."

The reports from the Chekists who had fought Liatoukine's doppelganger were rather garbled; neither Polly Bird nor Von Bork had understood the true nature of what had really occurred.

The German spymaster may have appeared untroubled to Polly Bird, but secretly, he was not pleased with the turn of events, having underestimated Liatoukine. This failure could easily be concealed from his superiors, who were not too informed about vampire matters.

"Of course," continued Von Bork, "Liatoukine may now come after me. But if he does, he will face considerably more opposition than he did with Kostaki. And even if he does not, the defeat of the Whites will render him powerless. He is too proud to return to your city, or maybe too cautious, given that his complete lack of a power base leaves him open to his enemies in Selene. You are operating in Novorossiysk. I think it is prudent to set another trap for him, through information I can make sure he receives. He will no doubt suspect a trap. If he had any common sense, he would avoid me. However, I think he will come for me. He will have no idea about you, although, of course, he must be looking for the 'White Lady'."

"I would favor that option," Polly Bird responded. "I would find it most reassuring to see that Liatoukine is liquidated one and for all. There are minor factions in Selene who are against our alliance with you. We cannot rule out his causing some trouble."

With that, matters were then set in motion.


Things went pretty much as Von Bork had predicted. The Whites were on the run. Boris Liatoukine walked through the streets of Novorossiysk. The town was teeming with people trying to leave. Evacuations had already begun to get everyone out. The military was headed to Crimea to make their last stand. The streets stank. Typhus was everywhere.

Liatoukine could have got to Crimea earlier, but he wished to follow various leads as to Von Bork's precise location, as well as dealing with the White Lady. She had continued her activities: a number of unwary lower orders had been murdered, causing more terror. She never killed military officers, or aristocrats, or even the middle class. Always the poor. For whom, of course, he cared nothing. However, it did cause more resentment against his side, given that the White Lady was considered an aristocrat.

The White Lady was portrayed as a provocation by the Reds in White propaganda. And indeed, Liatoukine considered this to be probably real. After his encounter with Kostaki, he suspected that the White Lady did work for Von Bork. He wondered if he knew who she was. There seemed to be something personal in her activities. It seemed as if her recent murder had gotten closer and closer to his base in Novorossiysk. Likely or not, this was just harrying them. The Red advance and the typhus were enough reasons for panic.

However, a murder had taken place just streets away from his headquarters, and he had to investigate. He approached the scene. A crowd had gathered around the corpse. They made way for him. There was a corpse on the ground: a young woman, her throat ripped out.

Kneeling next to her was a young man—her husband it transpired. He had been by her side when the attack had happened. He had been gibbering earlier about what had happened; but was now in some kind of shock.

Liatoukine had already heard the story from others, but he wanted to hear it from the husband. He grabbed him by the chin and pulled his head up to face his own.

"What happened?" he asked.

The man answered. They had been out last night in search of a doctor; his wife was ill. *Typhus no doubt*, thought Liatoukine. The man started to look fearful, saying:

"She appeared out of nowhere... She grabbed my wife and ripped out her throat with her teeth. I tried to stop her, but I could not move. She lifted a hand towards me and I still could not move!"

"Coward!" one of the crowd shouted—from well behind some others.

Liatoukine glared at the crowd. There were no more interruptions. The Vampire Captain was known by some as an officer not to cross. And the others who did not know him could sense that he was a dangerous man.

As he left, a old woman stepped in his way and held a cross up to him. He simply smiled. Seeing it had no effect, she moved away from him.

Liatoukine didn't like crosses, but it did not have the same effect on him as on so many other vampires. He would hardly have lasted so long in Russian society if they had.

Back at his headquarters, he considered the matter. The husband gave the usual description of the White Lady—a white dress, most likely a wedding one, black hair. It could be anyone. Was it someone he knew? He idly considered that it might be the Countess Marcian Gregoryi—an old foe. Then again, it could just have been a Russian aristocratic woman. The revolution had resulted in the deaths of many of the aristocracy. It was entirely possible that, in the chaos, one woman had been turned into a vampire. One missing aristocrat would hardly be considered odd at this time.

One thing he was certain of, the White Lady was a Red provocation, no doubt controlled by Von Bork in some way. She had used her mesmerism powers in order to stop the husband, but left him alive in order to relate what he had seen in order to spread terror. There had been an assumption that she left people alive in order to make a quick escape. Now, he knew otherwise.

He had also received information that Von Bork was somewhere north of Crimea, in Ukraine. He wondered about this. Was it a trap? Did Von Bork expect a visit from him? Perhaps. Liatoukine knew that, for his own safety, he had to eliminate the Bolshevik spymaster. However, he would take precautions.

Liatoukine used a secure line to get hold of Squadron Leader Raymond Collishaw, commander of the Royal Air Force's Crimean Group. The RAF had done excellent work in fighting the Bolsheviks. They—and other British units—had done much to destroy Red troops and equipment. It was unfortunate indeed, thought Liatoukine, that the just ousted General Denikin had bungled things so badly. His troops had committed atrocities, especially against the Jews. The Vampire Captain's only concern with this was that it detracted from military objectives. A lot of supplies the British had provided had even fallen into the hands of the enemy. Now, however, the British were due to pull out imminently.

Liatoukine was aware that there were some last attacks planned. Collishaw himself was involved. It was worth seeing what was scheduled. The Vampire Captain was well regarded as an "efficient" soldier by the British, due not only to his being an intelligence liaison, but his known battle skills.

Collishaw was forthcoming. He did indeed have an attack planned for the next day, the 26th of March. Conveniently, it would be on the encampment of Von Bork, in southern Ukraine.

Liatoukine was pleased with his good fortune. He could not rely on the bombing, but if anything went wrong, it may prove a useful diversion. He did believe himself invulnerable, but he certainly was more likely to survive a bombing than the humans. Time, however, was against him.

He gave orders to his remaining staff to immediately evacuate and retreat to Crimea. He himself had a mission to carry out and would join them there.

As Liatoukine started to leave, a lieutenant came up to him.

"Sir," he said, "I would just like to convey the men's appreciation for your staying to the end here."

"It is not required; we all do our duty," Liatoukine replied.

The Vampire Captain did not care about staying with the last troops until the final evacuation. He had only stayed due to the vampire situation, for it was very much in his own interest to find the truth.

Liatoukine left the town on horseback and went into the nearby countryside. There he walked into a field, which had a dilapidated barn in its center. But only the Vampire Captain could see it; there was a device he had appropriated from the Sepulchre that disguised it. It did not make it invisible exactly, but rather something not to be noticed. Further, it caused either feelings of foreboding or disinterest in those who came near it. If an entire army came past it, it might well notice it; but with smaller units, locals, looters, etc, the device ensured that it remained undisturbed.

Liatoukine let his horse go. He proceeded into the barn where there was an aircraft waiting for him—his Russky Vityaz. He had made certain modifications to it and it had served him well in the past.

The Vampire Captain had established the whereabouts of Von Bork. Perhaps a little too easily? A trap, he wondered? He had to deal with Von Bork—he just would have to be cautious.

Liatoukine landed his plane, with little trouble, a few miles away from where he knew Von Bork's train was. He walked the rest of the way on foot, eluding Red troops easily. Aside from his powers, he had dressed himself in Cheka style to help him get through. He had a low opinion of their fashion; it reminded him of the less than joyous style of the Sepulchre.

He had landed at night. By the time he reached the train, it was morning. If the raid was coming, he had timed it well. He was allowed to proceed towards the carriage. The Red troops made no attempt to stop him—either through orders, or fear of the Cheka uniform.

The Vampire Captain took note of the surroundings and the disposition of enemy forces. Once he had eliminated Von Bork, he felt he could elude them at speed, using his power—whether or not the bombing raid took place. This was arrogance on his part. That had been a failing of his in the past—but that attitude had also helped him many times.

Liatoukine noticed some green on the windows of the train. Clearly, the White Lady was present—presumably a vampire who, like him, could operate to a greater or lesser extent during the day.

One of the doors on a carriage opened. A Chekist beckoned to him. A trap then.

The Vampire Captain should have attempted a retreat at that point, but his arrogance prevented him. He did not wish to lose face. He entered, contemptuously tossing a kopek at the guard for his trouble.

He took in his surroundings in a split second. The usual comforts top Bolsheviks enjoyed, the overconfident Von Bork sitting behind an elaborate desk in an ornate chair, and, finally, the White Lady, who was indeed an old acquaintance—and ally—Polly Bird.

He was stunned by her presence, but did not show it. He also noted a rack of swords on the wall. Silver blades.

Deliberately ignoring Von Bork, who was merely human after all, he spoke to Polly Bird.

"It seems you have fallen low to work with such as these," he said, gesturing to Von Bork contemptuously. "You were once on the Vampire Council— what transgression have you made that has led you here?"

"My dear Boris," she replied, smiling at him, "you are so naive..."

No one had ever called him naive before!

"...I still am on the Council. I am here with their knowledge."

Now the Vampire Captain did show incredulity. But Von Bork spoke first:

"Selene has decided that an alliance with the proletariat of Russia—and the world—would be most beneficial. We, Bolsheviks, are the future. "

Liatoukine could hardly ignore him now.

"Vampires have no interest in the workers—aside from that of nutrition, of course. A bit like you, Bolsheviks."

*Antagonism would do no harm now*, the Vampire Captain thought.

Von Bork looked annoyed. Polly Bird laughed loudly.

"How has this come about?" Liatoukine asked. "The Bolsheviks are barbarians. They would reduce the world to a dull level, claiming equality, but providing the best only for themselves."

"Von Bork approached us with a proposition," replied Polly Bird.

*That made sense*, thought Liatoukine. The German spymaster, when he was working with the Kaiser, would certainly have come across organizations that dealt with the supernatural. The Austrians had the best one. Very likely, he had found much out about the Sepulchre from them. The war, however, had been devastating.

107

Unconsciously echoing Von Bork's own thoughts, he wondered if these organizations had been swept away by war? He did not know. In fact, he did not even know what had been happening in the Sepulchre of late. Until now.

"I offered autonomy to Selene," said Von Bork, "in return for certain services. We, Bolsheviks, seek only world peace."

Liatoukine could barely believe what he was hearing. He was also surprised that they were stupid enough to be discussing all this with him now instead of just killing him. And people thought he was arrogant!

"These people will simply destroy the Sepulchre when they can—or take it over and use vampires for their own ends," he said to Polly Bird, gesturing to Von Bork. "Their revolution has not even taken place in Serbia, where it is based."

"Boris Liatoukine," she replied, "you promised us that Russia would win the war against Germany and Austro-Hungary, that it would dominate Europe, with you effectively leading it. Our future, you said, would be secure. Instead, the Tsarist government was overthrown, and the Bolsheviks achieved peace with Germany by giving up large parts of their territory. Agreements can be found with the Reds. Furthermore, we can foresee a future where their power will extend beyond their borders. Peace with them now is acceptable to us and to them; as opposed to a conflict that would cost both sides dearly."

Polly Bird's words contained much truth. Almost too much for Liatoukine. Almost.

"That agreement has hardly been a huge success," he responded. "Far from allying with them, Selene should be devoting resources to destroying them—to restore the status quo."

"Why would we wish to do that, Boris?" She laughed again. "More to the point, why should *you*?"

"You wish to let these people have power?" he asked her.

"Who was it who kept saying we must not provoke the empires into attacking us? It was you. Furthermore, you seem rather, er, comfortable with them. Or at least, with the Russian one, which has not gone unnoticed. They all seem to have a great respect for God and the Church—even when the secular state is in charge. The Bolsheviks however, don't respect God, and neither do we vampires. Frankly, Red power is preferable to us. The fewer crucifixes around, the better."

Such a line of thought had not really occurred to him. Liatoukine had always managed to get away with minimal contact with the Church. However, whilst his first loyalty was to himself, it was true to say that he was a proud Russian. He regarded the Sepulchre as simply a source of potential extra power to him.

"They will not tolerate rivals," he said evenly.

"Not rival—allies," said Von Bork, slightly impatiently. "Let us get on with business. Your fellow vampires do not think you would ever come around to our way of thinking. Given that you have been quite a nuisance for my comrades and I, liquidating you is the best way forward. And your accomplice too, if you brought him along this time."

Liatoukine said nothing regarding his "accomplice."

"Your liquidation is a task for me," continued the German. "It seems the Vampire Council do not quite want to be seen directly dealing with you. Perhaps there are still some Liatoukinites about?"

Von Bork laughed, then brought out a pistol.

*Silver bullets, no doubt*, thought the Vampire Captain. Perhaps with ashes of burnt vampire hearts inside them, too? The silver would hurt, but the ashes may well destroy him instantly. He decided to play for time, sensing something, literally, in the air.

"What was the point of the White Lady?" he asked.

"To create terror and anti-White feeling amongst the populace as well as discreetly keep an eye on you," Von Bork replied succinctly.

Polly Bird suddenly jumped up.

High above, Squadron Leader Collishaw flew his Airco DH9 bomber towards his target. This was likely to be to be his last bit of active service against the Reds. British personnel were being recalled. They had made a strong contribution, but the Whites were not likely to win. Given their conduct, this was not surprising. Still, at least this would be a good target—trains were strategically important.

He dropped his payload.

The bombs hit with perfect timing. Von Bork's carriage was not directly hit, but it was flung off the tracks. All inside were thrown about. Outside, the locomotive was a write off; the other carriages were strewn around and many of their occupants dead.

There was silence for a moment—then, some moans and shouting from Red troops.

Liatoukine had heard the bombs falling; Polly Bird had done so seconds later. Their enhanced senses worked well for them. Von Bork only realized anything was wrong when Polly had jumped up. For vampires, having explosives dropped on you was not a good thing; physical damage sustained could take a while to regenerate. Liatoukine knew this from experience. He had reasoned that the raid may be able to help him out of a tight spot—he had been right, but this was too close. If Von Bork had just shot him rather than indulge in a conversation, the outcome may have been different.

In the mess of the carriage, Liatoukine threw off Von Bork's table, which had smashed into him, breaking many bones. The bones were already regenerating. He looked over to Polly Bird. She, too, was on her feet, shaken, but with fewer injuries. They made eye contact. In that moment, she knew that he was going to kill her. She did not fancy her chances in sole combat with him. Then, there was a moan—Von Bork was still alive.

In that split section of distraction, Polly Bird jumped upwards through the shattered carriage window, now above her, and ran away at inhuman speed—almost a blur to the still dazed troops outside. Her fear of Liatoukine must have been considerable, for she had escaped with a broken leg.

Back in the carriage, Von Bork got to his feet. His face was bloodied, he was dazed and probably could hear little—but ironically, he was less injured that his opponent, whose rib cage had been crushed.

The Vampire Captain could feel his bones regenerating, but not quickly enough! He could move, ignore the pain, but not much faster—if at all— than the German spymaster. This would be a fairer fight than he would have wished. Then, he saw what Von Bork had in his hand—a silver sword from the rack he had seen earlier. He saw another one—now, on the floor—beside him. He scooped it up and lunged at the German. Von Bork fought the attack off, almost a little too easily. He was known to be an excellent fencer.

They fought in the carriage; the clashing of the swords was all that could be heard. Neither combatant had the inclination for pointless prattle while they tried to kill each other. The vampire was not able to use his powers—although he could sense them coming back slowly. He needed time—a minute even. Then Von Bork slashed his face with his sword. Energy trickled into the air, before the wound healed. Such was the effect of silver.

The Vampire Captain could not believe that a mere human was starting to best him. The cut, though minor, held back his healing. They fought on, jumping and leaping over the wreckage of the carriage, their swords clashing all the while.

Outside, the Red troops had started to gather their wits. One was peering over the window.

Liatoukine realized his time was running out. If those troops entered the fray, he did not believe he could escape. A small amount of energy was returning. He summoned his double. It appeared next to him without a sword, and lunged at Von Bork, who thrust his sword into thin air. The double had vanished—the Vampire Captain did not have enough energy to sustain it. But the distraction had been enough. He exited in the same way Polly Bird had done, using up his energy for the leap. On the way up, he shoved the curious Red trooper down into the carriage—on top of Von Bork.

"Quickly!" he shouted to the soldiers. "Get inside and assist Von Bork"

He leapt of the carriage and ran off. Some soldiers obeyed him, the smarter ones pursued Liatoukine. But they soon lost him.

Liatoukine ran. His body regenerating, he began to pick up speed—but he still feared it was not enough. He ignored the pain. The fight, the leap, now the running. Was this the end for Boris Liatoukine?

Von Bork was not pleased at how things had gone. However, he knew that victory was now a matter of time—and not too long—for the Bolsheviks. Liatoukine would keep.

Later, the Cheka found a trail leading to a clearing where some locals had seen an aircraft taking off. Liatoukine had survived, of course. He ended up in Crimea with the last of the White Russian forces, now under the more capable command of Baron Wrangel. Despite a spirited attempt to fight back, the Whites were defeated. The Vampire Captain fled his own homeland on a French ship bound for Constantinople.

*Paris, 1928*

Boris Liatoukine returned to his fashionable Paris apartment from a pleasant night on the town—although not so pleasant for the unfortunate man he had drained for energy earlier on.

Before entering his apartment, he had noticed a tint of green through the windows. Further, there were a number of figures in the street. It would seem that Von Bork had finally caught up with him. He was surprised it had taken him this long. Whilst Liatoukine had taken an assumed identity, he could not—and did not want to—pretend that he was not Russian. And so he led the life of a White Russian exile in Paris. He did not mix too much with other exiles, but even so, he could not keep too low a profile—his ego prevented that. Clearly some clues about him had reached Moscow. After all, were there not Bolsheviks in France?

He could see that his opponents were a mix of humans and vampires—the Soviet/Sepulchre alliance still held in some form, it seemed. It would be difficult to elude them. He would go to his apartment and face whatever was there.

Inside, sitting on his expensive couch, was Von Bork. Did the man ever stand when someone entered? A number of others stood in the room, in the shadows. Only one lamp was on, illuminating Von Bork. Standing behind him was Polly Bird—in a clearly subordinate role.

*Things have changed*, Liatoukine thought.

In the Bolshevik's hand, held downwards as if it were a walking stick, was a stake built of silver—complete with a hammer and sickle engraved on it. Von Bork beckoned Liatoukine to sit down. The Vampire Captain did so; he was not confident against such a weapon. He would not attempt a last stand. He sensed that his destruction was not what Von Bork was after.

Von Bork got straight down to it.

"As you can see, we have finally caught up with you. Before you ask how, let us say that we are aware that, in the past, you have married wealth, and that your wives, rather unfortunately, were all mysteriously murdered soon after. Imagine our interest when we heard through our local comrades that a Russian exile's wealthy wife had died suddenly here."

Liatoukine knew exactly what he meant. He enjoyed an expensive lifestyle, which his recently deceased wife had paid for. He found wives an encumbrance;

and so he had murdered his latest one by draining enough energy only to induce a seizure. His arrogance had overridden his concern for his safety.

Von Bork waved the silver stake at him.

"Incidentally, I think this could destroy you if plunged into your heart, so you should reconsider if you think you can escape."

Liatoukine did not wish to test if he could. However, he did want to get on-to what Von Bork was really here for.

'What do you want from me?' he asked.

"I offer you the opportunity to serve world revolution, Comrade Liatoukine!" replied the German, smiling. "As you can see, I use a number of your kind to further the aims of the proletariat. Many former bourgeois oppressors have been successfully rehabilitated into our cause."

Liatoukine wondered if Von Bork actually believed in all that.

"You would employ me? Even under the laws of 'bourgeois' society, I am a murderer—a monster."

"Of course!" Von Bork beamed at him. "The revolution needs such people to further its aims!"

Liatoukine wondered briefly if the German was insane. Regardless, he better find out the terms that were being offered. The sullen-looking Polly Bird was clearly in a position he did not want.

"What would be my place?" he asked.

"You would work directly to me," Von Bork replied immediately. "Your powers and military knowledge would be used to their full extent. Your, er, dietary requirements would be seen to—we have many prisoners who cannot be reconciled to living in the worker's paradise. You would even have rank, above these certainly," he waved at the various figures in the room. "We are the future. Your Russia has gone. And soon, we will control the world. The only place you could have is with us."

Liatoukine's mind raced. Once, he would not have contemplated any such agreement. Yet, here was an opportunity, was there not? Von Bork would no doubt have methods of control other than the threat of a silver stake. And yet, the Vampire Captain was immortal, and Von Bork was not—and perhaps did not even wish to be. Soviet society could cover his true nature most effectively. Over time—perhaps even decades—he could change his position into something rather more congenial and more powerful. And if there was one thing he missed in his present situation, it was power.

*Let there be no further delay then*, he thought. He gave his answer.

"Your terms are reasonable. I accept... Comrade Von Bork."

*Over the years, Martin Gately has assembled a series of mystery tales starring Gaston Leroux's sleuth, Joseph Rouletabille. However, the chronology of these stories can be confusing because "Rouletabille and the New World Order" (TOTS 11) takes place between parts 1 and 2 of "Rouletabille Vs. The Cat" (TOTS 10). On Page 117 of TOTS 10, Rouletabille reflects on his adventure with Hugo Danner ("Rouletabille and the New World Order"), which involved the Sesqui-Centennial Exposition in Philadelphia held in May 1926. In the winter of 1926, ten years after the events of "Leviathan Creek" (TOTS 8), Cyrus West emerges from the rejuvenation cylinder at Glen Cliff and leaves New York on the yacht* Sea Silk, *with Missy-Lou. Subsequent to this, Rouletabille uncovers evidence which allows him to deduce what James Worth (son of Adam Worth, a possible inspiration for the character of Moriarty) was planning to do in the Pacific (see Page 75 of TOTS 11). And that is what this new story is about...*

## Martin Gately: *Rouletabille on Mysterious Island*

*July 2, 1927*

The first thing that the detective was aware of was a searing pain on the right hand side of his head, about two inches above his ear. He put his hand to it. Even the gentle touch of his finger tips on the wound was excruciating. He realized almost straightaway that the injury had been bandaged. Well, that was something. He propped himself up on his elbows and looked around. He lay on the sandy section of a small rock-strewn beach, roughly twenty or so feet from the gently lapping waves. And he had absolutely no idea how he had come to be there.

The most delicious smell emanated from almost directly behind him. He turned over to find that he had almost rolled onto a little campfire. Half a dozen silver fish, each about four inches long and impaled on bent sticks, were barbecuing over the blaze. A mysterious benefactor had prepared a meal for him.

Suddenly ravenous, he picked a fish from its improvised spit and greedily consumed it—scales, bones and all. It tasted marvelous, similar to whitebait. But the species was unknown to him. Yet, so many things were perhaps unknown to him. He knew his name—Joseph Rouletabille, and that he had been a journalist and a detective... also a spy and a soldier. He remembered something about a yellow room and the scent of a woman... That had been important. But it all seemed so long ago and far away.

The intense pain had formed a barrier in his mind, not merely disrupting his memories but also the routine pathways of cognitive thought. This much he knew: his mind had been an extraordinary one—swift and unerring, a computational machine that never fully rested. Now the linkages and chains of reasoning were snapped, useless. He... could... not... think... properly. It was maddening. He did his best to comfort himself. He had been awake for only moments. Perhaps, as the injury healed, his brain would return to normal.

He stayed by the fire until he had eaten all of the fish. He was unsure whether this was breakfast or dinner. The sun hung low in the sky and he could not tell for the moment if it was rising or setting. While he was considering this, and who might've lit the fire, he found, half-buried in the sand, a military-style water canteen. He took a few swigs of the water inside, then put it over his shoulder and began walking along the beach.

Within ten minutes, he had rounded a headland and the beach had almost completely disappeared; now there were just black volcanic rocks. He looked inland. There was a stubby peak that could almost be the shattered remnant of a volcano. He estimated that it was less than a mile away. He resolved to explore a little more of the coast and then head into the interior of the island—he supposed it to be an island, but until he had circled it, he could not rule out the possibility that it was a peninsula.

Up ahead, something was perched on the pyroclastic rocks—as if washed onto them during a tempest. As he got closer, he could see that it was the wreck of a boat, or more properly a yacht. The masts, rigging and sails had all been lost. The hull had been punctured by some of the more jagged pieces of basalt, and these rocks now held the wreck precariously like a clawed hand. The cabin was splintered as per the proverbial matchwood.

Rouletabille could only guess—was this the vessel that had brought him here? He moved closer and closer, seeking some clue. Finally, he climbed the great stones and approached the stern of the smashed craft. Hanging loosely was a wooden plaque bearing the name of the ship. He said it aloud several times. His tongue playing with the words, holding them in his mouth like he would with medicine he was not quite ready to swallow. *Sea Silk... Sea Silk... Sea Silk...* It was dimly recollected. But that was all. It was no key to his memory. He had seen it before. Seen it somewhere. The ship had been intact—but just how long ago was that? It felt like months.

"You've probably figured the whole thing out," the bearded man had said, as he lay there in the bed in the cabin.

And then, the visual and auditory recollection was gone. Impossible to retrieve. In its place was something else. A useless piece of information: sea silk is a rare fabric obtained from the pen shell—it is made from the fibers the mollusk uses to attach itself to the sea bed. He wished he could somehow trade that fact for something more relevant and helpful. But human memory cannot be bartered with at the best of times.

Rouletabille did not even seriously consider going aboard the wreck. It looked far too dangerous. He could imagine the deck giving way beneath him and toppling down onto the rocks. Or perhaps the grip of the rocks on the hull was not so firm as it seemed, and the whole thing would slide into the sea with him aboard. No, the answer did not lie in the wreck. His every instinct was that it was a doorway to death. He headed instead for the volcano, if, indeed, volcano it was.

So, he walked on, and soon realized that the pseudo-whitebait had been breakfast—the sun was rising. The morning was hot. He turned his mind to attempting to deduce his general location in the world. The vegetation was pretty sparse, just a few scrubby palms and hardy sedges. As he ascended the crumbling grey pumice slopes of the volcano, he was afforded a much better view of the island. It was small—perhaps a few hectares larger than a typical deer park—and largely barren. At one point, he thought he heard the bleating cry of wild goats in the middle-distance, but he never did see any, nor even saw any goat tracks.

He considered it most likely that he was somewhere in the South Pacific. There were volcanic islands in that part of the ocean. He knew that he was French, and it was not difficult to surmise that he was likely to be in a French Protectorate area, perhaps Boragora or Tagataya. Again, he had a fragmentary memory and another useless one. He had once been at a social function in Paris where he had been introduced to a criminal who had survived an attempted execution by guillotine and gone on to become a magistrate on an island in the Pacific.

It was getting even hotter; he was now perspiring freely; a wide-brimmed hat would've been advantageous. He paused to take a few glugs from his canteen. He also drank in the great sapphire vista of the ocean with one hand shading his eyes. And now, for the first time, he saw it.

There was a ship at anchor, perhaps only eight hundred meters from the northeastern shore. A large merchant vessel, some kind of cargo ship with two great cranes fitted to the stern. He was saved! It was a miracle that another ship had arrived here at the same time he had. Did he have the strength to swim out to it, or if it would be better to attempt to signal it from the shore.

He was about to turn around and start heading back down the slope when something stopped him. Not a memory, but something more akin to an instinct. There was danger for him down in that cargo ship, and a far greater one even than there had been aboard the rock-stranded wreck.

Now he was confronted by the gaping, uneven maw of the volcano. Fortunately, it seemed that it was inactive. While there was the aroma of sulphur, there were no more noxious fumes and no heat. The sun was high and shone like a searchlight into the depths of the thing. Far, far below was the suggestion of greenish blue water. There was a water-filled grotto within the volcano. More significantly, an intermittent throbbing sound emanated from the depths. There was something mechanical down there, an engine of some sort. The grotto was inhabited!

Better yet, his subconscious did not furnish him with any dire warnings about what might be in it. Quite the contrary. His anticipation was that it was a place of sanctuary and peace. Rouletabille looked gingerly over the edge of the volcano in the forlorn hope that there might be a way down other than a suicidal leap into the grotto's emerald waters. Without the climbing ability of a spider, it looked to be impossible.

He sighed and accepted defeat. He would simply have to head back down the peak and find another way in. There might be a cave or an undersea tunnel which could unite him with the grotto dwellers. He shot a last look back at the abyss and was astonished to see, now that the sun had reached its zenith, that a steel gantry was visible, perhaps five meters below the lip of the crater. He could not account for its presence or purpose other than it was obviously the work of the grotto-dwellers.

It was another hour before the detective had fully resolved and summoned up the courage to attempt to jump down to the gantry. He had spent a lot of that time squinting into the darkness beyond the steel walkway and he thought he could see a set of metal steps leading downwards. He stepped back a few paces and then launched himself over the edge. As his feet left the ground, he feared that the arc of his fall would not carry him as far as the gantry. Yet somehow it did, and the stairway railing whacked hard against one of his calves while the deck rose swiftly to meet his face. He was just able to bring up his arms, as one would for a break-fall in Baritsu or Judo, and this saved him from nasty facial injuries. Nevertheless, his palms and forearms were bruised. But it was a small price to pay for the progress he had made. He was convinced that he would soon be reunited with friends and allies.

He could see that there were electric floodlights far below in the water and on two craft. One was a long grey submersible with a horn-like ram on the bows, the other was tiny—some sort of metal sphere with trailing cables attached to it. Somewhat winded, Rouletabille stood up and only then began to understand how precariously the gantry and stairway beyond were attached to the inner wall of the volcano. His jump down had only served to loosen them further. The whole of the steelwork seemed to have been exposed to incredible temperatures, and some of it looked partially melted.

He started to pick his way down the stairs with great care, and with each step, they seemed more rickety. Down and down he continued. When he was perhaps seventy-five meters from the surface of the water, there was a sound like a gunshot, and his first guess was that he had been spotted by some enemy or guard and was being sniped at. But no, the noise was one of the supporting bolts from the stairway wrenching itself from the wall.

He instantly abandoned the idea of carefully traversing the stairs and began to run just as swiftly as he could. The more he ran, the looser and more disconnected the stairs seemed to become. The framework juddered and oscillated; the rhythm of the soles of his shoes on the steps was a hastening staccato drumbeat.

He dared not look back, but it was now obvious that the long section of stairs that he had already traveled was peeling away from the interior wall of the volcano. The steel was beginning to screech like a fearful woman.

Rouletabille decided to take his chances, vault the railing and jump into the green water below. He put his legs firmly together and pointed his feet so that he would make a smooth entry into the water. He just hoped he was executing his feet-first dive properly. The even greater danger seemed to be that the tangled mess of metal would land on top of him. But then, his ending would be so quick, that it seemed scarcely anything to worry about.

He maintained the diving posture for what seemed like an age as he dropped through the air. On the edge of his peripheral vision, the steel stairway tumbled away. The stairs hit the water first, propelling upwards a wide irregular fountain of the green-hued liquid. Then, it was Rouletabille's turn to slice into the grotto's watery depths.

The impact carried him a long way down. He held his breath and clamped his mouth shut. After another couple of seconds, he dared to open his eyes. It felt like he was still going downwards. All he could see was the all-enveloping milky jade froth, a churning mass of bubbles. He wondered if he was caught in some sort of tide or suction. As he tried to swim, he realized just how much his sodden clothes restricted him. Then, he cursed himself for a fool. He had become disoriented in the opaque water after the moment of landing. He was not being pulled down by suction, but rather rising in an inverted position. The movement of the bubbles around him now gave this away, as did the luminescence from the floodlights on the deck of the submersible. He righted himself in the water and began to kick upwards. Then he un-looped the canteen from his shoulder and discarded his heavy jacket. The ascent now seemed easier.

When his head came out of the water, he was surprised to see how close he was to the submarine. There was even a man on the craft with a boat pole trying to assist him, trying to help him from the water. So, the grotto dwellers were friendly. He had obviously made the right decision in attempting to come down here. Then the Frenchman's stomach turned to lead and ice. The man was no longer silhouetted by the lights. He was wearing a black and white uniform and sporting a black peaked cap with white trim. This was the uniform of the Catharus Society!

Rouletabille remembered about the Catharus Society and its plan to massively reduce the population of the world by means of a massive hemorrhagic fever pandemic. A plan he had just managed to avert with the assistance of the extraordinary super-human, Hugo Danner, and the courageous Captain Anthony Rogers (who had had no choice but to join the ranks of this villainous organization). [1]

---

[1] See *Rouletabille and the New World Order* in *Tales of the Shadowmen 11*.

His ability to recall was returning swiftly, just not swiftly enough. He was probably here to thwart another scheme by the Society or the unnamed rogue offshoot of the same organization that was commanded by James Worth, formerly a respected Philadelphian businessman.

He closed his fingers tightly over the end of the boat pole, and was then gently towed towards a rope and chain ladder, which would allow him to climb up onto the deck. He could've quite happily lain on the deck all afternoon recovering from the shock of his fall from the steel walkway. Yet, now he was starting to form the definite realization that he had secret allies here within the grotto, and he should make every effort to reunite with them so that they could achieve their mutual aims. The man with the boat pole suddenly shouted back to a figure on the submersible's conning tower.

"Tell the commander we've found another one."

Rouletabille was taken down a hatchway into the interior of the craft. The airlocks and so forth were not entirely unfamiliar to him. He had once been an unwilling guest on a U-boat. That had been during the Great War, off the coast of New Jersey. Kapitan Mors had been the commander.[2] But that craft was a paltry thing compared to this. This submersible was luxuriously appointed with gleaming brass at every turn and fixtures and fittings of coral and ivory. The walkways underfoot were of a material unknown to him—some kind of resin? He noticed that the raised lower bulkhead sections of the airlocks at floor level were highly polished as if by the passage of feet over many, many decades.

The guard ushered the detective into a grand state room where, incredibly, an organ had been installed. Somehow, it did not truly suit the room. It seemed new and garish compared to the other décor in the chamber. Then Rouletabille saw that two people were tied with ropes to two of the chairs. One was a handsome man of about thirty with black hair and full black beard, and the other was a dark-skinned woman of around forty. This woman possessed an extraordinarily beautiful face, albeit a haughty one. Yes, these were his allies. Although his imperfect memory would have it that it was months since he had last seen them. The detective's guard tied him to a third chair and then left the trio alone.

"Rouletabille! My God, how did you follow us down here in your wounded condition?" asked Cyrus West. "You should've stayed on the beach."

"I went along the pathway that led to the volcano and there is... or rather was a steel stairway down. I should say that I still have partial amnesia, from this head injury, but I know now that you are Captain Cyrus West—sometimes known as Harding. And that the lady is Missy-Lou Pleasant."

"Careful what else you say," ordered Missy-Lou. "The saying that walls have ears is not mere idiom aboard this ship."

"I'll remind you of the more salient points that it is safe to repeat," said West. "Following your experience in Philadelphia last year, you ultimately de-

---

[2] See *Leviathan Creek* in *Tales of the Shadowmen 8*.

duced that James Worth and his allies, an engineer called Hassett and a German scientist named Grierson, were trying to salvage Captain Nemo's ship *Nautilus* from the submarine grotto here on Lincoln Island. With the help of my lawyer, Crosby, you were able to trace Missy-Lou and myself to my property in the bayous of Louisiana. Traveling there to enlist my help, we eventually set sail for the South Pacific in my yacht. Unfortunately, during a storm... wait, someone's coming..."

Three men entered the room and the remaining mental barriers that had shrouded Rouletabille's mind melted away like an ice cube dropped on the ground during a summer party. Two of the newcomers wore variants on the officer's uniform of the Catharus Society, but instead of the Thrush emblem of that organization, they instead sported patches and epaulettes with a kraken or squid-like design.

One of the men in uniform was James Worth—the man who had bragged to Rouletabille that his father, Adam Worth, had been the real Captain Nemo, and that Prince Dakkar—regarded by many as Nemo's real identity—had been a fiction created by West to allow him to steal and patent Adam Worth's brilliant inventions.

The other man, he had only seen in police photographs, never in person. He as one of the most vile perpetrators in the annals of criminology: the infamous Ian Hassett. He had commenced his dreadful career by murdering his brother, and then his father. He had been deliberately entombed alive by the world's premier consulting detective within an old Roman lead mine adjacent to the Great Rutland Cavern in Derbyshire. But he had succeeded, eventually, in escaping this fate. He was arrested for murdering a street woman in London, but found insane.

And that, perhaps, explained the presence of the third man, Dr. Grierson. He was one of the French detective's oldest surviving enemies—a German master spy who frequently posed as a psychiatrist or asylum head. Once, long ago, Rouletabille had fallen into his hands in London, and was subject to the most appalling torture—agonizing intramuscular injections of camphor and electro-convulsive therapy. He had been lucky to escape with his life on that occasion.

James Worth fixed Rouletabille with his grey eyes and laughed derisively.

"Well, well, the little French journalist Rouletabille, and playing way out of his league as usual," said Worth.

The sadistic Grierson moved closer, grabbed the detective by the hair and examined his face closely.

"It is Rouletabille," he said, "or at least it looks like him, but he has scarcely aged since I last saw him more than fifteen years ago. He is still little more than a boy."

"Merely proof of his long and close association with West. He's been allowed access to what West's intimates call the *old E.V. fluid*—the *Elixir Vitae* of legend."

"Why are we wasting time on them?" asked Hassett, his voice sickening cold and detached. "We are fully occupied with cutting away the entire ocean door. Kill the men now, but keep the woman alive. I may wish to use her later as a plaything."

With a practiced accuracy, Missy-Lou spat in Hassett's face from almost three yards away. Mortified, he moved to strike her, but was restrained by Worth.

"You can't touch her," he said. "I need her in one piece most of all. Get back to supervising the divers on the cutting team."

"So, all these days here and you never did figure out how to open the undersea door into the grotto. You had to blowtorch your way in," said West. "You made a hole big enough for a diver or a Maracot bathysphere to get in, but now you need to get the *Nautilus* out."

"Yes," replied Worth, "but we both know that that portal is ancient in origin. It wasn't put there by Nemo, but rather by the advanced civilization that occupied this area ages ago."

"If you say so," said West, smiling secretly.

"Actually, there is something I want to show you, West. Something I can't really explain."

"Something aboard the *Nautilus* that you do not understand?" mocked Rouletabille. "How can that be when your father was Captain Nemo, and you know all of his secrets from reading that journal?"

"I invented the journal merely as a means of manipulating you, Rouletabille. But I know many things about this 'mysterious island' that you do not. For instance, the journey by balloon from Richmond to the South Pacific was no accident. And, of course, it did not take place in a Confederate observation balloon, but rather in a powered dirigible of my father's own design," said Worth.

"Is that truly what he told you?" said West. "It's nonsense."

"Was his father ever really here, Cyrus?" asked Rouletabille.

"Yes, but he sure as hell wasn't Nemo. In more pleasant circumstances, I'll tell you the story."

"I doubt if you'll ever be in pleasant circumstances for the remainder of your very short life," said Grierson, before adding, "I'll get the men to bring in the girl's body."

A few minutes later, two guards carried in a partially shattered transparent cylinder, set it down on the deck, and then left. Inside the tube was the body of a young blonde woman of about twenty-five. The remnants of an azure fluid—something like bluish, translucent mercury—still sloshed around in the bottom of the cylinder, just about half an inch worth. The girl had been dressed in a skin tight, futuristic looking golden fabric, but this had obviously been cut away by Grierson. And following that, a rib spreader had been applied. It was possible to see where the psychotic doctor had rooted around in her chest cavity with his scalpel.

"We had to smash the tube to get it open," said Worth. "There are a couple of others with men in them. This one was marked—*Mercurian Female—Rulu.*"

"And yet, I have examined her organs and she is definitely human," said Grierson. "What's more, she has dental fillings and bridgework of the exact type used in the United States. She has inoculation marks and an appendectomy scar. She is definitely of Earth. So what game was being played out on this island, West? What was really happening here?"

"You'll never know," replied West.

"Mr. Worth, would you do me the favor of shooting Monsieur Rouletabille in the head with your sidearm?" asked Grierson.

"Why not? He knows the least of any of us about the island and Nemo, so he is of little use," said Worth, tugging his automatic from its holster.

West paled. He had not fully anticipated the ruthlessness of Grierson.

"Very well," said West. "I'll give you the full answer, but it may stretch your credulity. Nemo had a machine which could erase a person's personality—essentially evicting it like an unwanted lodger—and install a new, better personality in its place. This woman was a prostitute, a thief and a murderess. But by the time she had been processed by Nemo's machine, she had no recollection of her old life. She was effectively a completely different person. She really did believe herself to be a woman from another planet."

"That's preposterous. What possible purpose could it serve?" asked Grierson.

"Nemo had a vision not totally dissimilar from that of the Catharus Society—although it didn't involve murder on an industrial scale. He wanted to remove the underclass from society and turn its people into hunter-gatherer tribes residing in very isolated locations. On this island, he succeeded in turning modern-day men into primitives, using his machine—he called them the *Volcano People*. They were pirates, criminals, the dregs of the Earth. But the conditioning was perfect; their original personalities never re-emerged. His biological experiments would've provided the megafauna upon which they could've subsisted. But that was not enough. He also wanted to create a group of ultimately beneficent overlords—the technological hierarchy so beloved of Mr. Worth here. So Nemo created another group who believed themselves to be aliens. And with access to Nemo's advanced inventions, that was exactly what they appeared to be. Their first job was to menace the primitives, but in the end, they would've become their moral guides and law-givers, had the experiment not been terminated by Nemo's death."

"I believe him," said Worth. "My father was a scientific wizard, not the criminal mastermind—*the Napoleon of Crime*—that some have painted. And it is from him that the concept of a ruling class with superior technology originates."

121

"Worth, you are an intelligent man under a strange delusion. What sign did Adam Worth ever give to you in his ordinary life that he was a genius?" asked West.

"Well, we had to live quietly and unobtrusively in Philadelphia. If my father had drawn too much attention to himself, his early life as a Civil War *'bounty jumper'* might've been exposed," replied Worth. "Besides, he told me so much about this island and it's all accurate—he must've have been here. And if he was here… then, he was Nemo."

"The world will be a better place when people cease to believe outrageous claims on bad evidence or on faith," said West. "Just because he was here—and I'll admit now that he was—that doesn't mean he was Nemo. And Nemo's real identity, I will take to my grave. Even the threat of death and torture of my friends would not pry it from me. It is too important."

"I would not torture you or your associates in order to ascertain something that I already know," smiled Worth. "We are about to leave this grotto in the *Nautilus* for the first time. Hassett's men have done a wonderful job in restoring power to the ship. This vessel will again be the terror of military and commercial shipping. Soon, no oceanic journey will be undertaken by any nation-state without proper tribute being paid to me. But I am a superstitious man, as are many of the men who serve on the crew with me. Many of them are adherents of Santeria and they are fascinated to hear that one of the most powerful women of the Obeah in the history of that great religion has come aboard this ship."

"And so…?" asked Missy-Lou. "What do they want from me?"

"They merely want to know if this is going to be a successful voyage, my dear," replied Worth. "They have prepared a *potion pour voir l'avenir,* so that you will be able to tell our collective fortune and see if we prosper in the future."

"It won't work unless I mix it myself… Besides, an Obeah Queen cannot drink of a Santeria sacrament. It is sacrilege for both religions," said Missy-Lou.

"Nevertheless, I would hate to disappoint them," said Worth. "Nezzar!"

Rouletabille twisted his head to see the doorway, a huge black man was entering the room. His face was covered with a satanic-looking mask fashioned from a goat's head. He was also stripped to the waist, and at his belt hung a vicious looking machete. Predictably, the container for the potion, which would afford Missy-Lou a view of things to come, was a human skull converted to be a bizarre ceremonial chalice. Less expected was the appalling odor emanating from the liquid—burnt hair, urine and candle wax could easily have been on the list of ingredients.

And then, from behind the goat-masked man called Nezzar stepped an Amazonian woman with red hair and sunburned skin. Her eyes were a cattish green, but there were two other notable things about her. Since her mouth was partially open, it was possible to see that her teeth had been filed to points, and her fingers were adorned with razor-sharp brass nails. This was Hell-Cat Maggie, an underworld enforcer recruited by the Catharus Society whose allegiance had passed to Worth.

"I helped cook it up, so I wants to hear what the Obeah bitch sez," said the woman with pointed teeth.

"Very well, Maggie," said Worth.

Rouletabille noticed that she was wearing a female equivalent of the Catharus Society officer's uniform, but with a rather immodest short skirt and black beret.

Nezzar got hold of Missy-Lou by the hair and pulled her head back. The Obeah Queen did not put up much of a struggle; perhaps she was more interested in finding out if the Santeria future-seeing potion worked. The liquid was poured into her and Missy-Lou gagged and spluttered.

"I don't know why you put any stock in this sort of thing, James," said Grierson. "It shows the lack of a scientific education. And it is wrong to encourage it in the crew. Rationality should be the way of the future. Not this sort of tripe."

The cold fury emanating from West was palpable. All now were silent. Waiting…waiting for Missy-Lou to do or say something. But she just rocked backwards and forwards in her chair—held fast by the restraints.

Then the silence was broken by a sharp whistle from the internal communications system. Worth put the brass listening tube to his ear. A few moments later, he related back to the room what he had heard.

"Well, ladies and gentlemen," he began, "Commander Hassett reports that the ocean door has been successfully cut away. He and his men are back on board. We are therefore about to maneuver carefully out of the grotto via the aperture. We will then surface and continue to run tests of the engines and diving systems."

Then came a powerful and rhythmic reverberation as the engine began to make revolutions. Within a few seconds, the propellers were engaged. It was a huge source of regret and shame to Rouletabille that he should be aboard the *Nautilus* in these circumstances, with this most marvelous of machines, under the control of his deadly enemies. Through one of the small portholes in the wall of the stateroom, he could see the now-unmanned Maracot bathysphere being left behind as the *Nautilus* commenced the short and shallow dive to the passable exit from the grotto.

At first, the detective did not understand why something, perhaps his subconscious mind, was drawing his attention away from the porthole and towards the rather out of place organ that Nemo had had installed in the submersible. There was something wrong… something even more out of place regarding the documents on the organ's music stand. There were several sheets of music on it, but in front of them was a small printed pamphlet entitled *The Polyphonic Motets of Orlande de Lassus*. The significance of this struck Rouletabille like a freight train.

123

"My God, West," said the detective. "As dire as our situation might already seem, it is infinitely worse. We cannot now make it out of here alive."

He glanced back at the porthole and saw that the vessel had cleared the tunnel from the grotto and they were in open sea. Then, unexpectedly, the nose of the submarine dipped and they headed down into the deep.

"We're supposed to surface, not dive," shouted Worth. "What the hell is Hassett playing at?"

Before Grierson could reply, Nezzar struck the scientist high on the forehead with his machete. The top of the German's skull was sliced off as neatly as a boiled egg on a breakfast table. Rouletabille saw the exposed cluster of grey matter from which so many twisted schemes had emanated as his enemy collapsed to the floor. His incomprehension was leavened with envy. Grierson was one of the few men Rouletabille would have killed without compunction.

Nezzar pulled off the goat mask. The Frenchman was astounded to recognize the face beneath, although it had been almost eleven years since he had seen it. It was Neb Junior, formerly the bodyguard of General Herbert Brown, latterly an officer of the Bay City PD, and, as Rouletabille would later learn, currently seconded to the US Secret Service.

Neb Jr. moved like a striking snake and freed Rouletabille from his bonds with a single stroke of the machete. Worth's reactions were slow. He was a talker, not a fighter. Nevertheless, his hand was already reaching for the automatic pistol in his holster as Neb Jr. commenced to cross the stateroom.

Far more dangerous was Hell-Cat Maggie, she of the deadly pointed teeth. Rouletabille launched himself straight out of his chair at her since she was obviously about to leap on Neb Jr. from behind. He tried to close his hands around her neck and throat, but his circulation had been badly restricted by the ropes around his wrists. Maggie shrugged off his pitifully weak grip.

It was at that moment that a sound like the cackle of a fairytale witch filled the stateroom. It came from Missy-Lou, who was now subject to the full influence of the *potion pour voir l'avenir.* Her pupils were so dilated that her eyes seemed to be swirling black vortexes. The voice from her lips was not her voice. She was in contact with something else, and it spoke through her. What it was or could have been was open to debate: was it the Goat of Mendes? The Lloigor? But what it said is not in doubt.

"You... are... all going to die," laughed Missy-Lou hysterically. "Soon the darkness will take you. You have boarded a ship of doom."

And while she said this, Worth was aiming his pistol at Neb Jr.'s face, and Hell-Cat Maggie's teeth started to break the skin of Rouletabille's throat. Cyrus West shook in his chair like an epileptic. He was undertaking a desperate and futile battle against the strong rope which held him in place. Time seemed to slow down. Neb Jr. jerked his head to one side while aiming a blow at Worth with his blade.

The pistol went off. The bullet excised skin and bone in the area of Neb Jr.'s right eyebrow, but was little more than a graze. Yet the muzzle-flash had caught the lawman in both eyes, and he was blinded by powder burns. Robbed of its momentum, the machete caught Worth in the shoulder, causing only a minor injury. Neb Jr. dropped his weapon and fell to his knees, clutching both hands to his eyes.

Rouletabille struck at Hell-Cat Maggie with all his strength. His palm connected with the underside of her chin, driving those deadly teeth away before they could do much damage. Still she was on top of him. And she was larger and stronger than he. In a moment, she had him by the wrists and had pinned his arms to the floor. He could feel now that her brass "finger nails" were cutting deeply into the flesh of his wrists. He arched his neck, looking to see if assistance was going to come from any quarter, but Neb Jr. was still incapacitated—now curled up in a ball. Missy-Lou, still bound, was just muttering gibberish—the same words over and over again, commencing with—*Ph'nglui mglw'nafh.*

Then he saw that Worth had slumped to the deck and put down his pistol in order to tend to his shoulder wound. He was dabbing at the gory cleft in his shoulder with a handkerchief, but it would not stop bleeding.

Rouletabille writhed beneath Hell-Cat Maggie, reaching as best he could for the abandoned automatic.

Now she was playing with him, as she had with so many of the men she had killed in the alleyways and brothels of Manhattan. She wanted to let him think he had a chance against her. She guided his hand towards the gun, almost letting him have it. Teasing him with it. Then she crooned and whispered into his ear the obscene talk and worthless promises that seemed to distract men even when they were on the brink of death. She could not bear to kill him quickly now—trapped in the tunnel-vision of the psychotic sadist, she only knew that she wanted to prolong their physical struggle for as long as possible. She could not bite into his throat now, so she sank her teeth deep into his shoulder.

"Get away from him," ordered Hassett. "I need to find out what they've done to this ship."

Hassett stood in the doorway with his firearm drawn, covering Rouletabille and Hell-Cat Maggie. But with her bloodlust boiling, the woman ignored the order to release her prey. She'd decided that she'd rather kill him quickly than not at all... and her teeth were now working her way to his carotid artery. Seeing this, Hassett calmly shot her through the head.

"The control surfaces have locked into a dive. The buoyancy system only allows descent. I've cut motive power, but we are still going down," he said. "How have you done it, and more importantly, can it be undone?"

"They can't have done it," interjected Worth. "We caught them before they got into the sub. But wait a minute! Nezzar is one of them. He could've sabotaged the *Nautilus* days ago."

"It's becoming academic," said Hassett, shooting a glance at his watch. "Unless we stop the descent in the next few minutes, we'll have exceeded the depth for a safe evacuation in diving suits… if the pressure doesn't kill us, the bends will."

"We're not evacuating, Hassett. I've gone to too much trouble to abandon the *Nautilus* now," said Worth, and his hand crept for his dropped weapon. "Get back to the bridge or the engineering deck, or wherever the hell you need to be and fix this. I pay you well, start earning it."

Without warning, Missy-Lou suddenly stood up—the ropes that had held her snapped with the accompaniment of loud cracks.

Rouletabille could not be sure if this sudden inhuman strength was as a result of the potion she had drunk, or if this was a manifestation of the Obeah woman's own strange powers. He stood ready to leap at Hassett to restrain his gun arm if he pointed the weapon at Missy-Lou. But Hassett suddenly dropped his hand to his side.

Missy-Lou's will permeated every atom in the room. She was a protean, irresistible force now, and everything was subject to her and her whims. The power broadcast from her was aimed primarily at Hassett, and his feeble mind and underdeveloped soul were no match for it. They were dust motes lost in the hurricane. Yes, the power was sexual in nature and, even as a secondary recipient or observer of the Obeah in action, Rouletabille would've gladly surrendered his eternal soul for just a minute alone with her. She was fully clothed, in her black blouse and snug black cotton trousers, and yet projected into his mind was an image of her naked. She was standing almost completely still, and yet, he could see her performing the most lewd, provocative and shocking dance—shaking dark tipped breasts an almost un-seeable blur.

No, nothing was happening. She was not moving. She was not speaking. It was all in his mind. It was all in everyone's mind. Then she stepped forward and took Hassett in her arms. Somewhere behind him, Rouletabille heard a choked whimper from Cyrus West—a man who believed himself betrayed by the love of his life. Rouletabille, too, was irrationally charged with jealously. How could he ever think of Missy-Lou in the same way now that she had sullied her lips with the flesh of the dreadful Hassett? A man who had killed his own family without any trace of regret.

Missy-Lou kissed him very passionately and their bodies melded hungrily together. The kissing continued. Hassett wanted it to continue forever. And then, Missy-Lou bit off Hassett's tongue. He staggered backwards and tried to staunch the flow of blood with his fingers, but it was no use. The thick crimson liquid was gouting everywhere. Hassett ran from the stateroom leaving a spattered trail behind him. The spell was broken.

Missy-Lou spat Hassett's tongue onto the floor, swiftly released Cyrus and then went to tend to Neb Jr. Rouletabille relieved Worth of his gun without him even noticing. The man was drooling and only half conscious, his head full of visions of Missy-Lou and her sacred *punani*.

"Help me get him out of here," ordered West.

The two allies manhandled Worth off the floor and onto his feet, then half-dragged him towards the air-tight door exit to the stateroom. West could hear in the distance approaching guards, doubtless coming to investigate what had happened to Hassett.

West slapped Worth hard across the face to bring him out of his reverie. He knew that those who lacked a basic moral core and principles were the most susceptible to the power of the Obeah.

"Worth, you need to die knowing that your father was not Nemo. Your whole life has been a lie… Adam Worth was there with us alright, under one of his many aliases… he was Captain Shard, the leader of the pirates," and without further explanation, West propelled him through the doorway and slammed the airtight door shut.

Missy-Lou noticed then how badly Rouletabille's wrists and forearms had been injured by Hell-Cat Maggie. She tore lengths of material from her own blouse to make improvised bandages, and did her best to clean the macerated shoulder with brandy from the stateroom drinks cabinet.

"How is Neb Jr.?" asked West.

"That bullet creased his forehead. I think he's only temporarily blinded by the flash burns, but he's in deep shock, and terrible pain," said Missy-Lou.

"That's no good. I need him in full working order right now. Even though he'll disapprove of my method of fixing him," said West.

West strode swiftly to the drinks cabinet and removed a crystal tumbler, then dipped the glass into the shattered cylinder where the body of Rulu, the Mercurian girl still resided. Scooping up some of the azure liquid at the bottom of the tube, he then dribbled it onto Neb Jr.'s injured eyes. Almost immediately the swelling began to abate and the tissue to regenerate.

"The old E.V. fluid!" exclaimed Rouletabille. "But what is it doing here?"

"Nemo suspended Rulu in it in an attempt to save her, but she was too far gone," replied West. "Those fools smashed open this healing cylinder—wasting the precious fluid. It would've taken decades to synthesize this amount, and I should know."

Rouletabille recalled how West had spent ten years immersed in the fluid in order to rejuvenate his entire body. He had once given some of the fluid to Rouletabille in order to speed his recovery from a near fatal drowning.

"If all four of us consumed some of the fluid before exiting via an airlock, might it allow us to survive the journey to the surface?" asked Rouletabille.

"Frankly, I doubt it," said West. "But I'll admit that the thought did cross my mind. However, we must now be hundreds of feet below the surface. I'd rather go out in a blaze of glory trying to retake this sub than by drowning or the bends. Which reminds me, you knew that the *Nautilus* had been most effectively sabotaged. How?"

"As soon as I saw the monograph on the *Polyphonic Motets of de Lassus by Altamont Sigerson*," explained Rouletabille, "I knew that Sherlock Holmes, Hassett's nemesis, had got here before us and sabotaged this ship. He must've deduced that Hassett's expertise in underwater operations would mean that he was likely to be involved in any criminal attempt to salvage the *Nautilus*. I can just see the great man now, persuading his brother that he needed to 'borrow' one of the Bruce-Partington E-Class submarines and its crew, travelling here and ultimately solving the mystery of how to open the ocean door. The *Nautilus* had become a trap for evildoers. He did not completely overlook the possibility that men on the side of law would enter the vessel. And his over-endowed ego provided the solution—any good man capable of finding a way into the grotto would have more than a passing familiarity with his work. The monograph was both a calling card and a warning."

Neb Jr. got to his feet, much restored by the ancient elixir.

"We've stopped sinking," he said, taking a look out of the porthole.

"We've reached a point of neutral buoyancy," said West. "Unless there are more tanks still to vent, we will just hang in the water now."

"Cyrus, there is something that I need to tell you," said Missy-Lou.

"What is it, my dear?" asked West.

"The Santeria potion nearly ripped my mind apart giving me a full understanding of the future and—oddly enough—the past. I have seen in my mind's eye how we get out of here, and it is in the way Rouletabille suggested. A terrifying swim to the surface... our blood bubbling from the pressure shift, our lungs rupturing... but our bodies and souls preserved by the power of the old E.V. fluid."

"I am no adherent of these cultish practices," said Neb Jr. "Like you, I would rather take my chances in a good scrap and trust to your engineering skills to fix this hulk and get her back to the surface."

"Don't listen to him, Master," said Missy-Lou. "I have seen the future so very clearly, you are re-enlisted in the US Army and again using the name Smith, promoted to colonel and fighting in a terrible war somewhere in Asia... albeit it will be long decades before all this comes to pass."

"I don't doubt that *will* come to pass, Cyrus," said Rouletabille. "But you are such a brilliant tactician that your final rank will, I'm sure, be general. You could be like a modern day Alexander or Hannibal."

"Your flattery doesn't help my decision-making. It's a pity we had to lose the element of surprise. Otherwise we could win a fight on this ship easily."

And then it seemed that the decision was taken out of their hands. A smoking red spot appeared on the airtight door into the stateroom. Hassett's men were starting to cut through with their acetylene torches.

"In less than five minutes, they'll have cut a hole big enough to shoot a carbine through," said West. "C'mon, let's fall back towards the rear airlock, but let's carry Rulu's cylinder with us."

West picked up the crystal tumbler and led the way towards the airlock.

Less than two minutes later, they had all toasted Rulu and drunk a glassful of the viscous metallic liquid from the bottom of the cylinder. Rouletabille could feel the injuries to his wrists and shoulder itching as they healed almost instantly. Then they crammed into the aft emergency airlock—and it was a tight squeeze. They all stripped to their underwear, apart, of course from Missy-Lou who only ever swam in the nude, whatever the circumstances. Rouletabille had been smitten with her physical beauty since the first time of meeting her, but now he regarded her as one might an elder sister, though not without great admiration. She was not a regular imbiber of the elixir; however, for a woman of more than forty her physique was exquisite.

West shut the inner door and primed the mechanism for the outer door. Outside they could hear gunfire as the *Nautilus* crew sprayed the interior of the stateroom with shots from their pneumatic rifles. Effectively, they had now made good their "escape," such as it was; only a madman would cut open the inner door and risk flooding the ship. With the *Nautilus* crippled by sabotage, Worth and the crew would most likely face death from slow suffocation—but that was likely to take weeks; perhaps the rations would run out first. Hassett would likely expire from blood loss unless someone assisted him by cauterizing his ragged tongue root.

The airlock swiftly filled with water and they all took deep breaths. Then the outer airlock door slid open. They kicked strongly through the door and out of the ship. West had warned them to ascend slowly, although he knew it was rather pointless since they would be unconscious long before they were anywhere near the surface. It was a matter of surviving drowning rather than swimming to safety. Quite what the protection of the elixir would be in relation to the bends, he was unsure. That had never been tested before.

Rouletabille took one last look back at the *Nautilus*, though most of his vision was impaired by the sting of the saltwater. Something was written in huge letters on the hull. And it did not appear to be in the alphabet of any language of which he was aware. There were two very similar words with a short word in between. He felt he ought to know what they said already, but he could not recall it. Was this the last vestige of his amnesia? If he lived, perhaps he would ask West about it.

The pain in his ears was excruciating. His chest was already very sore. It felt like his heart would rupture. He didn't think he would be able to ascend a hundred feet before he lost consciousness. Perhaps that would be a mercy. Black fog was already forming in his brain. His limbs were no longer obeying the instruction to swim and were just flailing.

At that moment, an immense curtain of silver bubbles erupted from the hull of the submarine. The last of the buoyancy tanks had vented. The *Nautilus* sank into the abyss. And the water here was miles deep. Realistically, no one would ever be able to salvage the vessel. The journalist in him regretted that he was unlikely to live to get the story into print.

Then his eardrums burst. There was a sudden urge to vomit, but that passed as quickly as it had arrived. His lungs were screaming for oxygen and his flailing converted into uncontrollable fitting—the beginning of death throes. He felt something touch him. He couldn't open his eyelids since his eyes were too painful, but he assumed he was about to be victim of a shark. No, it was hands touching him—pulling him close. Strong, yet unmistakably female. Then came the open-mouthed kiss. It was Missy-Lou. Was she doing it to say goodbye, because she knew that he did not have the strength to make it to the surface?

His brain started to unfog. She was forcing air into his lungs. Yes, much of her exhalation was carbon dioxide, but there was enough oxygen in her breath to reinvigorate him. She was pushing his eyelids open, turning his face, making him see, making him look, not at her but at what lay perhaps eighty feet above them. Was he hallucinating? It looked like a brass and enamel cathedral bell, suspended above them on long, white tether cables which reached up all the way to the surface. And then he understood! It was a Maracot diving bell, and it had been lowered towards the *Nautilus* by the ship that lay at anchor off Lincoln Island in some sort of rescue attempt.

Swimming strongly up towards the diving bell and pulling Neb Jr. as he went was Cyrus West—his endurance was prodigious due to the long years of exposure to the *Elixir Vitae*. Missy-Lou looped her arms around Rouletabille's chest and commenced a prodigiously powerful scissor-kicking action which propelled them fast towards the open bottom of the diving bell.

Rouletabille wondered if they might not be going too fast. Could this swift sprint to the sanctuary of the bell result in the horror of the bends? There was no time to ponder it. Within moment, he was being thrust up through the diving bell's moon pool entryway, and after that, the hands of Cyrus West reached down to him and hoisted him up onto the wooden bench which went around the inside of the bell. It seemed almost miraculous that the interior of the diving bell should be dry and full of air, and that the seawater remained at a low level just above the lip of the bell.

"*Venture* to Diving Bell One, *Venture* to Diving Bell One," said a crackling voice coming from a small speaker on the wall. "This is Captain Englehorn, can anyone hear me? Over."

Cyrus punched at the microphone button.

"This is Captain Cyrus West of the United States Secret Service, I have with me fellow special agents Neb Dobey Jr. and Louise Pleasant. Also with us is Monsieur Joseph Rouletabille, a French journalist. We are survivors of the *Nautilus,* all other hands are believed lost."

"That's good to know, Captain. We heard from our captors that there was a small opposing force aboard the *Nautilus*," said Englehorn. "My crew has reestablished control of our ship and placed all of the Catharus Society operatives in custody in the brig. Understand that we will have to bring you to the surface very slowly to avoid risk of decompression sickness... please be patient."

"I know Englehorn, he's a good man," said West. "Worth merely chartered the *Venture*, as film producers often do when they're making motion pictures in these parts. Englehorn has no real knowledge of this offshoot of the Catharus Society, and certainly no loyalty to it after his treatment at their hands."

Rouletabille's ears were itching insanely inside where the old E.V. fluid in his system was causing his ear drums to swiftly regenerate. Likewise the explosive pain in his chest was starting to ease off. Missy-Lou huddled up to him for warmth—all four of them were shivering.

"Well, is anybody a conversationalist?" asked Neb Jr. "Seems like we're gonna be stuck here with not much to do for quite a while."

"So, all of you are Secret Service agents?" asked Rouletabille.

"Yes," smiled West, "and I have been since my earliest days posing as a fellow 'bounty-jumper' in order to catch Adam Worth. Which reminds me? What day is it today?"

Rouletabille considered for a moment.

"I don't know. I'm not sure how long I was unconscious on the beach. Thanks for breakfast by the way..." said Rouletabille.

"I believe it is July 2," said Neb Jr.

"I thought as much. It's my brother Jim's birthday. Naturally, he's a Secret Service agent too. I wonder if he got that new Derringer I sent to him? I'll cable him when we get topside," said West. And then, he added, "Now is anything else about this little adventure puzzling you? There is still something of a mystery for you to unravel... let's see if you can do it before we reach the *Venture*. Or has that knock on the head when the *Sea Silk* was wrecked addled your deductive powers?"

"The final mystery is the riddle of Nemo's true identity. I know that he wasn't Adam Worth, and I know that he wasn't Prince Dakkar. For the moment, I will assume that you, Cyrus, are not Captain Nemo—although there is some evidence in favor of that, for I do believe that there are major time discrepancies in Aronnax's narrative and your adventures on Lincoln Island. I am beginning to doubt that your experience on that most mysterious of islands happened during the Civil War at all," said the detective.

"Go on then, you're on the right track. The enigma of Nemo's identity is akin to Mr. Poe's *Purloined Letter,* it is actually quite obvious. Direct then, your mind to the most obvious suspect," said West.

"I'm not sure I know how to do that, but I will tell you what I have noticed. The *Nautilus* is old. Very old. Ancient, in fact. It had the look of something refitted and refurbished many times, which I was not expecting. The walkways were worn smooth by the perhaps centuries' worth of passage of booted feet. Then I would guess that the craft is a product of the same ancient civilization whose remnants can be found both on the island and in the sea; the same society which constructed the ocean door into the grotto. And then we have Nemo's association with the old E.V. fluid—a product which takes decades to distill even in small quantities. I therefore deduce that Nemo is an extremely long-lived representative of that society and that the first iteration of the *Nautilus* was perhaps launched millennia ago."

"That's quite insane, Rouletabille. No one will ever believe you, so I suggest you keep your theories to yourself... However, you are quite correct," laughed West. "Then who is he? I want to hear you say it."

"I remember now, the motto of the *Nautilus*—*Mobilis in Mobile*—according to Aronnax's journal. But on the hull of the craft, it was not written in Latin. What language is it? Is that part of the puzzle?"

"It's Achaean," said West.

"My God, of course. The language of the proto-Greek sea-people," said Rouletabille.

The surface of the moon pool was violently broken by a figure emerging from the depths. He was wearing a self-contained diving suit with small cylinders of air strapped to his back. His face was obscured by his breath mask and he was brandishing a short divers' knife. The diving bell's occupants all sought to draw up their legs onto the bench to avoid the swishing arc of his blade.

As the diver got his bearings, he directed his attack at Missy-Lou. It could only be Hassett beneath the mask. But before the knife could reach her, Rouletabille jumped down from the bench and landed hard on the assailant, filling the interior of the bell with a high fountain of foam and driving Hassett back out of the pool. Rouletabille wrestled with the villain for the knife. When Hassett's grip stayed firm, the detective clawed at the mask and pulled the regulator from between his lips. Hassett's tongueless mouth attempted to scream, but instead projected forth a ribbon of blood.

Rouletabille uncurled the Englishman's fingers from around the handle of the knife one by one and then used it to at jab his adversary's face. The knife went straight through the glass of the visor and into Hassett's eye socket. He must've died instantly since he started to sink downwards straightaway. Rouletabille looked up and saw that the diving bell had risen to be quite a long way from him. He fought to get back to it.

Friendly hands met Rouletabille as he rose from the moon pool and helped him up to the bench. While the detective coughed up seawater, West spoke:

"A group of individuals with access to highly advanced technology inhabited the Mediterranean region several thousand years ago. They also had their own immortality serum, which they sometimes shared with their favorites. They were the original, the prototype of the technological hierarchy. And if you read the stories of the Greek Gods and the works of Homer in that light, you'll arrive at a very clear understanding of what was going on. There was a man of that era, a king, a great sea-captain, warrior and explorer… a man who had good reason to have a kink about war since he participated in one of the biggest wars of that time… and it ruined his life. Yes, there has only ever been one sea-captain using the alias Nemo, and he's been using it since he encountered the Cyclops."

At last Rouletabille understood. It was a truth that could never be told, because it would simply never be believed.

"The King of Ithaca… the father of Telemachus… he was and always had been Nemo," smiled Rouletabille.

Once aboard the *Venture,* Rouletabille, Cyrus West, Missy-Lou and Neb Jr. stood at the stern between the twin cranes and watched Lincoln Island retreat below the horizon as the ship steamed north eastwards.

"I wonder if any of us will return to that mysterious island," pondered Rouletabille.

"We will not," said Missy-Lou, emphatically. "But I have seen the future, and one day, a family will inhabit it. And just as Kapitan Mors' ship to the stars was launched from within a volcano, so this family will launch great red and silver rockets, and these rockets will bring succor to those in need."

Many days later, the *Venture* was docked at Puerto Baquerizo Moreno, on San Cristóbal, where Cyrus, Missy-Lou and Neb Jr. hoped to get passage on a freighter to Bay City in California. Rouletabille planned to continue with the *Venture* to Val Verde, where they would pick up an expedition from the New York Zoological Society. He wondered if they had encountered the strange and deadly creature which was occasionally reported in the jungles of that country, and if they had, perhaps he should pick up its trail; it might make for a good story.

Rouletabille waved to his trio of friends as they walked down the gangplank onto the docks. After a few yards, Missy-Lou and Cyrus stopped. They were talking about something. Oblivious, Neb Jr. kept striding on.

"Cyrus," said Missy-Lou, haltingly. "In the years to come, I am with him," and she pointed a long finger back at Rouletabille on the *Venture.*

Cyrus West merely nodded. She had waited ten years for him when he was little more than a corpse… waited to see if the *Elixir Vitae* would revive him. He could demand no further loyalty from her. The Santeria potion had shown her the life she was to lead, and it was not with him. There was no point arguing.

Rouletabille saw Missy-Lou turn and run back up the gangplank. He wondered what she had forgotten.

*Travis Hiltz has based the following stories on two remarkable French proto-SF novels: The first,* Spiridon *(1907; available from Black Coat Press, ISBN 978-1-934543-61-3), was written by André Laurie, one of Jules Verne's collaborators, and deals with a human-sized, intelligent ant; the other, Alfred Drious's* The Adventures of a Parisian Aeronaut *(1856; Black Coat Press ISBN 978-1-61227-067-8), is a wonderful social satire in which our satellite is reached via hot air balloon; it predates Verne's* Five Weeks in a Balloon *by seven years...*

## Travis Hiltz: *The Case of the Curious Cadaver*

*Paris, 1910*

*With the conclusion of the "Red Leech" poisoning investigation, I began to wonder if I would ever have a case that does not lead into that strange and fantastic world that seems to exist just beneath the surface of Paris. There are days where I long for the sweet simplicity of a robbery or kidnapping...*

From the Diary of Etienne Camparol.

Two figures stood under a flickering street lamp, watching a third stroll away into the night.

The stroller was an old man, with swept back, collar-length white hair, clad in a conservatively cut black suit. He carried a cane and had a large glass jar tucked under his arm. It was filled with murky brine, and an odd creature, resembling a red pickle with thin tentacles, bobbed about.

The old man paused at the mouth of an alley, turned back, and gave a brief salute with his cane hand to the duo and disappeared into the inky shadows.

The duo left behind, a man and a woman, waited another few moments before walking away. The man paused as a strange groaning noise drifted through the air and then faded away. He glanced about, then shrugged and continued walking.

The man was Etienne Camparol, a former undercover policeman, who, following his dismissal for some minor (in his personal estimation) professional transgressions, had become a freelance consulting detective. He was a nondescript man in his 30s who an equally non-descript suit.

His female companion was a few inches taller than Camparol. Her skin was white and smooth as ivory, her hair black as a summer midnight. Her dress was a balance of practical and fashionable. Her face held a youthful beauty and innocence, while her eyes seemed to hold ages of knowledge that were compelling, yet seemed out of place with her girlish features.

"Curious gentleman," Camparol said, nodding back towards the direction their departed companion had gone. "That Professor Omega..."

"It's 'Doctor'," the young lady replied. "And you have no idea."

"So, Mademoiselle Astarte," said Camparol, ignoring her comment, "the night is young... What next? Some light supper perhaps? I know I could use a drink."

"You require alcohol more than seems healthful or necessary," she said, matter of factly. "I do feel a bit peckish, though, but I was wondering... haven't we left Doctor Tasimoura unattended for longer than seems prudent?"

"Most likely," the detective muttered. "Dinning at home it is, then. I seem to do more chaperoning than investigating since the two of you came into my care."

He stuck his hands in his pockets, hunched his shoulders, and quickened his stride. His companion matched his speed with little effort and her features remained as composed as if they'd been carved from marble.

Stella Astarte was introduced to Camparol's friends as a foreign student, who had come to Paris to learn about French culture and history. What the detective neglected to tell them was that her place of origin was a celestial city on the Moon, and those who attempted to guess her age were generally off by several centuries.

Stella had come to Earth, hoping to locate Antoine Gerpré, a French adventurer, a friend of her family; only being immortal, she had lost track of time and discovered that her hoped-for chaperone had passed away, and Camparol was currently in possession of Gerpré's old house. She then assisted him with an investigation and decided that, not only did she wish to stay on Earth and continue her studies, but the notion of assisting the detective intrigued her. Camparol, reluctantly, took on the task, as he had also recently become the minder to the aforementioned Doctor Tasimoura.

Several minutes of walking brought them to a wide alley. There was a gate at the far end that opened upon a courtyard. Camparol and Stella walked through brown scrub grass to the back of a three-story house. It had seen better years, but had been well kept up.

Camparol fished out a key ring and let himself and Stella in.

The back foyer was narrow, dimly lit. A not overly tall, matronly woman in a starched dress and apron blocked their way.

"Oh, it's you!" she said, breathlessly.

"Yes, things ran a bit late," Camparol nodded. "Hope you can muster a bit of... What? What has he done?"

"You asked me to keep an eye out, concerning the Doctor's coming and goings!"

"Doctor Tasimora has been out?" Stella asked, pulling off her gloves.

"He went out on an errand and came back with a big bundle, rolled up in a rug..." the housekeeper explained, nervously.

"Damn," Camparol muttered, pushing past the stout housekeeper and hurrying through the kitchen and down a flight of rickety stairs.

The first room was the usual shelves bristling with kitchen supplies. The detective hurried past jars, crocks and utensils, through a room full of sheet-covered furniture into a narrow stone passage, which opened up upon a low-ceilinged room. It was dimly lit; its walls were lined with shelves, full to bursting with books and a staggering variety of medical implements.

In the center of the room was a heavy oaken table. Despite the covering sheet, it was obvious what was underneath it.

Camparol halted in the low doorway, before approaching the table. He pulled back a corner of the sheet, revealing the still form of a young blonde woman, possibly in her mid-twenties; her features had the slack serenity of death.

Camparol sighed and lowered the sheet.

A door, at the far corner of the makeshift laboratory, opened and a bizarre figure came shuffling out.

Doctor Tasimora was, in fact, a *nom-de-plume* for that unique medical researcher and notorious one-time celebrity, Spiridon.

He was an ant, but one the size of a man. He stood five feet tall. He had an over-large head, fronted by a small mouth with a set of pincers and topped with small, wire-thin antenna. The doctor wore a plain, black, ill-fitting suit. Sticking out of the baggy sleeves were black, bony claws.

The enormous insect paused in the doorway, studying his housemate with glassy, ebony, pupil-less eyes. Acting nonchalant, Spiridon walked up to the table and stood, waiting patiently, across from Camparol.

"Oh, a body," Stella commented, entering the room. "Where did it come from?"

"I was just about to ask the 'good Doctor'," the detective muttered, grimly.

Spiridon reached out a spindly arm and tapped against the edge of the heavy, wooden table. His unusual mouth rendered him unable to speak any human language, but he was able to communicate using his own version of Morse code. Both of his partners had learned this unique form of communication. Spiridon was quite capable of understanding French, English and even a few Asian languages. Camparol waited anxiously for the tapping to cease.

"What do you mean, you found it?" he exclaimed. "Not even in the worst, most depraved neighborhoods of Paris will you 'just find' corpses conveniently stacked up on the corner. How did you get this corpse?"

Spiridon tapped again.

"She was already dead," Stella nodded. "So, nothing to worry about then."

"Nothing to worry about?" Camparol asked, wide-eyed. "I'm relieved that you managed to get through the day without taking a life, but 'body-snatching' is not considered any more socially acceptable than murder. Where did you 'find' this corpse?"

More tapping.

"Rue Morgue?" Stella mused. "That is a particularly destitute area. Not to mention the poor hygienic conditions; it is most likely that she died from disease or malnutrition..."

"That's not the point," Camparol snapped. "Even if the police aren't aware of her death, someone will miss her... family, friends, or an employer... not every young, unchaperoned woman in the city is a recent arrival from the Moon. Someone knows her, or knows she is dead."

He pulled a wooden stool from under the table and perched on it, his elbows resting on the table, as he studied the cadaver.

"We need to know who she... was and what killed her," he explained. "We need information before I can decide how to proceed."

His partners nodded in agreement. The enormous ant shrugged out of his overcoat and began rolling up his sleeves.

"No dissecting," Camparol instructed, glancing up from the deceased girl. "You can take blood to discover if it was disease or something she ate, but no cutting... We need to be discreet."

He sat up, glanced over, noticing that Stella had stepped in closer and was peering intently at the body.

"So," he said, crossing his arms, "what can you tell me?"

"She was young," Stella said. "Thin, but not malnourished. If she is employed, it would likely be as a nanny, her arms aren't strong enough to be a cleaning woman and too clean to be a prostitute."

Despite the situation, the detective nodded in satisfaction at his charges' deductive skills.

Spiridon, on the other side, had a syringe clasped in one claw. He took a sample of blood.

"Hadn't thought about the arms," mused Camparol. "I'd discarded cleaning woman, due to how well-kept her fingernails are."

"What do you make of those marks?" Stella asked, leaning in.

"Marks? Where?" Camparol asked, looking over the corpse. Spiridon's over-sized head moved about, as he too, attempted to spot them.

"There, on the side of her neck. Quite small."

The detective leaned in, peering intently at the marks. He patted his coat pockets, retrieving a pair of gloves. He pulled them on and reached out to gently move the dead girl's head.

"Odd, look like needle marks... two of them, close together," he muttered. "Can't see how they are connected with her death... They look healed over."

Spiridon nodded in agreement, and then tapped out a message.

"What about the other side of her neck?" Camparol asked, looking up.

"I see what he means," Stella said. 'There's a thin line of... something... dried blood, perhaps...?"

Camparol turned the head, so the dead girl was now facing them and then stood up.

"There's another set of marks!" Camparol announced in surprise.

"If they are needle marks, perhaps she was ill and receiving some form of medication?"

"Or was poisoned," the detective suggested, absently. "Both sets are just about on the major veins on both sides of her neck."

He sat back down and glared accusingly at the over-sized ant, as though he brought this puzzling cadaver to the house with the sole intent of annoying the detective. Spiridon ignored his associate's scrutiny and focused his attention upon the body. He then shuffled off with the syringe of blood.

Camparol studied the body for another few minutes and then sighed.

"We need to see where she was found," he said, standing up. "Fetch your coat."

Soon, Camparol and Stella were strolling down the Rue Morgue. The detective alternated between anxiously glancing about the neighborhood and consulting the scrap of paper Spiridon had scribbled a rough map on.

He wore a plain brown overcoat and a dingy derby, not that he needed to put much effort into looking nondescript, as any attention that came his way, was directed at his companion.

Stella made no effort to hide her open curiosity that, along with her height and beauty, kept any passersby attention focused on her.

"She must have lived around here," Camparol muttered, as they walked. "Most of these buildings seem to be hotels and boarding houses…"

"It'll be difficult to find, with that crowd," Stella mused, drawing Camparol's attention.

He looked up from his map, peered at the group at the corner, and then over at his assistant. He sighed and tucked the map into his coat pocket.

"Come along. Focus on listening. Don't talk any more than you have to," he instructed.

They squeezed through the crowd, Camparol melting into it, Stella attempting to be discreet and, for the most part, failing.

He was soon able to piece together from snatches of gossip and various crowd mutterings that they had reached their destination, and both the neighborhood and the police were aware that some form of violent crime had occurred here. After making a circuit, the detective sidled up to Stella.

The young Lunite was standing by a dingy brick wall, looking over the crowd with unabashed curiosity and scrutiny.

"Well, the Doctor has put the cat amongst the pigeons," he said, in a low voice.

Stella glanced over, raised an eyebrow at her partner's arrival and nodded.

"Her name was Noel," she said, quietly. "She lived in the building on the corner."

Camparol nodded his approval.

"She was working a few jobs," she continued. "Cleaning and a bit of sewing. No whispers of gossip about her. Just a lot of 'that poor girl.' We should speak to someone who lived in her building."

"That'll be difficult," Camparol said, looking straight ahead. "Too many policemen around... oh, lord...!"

"What?"

"Inspector Ganimard," Camparol muttered, nodding in the direction of a heavy-set man across the street.

"If you know the Inspector, perhaps he can assist us in our investigations?" Stella asked.

"Unlikely," Camparol replied. "We were never friendly colleagues, even before my, er, dismissal. I tended to needle him concerning his obsession with Arsène Lupin. Attracting his attention would do nothing to help our case. Too many policemen about for us to get much done."

"Surely we can avoid the Inspector and his men's attention?"

"Possibly, but there are at least three other plain clothes detectives wandering the crowd," Camparol said under his breath.

"Are you sure?"

"Well, one of them might be a reporter, but I do have some experience with undercover police detectives," he replied. "If you want to be a detective, you have to learn it's not all asking questions. You observe, watch people, hopefully without it being noticed that you are watching them. People give away clues without knowing it, without meaning to. You learn to look for those signs and can piece together a great many situations. I'm no Dupin, but my own humble skills have gotten me this far."

"What are we looking for?" Stella asked.

"Since it appears young Noel was murdered, it's possible, likely even, that her killer is milling about. We want to look for unusual or suspicious behavior..."

"Like that dark-haired man who isn't breathing?" Stella asked, quirking an eyebrow in thought.

"Like what...?" Camparol asked, struggling to keep his voice low and even.

"The one by the mouth of the alley... dark-haired, rough looking, in a brown suit."

"Broad-shouldered?" the detective asked, glancing about in a casual manner. "He looks like a worker... a bit foreign perhaps...?"

"Yes."

"What do you mean, he's not breathing?"

"He's not. I don't hear a heartbeat either... It's been puzzling me since I first noticed it," the young Lunar Immortal replied.

"You can hear everyone's heartbeat?" Camparol asked, amazed.

"If I concentrate," Stella said, off-handedly. "This is simpler, as it's a noticeable lack of sound."

Camparol gave her a sidelong, puzzled glance, but then shook his head, filing it as a conversation for another day.

"We need to split up," he said. "I'll keep an eye on your mystery man, see where he leads us. Stay here and keep an eye on the Inspector..."

"Shouldn't I follow him?" Stella asked.

"The longer I stay, the more I'm risking a detective recognizing me. That would complicate an already precarious situation."

Stella nodded absently.

"How do I find you again?" she asked, her gaze focused on the surrounding mass of people.

"We'll rendezvous at the cab stand," Camparol said, sticking his hands in his coat pockets and hunching down into his overcoat. "Don't talk to anyone. Watch and listen."

He took a few steps backwards and melted into the crowd.

The detective had soon taken up a station at the mouth of a narrow alley, its opening blocked by discarded crates and assorted trash and refuse. He huddled up, leaning against the wall, for all intents, just a curious street dweller, more interested in staying warm and steadying himself after a night of liquid indulgence. No one gave him a second glance, including two constables who passed by. He had a good line of sight on the mysterious man without a heartbeat, as well as on Stella and Inspector Ganimard.

From under the brim of his hat, Camparol studied the mystery man. He was of medium height, broad across the shoulders. There was solidness about him and, while he stood quite still, even at a distance, the detective could feel the energy barely contained within him. He may have looked like a menial worker, but Camparol had the impression that he was looking at a hunter.

After several minutes, the man turned away and pushed his way through the crowd. Camparol, quickly, but unobtrusively, made his way along the edge of the crowd, keeping his quarry in sight.

They moved away from the neighborhood. Camparol followed the mystery man down a muddy alley, connecting two streets. The detective quickly crossed the street, lingered to read a tattered playbill plastered to a wall, patted his pockets, as though looking for something, and then sauntered down the alley.

Camparol glanced away for a second, to avoid a questionable looking puddle, and the next thing he knew was that it felt like someone had just struck him in the solar plexus with a sledgehammer.

Gasping to catch his breath, Camparol fell to his knees, reaching out for the wall to keep from collapsing to the muddy ground. He lost his hat, his eyes watered, and he had to bite the corner of his lip to keep focus and consciousness.

Hands grabbed the lapels of his coat and yanked him roughly to his feet. He found himself practically nose to nose with his quarry.

The man's face was broad and swarthy; his eyes like shards of obsidian.

"Why?" the man growled, his voice coarse and heavily accented. "Why do you chase Janos?"

He shook Camparol like a ragdoll. The detective struggled to break free of his assailant's vice-like grip. With each shake, there was another accusing growl. On the third shake, Camparol was able to focus just enough to notice that it was not only the accent that distorted Janos' speech. A pair of razor sharp, over-sized canines protruded from his gum line and added to his speech impediment.

"Leave me alone!" Janos snarled, hurling Camparol away from him.

The detective collided with the brick wall and then collapsed to the trash-strewn ground. As darkness closed in on him, Camparol's policeman's brain kept struggling to piece together snippets of information, and his last thought was the belief that he may have solved this mystery.

And vague concern over the fate of his hat.

Camparol had no idea how long he'd been unconscious. He just felt the world intruding painfully back into his mind, a hand shaking his shoulder and a muffled voice speaking to him.

Still half in a daze, he lurched forward, determined to return the beating he'd taken. Stella caught his wrists and with her leverage, standing over him, pushed him back into a sitting position.

"Monsieur Camparol?" she said with concern. "What happened? Are you hurt?"

"Where is he?" Camparol muttered, rubbing the back of his head. His hair was tacky with drying blood. "How long have I been unconscious?"

"Which of those queries should I answer first?" she asked, helping Camparol to his feet.

He leaned against the soot-coated brick wall, one hand clutching his forehead, the other gesturing vaguely as he spoke.

"He was here, ambushed… smarter than I thought... must have noticed me following… strong as an ox…"

"Who is he?" Stella asked, retrieving her partner's hat and brushing it off.

"Name is Janos… foreign, Polish, maybe… thick accent and… teeth…"

"He had thick teeth? Maybe we should get you home. Get some ice for your head…"

"Only if it's floating in brandy," muttered Camparol, straightening up. "We need to get back to the house... I don't trust the good Doctor to leave a fresh corpse un-touched. If I consult my files, I may have this figured out..."

He took a few steps, and then stopped, leaning against a crate.

"If you were a gentleman," Stella said. "You'd offer me your arm."

Under the disguise of gallantry, the detective leaned on his alien assistant, and they made their way to the nearest cabstand.

"What else did the Inspector say?" Camparol asked, as the duo entered the front foyer.

"This is the third girl to die in such a manner," she replied. "There have been a great many rumors involving Fantomas..."

"There always are," Camparol said. "No, I think we are dealing with something potentially worse."

He limped along, Stella trailing behind.

As they descended back into Spiridon's basement laboratory, both detectives paused upon hearing noises coming from behind the heavy door. Camparol quickened his pace, hurrying through the basement.

Noel's corpse had apparently woken up and the enormous ant was struggling to hold her down on the table. Spiridon looked up at their entrance. In his distraction, the pale, naked girl sat up fully and shoved him away. Camparol and Stella rushed over, nearly colliding in their effort to reach the table, going to opposite sides. They each grabbed one of her arms and struggled to hold the girl down. Noel writhed and thrashed, her eyes wide and crazed; her breath came in strange, ragged bursts, half snarl and half gasp.

Camparol struggled to keep the pale young girl down, holding her arm with both hands and leaning his full body weight against her thrashing form.

Stella also used both hands, but it seemed to take much less effort on her part. The detective felt like he was trying to tame a wild animal, while the tall woman seemed merely annoyed.

"What did you do to her?" Camparol shouted at Spiridon.

The ant shrugged, as he climbed back to his feet, looking, in his own manner, distressed at this bizarre turn of events. He frantically tapped out a narration of how he'd spent the last several hours.

"She just woke up?" Camparol asked, skeptically, after the tapping had ceased. "You have blood?"

Spiridon cocked his over-sized head quizzidly.

"Don't play innocent!" Camparol snapped. "Fetch some blood!"

The ant scampered off, rummaging through the shelves.

"What is going on?" Stella asked, rather calmly, considering the circumstances. "She doesn't have a heartbeat either."

"Really not... hmm... up to conversation... at the moment," Camparol muttered, as he fought to keep the girl down.

He winced. His banged up shoulder twinged painfully every time the girl's arm flailed. She lunged up, snapping at Camparol's arm with suspiciously familiar looking sharp teeth.

Spiridon came rushing back, clutching several test tubes of blood. He held them out to Camparol.

"Grab her arm when I take the blood," Camparol explained, through gritted teeth.

The two traded off, the detective snatching the glass vials, while the ant lunged for the thrashing girl's arm. He was struck several times across the head before pinning her down.

Camparol pried off the stoppers and, as soon as Noel reared up again, he dumped the contents of the three test tubes down her wide-open mouth. She slurped up the blood greedily, licking her lips and sighing in ecstatic contentment.

Her struggles became weaker and she lay back, savoring the sustenance.

The detectives quickly tied her down with thick leather straps attached to the sides of the table. Camparol tapped on the side of the table, instructing Spiridon to fetch any more blood he might have in his laboratory.

"Watch her," he instructed Stella, as he headed back towards the stairs.

He returned ten minutes later with a large tumbler of brandy and a battered looking ledger book. He alternated between sips and flipping through clippings and pages covered with scribbled notes.

"I think I may have…" he began, absently then drifted off as he glanced up at the two unusual women.

Noel, now strapped down, seemed to be sleeping or having lapsed back into her death-like state. Stella stood over her, staring down at her slack, blood-streaked face with a deep, thoughtful hostility.

He tucked the ledger under his arm and went to stand next to her.

"What are you thinking?" he asked, quietly, taking a sip of his drink.

"My people are the pinnacle of human development," she murmured, her gaze not leaving the pale girl's face. "We are immortal and pure of thought and feeling."

"You might have mentioned that," Camparol shrugged.

"We have reached the apex of what humans can be, physically as well as mentally. We have purged ourselves of our baser drives. Our emotions are in balance. Our energies are focused on learning and acting for the good of our society."

She brought her hand up and reached towards the other woman's face, stopping just short of touching her white skin.

"Yet, I look at this… this creature, this abomination, this mockery of all my people have accomplished and worked to become, and I want to… lash out. I want to see it destroyed."

143

"I would imagine it is quite easy to be pure and serene when you live in a walled off city full of 'enlightened' prophets," Camparol said. "Coming to Earth, those conditions do not exist. Your noble ideals will be tested and challenged."

"If you attempt to console me by saying 'You are only human,' I will be most disappointed," Stella said.

"What I'm saying is, we all have these dark feelings. It's how we act on them that matters; that is how we are judged," the detective replied. "This girl may be a monster, but she's also a victim. Doctors don't kill their sick patients, they search for a cure."

Spiridon came bustling into the room, his spindly arms loaded with a half dozen assorted containers of blood.

"Well, most doctors," Camparol muttered.

A corner of the young Lunar Immortal's mouth went up in the briefest of smiles.

"So, we invite this monster into our home?" she asked.

"It seems to be my lot in life," Camparol shrugged, looking at the other occupants of the cellar room.

He put his ledger down on a table and gestured for the ant to hand him a container. He handed his glass to Stella, who sniffed its contents, shrugged and took a sip. She made a face and reached over to dump the rest in a nearby sink.

Camparol was engaged in a tapping exchange with Spiridon, giving the ant instructions for watching over their new charge.

"...And no cutting her up!" he snapped, after several minutes of tapping. "If she wakes up, feed her, but anything else, come and get me."

Man and ant locked gazes for several minutes, the only movement being a slight twitch in Spiridon's tiny antenna. Finally, the ant nodded sullenly.

"So, are we finished?" Stella asked.

"Hardly," Camparol muttered, looking around for his glass. He frowned upon discovering it was empty. "We have no idea who or where this Janos is. We know more than Ganimard, but he may still be able to trail Noel back to us. Then we can worry about if our new charge will attempt to eat the housekeeper or not... You may be immortal, but I need some food and sleep before I can deal with anything else..."

It was at that point that the door to Spiridon's laboratory was kicked in and three men, two armed with crossbows, burst in.

"Oh, for god's sake!" the detective sighed.

"Monsieur Etienne Camparol, I presume?" the elderly, unarmed, member of the trio asked, in an accented voice. "We are looking for a young lady that I believe you are sheltering."

"And you gentlemen would be?" Stella asked, stepping forward.

"This is Professor Van Helsing," Camparol said, moving forward to stand next to his assistant. "But I'm not familiar with your... uh... chaperones?"

"You know him?" Stella asked.

"An elderly Dutchman always searching for vampires?" Camparol replied. "Narrows the suspect list a bit. I don't suppose we can have this conversation without weapons being pointed at us?" he asked the newcomers.

"Surrender the creature and then we can talk to your heart's content," one of the men growled, tightening his grip on his trigger.

"You are quite rude," Stella chided, stepping forward, until she stood directly in front of the crossbow.

"Step aside," the intruder said, reaching forward to move her.

The tall woman from the Moon took hold of his wrist, to keep him from grabbing her. He moved his arm to push her aside and found that, not only could he not break her grip, but also he could no more move her arm than if she was a statue. His expression of anger quickly shifted to confusion.

"Stella," Camparol said. "Let him go."

The man glanced over at Professor Van Helsing, who gave a brief nod.

When Stella released her grip, the man stepped back and lowered his weapon. He glowered at the tall woman.

"You will have to forgive young master Giles," the older man said. "He has only recently joined Dr. Seward and myself and has a great deal of youthful enthusiasm, but he is not wrong in his intent. You are harboring a dark creature that must be dealt with."

"I think, before anything is 'dealt with,' we should talk," Camparol said, pulling up one of the stools and perching on it. He gestured to a second stool.

"What?" Giles exclaimed, raising his weapon.

Van Helsing held up a hand to halt the young vampire hunter's protest and shuffled over to perch on the offered seat. He gave the strapped down young woman a long, studious glance, before returning his attention to Camparol.

"I share my associate's skepticism, but must admit to some... curiosity," he said. "State your case and then, perhaps, we can resolve this without further conflict."

"I don't know if I have a case, *per se*," Camparol shrugged, reaching for his ledger, "but I do have questions. I believe I've pieced together the events leading up to this little gathering, but it would help if you could tell me more. You and your men weren't originally after the girl, you were tracking the vampire, this man Janos..."

"Janos Skorzeny," Van Helsing said. "Yes, we have been tracking him across Europe for the past three months. After the... incident involving this young woman, we lost his trail near the Halles. We believe he snuck aboard a boat to Le Havre, and from there, plan to travel to America..."

"I almost feel sorry for him," Camparol muttered. He flipped through several pages, before stopping and turning the book towards the older man. "I assume you are familiar with the 'Bloofer Lady' incident?"

"How do you know about that?" Doctor Seward asked.

Van Helsing merely raised a questioning eyebrow.

"Am I the only one who doesn't know what you are talking about?" Stella asked, slim arms crossed and a peeved expression.

"Years ago, in England, there was a number of child abductions," Camparol explained, his eyes moving from the page to the face of Van Helsing. "The children were found, for the most part, unharmed. The culprit was never arrested. Rumors accused everyone from a woman, deranged with grief, to gypsies, to such supernatural beings as ghosts or vampires."

Camparol placed significant emphasis on the last word and then paused, focusing his gaze on the Dutch vampire hunter.

"Our young... guest is English, and just about the right age to be one of those children. She then came to Paris, with or to escape her family, following a lover or a dream, who knows..."

The detective shrugged, sparing a glance at his audience. Both of Van Helsing's assistants had lowered their weapons and were listening intently.

"But, despite her common appearance, there are things bubbling below the surface in her. Bitten, but not turned."

"We were concerned that the children might have latent... tendencies of some kind," Van Helsing said, stroking his chin thoughtfully. "But, none have showed any signs..."

"And most likely, they won't," Camparol continued. "I doubt our young lady would have, except she had the amazingly bad luck to be the victim of a second vampire attack, and then things began to happen... possibly nudged along by my colleague's efforts."

"She is a monster," Giles muttered, grimly.

"She is a victim!" Camparol snapped back. "You want to solve a murder case by arresting and executing the corpse! This girl is a unique mix of circumstances... We don't know what she will become and I don't consider murder to come under the heading of 'better safe than sorry.'"

"We will take responsibility for her," Stella said, surprising the others, including her partner. "One way or another, we can handle things."

She glanced over at Camparol and the detective nodded in reply.

He returned his attention to the elderly professor.

"So, we attend to the young lady, and you can continue tracking down Janos. Though, America is a big place... But eventually, someone there will be able to deal with him."

"Perhaps," Van Helsing said, nodding, either in reply or to himself was unclear. "I have... shall we say, concerns over this arrangement, Monsieur Camparol. So, do not take it amiss, but my associates and I will be keeping an eye on your most unusual household."

"Next time, be so kind as to ring the bell," Stella suggested.

"We shall," Van Helsing chuckled.

"Good," Camparol added. "On top of everything else, I'd like to avoid further upsetting my housekeeper..."

"If you mean the elderly woman with the suitcases that stormed past us, when we arrived," Dr. Seward said, in a sardonic tone. "I don't think that will be a concern."

"Of course," Camparol sighed, resting his elbow on the examining table, his head in his hand. He glanced over, remembered his glass was empty and sighed again.

"I will show the gentlemen out," Stella said, gesturing them towards the cellar stairs. "Your long night seems to be catching up with you."

"Yes, yes," the detective muttered. "And on the Moon, you never got tired or worried about who's going to do the dishes..."

He stood up, a wan smile on his face, and offered Professor Van Helsing his hand.

"Circumstances aside, it was good to meet you," he said.

"I, too. Perhaps, next time we can talk in more social setting and under better circumstances, hmm?"

He spared a glance at the form of the pale young woman and nodded to himself.

"Yes, perhaps we shall," he nodded absently, before turning to his two assistants. "Come along, gentlemen."

Stella gave Camparol a last glance before following the trio downstairs.

Camparol perched once again on the stool. He noticed Spiridon cleaning up, avoiding eye contact in the hopes of dodging yet another lecture.

He nodded to himself and closed his notebook.

"Did... did you mean all that?" a timid voice asked. "About helping me...?"

Noel sat up, as far as the straps would allow, the sheet sliding down awkwardly low. Camparol leaned forward and held it in place with one hand, while undoing the strap around her chest with the other.

"You heard all that, didn't you?" he asked, helping her to sit up.

"Yes, I did. They were right, those men... I'm a monster."

"Perhaps, but you may have noticed, you aren't the only one living under this roof."

They both glanced over at the bustling giant ant, which studiously ignored them as he rearranged his shelves.

"I seem to be collecting them," the detective added.

"You'd let me live here?" Noel asked, anxiously.

"Seems the best solution. You can't go back to your old home. Your old life, that is over... But you are welcome to stay and find out what happens next."

"I suppose I... If that old man was right... If I am... a monster... you'd... you would... stop me..."

"Let's wait until another day to have that conversation, shall we?" Camparol said, patting her shoulder in what he hoped was a comforting manner.

He then drew his hand back when he became aware that the shoulder in question was bare.

"Ah, yes…" he continued. "Maybe, we should concern ourselves with getting you a wardrobe and finding you a bedroom, then we can work up to matters of life and death. I think there's one, up on the third floor… have to do some dusting…."

"You are a detective?" Noel asked. "I… um… don't know how to do that. I won't be any help…?"

"Well, I am looking for a housekeeper," he told her, undoing the strap around her waist. "If you are going to stay in Paris, you'll need to keep a discreet profile. Perhaps, a different hair style, and a new name…?"

"A new name…?" Noel asked, thoughtfully.

"I was thinking perhaps… Dara Luc," Camparol suggested.

"Really?" Stella said, returning from upstairs. 'Why not just call her 'Ruth Venn' and be done with it? Human subtlety seems to be an oxymoron."

"Bit like Lunar modesty," the detective retorted with a faint smile.

"I think Dara sounds pretty," the young vampire said.

Camparol gave his alien partner a smug nod.

"Well, that's that then," he said. "Dara, welcome."

He then turned and wrapped a knuckle against the heavy wooden table.

"Do you hear that?" he said to Spiridon's back. "Dara is a member of the household. There will be no medical experiments preformed on her without permission. Understood?"

The ant nodded his enormous head, his antenna twitching irritably.

"We'll need to obtain a supply of blood," Stella said, tapping her chin in thought.

"And see that her that her 'death' is made official," Camparol added.

"Could I have some clothes first?" Dara asked, clutching the sheet around her.

148

*When describing Erik's stay in Mazenderan, Gustave Leroux wrote: "No one knows better than he how to throw the Punjab wire, for he is the King of Stranglers, just as he is the King of Magicians. When he had finished making the little Sultana laugh, at the time of the rosy hours of Mazenderan, she herself used to ask him to amuse her by giving her a thrill. It was then that he introduced the sport of the Punjab wire. [...] With a turn of the wrist, Erik tightened the noose around his adversary's neck and, in this fashion, dragged him before the little Sultana and her women, who sat looking from a window and applauding. The little Sultana herself learned to wield the Punjab wire and killed several of her women and even friends who visited her." Rick Lai built upon this passage to craft this untold adventure of Erik...*

## Rick Lai: *The Tomb of the Veiled Prophet*

*Persia, 1866*

"Shirin's body must be removed discreetly," insisted Anis-ed-Dowleh, the Shah's favorite wife.

Bending down to examine the young woman's corpse, Haji Abdu deduced that the neck had been broken.

"The mark of the Punjabi lasso. This is Erik's handiwork. What did she do to offend him?"

"She refused to let him kiss her."

"What woman would? Erik's skeletal visage is an obstacle to even an innocent flirtation."

"Are not you and Erik friends?"

"We are the best of enemies. Two years ago, you heard rumors of Erik entertaining Russian caravans. Your husband ordered me to find this magician and bring him here. Discovering a mutual enthusiasm for chess, we frequently played against each other during the journey back from Russia. Throughout our matches, we debated morality. Erik revealed himself to be a conscienceless killer. I advised the Shah against allowing him to become part of your entourage, but you convinced your husband to disregard my counsel. Shirin's death is a flower of evil grown from the monstrous seed that you planted."

"I had forgotten that you style yourself a philosopher."

"Being a Sufi, I seek to purify my soul by contemplating the glory of Allah. I also hope to purify the souls of others."

"An unusual aspiration for a Daroga of the secret police."

"When I joined the police, I believed that criminals could undergo redemption if they were treated fairly. Experience has taught me that most malefactors are remorseless predators. Like rogue tigers, they must be hunted down and exterminated. Erik is such a tiger."

"Erik was first a seed, and now a tiger. How do you really view him?"

"He is a consummate egotist with no regard for human life. The world would be a better place without him."

"A sound assessment!" interrupted a new voice.

A wall panel slid open to reveal a secret passage. The Shah of Persia, Nasir-ed-Din, emerged from the hidden chamber.

"Sire!" exclaimed Haji Abdu.

"Forgive me, my loyal subject. I needed to be sure that you harbor no qualms about extinguishing Erik's life. You are probably under the impression that he has functioned merely as a court illusionist."

"No, Sire. I am well aware that Erik has performed secret missions for you."

"You are better acquainted with Erik's activities than I imagined," replied the Shah, his eyes narrowing.

"Erik and I continue to play chess regularly. He was indiscreet during our last game."

"What did he tell you about *me*?" demanded the Shah.

"While performing tricks with his Punjabi lasso for your wife, Erik divulged its possible lethal nature. He also demonstrated a detailed knowledge of Afghanistan. Your wife immediately grasped Erik's true worth and summoned you."

"Elaborate on Erik's strategic value."

"Although you negotiated peace with the Emir of Afghanistan nearly a decade ago, his chieftains continue to launch raids on our borders. You dispatched Erik into Afghanistan to demonstrate his expertise with the Punjabi lasso."

"Subtle allusions weary me, Daroga. Speak bluntly."

"Erik was sent into Afghanistan to assassinate the chieftains harassing our borders."

"My assassin told you of these missions?"

"Yes, Sire."

"Erik was ordered not to speak of these matters to anyone else."

"I deduced that fact, Sire. Therefore, I wrote an account of Erik's indiscretions and submitted it for your perusal."

"Ah, I remember now. You recommended Erik's immediate execution. I chose to ignore your suggestion because Erik had claimed two intriguing rewards for his Afghan incursions."

"Erik never mentioned such rewards to me, Sire."

"Erik has architectural ambitions. He asked my permission to install a series of secret passages inside this building. I granted his request. The chamber from which I spied upon you is merely one of several covertly constructed during the recent renovations. Unfortunately, Erik has used his knowledge of these passageways to harass my wife's handmaidens. Shirin is not the first of Erik's victims. There were two others earlier. Erik is now feared as the Trap Door Lover."

"You indicated two rewards, Sire."

"Erik believes that the Moon Maker has a tomb in Khorassan. He wishes to lead an expedition to excavate it."

"A foolish notion, Sire. History plainly states that that heretic's remains were never retrieved for burial."

"I share your skepticism, Daroga. Nevertheless, you will accompany Erik to Khorassan. Once you have determined whether this tomb has any basis in fact, you shall execute Erik as punishment for the three murdered maidens. I considered being merciful in light of his prior services and merely plucking out his eyes. However, even a sightless Erik would still remain a formidable threat. His other finely tuned senses allow him to move stealthily in total darkness. As proof of his death, you shall deliver his head to me. His skull structure is quite unique. The Royal Physician is anxious to examine it closely."

"As you command, Sire."

Following Haji Abdu's departure, the Shah smiled.

"Self-styled philosophers are so gullible, my sweet. He doesn't suspect the real identity of the killer of the three girls. What prompted you to learn from Erik the usage of the Punjabi lasso?"

"Erik mentioned that he had been trained to kill with the Thuggee rope by the deposed Maharani of Pankot. Since a woman had been Erik's tutor, I suggested that he become my instructor. Of course, I needed test subjects to determine whether I truly mastered the lasso. Shirin and the others were chosen because their constant chatter had ceased to amuse me."

The Shah's court was located in the northern province of Mazenderan bordering the Caspian Sea. Khorassan was the northeast Persian province adjacent to Afghanistan. During the journey eastward, Haji Abdu and Erik always played chess.

Eventually, the archeological expedition pitched its tents for the night. In their conversations, during a game, Erik referred to the Daroga by his nickname, El Hichmakani, "the Man from Nowhere." Being a Frenchman, Erik had never mastered the Islamic calendar. In their conversations, the Daroga accommodated his companion by citing years based on the Gregorian calendar.

"How did you become familiar with Mokanna?" asked the Daroga.

"Through the works of an Irish poet whose name is probably unknown to you," answered Erik.

"You must be referring to Thomas Moore. *The Veiled Prophet of Khorassan* is one of four narrative poems comprising his most popular work, *Lalla Rookh*. I found the text somewhat amusing."

"How did you manage to procure a copy?"

"My English correspondent, Richard Francis Burton, sent it to me."

"Burton! The adventurer who visited Mecca by posing as a Muslim!"

"To be precise, Burton pretended to be a Persian Shiite. About thirteen years ago, I was performing my own pilgrimage to the holy city during Burton's impersonation. Penetrating his disguise, I befriended him. We have corresponded regularly for several years."

"The Shah would have you executed if he knew of your communications with Burton."

"You underestimate my monarch. He authorized me to initiate the Burton correspondence. It is in Persia's interest for a member of the secret police to feed information to an influential Englishman."

"Does Burton know you are the Daroga of Mazenderan?"

"He is totally ignorant of my ties to the secret police. Burton simply views me as a humble Sufi philosopher residing in Yezd province. All of his packages and letters are mailed to my ancestral home in Darabghird."

The Daroga took one of Erik's pawns with a bishop. Erik's response was to place his opponent's King in check.

"As you have noticed, El Hichmakani, I am adept at sacrificing pawns like Mokanna."

"Mokanna was a monster!"

"I humbly disagree. Let us review the facts. Around 780 A. D., a rebellion against the Abbasid Caliphate was inaugurated in Khorassan. The leader was an enigmatic personage called Mokanna, 'The Veiled One.' Hiding his face beneath a veil, Mokanna claimed to be the living incarnation of Allah. He recruited followers by performing feats of magic, including the creation of miniature moons. Consequently, Mokanna was dubbed the Moon Maker. While he generally wore a silver veil, Mokanna also occasionally hid his features behind a golden mask. He also owned a golden sword and golden tablets inscribed with his teachings. After some initial military successes, Mokanna and his adherents found themselves surrounded in a castle by the Caliph's soldiers. Mokanna ordered his disciples to commit mass suicide by swallowing poison. He then threw himself into a cistern filled with *aqua fortis*, better known as nitric acid. His flesh totally disintegrated. Mokanna's death was witnessed by a member of his harem who refused to drink the poison."

"Why are we searching for his tomb? There was no cadaver left to bury. There weren't even ashes to collect."

"The Shah granted me access to the Royal Archives. I discovered a most intriguing document. After Mokanna's death, his cult survived under the leadership of a man known only as Abd Dhulma. The Caliph's police tried to apprehend this associate of the Veiled Prophet. Their efforts failed, but the police confiscated a prophecy written by their quarry. The manuscript professed that he had been entrusted with Mokanna's mask, sword and tablets. Visiting the site of the Moon Maker's suicide, Abd Dhulma supposedly performed a mystical ritual to extract the 'essential salts' from the nitric acid. In effect, the ashes of Mokanna were somehow reconstituted. Abd Dhulma then buried the ashes alongside the golden relics in Khorassan. He predicted that Mokanna would inevitably be resurrected "

"If this document identified the tomb's location, surely the Caliphate would have looted it?"

"Abd Dhulma didn't reveal the site of Mokanna's memorial." Unfolding a parchment, Erik handed it to the Daroga before resuming the narrative. "During my earlier travels in Afghanistan, prior to becoming the Shah's assassin, I visited the mountain citadel of Yolgan. There I found this map. It designates a place in Khorassan called the Mausoleum of Moonlight. Perhaps this is a euphemism for the tomb of the Veiled Prophet erected by Abd Dhulma?"

"There are other pieces of writing on this map, *The Lord of the Empty Abode... The Lord of Illusion... The Lord of the Fourth Axis...* What is the significance of those words?"

"I have no idea," replied Erik truthfully. "The story of Mokanna has fascinated me since I read Moore. Mokanna professed that his veil hid a face of divine beauty. In actuality, his countenance was extremely ugly. Some historians claim that his visage had been scarred in combat during an earlier career as a soldier. Others assert that his horrific appearance was a birth defect... like my own."

"You identify with Mokanna. His early life may parallel yours."

"Yes, El Hichmakani. Despite having normal parents, I was born with a face that made me an outcast among respectable society. I was forced to live in the shadows. Since fleeing my native France, I have dwelt among Tonkin pirates, Indian Thugs and Afghan devil worshippers." Erik laughed. "Now I consort with the Shah of Persia and his secret police."

Upon reaching its destination, the expedition took four days of digging to locate the tomb. After forcing open the stone door barring the entrance, only Erik and Haji Abdu walked into the underground structure. Their attendants were ordered to remain outside as the torch-bearing pair penetrated the darkness inside.

The duo discovered an urn surrounded by a mask, sword and a stack of fifteen inscribed tablets. All were made of gold. Removing the lid of the golden urn, the Daroga saw that it was filled with ashes.

Lowering his torch over the tablet residing on top, Erik read the inscription:

"*To the Anointed One, invoke the Three Avatars of the All-In-One over my dust, and the reason for your earthly existence shall be divulged.*"

"Meaningless gibberish!" declared the Daroga.

"Perhaps not," said Erik, his yellow eyes opening wide. "Remember the writing on the map?" Erik looked down on the urn. *"The Lord of the Empty Abodes, the Lord of Illusion, the Lord of the Fourth Axis..."*

Instantly, the torches of the two were snuffed out. The chamber was plunged into darkness for a few seconds. A bright sphere appeared over the heads of Erik and his companion. Moonlight dimly illuminated the interior of the tomb. Both men found their muscles paralyzed. They were unable to move.

The dust inside the urn issued forth like a geyser. The ashes swirled and coalesced into a humanoid shape upon which flesh and muscle swiftly grew.

A naked man now stood before the two invaders of the tomb. His face was identical to Erik's, except his eye sockets were filled with black fire. The fiery orbs shifted their gaze toward Erik as a hoarse, rasping voice issued from shriveled lips.

"I salute thee, Anointed One. You have resurrected me by summoning the Three Avatars of Yog-Sothoth. Long have you suffered. The foul race called man has ridiculed and shunned you. You shall soon learn that your appearance is not a curse but a blessing. The promise of the golden tablet shall be fulfilled. You shall learn the rationale for your existence.

"Our histories are tightly linked. To explain your origins, I must expound upon my own. My father is the immortal wizard dreaded as Abd Dhulma, Through his study of ancient texts, he learned of the formidable sorcerers who had once dominated the lost continents of Lemuria and Attluma. The names of these necromancers have become obscure legends: Thulsa Doom, Kathulos, Rotah, Mardanax, Descales... But they altered the fate of nations! Each of those mages had performed an esoteric ritual, the Black Litany, to infuse their souls with the Torch Fire of Nug. The powers bestowed by the flames of Nug came at a price. The flesh of each enchanter's face was withered into a living skull.

"My father sought mastery over the Torch Fire. Vainly believing himself a handsome man, he was unwilling to bear the Skull Mark of Nug. While I languished as an unborn fetus inside my mother's womb, my father performed a ceremony to transplant the Torch Fire inside my embryonic form. Infused with the power of the Old Ones, I became a cannibal. Gnawing my way through my mother's stomach, I entered this world as a fully formed infant.

"Due to my awesome visage, my father was forced to raise me in seclusion. He tutored me in the occult sciences. Reaching adulthood, I became Mokanna in order to carve out an earthly kingdom. Unfortunately, I overestimated the extent of my powers. My army endured a humiliating defeat. The suicide of my followers and my own self-immolation was part of an elaborate ritual to gain much greater powers from the Old Ones.

"In order to appease the Lord of the Fourth Axis, I was forced to hibernate for centuries in my essential salts. During my reign in Khorassan, I planted my seed in many women. My father scattered my paramours to the four corners of the world. Once the stars were in proper alignment, my descendants would con-

154

ceive children bearing my face. One of them would be destined to trace his connection to me and find my crypt. You are that Anointed One. What is your name, my descendant?"

"I am called Erik. It is not my birth name, but a nickname derived from my sojourn among the cult of the Ruler of All That Was."

"Erlik of the Dark Star? His declarations of omnipotence are ludicrous. He is but a minor entity eclipsed by the cosmic splendor of the Lord of the Fourth Axis and his Twin Spawn, Nug and Yeb. Your yellow eyes must have led the adherents of Erlik to proclaim you a son of their dark god. None of my forebears had such eyes. Your pedigree must include other intriguing ancestors besides myself."

The burning eyes of the revived necromancer probed into Erik's own.

"I sense resentment in your soul, my kinsman. You blame me for all the misfortunes that plagued your life. You shall be amply compensated for every calamity in your unhappy existence. Mankind ostracized you by falsely declaring you less than human. You are actually more than human. This fact will become readily apparent when you are infused with the Torch Fire. You shall repay every slight and insult that mankind has heaped upon you. With a wave of a finger, you shall pluck out the eyes of any man who refuses to gaze on your face. Any woman you desire shall succumb to your lust. The vermin known as humanity shall be trampled beneath your feet. Do you wish such power?'

"Yes! With all my soul! *Yes!*"

Haji Abdu wanted to protest, but his tongue was stifled by Mokanna's magic.

The Moon Maker gestured with his right hand. The golden sword levitated off the ground. Its hilt faced Erik.

"Grip the sword!" commanded Mokanna.

Dropping his useless torch, Erik seized the hilt with both hands. The blade became surrounded by emerald flames.

Mokanna raised his head to gaze into the miniature moon suspended above.

"O Moon of Yian, Nug demands a Red Offering in exchange for bestowing his Torch Fire upon my kinsman. A foolish mortal accompanied my descendant into this fane. The Anointed One shall now skin this pathetic creature alive. Gorgo, Mormo, thousand-faced moon, look favorably on our sacrifices!"

As Erik raised the sword above his head, the eyes of the speechless Daroga reflected horror and despair.

Mokanna grinned with approval before reciting the Black Litany:

"O Masters of the Black Fires..."

Striking downward, the blazing sword bit sharply into Mokanna's head. As Mokanna's skull was split asunder, his flesh disintegrated into dust. Erik dropped the sword. Before the blade reached the ground, its mystical flame was extinguished. The Moon of Yian burst asunder. The explosion sent the Daroga hurtling into the ground. His head pounded into the earth. The tomb became shrouded in darkness as the Persian's consciousness was transported into the gulf of dreams.

Hours later, Haji Abdu awoke in a cot inside his tent. His first sight was Erik smiling benevolently.

"You suffer only minor injuries. After carrying you to safety, I ordered the tomb sealed with its cursed golden relics still inside. We shall inform the Shah that we found only an empty tomb gutted by grave robbers. Now rest, El Hichmakani. You must recover your strength for the long journey back to Mazenderan. Good night."

"Wait! You must tell me! Why did you refuse Mokanna's offer?"

"During my entire stay in Persia, only you have treated me as an equal. You are the only person here whom I would consider a true friend. I turned against Mokanna because the sacrifice he demanded was too high."

Following Haji Abdu's full recovery, the expedition left Khorassan. When the borders of Mazenderan were reached, the Daroga informed Erik that he had to briefly leave camp to take care of some personal business. Upon his return, the Daroga conferred with the Shah's assassin.

"Forgive me, Erik, there is delicate matter that we must discuss. It concerns your murder of Anis-ed-Dowleh's three handmaidens."

"What are you talking about? I slew none of them."

"Besides yourself, is anyone else in Mazenderan proficient in the Punjabi lasso?"

"Anis-ed-Dowleh. I trained her in its usage."

"That conniving temptress has made you a scapegoat for her own crimes. Before we left for Khorassan, the Shah ordered me to decapitate you for slaying the handmaidens."

"You must convince the Shah of my innocence!"

"Your innocence is irrelevant. The Shah must already know the truth. I am not as naive as he and his abominable wife believe. I ordered one of my men to undertake a discreet investigation. I left camp to receive his report. All of your subordinates in the construction of the secret passageways have disappeared. They must have been murdered on the Shah's orders. He desires to be the only man alive with knowledge of those passageways. That is his true motive for desiring your death."

"What you intend to do?"

"An escape route to Turkey has been arranged for you. I shall simply report to the Shah that you learned of the impending sentence of death and fled the camp."

"The Shah will behead you for incompetence."

"I hope to forestall that outcome. Before you depart, you shall surrender one of the European suits you brought to Persia. The secret police execute criminals every day. The decaying body of such a felon shall be dressed in your clothes and found along the Caspian Sea. If the Shah believes you dead from drowning, he may be merely content to exile me."

Erik gave the Daroga the suit.

"This will probably be our final meeting, Erik. Remember these words, old friend. In Allah's eyes, no one is above redemption. Not even men of the shadows like you and I."

Mounting his horse, Erik rode into the night.

The Daroga's ploy worked. He only suffered exile. With the help of Richard Francis Burton, Haji Abdu established residences in London and Paris. Rumors of his native Persia occasionally reached him. Anis-ed-Dowleh had become a maniacal killer. There had been further strangulations in the Persian court, but the Shah made sure innocent men were punished for her butchery.

In 1876, his tenth year in exile, Haji Abdu received in the mail a free ticket that entitled him to a private box at the grand opening of the Paris Opera House. It was accompanied by a note:

*I miss our chess games. Let us watch the opera together.*

*Erik*

*Black Coat Press recently published Frank Schildiner's mosaic novel,* The Quest of Frankenstein *(ISBN 978-1-61227-429-4), which continues the adventures of "Gouroull," the Monster of Frankenstein, as reimagined by Jean-Claude Carrière. Nigel Malcolm also wondered what could happen if it ever got back to Monsieur Lecoq that Sherlock Holmes had referred to him, in* A Study in Scarlet, *as a "miserable bungler with nothing to commend him but his energy." These are the starting points of the following tale that brings Lecoa back to Orcival, where he once solved a murder mystery. The story, per force, ignores the non-canonical events of the non-Gaboriau novel* Monsieur Lecoq's Daughter, *in which the detective apparently was murdered in 1886, and would take place between Carrière's first two Frankenstein books...*

## Nigel Malcolm: *The Adventure of the Orcival Rain*

*Orcival, 1889*

Shortly after the winter of '89, anyone reading the French newspapers would learn of a phenomenon in and around the town of Orcival where the locals might have chanced upon scattered wallets, coins, or mufflers. One lucky milkman even came across a fine gold pocket watch in a hedge by his cottage.

This sort of incident may not be considered too unusual in a quaint little town that boasts an annual festival. However, while the occasional dropped coin or glove may normally be considered commonplace, such an intense presence of bowler hats, or handkerchiefs draped off tree branches would suggest to the casual observer evidence of people so forgetful, they should not be allowed out unaccompanied.

By chance, Sherlock Holmes and I happened to be in Paris. Holmes had been employed by the French government in a delicate diplomatic matter, and we now found ourselves with a spare day in Paris before our return to London, where we were required to give evidence in not one but two trials at the Old Bailey.

However, while we were still in the breakfast room of our hotel, enjoying the coffee, a bell boy handed Holmes a telegram.

"It looks as though our holiday plans are scuppered, Watson," he said, before noticing the look of disappointment on my face. I had, after all, been looking forward to visiting the famous *bouquiniste* stalls by the Seine. "Although if it is any consolation, a M. Jean Saint-Clair's holiday plans seem to have been scuppered also."

The name rang a bell from our recent engagement with the French government.

"That's one of the young fellows at the Ministry of Foreign Affairs to whom we were introduced last week, right?"

"Exactly so. We are required to join him at his cottage in a town called Orcival in the Puy-de-Dôme."

So we found ourselves, within the hour, catching a train from the Gare de Lyon that took us to that quaint and charming little town. From the station we found a cab driven by a conceited Frenchman who, despite Holmes' impeccable French, still insisted that we told him where we wanted to go in English.

We eventually found ourselves at a large cottage with generous grounds that was Saint-Clair's inherited holiday home.

A brown bowler hat was lying on the front lawn. We both spotted it as we left the cab and its sarcastic driver. It seemed to foretell the strange events that were already happening around us.

We were shown into the drawing room, where we finally got to meet Jean Saint-Clair. At the time, he was in his early twenties, and so still virtually a youth, yet to develop into the assured man with a huge diplomatic career he was to go on to later.

"Gentlemen, thank you for coming," he said, a worried look in his eyes. "I don't quite know how to explain this."

"Remain calm and tell us what has happened," Holmes replied.

"There is a dead body in my back garden!" Saint-Clair blurted. "My man-servant found it lying half in the rose bed and raised the alarm. I did not know what to do, so I contacted the Ministry and they suggested I send for you as you were still in Paris and you performed such sterling work for us. I'm sure I don't need to tell you, a corpse found in the garden of a member of the Ministry's staff is a very grave matter."

"Quite so. Do you recognize this unfortunate fellow?"

"I've never seen him before in my life."

"Where is the corpse now?"

"It's been left where it was found. I have given strict instructions to leave it untouched until an investigator arrived."

"Capital—Come, Watson!"

The corpse indeed was dumped—for want of a better word—with most of his upper body in a bed of neatly kept roses, with his arms outstretched; his tweed jacket was open and spread out so that the lining, if there were a lining, was touching the soil. His legs were also spread wide. He was hatless, although the hat we saw in the front garden when we arrived would have complemented his apparel.

Holmes approached the corpse. He got down onto his hands and knees, and eventually onto his stomach, studying the neatly trimmed lawn closely with his lens. He half crawled and half slivered up to the corpse, where he rose from the ground and stood astride it, scouring it for clues.

"Is he always like this?" asked a baffled Saint-Clair.

"Yes, I'm afraid he is," I replied.

"He must have a very high cleaning bill."

I considered answering that comment, but decided that discretion was the better part of valor.

Holmes straightened up and beckoned us over. We joined him and helped him to turn over the body onto its back.

"Fascinating," murmured the great detective. "Utterly fascinating. Watson, what does your medical expertise tell us of this man?"

I examined the body. I noticed, as I looked him over, that had had quite a wild appearance for a yeoman. His neck was severely bruised.

"He's been strangled," I said.

"Yes, but was he dead *before* he hit the ground?"

I thought that this was an odd choice of words to come from him.

"Well, it's impossible to say from a preliminary examination. We would have to perform a full autopsy. But I would have thought it was a foregone conclusion that he was dead before he was placed here."

"Quite so, but you should know well enough by now that there are no foregone conclusions in our profession."

"But surely someone strangled this unfortunate fellow and then disposed of his body here in the garden."

"How do you think the murderer brought the body here?" Holmes asked.

"Presumably he climbed over a wall or a fence and dropped the body here before leaving again."

"There are no traces of the murderer's footprints on the lawn. There are some impressions of the manservant's boots over here, when he came up and inspected the body, before raising the alarm, but not the murderer's footprints. The impression into the lawn would have been much deeper if he were carrying something as heavy as a corpse. But the impression the corpse has made on the lawn and rose bed is what intrigues me the most. You used the word 'dropped' to describe it earlier, and you are not far from the truth. By the looks of the impression on the soil and grass, not to mention the scuffed lawn just here, he was slammed down so hard that he slid by an inch or so."

"The fellow who disposed the body here would have to be, well, almost supernaturally strong," said Saint-Clair, with a certain dread.

"M. Saint-Clair, how long have you lived in this cottage?"

"More than twenty years, on and off. It belonged to my father and he passed it on to me."

"Do you or your family have a dispute with any of your neighbors?"

"No, I think I get on well with all of them."

Holmes glanced around the garden, and spotted something on the roof of the house. I followed his gaze. There was a muffler dangling off the edge of the roof.

"How on earth did that get up there?" exclaimed Saint-Clair. "This is becoming ever more bizarre. There's no way that could have got up there. You'd need a ladder. It makes no sense whatsoever!"

"On the contrary, gentlemen, this incident is making increasing sense," replied Holmes. He turned to the young man. "M. Saint-Clair, has the weather been this still since earlier this morning?"

Saint-Clair erupted.

"There's a dead body in my garden, a scarf on my roof, someone is clearly trying to frame me, and you want to discuss the weather?"

"Yes, I would. Was there any sort of wind blowing here sometime in the last few hours? Anything more than a light breeze?"

Saint-Clair stood there looking exasperated for a moment, before answering:

"No. The weather has been very still and clear all day. There was a frost last night, I think, so it was probably still and clear all night. Yes, I remember that the stars were out."

"Well, *that* is the most baffling factor in the whole affair," said Holmes.

He looked at us and saw the confusion on our faces.

"M. Saint-Clair," he continued, "I still have insufficient data to confirm or denounce that the body was placed in your garden either to frame you, or warn you, or to damage your reputation. However, by the balance of probabilities, I think that this unfortunate man ended up on your property by accident. He certainly wasn't involved in any espionage or criminal activity; he is an innocent. He was a gamekeeper from a nearby village. He was strangled to death by someone as yet unknown to us, before being disposed of out of the basket of a hot air balloon."

We were both amazed.

"A hot air balloon?" exclaimed Saint-Clair.

"That is the part of my hypothesis that is weakest. Although this is ideal weather for ballooning, someone in the town should have seen it. Even at night. You can arrange to have the body removed now. We've gleaned as many facts from it as we can, aside from an autopsy, which I doubt will tell us much more. Where is your manservant?"

"Blanc is inside."

We found Blanc in the hallway by the front door. He was talking to an anonymous-looking man whom I would place in his sixties. He was dressed as a professional, but there was some dirt on his trousers and boots.

"Who is this gentleman?" Saint-Clair asked.

"This is M. Reno—an Insurance clerk, sir."

Reno bowed to us. Saint-Clair seemed to become tetchy.

"M. Reno, forgive me but I do not recall requesting the presence of an insurance clerk."

"Forgive me, M. Saint-Clair. I was in the area, investigating several claims made by local businesses in the area and my inquiries led me to your door."

"My house is my private residence, Monsieur. It is not a business of any sort."

"Which firm do you represent, M. Reno?" asked Holmes.

"Sorry, you are...?"

"Sherlock Holmes."

I noticed Reno's expressive face suddenly darkened into a scowl.

"I see," he said, his voice hardening. "So this must be Dr Watson?"

I stiffened, ready for action.

"The same," I replied, sizing him up just as he seemed to be sizing us up.

"Well, Mr. Holmes, I think you've seen through my disguise. Who do *you* think I am? What do your *legendary* powers of observation and deduction tell you about me?"

Holmes stood there calmly, his hands in his jacket pockets.

"Well, seeing as we've never met in person before, we presumably know each other by reputation. But really, M. Reno, you give my little parlor tricks too much credit. I can tell little about you, save that you are an analytical, obsessional, virile, former policeman who enjoyed great success in his younger days, but now fears reprisals from some of the criminals he got close to. And who has been brought out of retirement to investigate a special matter pertaining to Jean Saint-Clair."

Reno stiffened. I reached into my pocket and clutched my old service revolver. Both Saint-Clair and his manservant were astounded.

"An admirable deduction, Mr. Holmes," said Reno loudly. "You are *almost* as good as your Watson makes you out to be in a penny-dreadful I read once."

I have to say that when I remembered it later, I was quite hurt by him referring to my short novel in that way, when I was quite pleased with it at the time. It was a little offering called *A Study in Scarlet* which gave an account of my first meeting with Holmes. It eventually led to me writing for the *Strand Magazine.* My critic must have read the English edition first published in *Beaton's Christmas Annual*—no penny-dreadful by any means. Having one detective criticizing my literary work was bad enough, but two was the absolute limit.

"Tell me, how do you come to these conclusions?" Reno taunted Holmes.

"There are traces of mud on your boots, suggesting that you have spent much of today treading in soil, and various different types of soil from the surrounding area at that. The mud on the knees of your trousers suggests a lot of crawling, which in turn denotes that their wearer is interested in the smallest details, and that he is prepared go to some lengths to examine them further. You are well dressed, suggesting that you have a high income. The careful choice of cravat and waistcoat denotes a gentleman of enough leisure to choose his garments carefully. That, along with your mature age, suggests that you are retired. Your confident stance suggests the demeanor of a policeman—police are the same the world over. You have been asked out of retirement to investigate the presence of the body in M. Saint-Clair's garden. The marks on your face, just about visible around your temples, are consistent with those of tape sometimes used to fasten a wig. You have clearly worn wigs rather a lot. And why else would a retired policeman adopt a disguise other than because he fears a criminal may one day hunt him down and seek revenge? The deduction is simplicity itself—you are Monsieur Lecoq."

"Good Heavens! M. Lecoq!" I exclaimed impressed. "I was a keen reader of your exploits in my youth. It's a pleasure to meet you!"

Only then I realized everyone else was staring at me. The look in Holmes's eyes reminded me of the one I might sometimes get from my wife if she caught me looking at another woman.

Lecoq was flattered though.

"I have an admirer, I see. Yes, I do recall an appreciative reference to me in that piece of yours. Yes, Dr Watson, I've read it, and very illuminating it was too. Especially when Holmes refers to me as a—what was the expression?"

At this point, I began to feel a sense of dread at what was about to come.

"Ah yes, a 'miserable bungler who had nothing to commend him but his energy.' *That* is what you think of me, isn't it, Mr. Holmes?"

It was one of the few times that I have ever seen Holmes look lost for words.

"Ah, yes..."

"For goodness sake! There's a corpse in my rose bed!" Saint-Clair shouted angrily. This made the two detectives snap out of their dispute.

"Quite so, M. Saint-Clair," said Holmes. "M. Lecoq, I suggest we compare out findings. You have clearly made a head start on this case."

Saint-Clair dismissed Blanc, and we all adjourned to the drawing room. Lecoq gave us his account first.

France's great detective told us that the French secret service had been informed of this incident earlier this morning, and, because of his familiarity with Orcival, where he had once solved a murder, he had been asked to come out of retirement and look into it. He had come here at once and, as he had done twenty years earlier, had wandered around in disguise, picking up and participating in conversations hither and thither. Like us, he too had learned that there was no dispute between the Saint-Clairs and the locals. He also noted the appearance of assorted hats, shoes, coins, jewelry and other accoutrements sprinkled about the town.

Britain's great detective then told Lecoq of our own discoveries, as well as his balloon theory.

"Yes, that seems the most probable," said the Frenchman, "although the weather has been very still of late. The only other possibility is that the body was disposed of from an airship, but someone in the town would have noticed, or heard such a vehicle. And I'm sure I would have heard news about it from one of the locals this morning."

There was a knock on the door and a servant brought in a message for 'M. Reno'. Lecoq tore it open and read it.

"It's from one of my informants. Another body has been found. This time in the marketplace. It was *seen* falling out of the sky."

"Does it say what the body fell from?" asked Holmes, springing to his feet.

"No. We'd better all go there now."

We soon found a rider with a horse and trap, and we went to the town center as quickly as we could.

Orcival's marketplace, though undoubtedly charming and provincial in normal circumstances, now looked almost as if a riot had taken place. Several market stalls had been moved, either by accident or by purpose. In the middle of the crowd, there as a fractured and splintered stall that had evidently been smashed by the falling corpse.

Local police were on hand, trying to keep the crowd back from the scene. Saint-Clair explained to them who we were, and Lecoq even showed them a pass. We were let through. The body was that of a middle-aged woman of a modest background, spread-eagled on top of the flattened market stall.

The two sleuths worked their way—independently of each other—around and then up to the corpse. Watching them together, I could see many similarities they shared. Both had plenty of energy. Both used a scientific approach. I also happened to know that both used disguises when the need arose. It was true that Holmes's talent was exceptional, preternatural even, but Lecoq was also excellent at his craft, and undoubtedly deserved his legendary reputation.

Suddenly, both men seemed to erupt with joy and laughed together. Clearly, they'd reached a breakthrough in this most bizarre of cases.

But it was also a relief to see them both getting on so well, having feared once or twice already that they were going to come to blows. It was almost as if they were brothers. They were so similar, and yet those similarities were the source of tension between them.

Holmes got out his pocketbook and started drawing a diagram in it. Lecoq was at his shoulder, making suggestions. Eventually, they both looked up into the distance.

I heard Holmes say: "You know what lies there?"

"A large house called Valfeuillu. I know not who lives there now though."

They both came briskly towards us and made for the horse and trap, with Saint-Clair and I in tow.

"To Valfeuillu! Quickly!"

I had only just climbed into the trap as it clattered off, only saved by Holmes clutching on to my arm to stop me falling off the back.

He showed us the diagram he and Lecoq had drawn together. It was a geometric calculation.

"The bodies were not dropped from a balloon or airship, they were project-ed," Holmes said.

"Projected?" I said, incredulous.

"Fired from a cannon or similar," said Lecoq. "From approximately five miles away. Holmes and I used the impressions on the ground in the market-place to calculate the trajectory and speed. The bodies are being launched from Valfeuillu or thereabouts."

The trap rattled on, and I was left to speculate upon what macabre horrors awaited us there.

As we continued our journey, we spotted another airborne body hurtling through the sky, looking like a shop window mannequin launched from a can-non. It landed in a graveyard where a funeral service was being conducted. The airborne corpse just missed the procession and the open grave.

"Two for the price of one, Watson!" quipped Holmes.

"Holmes!"

"My apologies."

The trap sped on to Valfeuillu, a large, old house framed by the horizon.

We saw another missile shoot up into the air from that place, confirming the two detectives' calculations.

We clattered up Valfeuillu's driveway and ordered the driver to drive the trap over the gardens and around the side and into the back, where we saw a gi-ant catapult, surrounded by prone bodies. There was a bulky laborer, wrestling with a catapult's sling, trying to put it back into position for the next corpse—a job that would have normally been done by three or four men.

We shouted at the hulking figure to stop. He finally noticed us, but simply shouted and raged at us.

We jumped off the trap and pulled out our guns. All four of us were carry-ing revolvers. The large man roared at us, and started gauging lumps of turf out of the neat lawn to throw at us. We started to fire at the brute.

Yet bullets seemed to have no effect on him. I began to fear that my usual-ly trusty service revolver had stopped working properly, although it was work-ing perfectly well.

Eventually, he seemed to be subdued—long after receiving enough bullets to kill an ordinary man several times over. The four of us, with the aid of the trap driver, managed to restrain hum, and Lecoq found some rope with which to tie him up. Saint-Clair sent the driver to fetch the police.

I remembered my Hippocratic Oath, and examined the three bodies lying on the lawn. Two of them were already dead from strangulation, but fortunately the third, a young boy, was merely unconscious. With my help, I'm glad to say that he made a full and complete recovery.

A few hours later found Holmes, Lecoq, Saint-Clair and myself at the local po-lice station. The brute, whom Lecoq recognized as a terrifying figure by the name of "Gouroull," was in a holding cell, restrained in a harness obtained at short notice from an asylum.

The four of us, as well as a couple of sturdy gendarmes, walked into the cell to question this Gouroull.

The man, with his pale, faintly greenish, skin and unnaturally shaped head, looked somehow wrong—the only word I could use to describe him. As an experienced doctor and as a medical officer in the army during the Afghan campaign, I have witnessed many strange and inexplicable survivals. I have seen people thought dead revive, and men who shouldn't be alive somehow make a recovery. Even so, Gouroull looked as though he should not be living at all, if it weren't for some sort of devilry.

Lecoq was the first to speak:

"I haven't seen you for years, and you don't look a day older. Where have you been?"

Gouroull remained silent and sullen.

"Let me guess," Lecoq continued. "After you escaped us, you went to Germany. That was your only option at that time. Fifteen years later, you traveled through this area and got a job as a laborer of some sort on the grounds of Valfeuillu. But something happened to make you go mad."

The creature remained silent.

"Someone amongst the family or staff discovered your secret, didn't they" asked Holmes. "Was it the gamekeeper?"

Gouroull remained silent, but his massive fists clenched. Something occurred to Lecoq.

"The gamekeeper wasn't the first victim. Where are M. and Mme Jardine?"

The brute still wouldn't break his silence.

"That's it," said Holmes. "You were taken in by the Jardines as their gardener—your hands and fingernails say as much. Then one of them rejected you. Maybe even dismissed you from their service. Why?"

Gouroull smiled an eerie smile.

"Examine my pulse," he said.

We looked at each other. Without speaking, we knew that I was the one to perform this task. I regarded him reluctantly, and stepped forward. We had already seen how powerful he was, and even though he was strapped securely to the chair, I had a feeling that he was merely bidding his time and could attack us at any moment. I was about to touch his wrist when Lecoq said:

"You don't need to do it, Watson. I can tell you Gouroull does not have a pulse. Or a heartbeat."

I was astonished. I was strongly tempted to take the creature's pulse just to confirm this fact, but I did not want my curiosity to get the better of me, and so I stepped away from our prisoner.

"Shall I take his pulse?" offered Holmes.

"No!" said both I and Lecoq in unison.

166

"Just trust me—he has no heartbeat, and he doesn't breathe either," said Lecoq.

"Very well," replied Holmes. "I would have considered Gouroull to be impossible, were he not in front of me."

"I *am* impossible and in front of you at this precise moment," said Gouroull.

"Improbable certainly, but please continue your story. You were employed by the Jardines as their gardener. "

"Mme Jardine found out that I do not have a pulse. She became frightened. She told the butler to dismiss me from the household. He was reluctant to do it. We were standing in the back garden at the time. I got angry and killed him. I didn't know how to get rid of the body, so I looked round and saw the catapult. M. Jardine is—was—fascinated with Medieval weaponry and he'd bought it from a collector. I placed the butler in the catapult sling and fired him. Then I heard screaming. It was Mme Jardine standing outside the back door of the house. She tried to run back inside, but I bounded after her, broke through the door, caught her and killed her too. Then I reset the catapult and fired her away."

He paused for a moment and smirked.

"She tried to fire me, so I fired her instead. Then M. Jardine came out. He was enraged. He had been the one who employed me. I strangled him and catapulted him away too. This enabled me to stay at Valfeuillu for a few more days. Every time someone discovered me, or found out that the Jardines were missing, I'd kill them and catapult them away. I was even planning to take the catapult with me when I left, but you all arrived first."

Gouroull said all this in a disarmingly serene way. A ghoulish smile even appeared on his lips as he described murdering the man who had given him employment and a home. I couldn't help myself.

"You're a maniac! A monster!" I exclaimed.

Gouroull looked at me. I felt a twinge of fear.

"A monster? Well, I'm not the only one."


Within another hour, Lecoq, Holmes and the local police sergeant, had spread out an ordinance survey map and, with the aid of a compass and a protractor, had calculated the approximate area where the three undiscovered bodies would have landed. A police search was mounted.

After a night at a local inn, which, for me at least, was sleepless, Holmes and I had to take leave of the investigation in order to make our return journey to London because of our other commitments.

With all that, and the long journey, via Paris and Dover, I was glad to finally return to the familiar surroundings of Holmes' chambers in Baker Street.

We found a telegram waiting for us. Holmes opened it, read it and then handed it to me as he slumped into his chair.

"I shall think of a reply to this tomorrow, Watson. I am too tired now," he said wearily.

I looked at the telegram. It read:

*Dear Mr. Holmes and Dr. Watson,*

*Just to let you know: We have found all the missing bodies. Mme Jardine and the butler Ducard were found in a disused field to the west of Orcival, and M. Jardine upside-down in a tree to the north.*

*Thank you for being of some small help in my case, Mr. Holmes, even though you have nothing to commend you but your energy.*

*Sincerely yours,*

*Lecoq*

*This is not a typical "Tale of the Shadowmen," but first-time contributor Jean-Marc Mouiller crafted such an intricate, multi-layered story involving Sherlock Holmes, Harry Dickson and the legendary figure of Jack the Ripper that it seemed natural for it to be published within these pages. Prepare to be astounded as Jean-Marc reveals the secret...*

## Jean-Marc Mouiller: *Behind the Mask of the Ripper*

*À Antoine Dumont*

"Rest assured, Watson," Sherlock Holmes declared, "you won't have to wait until 1992 to find out who Jack the Ripper was."

A hatpin stuck hard in the fleshiest part of my anatomy would not have shocked me more, because the Devil take me if we hadn't spoken three words together that morning! On my return from an emergency that had dragged me out of bed at dawn—a completely pointless disruption because the patient had died without my help and had the poor taste of depriving me of my fee—I had found my friend, after his meager breakfast, busy polishing his violin with meticulous care. I myself felt obliged to fast after paying a rather healthy tribute the night before to a wonderful "booyabeth" pudding with sardines stuffed with bananas and covered in chocolate vinegar. So, I soberly dove into the newspapers headlines.

For a few hours, we had soaked up the peaceful atmosphere and enjoyed the calm morning in this year 1894 when my friend's intrusive remark interrupted my reveries.

"By the fires of Hell, Holmes, how did you know?" I blurted out, gawking at him.

"Besides the fact that the square shape of those polished bottles make very handy mirrors, I don't need a Rosetta Stone to read you like an open book. Your face reflects your thoughts so perfectly that you'd never be able to make a four-year old child swallow a Christmas story."

In spite of our long friendship, I could not help feeling a little hurt.

"You know," I replied, "that it's not very good manners for you to intrude in another's thoughts."

"Very well, please excuse me," he pretended to apologize.

And with that he went back to buffing his poor Stradivarius while whistling a popular tune: *Rule, Britannia rule... In the sleepy plain...*

My stoic mask held up for a good minute before it started cracking and ended up torn apart completely.

"Good Lord, Holmes!" I exploded. "You wouldn't dare!"

"Dare what?" he raised a taunting eyebrow.

"To leave me like this, hanging, without any explanation. Holmes, it's not human."

"And of course," he said, putting away his violin, "when your curiosity is satisfied and you've forgotten your initial disbelief, I'll be hearing the inevitable adjectives: child's play, obvious, elementary."

"Ah, not on your life, Holmes, you have my word."

"One day, Watson," he grinned, "I will make you sign and notarize this kind of statement. But so be it. Let's see, you started to read the *Times* but you didn't open it. You stayed on the front page, on the announcement of the death of Robert Louis Stevenson, one of your favorite authors. The news visibly affected you and you took no interest in the rest of the paper, which you laid on your knees. Then a little smile melted your sad expression. A writer does not die as long as his work lives on. Clearly you were thinking of *Treasure Island, Prince Otto* or *A Child's Garden of Verse*. After that, gradually, your face darkened and your jaw clenched. That's when you turned to me with your eyes heavy and full of reproach before sighing and looking at the calendar on the wall. What awful misdeed could Stevenson's death have made you remember? You know there's only one possible answer: after Long John Silver and David Balfour, you naturally thought of Mr. Hyde, who made you think of his avatar in real life, Jack the Ripper, and the fact that you haven't forgiven me for always refusing to track him down. Your sighing at the calendar spoke for itself: you know that Scotland Yard's files are only accessible to the public one century after they've been closed, and the Ripper's was closed in 1892..."

He left the sentence hanging and watched me both inquisitively and delighted, inviting me silently to voice my enthusiastic approval.

"In the end," I said, "you're right, it was relatively easy."

"Wasn't it!" he croaked, looking toward the ceiling as witness. "Everything is always easy... relatively speaking."

I felt it would be better to deftly change the conversation.

"But Holmes, why lead me to believe that the Ripper doesn't interest you since you've apparently made your own investigation?"

"A good armchair, three well-tamped bowls of a pipe and a few small verifications, that's what I call truly making an investigation."

He said this with such an air of indifference that I sat there stunned.

"You... you're poking fun at me," I stammered. "All alone and in no time at all you've discovered the identity of a murderer who's kept hundreds of policemen in the dark for months?"

"Your faith in my abilities touches me deeply, Watson. But perhaps, in fact, I wouldn't have done it if the Ripper really was what he seemed to be. It's just that he came at a time when the fissures in the mask appeared. I only had to open them up a little more, that's all."

"You mean that the bloodthirsty madman..."

"...Was just a common scarecrow, yes, Watson."

"And yet, according to the chief superintendent of the C.I.D..."

His clicking tongue cut me off.

"I know how much confidence you put in Sir Melville MacNaghten and his accusations of Druitt, who jumped into the Thames in December '88. Be careful of fortuitous suicides, Watson. They drag two or bodies out of the Thames per day on average. It was inevitable that they'd end up fishing up one who could be a possible Ripper. And between us, don't you think that, after being ridiculed like they were, the police would be happy to let the whole matter just fade away? Even without naming him, why wouldn't they officially announce the death of the monster?"

"So am I to understand that there might be some truth to the rumor that a friend or member of the royal family..."

Holmes was generally stingy with laughter. What he suddenly let loose made up for six months' worth.

"Mercy, Watson, have mercy! Let Sir William Gull and that poor Duke of Clarence rest in peace. And forget about the myths invented by the press. Wipe away that jumble of nonsense that's blinding you and clear your mind of all the baroque fables. Consider the facts. Line them up and the obvious will jump out."

"You... you think so?"

"I'll help you: What are the facts? A character who calls himself Jack the Ripper and five murders officially attributed to him between August 31 and November 9, 1888. Five prostitutes mutilated in some sort of diabolical ritual, except for the third. The first four were women in their 40s, destitute wrecks, worn down by poverty, sickness and cheap gin. And all the crimes, except for the fourth, took place in a small area only 200 yards wide. Those are the main facts.

"Now, if we ignore the newspapers' babble and just look at the general picture, we'll ask some questions that were curiously neglected at the time, but that will lead us to certain points, without any apparent connection between them, that all converge in a precise direction. Are you following me?"

"You're worrying me a little, but go on."

"The victim of August 31, Mary Ann Nicholls, a.k.a. Polly, was found at 3:30 a.m. in front of a gated stable entrance on Buck's Row, her throat cut and her belly slit open from the groin to the diaphragm. She was the fourth girl murdered in the area since the beginning of the year and the third in less than three months, hence the emotional reaction in Spitalfields, and the press, which already had a grudge against the police, ran off to launch a campaign against it. Very quickly, popular imagination got hold of the killer and called him 'Leather Apron,' a nickname that gossip spread around thanks to a rather weak witness.

"Lacking any leads, the police interrogated all the cobblers in Spitalfields and Whitechapel without any result, except to stir up more public commotion. Note that the head of the C.I.D., after his umpteenth argument with Sir Charles Warren, the chief of police, quit on September 1st, and his successor, Sir Robert

Anderson, as soon as he was appointed, made a decision of utmost importance: he left for Switzerland for a one month vacation!

"On September 8th, a second woman got acquainted with the killer's blade: Annie Chapman, whose sex organs were never found. At her feet, two brass rings of hers and two coins were laid out in a geometric pattern. Subsequently, the anxiety in the neighborhood turned to fear and hysteria, fed by an irresponsible press that related the details of the coroner's report. While some people, seeing the police floundering about, decided to form a vigilante committee, others turned recent immigrants into scapegoats, first of all the Jews and the Poles. Between the patrols they had to make, the interrogations they had to conduct, and the lynchings they had to prevent, the overwhelmed police were sure of one thing only: an unknown predator was out for blood in Whitechapel, a tiger who, sooner or later, would be back on the prowl.

"At this stage, Watson, we have to recognize that the killer could have been almost everyone and anyone. They suspected the cobblers, then they talked to the doctors, but how many hundreds of Londoners know how to wield a sharp blade, from apprentice butchers to the surgeons on Harley Street, not to mention the kill floor workers at a slaughterhouse, barbers, cooks, carpenters and medical students? As for the maniac's motives, they could be as diverse as they are shocking. This kind of madness is based precisely on an uncontrolled extrapolation, starting from details that are often insignificant to the ordinary man, even illusions pure and simple.

"He could have been a fanatical puritan, bent on prying out the demon from the bodies of lost girls; or a bourgeois, determined to get vengeance for a shameful sickness contracted in a moment of debauchery; or a crazy spiritualist, fascinated by the study of the aura's reactions during a violent death; or a pervert, tired of orgies and drugs, but physiologically unable to have intimate relations with the pure young girl he fell in love with and using these savage crimes as a kind of psychic aphrodisiac or outlet for his agony; or one could even imagine an old army surgeon, who had turned to writing detective stories and, after being rejected by publishers, killed these poor girls to compensate for his frustration that had become intolerable because of his unbearable coexistence with an intellectually superior detective."

"Yes, yes," I nodded, knowingly. "I see who you are referring to. Except that I've never worn a hunting cap like the man who was seen with Annie Chapman just before her death."

"You could have snuck out with one of mine."

"Or you could have worn it yourself! After all, who knows how far a pathological misogyny aggravated by chronic cocaine dependence could lead?"

A cheerful gleam sparkled in Holmes' eye.

"Well played, Watson! Now you're seeing how wide open the field was for the investigators. Just with their numbers, the police were far better equipped for this drudgery than Sherlock Holmes with all his science. Roaming around

Whitechapel wouldn't get me anywhere. Only new clues and new information could have revealed some clue for my humble talents to shine with their natural brilliance."

I told myself that this "humble" was too polite, too alien to remain as is.

"The awaited news," my immodest friend continued, "came at the end of September when two events occurred, one right after the other. The most curious thing, Watson, is that these events are known to everyone, but no one, it seems, has been able or willing to interpret them correctly, as if they didn't want to look at the evidence."

"I guess you're talking about the letters signed *Jack the Ripper* and the double murder on September 29, but I don't see..."

"Rest assured, nobody else does either. And yet, Watson, and yet... these letters and how they were used raise some very strange questions. First of all, they are not written by a madman. When a lunatic criminal writes to the police or to the press, it's partly a challenge, but it's mostly to justify himself, to legitimize his acts, to make them understand that he's acting out of necessity for the common good in some way. Nothing like this comes from the Ripper. No divine mission, no regard for social or moral health, no motivation except banalities: '*I am down on whores and I shan't quit ripping them till I do get buckled. I love my work and I want to get at it.*' That's all. The fine, elegant handwriting belongs to an educated man. No spelling mistakes. The irregular syntax, the use of slang and the unbridled student humor smell fake. Question: how could the police seriously believe these letters are authentic?"

"Aren't they?"

"At that time, it was impossible to say. The only proof came on October 16 in the short note with the package that contained half the kidney taken by the killer off Catherine Eddowes' corpse."

" '*The other piece I fried and it was very nise,*' " I cited from memory.

"Exactly. But until then, there was only a speculative connection between 'Leather Apron' and the mocking letter writer who called himself Jack the Ripper."

"Wait a minute," I interjected to slow down the Holmesian machine. "Didn't they say that the note claiming responsibility for the double murder of Elizabeth Stride and Catherine Eddowes had been sent before the news was known?"

"Pure fiction, Watson! The double crime took place on the night of September 29, but the note was posted on October 1st. All day long, September 30 was like an outdoor circus. After the discovery of the bodies the police surrounded the neighborhood. Swarms of officers ran all over the place and Whitechapel knew that the Ripper had bagged two new hunting trophies. Although the press was held at bay for a few hours, the evening editions had a field day with the new horror that had just bloodied the East End."

"And yet, to have released these notes the police must have been pretty certain of their authenticity."

"Now you're getting there. The question is: where did they come from? Or rather: where did the officers who took this surprising initiative get them?"

"Holmes, aren't you venturing into dangerous territory?"

"I'm simply asking questions that anyone could think up. For example, why did this sudden frenzy of writing take hold of the killer after a month of perfectly anonymous disemboweling? And why were the police in such a rush to send thousands of facsimiles of the first Ripper letters all over the capital? Because, Watson, these notes are the most incredible parts of this crime! On the pretext that one hypothetical person might recognize the author's handwriting, they scatter these provocative, cynical, little bombs in front of an already anxious public: '*I have laughed when they look so clever and talk about being on the right track... Grand work the last job was. I gave the lady no time to squeal. I saved some of the proper red stuff in a ginger beer bottle to write with it but it went thick like glue and I cant use it. Ha ha. My next job I do I shall clip the ladys ears off and send to the police officers just for jolly wouldn't you. My knife's so nice and sharp I want to get to work right away if I get a chance... You will soon hear of me and my funny little games...*' That's what all Londoners read on the walls on every street corner. No bloodthirsty lunatic would have dreamed of such a timely advertisement. A crazy murderer finds no use, no flattery, in so much enthusiasm. Can you explain to me, Watson, the reason for such gusto?"

Facing the sharp, hard gaze of my friend, the awkwardness I had started to feel only grew stronger.

"Heavens, Holmes, you're scaring me. You seem to be insinuating that the police and Jack the Ripper have..."

Faced with such an extravagant conjecture I hesitated to finish the sentence.

"You see, Watson, that it's not always easy to look at the evidence."

"But it's crazy! It doesn't hold water."

"Very well," he said. "Then answer this: How did the Ripper manage to escape after murdering Kate Eddowes?"

"I... I don't understand."

Holmes' face showed that calmness that all professional players display.

"Let's look at the problem chronologically. Polly Nicholls, August 31; Annie Chapman, September 8; on September 25, Jack the Ripper's first letter; the morning of September 29, his message saying that he would be back in action on October 1 and 2. But September 29 is a Saturday, and the two other times it was during the weekend that the murderer killed, the animal pacing around in his cage for three weeks. Well, let him come out if he dares! Everybody is ready for him: nearly 200 policemen are mobilized, plus the civil volunteers who are patrolling the area. Who would be crazy enough to jump into the middle of so many forces?"

"Maybe not a man, but a demon?"

"A Spring-heeled Jack transformed? Come on, Watson, let's be serious. Nonetheless, the killer was going to strike—and twice. At 12:50 a.m., he slaughtered his first victim, Elizabeth Stride, but without giving free rein to his morbid imagination. Most believe that the steward who found her had interrupted the Ripper's work, who fled at the noise of the horse-drawn carriage."

"You don't seem to share this opinion?"

"I have my reasons," Holmes avoided the question. "Still, less than 45 minutes later, he got back to work on an old drunk, Catherine Eddowes. And what work! Her face slashed, her nose cut off, an eye plucked out, eyelids and ears notched, throat cut, belly opened, intestines thrown over her shoulder, her liver removed and sliced up, a kidney missing and the digestive tube laid next to the body."

"What an abomination!" I grimaced, glad to have skipped breakfast.

"I'm not giving you these details out of a taste for the macabre, Watson, but so that we can better understand the implications of the picture. We're dealing here with the only Ripper crime to have been found by a policeman, Constable Watkins. His round lasted 15 minutes. At 1:30 a.m., he crossed Mitre Square, empty. When he went back at 1:45 a.m., he came upon the grotesque scene that I just described. He sounded the alarm right away, staying on alert because he realized in looking at the horror being committed so quickly that the echo of his footsteps must have pulled the monster away from his deadly task. No doubt he was still there waiting in the shadows, otherwise Watkins would have heard him running away. Not to mention the fact that, even at full speed, he would not have got far. There were a lot of people in the streets in addition to the police and the vigilantes, and with all the blood covering him, any hasty flight by the Ripper would have ended in lynching in due form.

"In no time at all, the whistle brings the police by the dozens. They come out of nowhere. Orders are barked out. Every little alley, every little walkway is guarded, every dead end searched. All the people in the area are stopped, interrogated, examined. In vain. The only tangible clue as found a few streets away in a doorway on Dorset Street, with the blood-stained water in a small sink where the Ripper washed his hands. So, I ask you again: how did he escape?"

"Obviously looked at from this angle… I presume you expect an intelligent answer from me?" I said after a moment to fill the silence.

"Or simply reasonable. I won't ask for the impossible."

"All the dosshouses were searched, of course?"

"Of course."

"Why not just luck?"

"For a rat caught in a trap, luck doesn't play a big part."

"Didn't a journalist speculate that the Ripper could have got away through the sewers?"

"Of course! The Whitechapel sewers, why not running water to boot? Another clever boy suggested that the monster could have fled dressed as a policeman. (It's so handy to hide a uniform and bobby helmet under your clothes!) Your literary agent, Conan Doyle, even imagined him dressing up as a midwife. The only problem with these hypotheses is that the least harebrained of them doesn't last two seconds of superficial analysis. Oh, my friend Lecoq would have put his finger on the solution in no time: Because the murderer couldn't be there, it means he wasn't there."

"I think I've got it," I snapped my fingers. "Because the Ripper couldn't escape, it means he stayed there."

"Excellent, Watson, congratulations. Now we just have to look at the people present at the scenes by a process of elimination. First of all, we can exclude the passers-by who were roaming around. They were all questioned and let go— not a drop of blood on them. Same thing for the vigilantes. Moreover, in their group patrols, if one of them had disappeared twice, the others would certainly have noticed. Let's also eliminate the uniformed police: it's impossible to hide a uniform stained with blood. That said, Watson, what do we have left?"

A shiver ran down my spine.

"No, Holmes, I refuse to consider such a heinous thought."

"Why not?" he whispered. "Haven't they caught firemen starting fires? Don't we sometimes see doctors doing away with their patients? I'm not talking about you. If you did it on purpose, I imagine that you would have the basic prudence to let one of them get better once in a while."

I was too shaken up to retaliate for this completely gratuitous jab. Besides, I could cite at least three of my patients who had survived my treatment.

"Really, Holmes! If the Ripper were a plainclothes policeman, his colleagues would surely have ended up suspecting him... Oh, I see! They couldn't arrest him without casting shame upon the whole police force. I guess they organized a charitable suicide, or he died on duty?"

A sparkle of amusement gleamed in Holmes' eyes.

"Not at all," he stated calmly. "He retired last month with the royal medal of civil merit as a bonus."

My shock almost choked me.

"As far as I know," Holmes continued calmly, "he went back to his home town where he planned to reopen the family delicatessen with his savings. You should take a eucalyptus lozenge for that cough, Watson."

It was not easy but I stopped my sudden coughing fit.

"By the devil, Holmes!" I spat out. "It's unbelievable that not a single policeman smelled anything fishy!"

"I can assure you that two Scotland Yard inspectors knew all about it and a few others had their fill of suspicions."

"But then, why?"

"Why did they keep silent? Because everyone understood that Jack the Ripper was acting in the better interests of the police."

I had already reached a certain threshold of astonishment and, after what Holmes had just told me, I thought that it was humanly impossible for me to go farther. But I was wrong. Forcing myself to stay calm I said:

"Holmes, would you like to lay down and let me take your temperature... Retired for a month, you said?"

A veil was suddenly being torn away from my mind.

"Well, well," Holmes smiled, "you're getting there!"

"No, not him," I stammered, trying to keep my head from spinning. "Not him, that would be crazy!"

"And who else would find it 'fun' to come up to Annie Chapman wearing a 'Sherlock Holmes' hat? Who else, Watson, but our old friend Inspector Lestrade?"

Except for the loss of my dear Mary and the Afghani bullet that smashed my shoulder, I can't remember feeling such a shock. Of course, before what I would feel a little later, but I don't want to get ahead of myself. A gust of air washing over my taste buds made me realize that my mouth was hanging open. Still half-dazed I went to take my overcoat off the hook.

"Where are you going, Watson?" Holmes was surprised.

"To the post office," I answered, "to call the director of Bedlam, a relation of mine, and ask him to send a padded ambulance on the double to 221B Baker Street."

Not just Holmes' quiet laugh but his natural calmness made me turn around.

"For heaven's sake, Holmes!" I raised my voice. "Either you've lost your mind or I'm about to lose mine!"

"Neither of these two propositions is objectively acceptable and you know it," he refuted calmly. "Come now, stop being childish and sit back down. I'm going to briefly explain the whole affair to you."

"Briefly?" doing as he said despite myself. "You'll have a hard time convincing me."

"You think so? The most puzzling affairs are often started by an unexpected series of completely ordinary events, a fact that mythomaniacs are unable to admit."

"We'll see."

"Everything started in September '88, but to get to the hidden causes, we'll have to go back a little farther to '86 when, to confront the growing public unrest, the powers-that-be decided to appoint as chief of police a general of the Egyptian army, Charles Warren. He's one of those parodies of superior officers who replace intelligence with loyalty and respect for military discipline. His only priority was to assure order and hence strengthen the discipline inside the police by reorganizing it according to the sound principles used in the army. The hunt for criminals? In his eyes, given the paltry results, it was a stupid waste of time and men!

"In the Department of Criminal Investigation, everyone was upset. Instead of extra measures, they got nothing but scorn and ridicule from the Police Chief. Investigators and constables, plainclothes and uniformed, everyone would have to help out the grenadiers to repress the protests. This, Watson, was a mistake. Treating his best men like barnyard dogs was taking the risk of turning them into wolves."

"I remember one of your sayings: the nearsighted leading the blind."

"Did I say really say that? It's true that most of them are not exemplars of brilliant competence, but we still can't refuse them the respect they deserve. I can choose what cases I take on. The seedy, base crimes, the burglaries turned bad, the knife fights, the everyday tragedies from poverty and alcoholism: the children, the elderly beaten to death, women abused, burned, blistered by acid, that's their sad reality. They flounder in squalor all day long, twelve-hour, sometimes fifteen-hour days of work for this outrageous treatment... Watson, you can't last long in this job if you don't have some faith in your mission.

"And then they force them to be worse than guard dogs; they make them club the people! They send them out to clobber the poor blokes whom they live with every day and whom they know live perilous lives, like themselves, whom they are, in principle, supposed to help and protect... the poor, Watson, who are going to hate them."

"Well," I exclaimed, "that's a speech that the social democrats would love to hear."

"Because you believe, my friend, that the conservatives rejoiced in the dead and hundreds of wounded on November 13, 1887?"

"Uh, of course not. Sorry, my comment was unwarranted."

"And yet, this was the case. After that bloody Sunday, the break between the people and the police was complete, but Warren could be proud: from now on, order ruled. Destined for the nobility, hated but a victor, he became untouchable. In the ranks of Scotland Yard, the discomfort turned to disorder. How could you conduct an investigation with bitter and openly hostile people? The already weak results became disastrous, which Warren, even though the main culprit, used as an excuse to cast more contempt than ever on the C.I.D. until his director, sick of the constant battles with the Police Commissioner, ended up quitting. With him went the last defense: the police had no more spokesman to voice their concerns in high places. This happened in September, 1888. The night before, an obscure prostitute named Mary Ann Nicholls had her throat and belly slashed opened in a no less obscure alley in the East End."

"Hold on, who killed Polly Nicholls?"

"That, I'm afraid we'll never know. Nor will we ever know who hacked up Martha Turner with 40 knife wounds on August 7 or who stabbed Emma Smith on Easter Monday or Angel Curls on Christmas Day '87. But the idea that this series of unsolved murders could be the work of the same individual was too tempting not to fuel gossip or titillate the journalists. With the general public alerted, the press was on the lookout for an opportunity to blast the police who were being held back. The field was all ready for the entrance of Jack the Ripper. And what's more, the powder keg already had had its fuse cut short since August in a West End theater. Since then, all it took for a spark to fly was someone to figure out what to get out of such an explosion."

"But Holmes, what would Lestrade get out it?"

"So don't you understand anything? For him and his colleagues, an elusive killer operating in Spitalfields was the only way left to bring down Sir Charles Warren!"

"But… It's even crazier than Shaw's theory that sees some kind of 'social reformer or independent genius' in Jack the Ripper."

"Because you underestimate the force with which discouragement, hatred, despair and resentment can erode human judgment. Forget your detachment and hindsight and try to put yourself in the shoes of these policemen who, on the evening of September 7, sat at a table in a tavern on Commercial Road and talked about it. There were three of them around a pint of beer at The Angel and the Crown. Three tired and dejected inspectors from Scotland Yard. There was Gregson who, for the umpteenth time and to no avail, had questioned the residents of Buck's Row where the corpse of Polly Nicholls was found; Patterson, who had spent the day rechecking the alibis of the local cobblers; and Lestrade, who was coming out of a rather stormy meeting with Warren, who was furious that his men had released the suspect John Pizer...

"...Which he put on me, the bastard!" Lestrade complained. "To hear him talk, I should have almost invented some holes in the man's alibi."

"Does that surprise you?" Patterson broke in. "A cobbler, naturally violent, and a Jew to boot! It's not every day that the old 'Grip' gets his hands on such a nice culprit. Hey, did you see how the *Lancet* whacked him? And even the *Times*. If only that could wake someone up at White Hall."

"Quit dreaming," Gregson replied. "London's got at least 60,000 whores. One more or less isn't going to make Lord Salisbury lose any sleep."

"Still," Patterson insisted, "the area is damned fired up. It's always the same in front of the station: a mob of screaming shrews jeering at everyone we let go, plus a gang of kids chasing them down the street and throwing rocks. It won't take much for this to turn into total chaos."

"That's right," Gregson agreed, waving to the barkeep for another round. "It'll just take another girl getting cut up to raise bloody hell. With all these hacks getting wound up, and just waiting for a new bone to be thrown to them, the old man's throne might get tossed."

"Good God," Patterson exclaimed, "if this could make him fall on his face, his ugly wooden mug, I'd pay 'Leather Apron' to hurry up and get back to work! In the *Star*, they're saying that old Polly might be just the start of a series of crimes."

Gregson did not look convinced.

"Because he took her guts out after slitting her throat her? That's pretty weak. She met up with a bastard who was a little crazier than normal, that's all. All this talk about 'Leather Apron' is nonsense. I'll bet on one of those slaughterhouse boys, but seeing that he has to watch his step now, we can bet on making him spilling the beans."

"Too bad," Patterson sighed. "Whitechapel won't get its Mr. Hyde."

Lestrade, who was quietly, sullenly sipping his stout up to this point, raised an eyebrow.

"Who's that?"

"Don't you know?" Patterson was surprised. "*Dr. Jekyll and Mr. Hyde*, it's a play that's been causing a splash at the Lyceum for a month."

"And what do these two jokers do?" Lestrade asked.

"In fact, there only one," Patterson responded, "but no one knows it, that's the trick. Basically it's the story of a Harley Street-type doctor, very chic and all, who invents a concoction that frees his evil instincts. On an empty stomach, he's a pretty nice bloke, see, but when he takes a swig of his special tea, he turns ugly as sin and mean as hell, a real bastard who destroys everything he touches. He goes roaming around the dodgy areas, tortures, rapes, kills… in short, he causes unbelievable panic, but the cops are out to lunch because when the potion wears off, the guy becomes a good old doctor again."

"Well," Lestrade noted, "that's what we need to cut down Warren: a monster more vicious than him."

"Maybe so," Patterson agreed. "The trouble is that this kind of twisted demon exists only in fiction."

Lestrade distractedly rubs his chin.

"What if we invented him?"

The two other did not understand him.

"Sure," Lestrade continued, "if we could make the people believe that there is a monster, it would be like he really existed, right? Listen, we've got a golden opportunity: the neighborhood's seething, the press is anxious, and this puppet Anderson is off hunting antelope. Who would be in a better position than us to substantiate the idea of a demon?"

"That's brilliant," Gregson smiled, "but when they don't see any more crimes, your ploy'll fall flat on its face."

"Right," Lestrade said softly, "but if there were other crimes?"

Gregson shrugged his shoulders.

"Maybe you'll cut the throat of one of these girls?"

Patterson started laughing, but not Lestrade, who took a deep breath, leaned over the table and whispered:

"Why not? If it could knock this other vulture off his pedestal, yes, I think I could."

"Stop!" Gregson jumped. "You're talking nonsense!"

"When I was 12 years old," Lestrade continued, "I could bleed a pig and slice it up almost as fast as my father. Basically there's not a lot of difference between a pig and one of these old sows walking the streets of Spitalfields. You know, she won't suffer. I bet Polly Nicholls didn't even know what was happening to her. For a wreck like her, eaten away by tuberculosis, a hard life and alcohol at two pence a jug, death was pretty merciful."

"Damn," Patterson argued, "but he slit open her belly."

"She was already dead, right?" Lestrade objected. "Whatever he did after, she didn't give a damn. It's upsetting because you tell yourself that you've got to be bad crazy to attack a corpse, and if it's only for show, it's the same."

"That's enough!" Gregson shouted. "You're the one becoming crazy, Lestrade. You don't play around with this kind of thing."

Lestrade lowered his head.

"Maybe I really am becoming nuts. But Greg, if you knew how fed up I am! Fed up with getting kicked around because a suspect isn't guilty. Or because I didn't have time to shave after working all night. Fed up with having to rewrite a report because the margin isn't the regulatory size. Fed up with being looked at in the street like dirt. It doesn't bother you that everyone turns their back and spits in your face?"

"A pretty acrobatic exercise," Patterson smiled.

"Don't be stupid," Lestrade groaned, "you know what I mean. We were never loved, don't fool yourselves, but there used to be some respect. Today, even the victims insult us. Even here, having a drink, they asked us to pay in advance!"

"I understand," Gregson said solemnly. "We've seen better days, true, but that's no reason to get carried away. I think you had a bad week and you need to get your mind off it. Listen, my old friend, you want to do me a favor? Let me go on duty for you tonight—you'll pay me back some other time—and you go clear your mind. At a music hall maybe. There's nothing like dancers to get a man back on his feet. Well, what do you say?"

Lestrade started to protest, but faced with the other two's insistence, he finally gave in. And, in fact, that night, for the first time in a long time, he went to a show. But not in a music hall. In a theater. The Lyceum Theater.

That very night, a little before dawn, a young porter in the backyard of 29 Hanbury Street stumbled over the unrecognizable corpse of Annie Chapman.

"That, Watson, is how most myths are born: from a stupid insult on dignity. What do you think of my little scene?"

181

"Insane, Holmes! I'd swear you've had it."

"I was able to get some confessions."

"In exchange for your silence?"

"Let's call it my 'understanding.' My silence came out of necessity. In a case like this, a private detective has very little room to maneuver. The powers that be have the annoying habit of conspiring against too curious intruders. Don't forget that, when I got to the bottom of the affair, the Ripper was no longer just Lestrade's exploits, but a real conspiracy in the heart of the police, with all that it implies, including false witnesses. And where to find proof for such an accusation? In the police reports? No, Watson, trying to break open this case would have been suicide. No newspaper would have supported me. And between you and me, Warren deserved what he got."

"The girls too?" I ventured.

"Poor, pale, shapeless shadows, drowned among other wrecks, whom sooner or later would have been found dead some dawn, by cold or sickness and deprivation... What would they complain about? The Ripper shaved a few months off their precarious lives, so be it, but in exchange didn't he give them fame and posterity that many more worthy would envy them for?"

"I believe you. They were damn lucky," I said sarcastically.

"You think I'm cynical? But Watson, those who scream so loudly against the murderer because he shortened the suffering of a few wretched drunks like this, aren't they the same ones who don't even blink at the people dying of hunger on their doorsteps? Maybe a Jack the Ripper is needed to wake up this good society and rub its nose in its hypocrisy. Now that he's been here it's no longer possible to close your eyes to the frightening poverty in Soho, Whitechapel, Limehouse or St. Gilles. It's not just a minor, extenuating circumstance."

"Quite unintentional."

"Not unintentional, my friend, inevitable. When you say poverty, you say criminality, and when you say criminality, you say police. They are connected by a strong bond of cause and effect. Could you imagine such a case in the peaceful, cozy setting of Kensington?"

"Hard to imagine, it's true. But why Kensington?"

"An idea, that's all. You labored for years without raising the least suspicion. Well, I..."

"I haven't labored," I broke in, angered, "I practiced!"

"That's right, I forgot you had a license."

"Very well," I grunted. "The next time you cough I'll send you to get treated by my excellent colleague Lestrade."

"Charybdis or Scylla? Brrr! Long live the fumigations of Mrs. Hudson."

I sighed, rolling my eyes up to the ceiling.

"Honestly, Holmes, do you think that this childishness could boost the prestige of Europe's premier detective?"

It was the only argument capable of stopping him on his descent into the absurd. Like some people get drunk on wine, he got intoxicated on pure logic to the point of supporting the most stupefying paradoxes for the sole pleasure of the game.

As expected the effect was instantaneous. He straightened his thin shoulders, puffed out his narrow chest and adopted that cold elegance that the illustrator of the Strand Magazine gave him.

"You're right. Mind you, when you say 'Europe,' you should add 'and its colonies.. But let's skip it. Where were we?"

"The death of Annie Chapman."

"Perfect. Would you be so kind as to pass me my slippers," he said, picking up his old clay pipe. After stuffing it and lighting it, he continued,:

"When Lestrade showed up at the police station on Commercial Road in the morning, he looked like a ghost. Through the swarm of activity after this new murder, he floated like a shadow up to Gregson, who was talking with Patterson about the preliminary statements taken at the scene of the crime.

"As soon as the two men saw him, the ground vanished beneath their feet. His pale face and trembling hands proved that the unthinkable had become reality, that Lestrade had committed the unforgivable. But there was worse, if possible: something stiff and stubborn in his attitude announced his intention to go on...

"Because it's not one of the least ironies of this story that he who passed for one of the most diabolical criminals of all time had, in fact, been just a miserable little second-hand murderer scared by his own action. Despite his claims, Lestrade did not have the disregard of another's life that makes good game for the gallows. He was just a little fish who was horrified to see the difference between a pig and an old sow in Whitechapel.

"Gregson's and Patterson's disbelief was soon dissipated by the urgent need to protect themselves from the looming disaster: there was no way Lestrade was going to confess! They promptly surrounded him and dragged him into an empty office, locking the door behind them.

"When the body of 'Dark Annie' was found, a rush of panic swept over Whitechapel. The atmosphere was heavy and morbid, an atmosphere you could cut with a knife, a lurking dread that gnawed at the nerves, vexed the mind and might, with the slightest excuse, would topple over into collective madness. If they had the bad luck in such a noxious climate of revealing to the neighborhood that the woman slayer was one of the dirty cops they despised, the reaction of the crowd would soon get out of control: the swelling hatred, then the fury would turn into a tidal wave and the police stations would be assaulted, the officers lynched—carnage everywhere!

"That's what Gregson explained to Lestrade. Now that the damned thing was done, they couldn't change it but above all—above all!—they had to keep quiet! And, if possible, make an effort to act like normal policemen. It took them almost an hour, but with a persuasive speech—and a few swigs of whiskey—they managed to restore a little energy to Lestrade, enough at least for him to forget about surrendering, am honorable but suicidal idea."

"Holmes, don't you find it shocking how easily policemen, who are not novices for sure, could break the law in a heartbeat like seasoned veterans of crime."

"But they are seasoned veterans of crime, Watson!"

"The crimes of others!"

"It's still crime. Besides, what never changed is that none of them at any time acted for personal profit. They broke the law, yes, but in the interest of the public good, which is the purpose of the law, an approach that was radically different from Warren's. In the end, as the saying goes, 'The first step is the hardest.' That's what Lestrade had taken. Almost in spite of themselves, Gregson and Patterson took the second, whereby they went from involuntary witnesses to active accomplices. All that was left was to take the third, which would make them offenders."

"A giant step, Holmes! Do you find it so natural?"

"The beauty of the Devil, my friend, is not a concept reserved for theological debates. There is pleasure in doing what's forbidden, otherwise crime would be just a crude, unexciting act. This murky pleasure is more subtle still in our case here, insofar as the protagonists have one foot on each side of the fence. Gregson and Patterson were not so reluctant to participate because Lestrade's guilt didn't weigh heavily on their shoulders. Remorse was not for them. Not yet...

"Little by little they would get intoxicated by the whirlwind of emotion and commotion that their colleague's action caused. Day after day. 'Leather Apron' kept making headlines. The alarmist or outrageous articles poured out one after another. He became the main subject of conversation in London and in port taverns, where they evoked his name with fear and respect, in salons where he made the ladies at teatime shiver deliciously with horror. Buckingham Palace itself was affected by the common phobia. The Queen wanted to stay personally informed about the development of the investigation and, through her home secretary, sent countless notes to Warren, whose situation was turning more and more uncomfortable.

"Gregson and Patterson were forced to recognize that Lestrade's crazy action was working its magic. They delighted in the worry that surfaced on the face of the Police Commissioner, a face that formerly abused them and left them helpless and bitter. In the stations, they started playing darts and the target was the latest cartoon of the chief cut out of the *Star*, or of Anderson hunting daisies. Then the reporters came to question the two inspectors about the 'monster' and they became talkative right away, painting a melodramatic picture of the bestial ferocity and diabolical cold-bloodedness of the elusive human tiger. That was their first contribution to the Ripper myth.

"The idea of going further came when Warren smeared himself with ridicule by bringing huge hunting dogs into Whitechapel to sniff out the killer's trail. In a reeking district that has a slaughterhouse or butcher shop on every block, the scent-crazed dogs ran off terrorizing half the residents before vanishing into the wild. The next day, the wanted posters for these poor animals made the capital break out laughing. The branch on which Warren was perched was starting to crack wide open. A branch that one good swipe of a sharp blade could snap in two.

"A blade like the Ripper's.

"Gregson and Patterson approached Lestrade again, dropping some hints, first rather vague, then more and more obvious... but with his conscience overwrought, he turned a deaf ear. They insisted, showed him the almost flattering article by George Bernard Shaw, suggesting that it would be a pity to give up when so close to the goal, that this poor Dark Annie would have died for nothing and that he, Lestrade, was making a good show for a little no-account murder. Without results. In desperation, they offered him a magnificent full-sized portrait of Sir Charles Warren smiling in his golden frame... The effect was instantaneous. It took them almost fifteen minutes to calm Lestrade and keep him from jumping feet first through what remained of the damaged painting. They had succeeded: the Ripper was reborn!

"But this time, it wouldn't be a hasty act committed on the spur of the moment. After the firecracker, they needed a bomb. They needed to shock popular opinion and leave the city speechless with fear, gasping in horror and dread, and burying Warren for good. For this, they couldn't be satisfied with the ghostly Leather Apron. They had to stamp the image of the real Mr. Hyde on people's minds, a pure, satanic incarnation capable of openly taunting the authorities, of announcing his attack and striking in the midst of the biggest concentration of policemen, of acting like the forces of order didn't exist... You look doubtful, Watson. What's bothering you?"

"By Jove, I admit that I can see how the letters and posters came in handy, but honestly, I have a hard time picturing one of your three musketeers writing them. I mean that Jack the Ripper's style is so unlike what you'd expect from a civil servant."

"Excellent observation, Watson. The sarcastic spirit of an evil imp, relishing in provocation, skillfully manipulating bitter irony in the style of a professional."

"A professional!"

"A playwright without fame or money, whom Patterson went to find. On his own initiative and most surely the only real bold stroke in the entire affair."

"Or pure madness."

"I won't deny that. Fate would have it that he found the only man probably in all of Great Britain who could be tempted to participate in such a twisted story, but one which was too seductive to the person's murderous sense of humor and apathy."

"But it was a great risk!"

"Patterson, as I was led to believe, would have presented it as a hoax meant to flush out the murderer, but I don't think he could have fooled him. I think rather that, as a playwright, and especially as an Irishman, the author couldn't resist the desire to bring the stage to life and avenge himself at the same time on the English who ignored his genius."

"His name?"

"What does it matter? As far as I know, he's still poor and controversial, although a little less anonymous, perhaps. Let's call him Bugle or Horn since the Ripper must have a scratchy, howling, coarse voice."

"Don't be ridiculous," I was disappointed.

"Well, let's close this parenthesis and move on to that memorable night of September 29. Here, my friend, you're going to lose another illusion because he who, with hindsight, looks like a model of sadistic efficiency, a bloody jewel, a black hymn to the glory of crime, only by happenstance ended in a resounding flop."

"You're referring to the steward who almost caught Lestrade?"

"The steward almost caught nothing at all. It was worse than that. I myself, at the time, believed that I saw a diversion in the first murder, the killer using the crowd's confusion to walk calmly away, a little farther on, to slaughter his second victim in good order... That was giving the Ripper an intelligence and determination worthy of the late Moriarty himself. The truth is less exciting: Lestrade buckled under.

"In spite of the enthusiastic support of Gregson and Patterson, he had attacked the night in a trance, tormented by anxiety. All his will could not chase away the image of Annie Chapman, which wouldn't stop haunting him. Hesitant and nauseous, he wandered aimlessly through the dark and seedy alleys. It was already past midnight when a hoarse, stammering voice called out to him from the shadows, an awkward call that promised him an overused but cheap paradise. Lestrade was tortured. Did he have the strength? *Don't think about it,* he repeated to himself, *don't think about it. Think about your friends, only them!* He let himself be dragged away by the blurry shadow, closed his eyes... When he opened them again, Long Liz Stride was lying at his feet with her throat slit.

"Then he was awash in an overwhelming disgust for himself. He started trembling, broke out in a cold sweat... and he ran away. A burst of conversation slowed him down. A desperate wreck, more dejected than a beaten dog, he walked blindly, lugging around his pitiful confusion like a ball and chain, instinctively avoiding the pools of light that the few lamps cast upon his path of darkness.

"He was well known to the policemen and vigilantes, but whoever he passed only glanced at him, figuring his silence was due to the tension in the neighborhood. In the surrounding darkness, none of them thought of pointing their lamps at him and nobody, therefore, saw his blood-splattered hands. He himself was only looking at Dorset Street. He hurried to wash his hands in a sink and, after sprinkling his face, a single idea arose out of his mental confusion: forget about everything and go home. That was probably what he would have done if a vicious destiny had not put old Kate Eddowes in his way. And she really had to make an effort. Just coming out of a gin-soaked sleep at the Bishopgate's post office, far from being completely sober, she was bound to do the one stupid thing she shouldn't. The last also.

"She recognized Lestrade and figuring he was slinking around out of fear of the Ripper, she started making fun of him and heaping insults on him. 'Yer scared stiff, eh? she yapped. 'Yer runnin' off to hide somewhere, is that it? When your beating up the poor, yer a fine one but when the game's a lil big, aye, there's no one around.'

"Lestrade tried to pass by her but she grabbed his coat and sneered, 'Eh, don't think you can run away like that, big boy! Yer just a sissy, I'm telling you! Got nothing in your shorts! You git me, eh, you dirty rat.'

"In the distance, some night owls were approaching. Lestrade swung around, caught a glimpse of officer Watkins coming out of Mitre Square and heading in the opposite direction. 'Nothing in my shorts? Come closer and I'll show you,' he muttered, heading for the small square.

"The old lush followed him, suspecting that by ribbing him, she had snapped him out of his lethargy, sparking his shame for almost failing his mission, a shame that was now stronger than his remorse. 'Stop, you got me,' she taunted. 'Eh, it's two shillings! No gift since I don't need you to defend meself! Even this damn bastard ripper can come if he wants! He'll see who he's dealing with, the swine!'

"Lestrade, who had stopped in the middle of the deserted little square, was nothing like the pathetic wandering dog, trembling and confused, a few minutes earlier. His eyes were blank as they stared at, without seeing, the worn-out, red-faced bat spitting her pathetic venom. Not even a caricature of a woman... a bitch in heat, maybe? Yes, that was it, nothing but a wrinkled old bitch who talked far too much.

"Katherine Eddowes let out one last smutty sarcasm, then a glint of metal flashed while Lestrade let his anger overtake him. Constable Watkins, who was making another round, missed catching him at work. Lestrade barely had time to jump around a corner into the shadows.

"As Watkins leaned over the corpse, he snuck out of Mitre Square but didn't dare run over the loud pavement, choosing instead to hide in the darkness of a carriage entrance. So, only then did he realize that he held something warm and spongy in his hand. His heart was racing, but his lucidity, jolted by the danger and the urgency, was sharper than ever. He knew what he had to do.

"While frantic whistle blowing echoed through the night, he acted without hesitation. He dropped his knife and the soft thing into his pockets, wiped his hands on his bloody jacket, took it off, turned it inside out and put it back on. He barely got his gloves on when the first boots came echoing down the road. He came haughtily out of the shadows and went to meet the officers running towards him, barking a few orders to guard all exits. After this, he hurried over to Watkins as if he had just arrived at the scene."

"Incredible," I said as Holmes stopped talking to light his pipe. "The whole trick hinged on his reversible clothing."

"The simplest things are always the most effective. Gregson's idea, by the way. The old foxes often have a nose for these kinds of things."

"But the soft thing Lestrade was carrying?"

"Watson, you're sleeping! It was the famous missing liver, half of which would be sent in the mail a few days later to the head of the vigilante committee. Would it be useful for me to linger over the consequences of this double murder? The outcry was absolutely fantastic. London started looking like a huge insane asylum. The journalists jumped on the new 'exploit' like pirates on a Spanish galleon. The morbid passion burst out of the British Iles and the name of Jack the Ripper—since this was what he called himself—spread like wildfire across Europe and the whole civilized world.

"It was not difficult to see who was going to pay the price for the scandalous glory that was so unflattering to the Crown and its police. Sir Robert Anderson saw his vacation plans ruined for good. As for Warren, although they held back from demanding his immediate resignation, it was only for the sake of propriety. With the public condemnation, his expulsion was inevitable and planned. Jack the Ripper could now stow away his cutlery in the prop museum and abandon his cynical specter to the tormented dreams of the storytellers. That's the whole affair, Watson."

I looked at Holmes without trying to hide my astonishment.

"Well, wait a second. The whole affair, you say? You're joking. What do you make of the grand finale, the last murder, the most gruesome, that of Mary Kelly?"

"Oh, that one," Holmes replied, looking at his pipe wearily. "Just a minor detail."

I was flabbergasted.

"A body that the doctors had to work on for more than six hours to give it a human appearance… you call that a minor detail!"

For some reason I could not fathom Holmes seemed uncomfortable talking about it.

"To push it might not be a good idea, Watson."

"Holmes, I want to know!"

"I warned you," he sighed. "First of all, the Ripper never took credit for this crime."

"And yet, the technique was the same."

"Let's say that the resemblance was rather convincing indeed. Secondly, since it's obvious that you're aware of the coroner's report, something about Mary Kelly's state should have gotten you thinking."

"You mean, the state in which the butcher left her?"

"No, irrespective of the murder."

I struggled to remember.

"Well, outside of the fact that, contrary to her sisters in misfortune, the girl was young and very pretty…"

"…And pregnant, Watson," Holmes finished with a half-smile.

Now it came back to me.

"Oh, I see where you're coming from. The same old song, right? A shameful liaison, incriminating fruit…"

"Exactly. And its twin brother—blackmail, if the presumed culprit had a pretty little fortune or a bright future. You can be certain that Mary Jane Kelly was not the kind to let such a windfall escape and she meant to get a cozy little place in the sun out of it."

"How can you be so sure?"

Again, Holmes looked hesitant.

"Keep this to yourself," he said reluctantly. "At that time, my brother Mycroft had to face a similar problem resulting from a weak and foolhardy moment with a little hussy like that. No, believe me, the girl only got what she deserved."

"Holmes!" I started, indignant.

What he was saying offended me almost as much as his apparent lack of coherence. But I was bound to be blind to the end. However, Holmes' attitude was nothing less than natural: the excited glare and the weird stare in his eyes, that mixed expression of fear and defiance that I had never seen before and the nervous tic in the corner of his mouth—all these details should have alerted me. Instead I said flatly:

"That's a little harsh. Besides, you didn't answer my question."

"Ha! The truth!" he had a cold grin. "The sacrosanct, unvarnished truth! You want it all, don't you?"

"My God, I would like to understand," I confessed with appalling naivety.

But how could I ever have imagined hearing these words that would haunt me to my dying day? These revolting, sickening words, more frightful than in the worst drunken nightmare.

"Well, too bad for you," Holmes' now almost unrecognizable voice sneered. "Knowing what I knew, it was obvious that a crime committed in November '88 in the style of the Ripper would be automatically blamed on him and that no investigator would take the trouble to go searching any farther. What do you want, Watson? There are favors that I cannot refuse my brother… And then, just between us," he added nonchalantly while I looked on aghast, "haven't I earned the right to let off a little steam too?"

After such a blow, being thunderstruck and unable to utter a sound, with my poor little brain paralyzed, gone soft and trembling like jelly, I sank into a kind of trance. After an indeterminate time, I snapped out of it and automatically reached for my medical bag to take out some objects that jingled softly.

"Come now, Watson," I heard through a thick fog, "put away that cocaine. You know very well that I stopped using such measures."

Without answering I filled the syringe and struggled to my feet. With faltering but determined steps I reached my room, locking the door behind me, carefully took off my coat and sat on the bed.

Very far away, on the other side of the door, the ironic voice of a violin started up, distorting an old and sinister lament:

*"It's been a day ripper, One-Way ticket's knife..."*

I rolled up my shirtsleeve.

### Baker Street, November 9, 1933

After he finished reading, young Tom Wills looked up. He looked so stupefied and devastated that Harry Dickson, the famous detective, could not hold back his laughter.

It was one of those very rare free evenings when crime sometimes granted the righter of wrongs a brief respite. The approach of winter seemed to have swallowed even the crooks in London and Mrs. Crown, their housekeeper, had cooked up a dinner worthy of a prince.

After the feast, the young assistant had asked for the opinion of his master about a theory that the press was batting around, according to which the blood-thirsty Jack the Ripper must have been a Frenchman. According to the article in the *Daily Mirror*, a certain Dr. Drum had proven that the Whitechapel killer showed symptoms identical with those produced by the abuse of absinthe, the typically French liquor that had once so ravaged the frog eaters.

Dickson was amused for a few moments but, as Tom seemed determined not to change the subject, he had finally got up and gone into the library. He came back two minutes later with a bundle of yellowing paper that he handed to his student.

"This, dear Tom, is a rare gift that Arthur Conan Doyle gave to me a little before his death. Since this old mystery fascinates you, I leave it to you to find the truth regarding the terrible Jack the Ripper."

While the delighted young man started devouring the manuscript, Harry Dickson nestled into his armchair next to the fireplace, his feet stretched out to the flame and his Navy Cut pipe in his mouth. The fierce, determined avenger lost himself in the delicate poetry of Samuel Smiles.

"Come on, Tom, don't look like that. I'd swear you'd just met Count Dragomin in person."

The young assistant was too stunned to return the jibe. Instead, he stammered:

"Boss, this is… it's monstrous, abominable, it's…"

"Spare me your exaggerations," Dickson cut in, laughing, "and have some more of that excellent cake that Mrs. Crown left us. We shouldn't upset her."

"Thank you, but I think that what I've just read will ruin my appetite for a month."

"Bah! You've become too sensitive."

"Still," the young man protested, "finding out that Sherlock Holmes, the great Holmes, doubled as a vile murderer!"

"And a trifle like that put you in such a state?" Dickson poked fun.

"A trifle? A man whom I've always admired, whom I revered like… like a spiritual father, a model, a exemplar of righteousness, of self-sacrifice, of honesty… what a deception!"

Hearing his assistant's voice tremble, Harry Dickson felt that his emotion had brought him to the brink of tears.

"Think, Tom! Think!" he said coldly.

Spoken curtly, these words had the effect of a cold shower on the young man. He opened his stunned eyes widely.

"What is there to think about? I don't understand."

"That's the tragedy," Dickson smiled. "You don't understand, you don't see, you don't think! As usual, you let your impetuosity get the better of the most basic prudence, including intellectual prudence."

"But this story…"

Harry Dickson settled into his armchair.

"Tom, do you know the meaning of the expression: to lead someone up the garden path?"

"Of course, but I don't see what…"

"Think, I said! Do you think that, after a revelation like that, Dr. Watson could have put up with being around Holmes for even one more day?"

"I… I guess not."

"And yet, their life together lasted until 1903, the year when the old detective retired to South Downs to raise bees."

"You mean…?"

"That this so-called confession of Holmes was purely an invention of Watson."

"But why?"

"Because he realized that, on the pretext of revealing the secret of the Ripper, his friend had given him a crazy fable, a charlatan's tale."

"So the whole story was just a… a joke?" Tom was abashed.

"Exactly. I guess that since '88 Watson could not help but criticize Holmes for not investigating the monster of the East End. Holmes was irritated but, with his Victorian elegance, he couldn't tell his old partner, 'My friend, you're annoying me!' So, one fine day, he decided to fool him. He took the most unreasonable suspect of all, Lestrade, and had some fun turning him into Jack the Ripper. Starting from this premise, he constructed an entire saga, cleverly of course, and seemingly logical, but totally fictitious. Honestly, Tom, have you ever heard such an outlandish motive? Killing prostitutes to ruin the career and reputation of the police commissioner! Not to mention the outrageous idea that Bernard Shaw would write the letters signed Jack the Ripper."

"George Bernard Shaw?"

"I quote: 'Let's call him Bugle or Horn.' At that time, Shaw wrote musical reviews for *The Star* under the pseudonym Corno di Bassetto. Holmes went really too far there, and, of course, Watson, being occasionally a little slow, but far from stupid, understood that his friend was feeding him a huge lie. I quote him speaking about Holmes: 'Like some people get drunk on wine, he got intoxicated on pure logic to the point of supporting the most stupefying paradoxes for the sole pleasure of the game.' This remark wasn't made by chance. Also, by recording this ridiculous story Watson, in a feat of good-natured vengeance, didn't hold back from ending it with a scathing finale of his own invention—the very one that shook you up so much?"

"But then, why tell me that I'd find the truth about Jack the Ripper in it?"

"Ah, simply because it's there. Very unexpected and only briefly, I admit, but it's there. Of course, this story was just a game between two old partners, and even though it was never meant for publication, it's just possible that, in some distant future, it might be seen by someone. Although Holmes told Watson nothing about it, he was fully aware of the secret identity of Jack of Ripper. Since he had his pride as a detective, and he didn't want, even post mortem, to come off as a common jokester, he took care to slip in a pretty clear reference for those who, in 30, 50 or 100 years, would know the truth about the Ripper, and, upon reading this story. would understand that he, Sherlock Holmes, knew it too."

"A reference, you say?"

"A short but meaningful passage for whoever can read between the lines. Remember, Tom, that after talking about the first two murders, Holmes admitted that, at this point in the investigation, the killer could be almost anyone. And he went through a series of suspects, half in jest and half in earnest, among whom was 'a pervert, tired of orgies and drugs, but physiologically unable to have intimate relations with the pure young girl he fell in love with and using these savage crimes as a kind of psychic aphrodisiac or an outlet for his agony.' That's rather accurate for a random hypothesis, isn't it?"

"Accurate, accurate, that's only your point of view," replied Tom, looking doubtful.

"Get your brain working, your lazy boy. We know a few things about the Ripper. Firstly, the police would never give his name and would probably never even arrest him. We can rightfully deduce that he wasn't just anyone—far from it. Secondly, in the beginning of February 1889, in Whitechapel, when a head of the vigilante committee got worried that the police would do away with their security measures, he was sworn to secrecy that they were certain that Jack the Ripper had killed himself. Now, to sum up: a very prominent but unstable person, delving in drugs and wild parties, who would fall madly in love with a young woman, almost a girl, and who would commit suicide in December '88 or maybe January '89... Really, Tom, doesn't that remind you of anyone?"

The young assistant suddenly turned as pale as wax.

"My God," he muttered. "My God... Mayerling!"[3]

"Shush, Tom," Dickson whispered. "In an affair like this, one name, even the name of a place, is already one too many."

"But why? Why after more than forty years not reveal the truth to the world?"

Harry Dickson started laughing.

"To destroy at once, just by relating them, two of the biggest mysteries of the modern age? My young friend, the fans would never forgive us! Even the shoeshine boys down at Victoria Station would stop reading our adventures."

A few hours later, while Tom Wills was sound asleep, a tall, dark silhouette slipped silently into his room. Dickson smiled paternally and leaned over the peaceful face that sleep made look even younger.

"Ah, the young," it whispered so quietly that it was like a sigh from some forgotten world, "how I love your idealism... but you'll believe anything as long as we spare your gods!"

Then, as the cuckoo poked out its head to announce two o'clock, Harry Dickson gave it a quiet "shh!" along with a knowing wink and tiptoed back out of the room.

*Translation by Michael Shreve*

---

[3] The Mayerling Incident is the series of events leading to the apparent murder–suicide of Crown Prince Rudolf of Austria and his lover, Baroness Mary Vetsera. Rudolf was the only son of Emperor Franz Josef I of Austria and Empress Elisabeth, and heir to the throne of the Austrian-Hungarian Empire. Rudolf's mistress was the daughter of Baron Albin Vetsera, a diplomat at the Austrian court. The bodies of the 30-year-old Archduke and the 17-year-old baroness were discovered in the Imperial hunting lodge at Mayerling in the Vienna Woods, fifteen miles southwest of the capital, on the morning of 30 January 1889.

*Christofer Nigro introduced the character of Felanthus, Felifax's brother, in our last installment of* Tales of the Shadowmen. *He continues to chronicle his adventures here, teaming him up with Judex (who met Felifax in "Eye of the Tiger-Man" in* The Shadow of Judex*) and pitting him against the villainous Dr. Cornelius Kramm from Gustave Le Rouge's* Mysterious Doctor Cornelius...

## Christofer Nigro: *Justice and the Beast*

*Paris, August 1936*

The underground laboratory was lit by an unusual luminescent silicate imbedded within the rock from which the walls were built. This provided the large chamber with an eerie ambience, which was quite apropos considering the nature and purpose of the two scientists having an amicable but tense conversation over cups of the finest imported herbal tea.

Professor Tornada's shiny bald head was wracked with its distinctive series of jarring tics as he spoke to his newest comrade-in-arms.

"I am thinking this pooling of our resources in such a manner over the past five months has borne resplendent fruit for both our operations, *n'est-ce-pas?*"

Dr. Cornelius Kramm took a sip of his steaming tea while appearing to keep a cautious gaze on his unnerving ally.

"My brother Fritz and I agree with you for the nonce, Tornada. This arena of ours has been a marvelous way to earn a sizable degree of money to fund the operations of both the Red Hand... and your own endeavors, of course. The substantial percentage that is allocated to my own scientific experiments is a boon to both our profit margins and the overall advancement of knowledge."

"Ha!" Tornada saluted Cornelius with his tea cup. "To the advancement of human knowledge indeed! That is what science is ultimately designed for. The pursuit of material advancement should be but a secondary fringe benefit, and of mere necessity to continue funding the quest for progress."

"To the contrary, Professor," Cornelius glowered. "Advancement of the human species is certainly an important goal, but profit is what drives the civilization we have established. Its importance must never be downplayed, for all the progress we achieve must remain primarily accessible to those who sit at the top of the fiscal food chain. Or are you perhaps a supporter of that recently elected imbecile Blum and his petty charitable institution posing as a political party?"

"*Pour l'amour de Dieu*, most certainly not! Compassion and morals have long been an impediment to progress, and you can rest assured I have no love for Blum's Popular Front! It is equivalent to having Poincaré take the office a *third* time, *Dieu nous protège!* I fully concede which direction the cash must always flow, as those of our contributions have every right to live above the rabble."

Cornelius's edgy glare softened.

"That level of agreement between us will suffice."

"*Parfait*! Ha ha!"

Tornada's spastic movements while laughing caused him to knock over his cup and spill the remainder of his tea on Cornelius's lap. He made no effort to apologize or even acknowledge the accident before jumping onto the next topic.

"So, Dr. Kramm, are you impressed with the incandescent silicate that some of my laborers discovered in that subterranean cavern in Egypt? It was the same locale they retrieved that strange humanoid creature who makes up one of the reluctant gladiators of our arena. You never gave me due appreciation for the vast amount of lucre that saves us in electricity."

"Because I would actually have preferred resorting to the expense of electricity, as the illumination provided by that silica of yours is inadequate by comparison. And you say there are remnants of a Sumerian civilization in these subterranean caverns along with creatures such as that... mole-like man you brought back for the arena?"

"Oh yes, but that is my discovery, Doctor, so let us have no more words about that, save for its applicability to our joint project. Now that we know how many wealthy Parisians are willing to pay so exquisitely to see such creatures battling each other to the death, we must continuously find more 'gladiators' to replace those killed or too maimed to recover."

Cornelius huffed in annoyance.

"Very well. On that front, my studies of those Deep Ones inhabiting the ocean of the northeastern United States have borne much metaphorical gold. The ease with which their genome splices with the chromosomes of virtually all other organisms on this planet is remarkable. The gene seeding project resulting from those studies in Brazil have spawned an able combatant for the Arena: a fresh water dwelling creature resembling a humanoid cephalopod similar to the more intelligent breed inhabiting those caverns near 'Dead Man's Point' in the U.S. state of Florida."

"*Magnifique*! How did you develop that creature so quickly?"

"It appears that the Deep Ones' highly adaptive genome can be stimulated with repeated bursts of a few exotic frequencies of radiation. Prolonged exposure to large amounts of conventional radiation will also stimulate their development, but that route takes far too long. We needed a new contestant with due promptness. The renewal of our supply of combatants demands no less."

"And speaking of unique frequencies of radiation, those queer meteorites that have bombarded the Earth at periodic intervals throughout human history are wondrous sources for such genome-altering energies. They appear to materialize in the planet's orbit from some type of spatial disturbance I have yet to fully understand, but which may open portals to alternate planes of reality, or far off locations in space. I have christened it the Gordian Anomaly after the colleague who discovered it and revealed its existence to me."

Cornelius looked genuinely fascinated by the mention of these strange rocks from space.

"That may well explain why these specific meteors do not fully burn away in the friction of the planet's atmosphere. One of them is allegedly responsible for the enhancements seen in certain lineages connected to a group who were in close proximity to such a landed rock in Wold Newton, England, over a century past. Another has just recently been retrieved by my former colleague, Dr. Alex Zorka, who refuses to share samples of it with me or anyone else. The narcissistic bastard! Little is he aware that I informed many governments about that rock in his possession."

"Ha, good retribution there, *mon ami*! I have my protégé, Dr. Nolter, to thank for one of our most intriguing additions to our roster of monstrous combatants. This is connected to his work in combining the genetic material of plants to animal physiognomy. You will likewise marvel at another of my recent acquisitions, a creature I had captured for study on a previous occasion."

"I look forward to the unveiling, Tornada. Just make sure this new acquisition is revealed to me before tomorrow has ended."

Felanthus opened his eyes wearily as the noble beast-man returned to consciousness. The product of an early pioneer in genetic engineering inseminating an Indian woman with an altered zygote that combined human and tiger DNA, the feline senses he possessed were more than adequate to discern the nature of the surroundings he now found himself in. His slit-like pupils in the center of yellowish-green irises could detect heat patterns beyond the visible spectrum. But all he could see was a cage with no heat emissions beyond his own body.

He lifted his sensitive cat-like nose and sniffed the air. Several strange scents beyond the musky odor of his cage were detectable, all of which were nothing like any human or lower animal he had ever encountered during the days he ran loose in the forests of Britain. These scents were clearly from disparate entities, but all utterly alien and thus unsettling to him. His keen ears suddenly perceived the sound of human footsteps echoing in his direction. He stirred and snarled with rage when the scent of one of the two human beings now approaching him proved hatefully familiar.

"*Bonjour, mon ami,*" the voice of Prof. Tornada said as he stepped in front of the cage beside Dr. Cornelius. "I thought you were lost to the world forever after I heard you had fallen into that chasm during your struggle with Gouroull.[4] All believed you had died, even Felifax, that meddling beautiful brother of yours who sought you out and ruined my previous enterprise in the course of freeing you.

---

[4] See *The Noble Freak* in *Tales of the Shadowmen 11*.

196

"But my knowledge of geology made me realize there was a possibility you didn't plummet all the way to the bottom of the chasm. Indeed, the search party I organized found you laying on a large precipice a mere twelve meters down in a state of catatonia. With an emphasis on the word *cat*. Ha ha!"

The hairless scientist elbowed Cornelius to emphasize the pun he had just made.

"Your immature grasps at humor are wasting my time, Tornada! The ministrations you gave to this cat-like man to enable him to recover from his injured state are admittedly impressive, though. And you say this beast is actually Felifax's sibling? Remarkable!"

"And I assure you that he will prove a most formidable addition to our stable of monstrous gladiators..."

Tornada was cut off as the enraged man-tiger hurled himself against the steel bars of the cage. The two scientists leapt back as Felanthus made a loud clanging sound upon hitting the metal barrier. The bars held fast, but the cat man still managed to slash through Cornelius's lab coat, leaving a long bloody gash on his left arm.

"Arrgh! Tornada, your beast slashed me! The creature has just signed its death warrant!"

The co-leader of the dreaded Red Hand pulled out a World War I Luger and pointed the firearm at his attacker and pulled the trigger. But the shot went wild and bounced off the hard strata of the far walls as Tornada grabbed his colleague's arm and spoiled his aim.

"Cornelius, what do you think you're doing? This animal-man is a prize to us! Are you not man enough to endure a small scratch on the arm?"

Cornelius wrenched his limb free of Tornada and utilized every iota of his willpower to resist pointing the firearm at him. Both scientists held fast with their simultaneous scowls of dominance, which appeared to cancel each other out. The seeming impasse ended a moment later when Cornelius slowly holstered his Luger; he then squeezed his badly torn arm as hard as he could to staunch the bleeding until he could get the wound stitched.

"Very well. But if this animal so much as hisses at me again, I will have him gutted right before your eyes. And I will make you eat all of the entrails that spill onto the floor, understood?"

Tornada's head gave a slight tic as he gritted his teeth while maintaining his unwavering glare upon Cornelius's anger-ridden eyes.

"Yes, I quite understand, Doctor. But we shall see which creature is triumphant in the Arena, and you will be quite grateful to me for staying your hand."

Jacques de Tremeuse sat quietly before the dancing flames of the fireplace that occupied a prominent space in the middle of his huge den. He had his elbows on his office desk while a pensive expression adorned his still young-looking visage.

Much had happened over the past few years to this man who had devoted a good 20 years of his life to meting out justice to the forces of evil. He had thus taken to spending his quiet moments reflecting on all he had gained and lost during that time. He was only interrupted from his meditative musings with a knock on the oaken doors that separated his den from the rest of his stately manse.

"Jacques, it's me," he heard a familiar voice utter from the opposite side of the doors.

It was none other than Detective Cocantin, a young man who had been a trusted friend and resourceful ally ever since his childhood when he was known as the Licorice Kid.

"I know you don't like being bothered by anyone lately," said Cocantin, "but I was just handed something by one of my trusty contacts that you really should see."

Jacques peered at the door silently for a moment, as if debating whether he should respond even to such a valued visitor.

"Please do come in, *mon ami*. My apologies for this seclusion."

"No apology necessary," the detective told him with a rascally smile as he entered the room. "I sure know all that you've been through, since I was there, and..."

"Please give me this important information before you step into an unrelated tangent."

"Hmf. OK, if that's how you're gonna be. Take a look at this."

Tremeuse was handed an elegantly embroidered invitation to some event scheduled the following night at a secretive location called "The Arena." It was obvious to him that this was a highly exclusive show, something only offered to a portion of the wealthiest citizens of Paris. Though he was indeed among those ranks, he was never considered as being part of the more decadent faction. This forced him to wonder why he was suddenly trusted with an invitation to such an exclusive event, which had obviously been going on for an extended period of time without catching his attention before now.

*I must find out what this mysterious 'Arena' may be,* he immediately thought. *Something about it bodes quite ill to me.*

"What information do you have on this 'Arena'?"

"Not much at all, since it's been kept hidden from my eyes for a while now. But don't worry, I have my contacts on the street and in the police working on this, and when have I ever failed to deliver the goods before, huh?"

"*Très bien.* In the meanwhile, I shall begin cleaning my firearms and salvaging my hat and cloak from where they have been languishing in storage for too long now."

The following evening a chained Felanthus found himself prodded by several armed guards through a corridor which led directly to the sprawling Arena. The tiger-man resisted as much as could be expected, but the searing pain caused by the touch of the electric prods provided for these security guards by Dr. Cornelius nevertheless prompted him forward.

Alongside him, also in chains, was the subterranean entity that Cornelius had referred to as the "mole-like man." This creature, christened Burrkos by Tornada, was distinguished by a thick, tan exo-skeletal layer of chitin covering his entire roughly human-shaped body, further differentiated by a pronounced hump on his back. The creature also boasted round black against green eyes, no body hair, and very large spade-like hands with extremely long and thick talons protruding from each finger like stone-sharpened daggers. This being seemed quite intelligent, and was actually clothed in a flowing robe-like garment, but he uttered incomprehensible sounds which didn't resemble any human language that Felanthus had ever heard.

As the two hapless non-human combatants were forced towards the Arena, the keen hearing of the tiger-man caused him to cringe at the loud screaming throngs of the hundred wealthy Parisians cheering for the bloody slaughter to begin. Among those in attendance were Tornada and the brothers Kramm. Cornelius held a sophisticated microphone that enabled him to act as master of ceremonies. They were sitting in a special cubicle located in the center of the audience, separate from the crowd.

The basic construction of the Arena was much like that of an old Roman coliseum, with the audience seated in rows attached to an elevated stage that protected them from any possible attacks by the combatants. This modern version of an ancient coliseum likewise included the presence of several portals sealed by heavy wooden doors that could be automatically lifted to allow the conscripted gladiators to enter the main chamber, where the combat took place.

"I must concede to being impressed by your contribution to this team-based bout, Tornada," Cornelius admitted to his ally. "How did you happen to come by such a life form?"

"The Triffid is an ambulatory plant artificially created by certain Russian colleagues of mine who worked from Dr. Nolter's notes on radical alteration of predatory botanical life," Tornada explained. "They were among a handful of truly remarkable plant species developed by exposure to unique frequencies of radiation emitted by those mysterious meteorites which we discussed. Exposing apparently naturally evolved predatory botanical life such as the Venus fly-trap and cobra plants to a combination of such radiation frequencies and splicing with the recombinant DNA of certain carnivorous animal species, have yielded not only two different species of Triffid, but other large vegetal predators of more limited mobility.

"This includes preda-plants resembling larger fly traps and cobra plants, two species of black orchid with stinging tendrils similar to that of the Triffids, and a large Black Swamp flower that devours leopards and appears to have formed a strange symbiotic relationship with the crocodiles dwelling there. All of these have been seeded in the African continent, where they are able to survive quite well in such a tropical environment. They are not nearly as environmentally adaptive as the Triffid plants, unfortunately.

"The species of Triffid which will be engaging in combat here is a further evolution of those which merely utilize a deadly stinging tendril; this alternate species possesses the additional characteristic of grasping and tearing with their powerful limb-like branches."

"Most impressive!"

"You will see that the entirety of my work is impressive, Doctor."

"To those who lack your level of skill and accomplishment, no doubt. Now, let us begin the event which our customers have paid so handsomely to view."

Cornelius quickly checked the microphone to insure it was in proper working order, and his deep voice began blaring to the excited assemblage of debauched bourgeois who paid richly to see the spilling of blood.

"Esteemed ladies and gentlemen, that which you have eagerly awaited is now set to begin! This battle will feature two wondrous and deadly life forms pitted against two others in a four-way battle of primal supremacy.

"From the left of the Arena comes the Octaman, half-human, half-octopus, and all-lethal. Alongside this marvelous aquatic engine of destruction is the Triffid, a moving plant the size of a man that attacks and devours anything it encounters, which it will now attempt to do to its opposition, all for your viewing pleasure!

"As to that opposition, emerging from the right of the Arena is the savage beast called Felanthus, half-man, half-tiger, and fully prepared to kill anything that dares challenge it! Alongside him is Burrkos, a mighty and barbaric creature from beneath the Earth with claws sharper than a sword, who is eager to put those natural weapons of mayhem to good use for your entertainment value!"

The audience began roaring louder than the loudest beasts of the jungle, demanding death for reasons entirely unrelated to either the requirements of food or self-preservation. These people wanted blood for the sheer thrill and entertainment value of seeing it spilled, a trait that marks humans as all but unique amongst the Earth's fauna. This characteristic of the human race had long proved extremely useful for those like Cornelius and Tornada, whose relentless pursuit of profit and power absolutely depended upon exploiting the more loathsome aspects of the human species.

Felanthus and Burrkos would have preferred not to engage in such a ritual merely to amuse a group of humans, but the matter of self-preservation made it a necessity. After Cornelius provided the necessary signal, his guards on each side of the Arena prodded both sets of combatants into the center of the chamber, closed the doors behind them, and then opened their restricting chains by remote control. The battle was on.

The Octaman was the first to strike, emitting a hissing growl from a completely circular mouth ringed with numerous sharp teeth. Standing over seven feet tall, this octopoid possessed a huge rounded head and lidless orange eyes with vertical pupils. His skin was a grayish-blue with four long grasping, suction cup-covered tentacles—two each in place of where arms would be on a human being, whose form this creature partially imitated—on two thickly muscled human-shaped legs with a tentacle protruding from the back of them.

The tiger-man was determined to meet the amphibious monstrosity's attack with a powerful lunge of his own. Emitting a snarl of defiance, Felanthus leapt several meters at the Octaman, who quickly took the advantage by catching the felinoid in the grasp of all four tentacles, the suction cups biting into his skin.

Before the cat man could rake the twisting quartet of limbs with his claws, the intelligent octopoid effortlessly lifted Felanthus off the ground and slammed his hirsute form several times against the nearby stone wall. The man-cat was thoroughly dazed, and while he stood limp in the seemingly unbreakable arms of his semi-aquatic opponent, the Octaman moved in for the kill.

In the meantime, the mole man Burrkos took the initiative and rushed towards the Triffid. The botanical grotesquerie moved forward to meet the challenge slowly but methodically, its own set of four grasping limbs seeking to entwine its opponent. The steady clicking sound produced by the giant moving plant had an unsettling effect on all who heard it, but Burrkos's own wailing cries drowned it out as the battle was met.

The Triffid quickly caught both of Burrkos's arms as he attempted to slash it to pieces with his incredible talons. Though the mole-man's strength rivaled that of the plant, the latter was able to hold him in a single spot just long enough to project its deadly stinging tendril. The naturally armored warrior howled in agony after the plant's harpoon-like barb struck the middle of his forehead.

As the Octaman moved closer in an attempt to crush Felanthus to death in the unyielding grip of his tentacles, the cat-man used the strategy of what humans called "playing possum" to good effect. Though he was still unable to wrest his arms from the creature's four tentacles, the tiger-man quickly flipped his legs upwards and kicked forward so that the long claws on his toes punctured the pale blue flesh of his approaching adversary. He then quickly pulled his feet downwards, horizontally ripping open the creature's abdomen from the diaphragm to the bottom of his stomach. The octopoid screamed in agony while he involuntarily backed away and loosened the grip of his tentacles.

Taking advantage of this, Felanthus used the full degree of his superhuman musculature to pull free from the tube-like limbs and rush his opponent. Still determined to remain on his feet, the Octaman blindly swung his tentacles at the cat-man with incredible force.

However, the quick moving man-beast slumped down to all fours and ran underneath the flailing limbs, avoiding what would have been debilitating blows. The tiger-man then came up close to the creature's ripped abdomen, plunged his orange-furred hands deeply into the wound, and used his talons to tear the Octaman's gut completely open.

The beast wailed horrifically as his internal organs spilled onto the dirty ground with a sound resembling a wet towel being dropped. The octopoid gladiator fell to the floor unmoving, while the crowd cheered the triumphant Felanthus, who stood with blood and pieces of his opponent's viscera dripping from his claws.

A minute earlier, the Triffid discovered that it was unable to puncture its stinging barb all the way through Burrkos's chitinous armor, even at a typical weak point like the forehead region. It was thus unable to inject its agonizing venom into the mole-man's bloodstream.

Burrkos took full advantage of this by managing to wrap his fingers around the plant's tendril-like branches and tear through them with a combination of his razor-like talons and a heave of adrenaline-fueled strength. Greenish blood-like sap spewed out of the torn branches as Burrkos pressed the advantage and leapt at the Triffid. A second stab of its poisonous barb missed the intended mark of Burkkos's left eye, and the mole man swiftly slashed at the plant's head-like flowery bulb with his dagger-like claws. The plant released a disturbing wail that strongly resembled an animal screeching in pain, and the now mutilated botanic nightmare dropped to the ground in a large puddle of thick, chlorophyll-tinted liquid.

The audience continued to cheer to the point of seeming orgasm as the victorious mole man shook the green leafy debris from his claws.

For a moment, Felanthus and Burrkos stood back to back in preparation for opposing the attempts of the security guards to recapture them, but Cornelius had prepared for this eventuality. He had equipped the guards with guns which projected darts filled with the universal, physiology adaptive anesthetic he had developed. The compressed air mechanism that fired the tranquilizer darks sent the projectiles through the air fast enough to even penetrate Burrkos's thick exoskeleton. Within seconds, both man-monsters were rendered insensate, and able to be dragged away to their cages with no resistance.

Cornelius was quick to grab the microphone and bellow the closing monologue to the satiated crowd.

"And the winner of tonight's battle is... the team of Felanthus the Tiger-Man and Burrkos the Mole-Man! And what a spectacle it was, one such as only the Arena can provide to Paris's finest citizens!"

"It's really quite clever, if you ask me," Detective Cocantin said as he handed a manila envelope filled with much requested info to Tremeuse. "Not many people know of those caverns beneath the Louvre, so that was the perfect place for the Red Hand to build this Arena. There are many such underground locations beneath the streets of Paris. Do you think the Phantom of the Opera built all of those underground digs of his under the Garnier Opera House on his own? No, he just expanded on what was already there, and considering how the Louvre was first conceived as a military fortress, it should be no surprise that these caverns were under there too, just waiting for scoundrels like these guys to make use of them."

"If the Red Hand is involved in this venture, then it's certainly of no benefit to the people of Paris," said Judex, after he perused the handwritten notes with a look of deep concern. "And the additional involvement of Professor Tornada has me doubly certain that this operation needs to be stopped at once."

"Truth is, Jacques, I'm not sure those miscreants are really breaking the law. I mean, what laws protect, well, creatures like these from being forced into fighting? Cock and dog fights are held in all sorts of places across the world. Even I have enjoyed seeing the bull fights in Mexico when I went there. They were less harmful than the food, which did a real number on my bowels. I don't see you dispensing justice on the fools who make those burritos that give tourists the squirts—now *that* should be an international crime!"

"Your mirth has a place in this world, Cocantin, but it's ill-suited to understanding the matter at hand. The truth is that we know nothing about the nature of the beasts used to provide such entertainment to these Parisians who believe they stand above the masses."

"You mean, folks like yourself?"

"Not like me. I have dedicated my life to serving the greater good rather than the banal pursuit of profit. I do not use my financial position to indulge my darkest whims in a manner that is destructive to society."

"Oh really, Jacques?" said the detective smirking. "I think many may argue otherwise if they knew about certain, well, evening activities you have enjoyed engaging in."

"That is enough, young man. Your remarks suggest the same concerns your adopted father often expressed in the past, but the comparison is ill-suited. As you know, I've sacrificed much for my work as Judex, whereas these wealthy people who glean entertainment from this Arena have not."

"It's not important that we argue this out right now. What is important is that I'm not sure you can get the police to shut this operation down. Who knows how much money is being poured by those people into kicking Blum out of office and getting ready for the war with Germany? The Préfet de Police will have to consider the big picture..."

"This 'big picture' of yours matters not. Justice is a force above the laws of men. Further, keeping such strange creatures in the city may pose a potential threat of great magnitude. Of equal consideration is the fact that the anthropomorphic features of many of these beg the question of whether they are more than mere animals. I'm not certain why I was given this invitation, but since I have, I will attend the next event and put an end to this atrocity."

"I think you just want an excuse for another crack at Dr. Cornelius, but considering how much I've always hated that guy, I'm gonna give you my usual free pass. I'd help you more directly, but a guy in my position can't be seen down there. I could try one of those disguises of yours, but considering how I always flummoxed the acting thing before…"

"Your looking the other way is sufficient help, along with this precious information you've brought me. I shall handle this alone."

When the evening of the next event arrived, Judex found himself moving through some of the lesser known sections of the famed building known as the Louvre. As the world's largest museum, its vast size provided no difficulty in hiding ingress to any number of hidden locations, many of them harkening back to the building's distant past.

The honoring of his invitation required him to arrive not a second later than a specific time on the clock. Further, he had to be led down the passageway sequestered behind the De Vinci exhibit alongside the entire attendance roster of wealthy patrons who had received similar invitations. They were only allowed to advance single file into the underground passageways beneath the great museum as a group; a contingent of armed security guards escorted them every single step of the way. The reputation of the Red Hand was well-known and feared, and there was no doubt in the minds of anyone present that their security force would react to any breach of protocol quickly and without anything resembling mercy or deference to social status.

After a full twenty minutes of descending these musty passages, decorated with expensive paintings to break the barren nature of the caverns, they were guided into the main seating area of the Arena. It was deliberately designed to seat at most a hundred and fifty at a time, as clearly this was not a show intended for mass attendance.

Though he and the rest of the patrons were thoroughly searched for any possible weapons, Judex had long since designed firearms that could be disassembled into minute component parts and hidden in carefully stitched pockets throughout the entirety of his clothing. With hours of practice, he mastered the art of promptly retrieving each part and re-assembling them with a speed that would have impressed Hermes himself. The identifying black cloak, slouch hat, and other features of Judex's distinct apparel, were similarly hidden within an expensive tuxedo that was tailored specifically for this purpose.

Upon being seated, the vigilante forced back the desire to act immediately when Cornelius appeared in the center cubicle. He was accompanied by a strange-looking bald man of curious bodily movements that could be none other than one of the less scrupulous members of the legendary Tornada clan.

*Soon Lady Justice will have her reckoning with you,* Judex assured himself.

"Esteemed ladies and gentlemen," Cornelius blurted over the microphone. "We have quite an event planned for you this evening. The two winners of the previous contest will now be pitted against an assemblage of deadly gorillas culled from a hidden region of the Dark Continent and directly bred by their long gone handlers to be brutal killers, all for your glorious entertainment! Against such odds, can even the likes of Felanthus the Tiger-Man, the bestial sibling to the great Felifax of India, and Burrkos, the Mole-Man from beneath the Earth, possibly prevail?"

The expression on Judex's already dour countenance took on one of alarm.

*Did Cornelius just say that one of these creatures is a sibling of Felifax himself?*

Not only had the jungle lord of India become quite famous over the past few years—particularly following a spectacle-ridden celebration that occurred outside the Notre-Dame cathedral a few years previous—but Judex had encountered the noble and formidable Hindu champion many years earlier during a journey to India of great personal importance. Despite being in opposition that time, Felifax had earned his respect.

*If this creature is truly related to Felifax...*

In the center cubicle, Tornada couldn't help inquiring about Cornelius' latest acquisition for the Arena.

"Wherever did you find these incredible primate specimens? Despite popular conception and notable exceptional incidents, all who have studied the nature of gorillas are well aware that they are generally docile creatures who do not wantonly attack humans, or any other animals."

"These gorillas are no product of natural evolution," Cornelius responded. "Their genetic nature has been tampered with by ancient human hands, using scientific means that were well in advance of anything at my disposal... or yours, for that matter. A fledgling theory is that these simians may be remnants of ancient Lemurian genetic engineering, whose brilliant scientists mastered the science and developed very aggressive versions of common species for use as living weapons against their opponents from Atlantis. Aggressive simian species of many sizes and forms were created, and this may include the rarely seen giant Kongoid species.

"This particular synthetic species of apes, however, are slightly smaller than the two types known to conventional science, but faster as a result, and no less powerful. These remnants are descended from some abandoned specimens who somehow managed to establish a small breeding population in a very remote region of Africa long after Lemuria sank beneath the Pacific. They were later forced into servitude and put to use as guardians of the precious diamond mines owned by the kingdom of Zinj, whose civilization vanished two thousand years ago.

"I have further theorized that periodic inter-mating between these primates and conventional mountain gorillas may have resulted in persistent reports of seemingly common specimens who exhibited unusual degrees of aggressive behavior towards humans, and such genetic tampering may even have given rise to the now nearly extinct but highly intelligent primates known as the mangani."

205

"*Merveilleux*! I anxiously await seeing how our two champions fare against a troop of such gorillas! Ha! But remember, should the tiger-man not prevail, I will be given possession of whatever may remain of the creature for my own purposes, as promised."

"Of course, Tornada, there was no need for such a 'friendly' reminder. Now why not sit back and be entertained by what follows like the rest of our audience?"

Jacques de Tremeuse had seen many amazing things in his long career as Judex, including the likes of werewolves, vampires, demons, and gargoyles... but he still bore an expression of awe when he saw Felanthus and Burrkos forced into the combat chamber. As for their opposition, he had seen and faced killer gorillas before, but never of the type now released from their chains: these apes from the African region surrounding the ghost kingdom of Zinj were gray in fur and sleeker in build than familiar mountain or silver-backed gorillas, with the males of the species all but lacking the distinct cranial crest.

The six gray simians began hooting and slavering menacingly at the sight of the tiger-man and mole-man before them, and being accustomed to attacking in groups, they began surrounding the two.

Felanthus and Burrkos stood side by side, both prepared to meet this most formidable challenge. But they wouldn't be meeting it as a mere duo. Upon seeing what was about to occur, Tremeuse used his great skills of stealth to slip out of his seat in the auditorium section, locate a sufficiently darkened corner outside the sight of either the patrons or security guards, and quickly change into the garb of his dark alter ego. It took him mere moments to fully remove the components of his firearms and a nylon dagger from where they were hidden in the stitches of his clothing and fully assemble them.

The first of the six gray apes howled viciously and lumbered towards Felanthus with surprising speed on its knuckles and feet. The cat-man was equally fast, however, and he growled defiantly while slashing a chunk of flesh out of the gorilla's right cheek with his fearsome talons. The gorilla bellowed in pain and leapt back as blood spurted from its maimed face, while another took advantage of the distraction and leapt upon Felanthus from behind. The strength of this simian was incredible, and the felinoid warrior was slammed to the ground while his attacker prepared to pummel him with its pile driver fists.

Two of the other apes jumped on Burrkos, who wasn't fast enough to strike before they were upon him. They pounded the mole-man in unison, and the mighty being found himself battered to the ground by the display of primal strength directed against him. His thick exoskeleton-like dermis remained intact but still suffered a severe beating, and he struggled to gain some footing that would enable him to strike back.

Finally managing to do so, he put all of his fading energy into plunging his ultra-hard, several inch long claws into the throat of one of his adversaries. The ape let out a hoarse gurgling sound as blood spewed from the wound like a crimson mini-geyser, quickly expiring in the process. However, the other gorilla redoubled its efforts to keep up the attack, and another which waited on the sidelines rushed in to join the assault.

As Felanthus grappled furiously with the ape that leaped upon him from behind, the first attacker with the severely raked face re-entered the fray. But just then, behind the charcoal-haired simian, appeared a curiously human figure dressed entirely in black, his cloak billowing about him like the wings of a gigantic bird as he leapt a few meters from the wall separating the audience from the combat chamber.

Judex's well-honed legs took the impact of the landing well and he swiftly shot the ape through the back of its head, the bullet exiting from its gullet in a spatter of blood.

The tiger-man continued his brutal battle with the other ape under fairer conditions, and the two beasts rolled about the floor ripping and tearing at each other in a savage frenzy.

The two remaining gorillas moved towards the darkly attired newcomer with their usual impressive speed. Realizing the first would reach him before he could dispatch it with a shot, Judex back-flipped out of its path, just barely evading a crippling blow from its bludgeon-like arm. This maneuver put him in position of being attacked by the second ape, who grabbed him from behind in a steely grip, the likes of which Judex had rarely experienced before. He knew his ribs would be crushed within moments.

Seeing this strange intrusion into the combat section, the audience didn't know what to make of it, so their continued cheers were joined by queries of befuddlement. Cornelius, on the other hand, knew *exactly* what to make of it.

"Damn it all to Hell!" he shouted. "That's Judex!"

"*Bon Dieu!*" Tornada shouted. "How did that vigilante learn of the Arena?"

"How can I know, idiot? All of the invitations were sent by me alone, and I only sent them to reliable patrons whom I was certain knew the protocols of discretion! We need to make sure he does not leave this coliseum alive, or all is lost!"

"Do your best to make that happen, *mon ami*, but I think it's now time I take my leave. This arrangement of ours was fruitful while it lasted, but it's now clearly at an end."

Tornada shoved Cornelius aside and fled through the door leading out of the cubicle. The co-leader of the nefarious Red Hand shouted an obscenity and fired at him with his pistol, but the hastily aimed bullet bounced off the wall near the door just as the scientist slammed it shut.

*I'll deal with that treacherous fool later,* Cornelius thought. *Right now, I need to call Fritz and let him know that we must abandon this operation.*

Two minutes earlier, Felanthus brought his savage one-on-one battle with his simian adversary to a culmination when he finally gained enough ground to sink his knife-like teeth into the ape's throat and tore out its trachea with a single mighty heave.

As Judex was in the process of being crushed in the grip of his own attacker, he quickly positioned his firearm directly under the ape's chin and fired. The vigilante was showered with the primate's blood and brain matter as its grip on him was released. He was still nursing bruised ribs, however, and was thus unable to avoid the attack of the other ape waiting in the wings. The creature ran towards him with amazing speed and swatted him down, causing him to drop both of his firearms. He tried reaching for the dagger in his boot, but was prevented from drawing it when the ape leapt upon him.

All appeared to be lost until Felanthus, having just dispatched his own foe, lunged on the ape, the force of his assault knocking the beast off of Judex. Realizing the cat-man had consciously saved his life, the dark-garbed avenger pushed to his feet and retrieved his firearms.

He turned to see the other two apes pounding upon the now nearly unconscious mole-man. Feeling that this being was also more than a mere animal, Judex ran behind one of the apes and pressed the turrets of his pistols to the back of its skull. Both of the ape's eyes were blown out of their sockets from the subsequent shots. The other simian was startled by the sudden boom of the twin firearms as the bloody facial material of its slain brethren splattered over its brow.

Burrkos then forced himself to his feet and slashed his claws at the ape's barrel-like sternum. This move tore off several layers of flesh, leaving three of its ribs exposed. He then smashed his powerful hand through the protective bones and grabbed the beast's heart, tearing it out of its chest. The terminally injured primate vomited a stream of blood just before it fell to the ground in an unliving heap, while the mole-man tossed down the ape's no longer beating heart.

Judex and Burrkos then turned to see Felanthus furiously battling the last remaining ape while the audience began trampling each other in their haste to flee the coliseum, having now been alerted to what was happening. The cat-man rose victorious from the corpse of his simian adversary after finally managing to rip out its intestines in his feline jaws.

It was then that the vigilante and his two bestial allies realized that Cornelius and Tornada had fled, the former having taken his security guards with him. Judex motioned his hands to encourage the monstrous victors of the battle to follow him out of the Arena, whose location he had now compromised and shut down.

A smartly dressed elderly man of regal bearing who exuded a tremendous degree of power entered the now deserted coliseum, accompanied by a quartet of heavily armed guards clad in tux. The ominous looking man looked at the mutilated corpses of the six gray apes strewn about the combat chamber and beamed in sinister fashion.

"Ah, it was so generous of Monsieur de Tremeuse to accept the invitation I secretly sent him," noted Colonel Bozzo-Corona, the nefarious leader of the crime cartel known and feared across the world as the Black Coats. "I couldn't let the Red Hand continue this operation and remain the chief benefactor of the government, not when we have a socialist in office to dethrone and a war to start, could I now?" He then released a throaty laugh in answer to his own rhetorical question. "Only the Black Coats can be allowed to prosper from such a position, as we have a world to win when the war begins and the fascists conquer all."

Just over twenty minutes later, Judex led Felanthus and Burrkos out of a hidden back entrance to the Louvre, where they all stood in deserted streets due to the time of night. The mole-man put his huge hand on the vigilante's shoulder while uttering a series of grunting sounds that appeared to be some unknown language. Though he couldn't understand the words, their tone and accompanying gesture made it clear he was being thanked. He nodded his head in understanding.

He then turned to Felanthus, who stood in a crouching "at ease" position.

"I know you are related to Felifax," Judex said. "I'll use my resources to see to it that you are flown back to India to rejoin him."

"No..." the tiger-man replied in a grating pattern of speech that was still discernible. "Do not... trust you. Even though you... helped and are... not bad like those other men, you are still... human... and I don't trust. I will find my... own way back to brother."

Before the vigilante could utter another word, Felanthus moved down to all fours and raced out of the darkened neighborhood on a route that would lead him out of the city and into the forests.

Judex was wary of this creature being loose in the wilds of France, and wondered how he would possibly find a way back to India on his own. Nevertheless, he knew this beast was of noble mien, and should be afforded a measure of trust, however grudgingly.

"Godspeed," he said quietly.

As he turned back to Burrkos, he noticed the mole-man burrowing into the ground from his lower extremities on down with the use of his incredible claws. Within seconds, Burrkos had disappeared into the depths of the earth, apparently also mistrustful of human aid despite his gratitude to Judex, and equally determined to make his long way home entirely on his own.

The avenger of the night was confident that justice was served this evening, but he couldn't ignore a strong premonition that something even more sinister than the machinations of the Red Hand were on the horizon.

*Pierrick Rival is a French author who is making his first contribution to* Tales of the Shadowmen. *He portrays here the famous Long John Silver of R.L. Stevenson's* Treasure Island *along with a legendary figure of French buccaneering, Robert Surcouf (1773–1827). Surcouf, like d'Artagnan, is a historical character who has served as fodder for several swashbuckling novels. He was a French privateer who operated in the Indian Ocean between 1789 and 1801, and again from 1807 to 1808. He preyed on British, American and Portuguese merchantmen. He was eventually awarded the Legion of Honor and amassed a huge fortune. In 1816, it is said that he challenged twelve Prussian officers to a duel and defeated all of them except for the last, which he let go "to tell in his country how a former soldier of Napoleon fights." Surcouf became the hero of two 1966 films* Surcouf, l'eroe dei sette mari *(released in the US as* The Sea Pirate*) and* Il grande colpo di Surcouf, *both by Roy Rowland.*

## Pierrick Rival: *The Inn of the First Voyage*

*December 178\* - One dusky evening, between Dinan and Cancale, in Northwestern France.*

Whilst the land was already partly covered by darkness, a stagecoach fought bravely against the cold, rain and icy wind. A wicked storm on the coast had made the English Channel furious and the entire carriage shook. Under such conditions, the coach could not pick up speed and had trouble climbing a steep hill before coming to rest at the top.

An old, awful-looking man scrambled out clumsily. Anyone observing him would have noticed his crutch, the missing left leg, and then his face, incredibly wrinkled, ugly, grotesque and pale, with hollowed out cheeks, a glassy stare, hesitant, dazed, betrayed, however, by little sparks of intelligence and the will to look good; concealing, but unable to hide, his profound suffering and weariness; full of fear and valor at the same time, of spirit, cunning and sincerity... His toothless mouth with it fake smile, wheezed and panted. A hideous scar was barely hidden in the folds of his neck... A few long strands of white hair, which must have been blond once, stuck out of a short-brimmed, three-corner hat. It was hard to tell exactly what age he was: at least 70, but maybe a lot older...

The old man's trunk was hurriedly put on the side of the road. The coach sped away, abandoning the passenger in the middle of the storm. He looked like he should melted into the countryside, but his figure stood fast against the wind. He was tall, fat, clad in a well-fitting, black frock coat—a moderate luxury. He had no doubt once been rich... How else could he have lived so long? He was an old crow full of history, no doubt more dangerous than his appalling decrepitude

210

suggested: a bulge in his pocket bespoke the presence of some dangerous weapon.

Favoring his right leg, grimacing, he grabbed his crutch with both hands and pushed the trunk under a thorny bush. He took no pains to hide it and started stumbling down a narrow path that ran perpendicular off the road, barely visible. The wind was starting to die down and the cold rain fell to a drizzle. How could such a path, muddy, maze-like, surrounded by shrubbery, sometimes intersected by branches of firethorn, bristling with their dangerous thorns, barely able to let a horse through—not to mention a cart—how could it lead to what he would consider his most lucrative investment?

*The Inn of the First Voyage...* The name he preferred, long before the defunct *Spy Glass*, which had made them laugh so much... What irony of fate on this perhaps baneful night!

His lamented "wife" had always been very shrewd in placing their money. What he had reaped, she knew how to grow. As intended, in the end, he had become independently wealthy. Thus, this inn, where he had never felt the desire to set foot in, represented one sixth of his fortune, guaranteeing regular, steady income that flowed into several banks. The Inn, by nature, was a melting pot of stories and legends, a luxury brothel of experienced whores, a place famous for being almost impossible to find, a place to make and break distant alliances, an absolutely neutral place, the favorite resting spot of adventurers... The craziest stories were told among the initiated... It was rumored that dreams of men were sometimes incarnated there... Famous sailors from remote times, bloody pirates and bold corsairs, crafty merchants and legendary discoverers had all crosses its threshold...

This made him smile: He was very familiar with the rum that landed in the storeroom every month; a very rare rum with morbid effects. Nothing is more dangerous than rum, he was in a position to know...

There were three or four of them against one and, in spite of the incredible naivety of Squire Trelawney, in spite of the boy, they had failed! It does not matter what boy, really, but still... If anyone dared to write about this episode, it would no doubt be very funny, but not for those who lived through it... He had not drunk for almost twenty years. No rum, no cognac, no eau-de-vie, nothing at all. Not a drop in spite of all his pain that the medicinal plants helped less and less. Never drunk, his word was like his only weapon, even though he found it more and more difficult to be obliging. He was older than ever, much more cultivated too: he would never have imagined that he would one day be able to speak French so well...

He heard the delightful cries of the seagulls and he filled his nostrils with the salty air that the wind, lighter and lighter now, wafted to him. What wouldn't he give to see the proud storm as he perched on the walls of Saint-Malo! To hear the rumbling, then the crash of waves and the screeching pebbles driven by the sea… To have given everything up in Bristol would not have bothered him. It is retiring far from a ship that was really heartbreaking.

At first, his "wife" had wandered from port to port in his place, then Mary, their adopted daughter, free as the sky… When he thought about it, he did not think that his "wife," who could be spotted in a crowd, had ever been followed. But although he believed himself forgotten, safe from all surveillance, as the last, darkening port of call was in sight, *they* had found him.

It was not an English inspector or a French customs officer who had found him, but *his own people*—but he did not know which ones or why. Even though he had let almost nothing show, he felt an untold terror on seeing the thin piece of paper, cleverly scorched by a flame, on the back of which were a few words in his native language: "*You have until midnight, six months to the day. Last voyage.*"

Six months was a long time… but who could still have it in for him? Most of his old partners had passed on, he was sure of it… Alcohol, malaria and madness had long ago consumed Dick, old Tom Morgan and the third acolyte… A relative of a member of the expedition? The list would be long! Not likely after all this time. A bad joke from some rival trader? Yes, but how in Heaven's name would they know? This was definitely one of the worst periods he had ever embarked upon… A faceless enemy…

Six months? A pirate would never had given him such a deadline. Furthermore, when the black spot had been given to him, it was not done in the full light of day, from pirate to pirate. Some wretch off the street was used as an intermediary. They were far from Pew meeting Billy Bones. So why bother with this ridiculous formality?

The fateful hour of that infamous midnight was tonight. In spite of his old carcass, he had crossed France. Maybe this would be enough… Mary had wanted to come with him, but he had absolutely refused, despite the storm of arguments that she had unleashed upon him. He had hired three trusty henchmen and left immediately with them. For six months, they had taken the main roads to travel fast, and then complicated detours to cover their trail. In three carefully chosen places, each henchman had paid and disguised three lame men to limp along with them and add a little more confusion to the affair. The voyage had taken much longer than expected. The trickiest part was to dig up three men who were lame in the left leg. At no time did he tell his companions about his final destination.

He was alone now. When it came to a black spot, it was in fact necessary to disappear without leaving a trace. To be surrounded by people was to multiply the risks of betrayal and increase one's suspicions… Before leaving, he had asked Mary to hide also, for fear that she would be questioned. He would write her a letter after the deadline had passed to tell her where he was. If no news came in the next few months, she could make inquiries in the different inns where he had invested his fortune.

The deadline... In pirate past, he had never heard of a deadline being missed. Usually it was only a matter of hours because they would watch the spot being delivered and allow no possibility of escape: someone had to die and it was more often he who had received the spot than those who had given it... What would happen if no one came to meet him at midnight? Would they leave it there? Would he get a second black spot? In the inn, he had been told, no one would ever try to kill anyone unless it was a guaranteed death sentence. But could he really trust this? This was a rule respected in the area, not a law decreed by piracy... Therefore, he could not count on it being applied without fail.

Twice, he almost fell, but he managed to climb down the uneven path to the bottom. Not a drop of rain. Not a breath of wind. But a sound, a stealthy sound, on the port side.

He was barefoot, numb, exhausted and hobbling, but still fighting against the strong wind. The rain lashed his face and soaked his clothes. He had to plow on, no question of turning back. The taste of blood was still in his mouth. He had spit nothing out. It was the taste of revolt, vengeance and freedom! He had made his decision and he had to stick by it. The taste of blood boosted the little strength he had left. He would use it until his body twitched its last.

His mind, as if frozen, could only think with difficulty: it had been several hours since he had stopped thinking of the consequences of what he had done. Walk and not get caught. Reach the manor, howl out his dreams and outrage! Walking made him feel the cold less. He could not run. With his feet already blistered he was starting to feel a pain in his chest. Seven or eight leagues, because of the detours, to take this trip. Spotting the men and the horses in the storm, hiding, getting ready to jump out, changing tack, hiding, leaving again. All the way to the big oak. The bend down there. The chestnut now. Buck up! Gulp down the weariness. The grove. The rock. The hill. Walk. He had spilled the blood of a man and he felt entirely like a man. He would start again as many times as necessary.

At the moment when the last rays of daylight were disappearing, his head emerged for a few seconds in the eddy of water and wind that encircled the path in the heart of the storm. Suddenly, he heard the recognizable sound of wheels sliding over the ground and the whinnying of horses.

In weather like this, his faithful, two-shot pistol might have wet powder. No sooner thought than done: he brought out his big cutlass and stepped back. It had been a long time since he could jump around as light as a lark with his crutch, but he could still put up a fight. Someone nearby was trying to hold his panting breath... An opening in the bushes on his left... A hoarse cough came out of the black lair... Choked back and held in, then let loose openly. By the devil, it was a child's cough! He knew perfectly well that crime had no age limit, so he stayed on guard.

"Who's there? Come out, kid, let me see you! Slowly and bring your hands out first where I can see them! Hurry up or I'll open fire and it'll be at point blank range..."

A bloody foot poked out of the bushes.

"I said your hands!"

The foot froze.

"Are you English? An English sailor? You're not chasing me?"

While asking these questions, the child came out, hands in front this time. He was around twelve years old and trying not to stumble. Tanned skin with drops of water running between his freckles. His clothes were tattered, torn, black in spots, as if he had been caught in a cloud of ash... Out of his firmly tied hat a shock of hair stuck out whose color was hard to determine in the night. A boy! He was worn out but his build, his well-developed muscles looked like they could draw on his reserves far more than others could do... A bold and violent flame seemed to fill him in spite of the cold gnawing away... His small, feverish eyes gleamed in the dark, more curious than frightened... If he were less tired he would have had a good face full of vitality but the blue in his lips was disturbing. At ten years old, he looked like he was thirteen. The man put away his cutlass.

"Are you English?" the youth repeated, examining him from head to toe. "What battles? Ushat? Chesapeake? Cuddalore?"

To know about these battles, he must have been the son of a good family, a sailor or an innkeeper at a port.

"Calm down, kid, I speak French too well to still feel English and more than one subject of His Majesty has dreamed of seeing me hang at the end of a rope. Doesn't matter anyway, I'm retired from those old days now... We're on the same side, maybe a lot more than you think. What are you doing here?"

"My teacher wanted to give me some lashes, so I ripped up his leg with my teeth and ran away. I'm going back home. I'll never become a priest because I'm a sailor!"

The old man laughed thunderously and his eyes, too, flared up.

"What you did there is a lot less serious than my offenses. But I like you, kid, and I want to know your name."

The boy gave it. If anyone were spying on them they would not have heard it: a sudden blast of wind made it inaudible to anyone but the two of them.

"Glad to meet you. In memory of a brave boy who changed my destiny, I'll call you Jim, nothing against you. My name is John. Where's your school and where are you going?"

"Dinan, and I'm headed for Terlabouet."

"That seems far in this cold. You're coming with me to an inn I know, a little ways on. I'll offer you a meal and a good fire. If you don't get your strength back, you'll never arrive safe and sound. I'll talk to you about ships, if you want, and maybe I could teach you a thing or two."

214

"There's no inn around here."

"You see, I do have some things to teach you. At the end of this semblance of a road is *The Inn of the First Voyage*, a good quarter league from here. A sailor's hideout that's only available to the initiated. You told me you're a sailor... I believe you so I'll open its doors to you... and you'll be able to help me if it gets too slippery."

John started walking again, cautiously but confidently. The kid was in no condition to carry his trunk. If he were going to be an ally, he would have to take care of him. He was sure the kid would follow him because his arguments had been simple but true. The boy coughed again. After a few seconds, he caught up to him, even though he was a little uncertain: he had never heard of any inn around here. But he knew how tired he was, so if the inn really existed, it was an opportunity he had to take.

The mysterious old man fascinated him, too. Corsair? Pirate? A sailor anyway... If he wanted to kill him he would already have tried. But why would he want to kill him? The devil's sidekick? No, he did not feel this from him. The old man seemed worried and more on the defensive than on the prowl. An escaped prisoner? Too well dressed. The fact that he was originally English raised even more questions. In any case the kid had no real choice, as scared as he was. A good fire, a good meal, that was what he needed before resuming his journey.

As they winded through the night John kept turning everything over in his head.

Who? Who wanted to kill him before he died of old age? He went over and over the names of those who had anything to do with the expedition: old Flint to begin with, Billy Bones, Pew, Black Dog, the whole crew more or less under his orders, all those whom he had to get rid of, like Alan and Tom and those he took care of himself in the good old days when he could sometimes walk without his crutch or use it like a weapon. Struck against the back, breaking the spinal column, followed by two, expertly delivered thrusts with the cutlass before the blade totally disemboweled whoever dared to challenge him...

The survivors, then, like Ben Gunn and the three darkies who took his place... A partner of George Merry could certainly want a piece of him since he had done him in with two pistol shots in the ditch where Flint's 700,000 pounds should have been... But very few knew about the Bible! The three darkies and Jim, for sure, dear Jim who must have told everything from A to Z...

When they had turned against him, it was that numbskull Dick who had mutilated the Bible so that George could make the black spot. He remembered, too, having threatened him when he found out. On the back of the page where the decision was written something was printed that said something like, "In the outer dark are dogs and murderers." Was it God and his cronies who had tracked him? Maybe... They had been pretty patient with him so far... But with regard to his past actions, it had been a long time since he reported back to duty! Otherwise maybe the story had really been written down or told, read or heard in this world down below. And since he had cut himself off from English civilization, he had not found out about it... But he was almost certain that no one had followed him these last six months. All these questions gnawed away at his sanity little by little. To know who his enemy was would be a relief... as for the rest, wait and see.

Nothing in the muddy ground hinted that this path had ever been taken before. The farther they advanced, the more they were swallowed up by nature. The spiny bushes, growing thicker and thicker, narrowed along either side of the path until they were almost touching, but not quite, as if some invisible force held them back. The menacing branches, however, loomed over the gloomy corridor. The boy was in agony because of his blistered feet but he still managed to help the old man who tripped a couple of times in the mud on pushing his bent body through the brambles and branches. How he was able to make it this far along the steep path on only one leg was amazing to the boy. Luckily, the layer of mud was not so thick at this point.

A light, at last!

In the middle of a clearing surrounded by ancient trees, sharp rocks and impenetrable bushes, a strange building stood... They both noticed another path off to the left, which also ended up in the clearing. Another narrow path but that at least deserved to be called a path more than what they had just come out of.

Lit by seven or eight lamps, the imposing *Inn of the First Voyage* looked made of all the materials that architecture had used since time immemorial. The main walls were built of natural rock that the hand of man had skillfully finished off with various methods of construction: branches and hides for certain additions to the side, primitive or well-hewn timber on the front, waffle and daub mixed with different kinds of wood, a motley combination of sod and plant fiber, blocks cut out of granite, limestone, sandstone, schist—blue-green, black, gray and purple—pebbledash, sealing and mortar that were all thrown together with no order, interlaced with straw, slate and tiles... It was all very unsettling.

The inn seemed ancient, monstrous, artificial and authentic at the same time. The heavy oak door that barred the entrance and the planks of wood hanging over the few windows made the building even more secretive. The plants that grew wild around and between all this material gave it a life of its own.

The storm here had calmed down but silent bolts of lightning flashed across the horizon.

"Listen, I didn't tell you everything. I'm in a delicate situation with a stranger who's trying to pick a fight with me like your professor. Maybe we should both take the helm to save our hides. It's highly probable that one of your professors or my chap is here, but if so, it would be best if you do as I say... We enter together, kid, you're my guest."

While they were talking life seemed to flow back into his eyes: he was a sailor who was finally climbing back on the deck after 20 years on solid ground. So, after they opened the heavy door, as the old man looked over the place, concentrating on the men, trying to flush out his invisible enemies, the young runa-way could gaze at a scene right out of his dreams… Sights and smells… Wide-eyed and sniffing… Everything in wood, sea, metal and canvas… Barrels used as tables, trunks as benches… Tobacco smoke and whiffs of alcohol… A ship's décor, the deck and piles of maritime objects: fittings, gear, pulleys, cables, cap-stans, iron bars, hooks, a figurehead, a carronade and cannon balls, ramrods and cartridges, pistols and blunderbusses, sabers and cutlasses, sails hanging from the wall, spyglasses, compasses, exotic shells, sea charts, both real and false, fishing rods and hanging hammocks… he even thought he could smell salt, powder and tar… The fire in the fireplace under a roasting pig flared up when the heavy door closed. The customers, amazing and frightening, did the same. Oh, this inn well deserved its name! He was already starting to well better.

Except for the oaken clock of English workmanship, which was ticking off the last minutes before midnight, and a dismally empty parrot cage, John did not look at the surroundings. He counted five tables, one old sea dog alone and the innkeeper with a young serving woman. Nineteen people in all, most of whom would have been a delight to a portrait painter specialized in old sailor faces… But he could see that other rooms were off to the sides, not to mention the up-stairs!

He headed for an empty table in the darkest corner, not far from the bar and the back door. He sat with his back to the wall and asked the boy to sit across from him. The conversations stopped suddenly. Everyone, or almost, turned and stared at them. He did the same, while respecting the custom: Long John Silver stuck his cutlass in the table and from his deep pocket he took out his pistol and laid it in front of him. How surprised his young guest was!

"Don't worry," John said, picking up the cutlass, "they usually don't kill in this inn. This is just a kind of password so that everyone can see that we didn't come here by chance. Look, the table's covered in nicks. Some of them were obviously made by big swords. Now it's your turn."

"I don't have any weapons."

"Then bang your fist on the table, Jim!"

The kid almost corrected the old man about his name but changed his mind, figuring it was of minor importance at the moment. He did as he was told, dealing a loud, sound blow to the table… and without breaking his hand, which, given the force of the blow, could easily have happened to a child his age.

The strength of the blow assured Long John that his companion was a seri-ous young man. He put away his weapons, aware that they could come out again at any moment. He had to get back to basics right now: some customers might be on the list of suspects. Like the pale guy there with two fingers cut off his left hand like Black Dog, whose son he could be! No, he would be older and it was completely stupid because amputated fingers are not passed on from father to son… That other guy at the same table, dark-skinned, with earrings, squinting a little as he drank his rum—he looked a little like Arrow (not the sharpest one, him) whose feat had been to kick the bucket. Yes? No? He did not know... Every night for six months he tried to call up his memory of forgotten faces... At the next table the two men who were whispering to each other looked like Alan and Tom. It was just a vague feeling, however, because he could not find a single detail to corroborate his impression. They were two of the customers who had stared at him the least, which was also suspicious.

When the young woman came to ask them what they wanted to drink, Silver told her but kept his eyes on the room. She looked surprised as she went behind the bar. The old sea dog who was sitting alone had not even bothered to turn around. He kept his eyes fixed on a big glass of rum. His clothes and his build were typical of a pirate and Silver suddenly thought he saw them all in him! A second glass next to the first, empty and turned over, made him feel a little better but...

While continuing his meticulous scan of the horizon, he figured it time to deal with the kid. The innkeeper came in person with two fuming plates, went to the fireplace, cut off two big pieces of meat and brought it all to their table, but not before stopping twice on the way: once by the guy with two missing fingers and once by the two who looked like Alan and Tom. A jug of water for him with an empty glass, and a glass of rum for his charge, a true ship's rum, as he had ordered. While the boy attacked his plate and started gobbling up the food, the innkeeper, who was holding the bottle of rum he had just opened, mumbled that only those three had an English accent. Then he listened carefully to what was whispered by his main supplier of rum and went back to the bar.

Long John drank the refreshing water slowly and ate very little, though he still appreciated the quality of the food: his culinary tastes had only improved over time and he had become more and more demanding... His young guest had already finished his plate and was starting in on the rum, with the elated look of someone discovering the world. The old man had the absurd feeling that a budding destiny was taking shape right before his eyes. He who called himself a sailor seemed to be becoming one with the inn: he observed everything, taking in everything around him, constantly doing double takes, eagerly fingering every nick in the table... And in reaction the inn resumed its life and sense in his presence: the setting drew from him and became a force begetting the future... Almost enough to forget the black spot...

Long John Silver got a grip on himself. The problem was that the room was too calm now, impossible to try anything without being seen. Was it really necessary to try something? He could just as easily wait, keep on storm watch... There was much time left... Jim, dear Jim, I could have taught you so many things.

As the boy turned to look at him, the old man became excited and decided to talk.

He asked him about his family, trying to judge his financial possibilities with regard to his career plans, then he flooded him with advice of every which kind. Had he already sailed? For his body, no problem. His sense of balance? Did he climb to the tops of trees? In the rain? Had he seen death? A cabin boy to start with... A merchant ship... Navy man or pirate... The slave trade, why not? A ship owner in the end... Invest during his whole life to be free forever... At sea, on land, ships, houses... A corsair rather than pirate...

He did not want to say openly that he himself had been a man of fortune and this muddled his speech, the more so since he was trying to watch the three suspects at the same time.

Pirates were not what most people thought... Quite the contrary in fact... They sought riches, certainly, but first all freedom... With rules, however, efficient, frightening seen from afar, but for a noble cause... Fewer and fewer of them, hunted everywhere... Maybe a corsair would be better... They had the law on their side... Legal hypocrisy... They had a camp and attacked the enemy, which looked a little simpler morally... And to dole out the booty had to be a lot easier... he could die in battle just like a pirate but he would rarely end up hanged... Had he seen a hanged man yet?

He had the feeling that the two guys who looked a little like Alan and Tome were listening to him. True he might have been talking a little loudly and they were not the only ones turning around. Therefore, he could make no definite conclusions. He resumed.

The gallows... The gallows, in all its horror, with the clicking of the useless chains, devoured by birds flitting about, supper... No one is bad with a rope around his neck, all the actors in the tragedy make a big splash in the atrocious show, but at what price! Corsair, then, privateering, that's better, more prestigious too... But constant obedience, less solidarity, less democracy...

His young companion did not understand a thing. He was as much horrified by the confusing words, by the things unsaid and the old man's allusions to his past, as by he was fascinated by the prospects of adventure opening before him and certain very descriptive phrases. He tried not to let anything show: he would sort it all out later. The rum was making his head spin for the moment. He did not finish his glass. His mysterious professor also seemed drunk even though he was drinking only water.

And the art of commanding, the art of the word, the art of cunning! That's important! As important in speech as in battle! To know how to evaluate a situation, make the right decision at once. To be tough when you're the strongest, to confuse the issue, make a mess when you're trapped, so you can get the upper hand again later. Never a face-to-face combat, one on one, without a trick up your sleeve. A duel, nothing is stupider than a duel... The king of the seas is a good sailor, a quick decision-maker, a businessman, a clever talker, a wily, cunning fellow, a lover of oceans and well planned adventures... And when you plan well you can always win, even if you're inferior... And lift anchor when you have to!

"But you're not there yet, kid, even if I know you'll go far. You're a sailor in your soul, Jim. When I look you in the eyes I see the sea and the adventures that I miss so much! I started as a cabin boy not much older than you... There were traditions to see if you're made for it and if they can count on you... I'm going to break you in, if you want. I know how it works in France... Don't mess up the start..."

He launched into a long account, a little more coherent, in which he unloaded his wealth of maritime knowledge. The student looked captivated. He was going to be able to use him—he did not have much time left!

Either he had nothing to fear or it was going to happen in the next thirty minutes. What nagged him was that if one of the three did something, seeing that apparently no one had followed him over the last six months, it meant that someone close had talked about this inn or other places he had invested in... Mary was too shrewd to get trapped... One of his lovers? And then could he really be sure that his adversary was English? If it was the nipper of a member of the expedition but not strictly speaking a pirate, he could have given the job to someone else... Likewise if it were not a pirate maybe he would have more chance that the neutrality of this place be respected... Were they going to try to drag him outside? And why would they come here rather than another inn? The storm resurged in his head...

Now he told himself that he was stupid to come here... He had thought that he would end up in this safe harbor much earlier than on the last night of the six months! He would have done better to hide out in the bushes and wait for the tide: it would only be one night to endure the cold. At the same time he wanted to know the truth! And he would have missed this strange meeting with the boy. Now he was not going back out. Should he take a risk to earn some time or wait it out? All of these thoughts got mixed up with his maritime tales... He would pull through, however, if he managed to steer the two ships at the same time... He had made up his mind... The kid had not finished his glass, it was a good thing... His last card...

The voices rose in the smoky room, the spirits heated up, the tongues loosened, a hubbub, like a cloud of dust, started to cover their minds already clouded by alcohol. Some prostitutes with no more clients had entered the room, which started a game of musical chairs. No more time to think, he had to use the commotion to act... Silver whispered to the boy, who barely heard:

"Jim, you're my spitting image when I was young. It's time that you went to tell your family in no uncertain terms that you want to become one of the elite sailors. We could have done great things together but our paths have to separate. I need a little help, which will have no repercussions on you. I'm asking you to trust me. I've lent you a hand, you can lend me a hand in return... Remember that I told you that a stranger was looking to give me some trouble... It's no doubt a pirate and the worst kind, believe me, so helping me will be good work... I have to hold out until midnight and I'll be saved! We'll be partners, the two of us. I'm going to drink the first glass of rum I've drunk in a long time and the effect will be devastating... Don't worry about me, it's trafficking, or overacting, nothing more... A little rehearsal before taking the plunge for real."

The pirate used the clamor, the boy and the bustling prostitutes and customers in the inn as a screen. It was not him but the girls that the three others ogled... He poured a glass of rum, took out a one louis coin and a small vial, then grabbed a piece of paper and a bit of lead. He poured the contents of the vial into his glass. Right away he wrote a few lines and resumed talking.

"There you go. I'll just ask you to give this, as discreetly as possible, to the innkeeper behind the bar, but start with the louis here. If he has trouble reading it, I want you to repeat these words to him: 'As planned, you must run to him when he falls, examine him, and say that he died honorably while drinking his rum. Give the customers some time to examine the body if necessary. Make a fuss if anyone takes out a weapon! Then bring the body upstairs, into a room, and lock it, leaving a double of the key inside. Watch their reactions. Burn this note.'"

He repeated the instructions three times.

"You, Jim, get near the exit and take off when the wave hits me. There's no way you should take any more risks for my noggin. Don't worry, nothing will happen to me. I've been taking medication for years for the pain that the loss of leg causes in the rest of my body to compensate for. I know plants well and this concoction is absolutely marvelous. They'll think I'm dead and leave me alone."

The rum was still affecting the boy and he was less afraid that he would forget the instructions than that he would keel over on standing up... He nodded in agreement, although the logic of his decision was not really clear. He took the paper and the coin, stood up and made it a point of honor not to look ridiculous by falling down. Just before going to the bar to accomplish his mission he reminded the old man of a detail that was important to him:

"My name is Robert Surcouf."

For one of them everything happened pretty much as planned; a little less so for the other.

When Long John had downed his glass of rum, those watching him saw him jump up, grab his throat, sway a little and fall face down on the floor. The innkeeper played his role the best he could, for which he had been paid. The body was carried upstairs. When Silver came to, one hour later, he felt more alive than ever. On the nightstand were a note and a letter. The short note was obviously from the innkeeper saying that no strange reaction had been noticed. As for the letter, he recognized the handwriting right away. It was addressed to him with the same date as the fateful deadline with the addition "Not before midnight." And what a letter! His mind was assailed by a multitude of reactions: curiosity, stupor, anger, desolation, then after some thought, pity, compassion and forgiveness.

Mary, oh unpredictable Mary... She had played this wicked game in the hope of curing him... For two years already he had progressively faded away into an empty body, worn down by the certainty of an imminent end... He talked less and less about the sea, adventures, his fight for freedom, had even lost his taste for concocting his delicious meals... Several times she had offered to go with him to the coast, to a port, on a ship, to live again, to take full advantage of his remaining days in this universe that he loved so much, and hoist a sail, as she said, that would flap in the wind again... She had not understood his obsessive fear of being captured and hanged. As she said several times only a few dusty archives could still prove that he was wanted and he was not taking a great risk... Then she decided to force his hand: a fake black spot so that he could find that he could take a voyage, that adventure could once again fill his body and make his heart sing... She had sent this letter to all the inns that had built his fortune, betting that according to his final instructions he would end up at one of them... She was convinced that the spark of freedom had lit a fuse in him and now she was hoping that a cannon would boom forth... She explained, moreover, that most of the inns were not far from the coast and he might continue his adventure a little farther... The letter ended with a string of excuses and asked for forgiveness.

Standing up straight on his crutch, he put the letter down.

He had to get his trunk back. His new wooden leg, the one Mary had given him for his birthday, was inside. He would have to get used to it. In the long run it would be less painful. Saint Malo would be his next stop.

Robert Surcouf ran through the cold, winter night. The wind was starting to blow again. Oh how passionate that old crow was! The boy could have listened to him for hours. Of course he would become a great sailor, he did not need to be told this. He was both happy to have helped the old man but also regretted having helped a pirate... He would have liked to know all the details and the final outcome of his story.

On leaving he had heard no gunshots, no screaming, not a sound, not even voices. A veil of silence seemed to have covered the inn... It was not possible that all this really existed. It was too supernatural for his taste! Stumbling through the thorny maze he had the feeling that the branches were closing in behind him... The wind? The rum? Could he come back here some day? But if his parents found out that he set foot in such a place and they managed to find it, they would never let him become a sailor...

For the moment he had to concentrate on the path. The rum was not really protecting him from the cold, he knew... The night made his journey harder: he had no points of reference to mark his way. Maybe he was in more danger than he thought.

His chest was hurting more and more...

The energy he had found at the inn was already starting to slip away...

He would probably have died if he had not been found by the fish sellers. They recognized him; they knew him; feverish, delirious, his face almost blue, a hair's breadth away from pulmonary congestion. They carried him to the family estate. They were given a well deserved reward and the smell of roasted pig, rum and tobacco that the boy exuded faded away into the abyss of history. It was still something that he had to answer for. He did not want to talk about the inn, so he had to lie and be persuasive, which was not the end of the world: there was more than one tavern in Dinan.

For his parents, whatever the case, it was out of the question that their son enter the priesthood...

*Translation by Michael Shreve*

*Jean Kariven is a dashing 1950s archaeologist created by French SF writer Jimmy Guieu. Kariven is often involved in an age-old, secret interstellar war that pits the good Polarians against the evil Denebians, with Earth stick in the middle. Guieu's six original novels will be available in translation from Black Coat Press in a two-volume edition in 2016. In the meantime, here is yet another incident from that war as told by Frank Schildiner...*

## Frank Schildiner: *Ancient Space Lizards and Other Visitors*

*London, 1954*

Jean Kariven liked the British Museum. It was a place where a scholar like himself could lose himself for days, weeks, even months. The antiquities, a few of dubious provenance, were stunning. The solitude the rooms offered its patrons was conducive to proper archaeological research. But not today.

Today, Kariven was there to consult and offer an opinion as to the Museum's latest find, obtained from a collector. The Museum Director had delegated the task to one of their lesser curators, a wealthy coin expert reputed to be more interested in animals than his current career, whose name was Fink-Nottle.

Fink-Nottle appeared to resemble a fish rather than a member of the British upper crust. He was comfortably rotund, wearing large spectacles, and possessed an unusual manner of moving his head about. He was chattering away, obviously ill-at-ease around Kariven.

"...And this was bought during the War by one of our most generous patrons. The new Baron was gracious enough to present the Museum with this object of ancient antiquity," Fink-Nottle burbled.

Kariven was scarcely listening as he moved easily through the familiar back rooms of the great building. A tall man with dark hair, a pencil mustache and slightly protruding ears dressed in a well-cut Savile Row suit, he looked more like a matinee idol than an expert on the ancient treasures of the world.

"Normally the museum would entrust its appraisal to one of the more experienced curators," Fink-Nottle continued, "but all our Eastern experts are at a special conference, meeting with the Americans to discuss the fate of certain items seized prior to the war. Therefore, at the suggestion of one of our trustees, the Duke of Denver, your expertise was requested."

"Yes, I know as much," Kariven replied, hoping to cut off the man's incessant narrative flow.

But Fink-Nottle was not to be deterred, obviously having practiced his speech for days prior to Kariven's arrival.

"And here we are!" Fink-Nottle exclaimed, throwing open an old metal door with shiny brass hinges.

The door creaked loudly and crashed audibly as it struck the wall. A room was revealed, square shaped and featureless, other than unpainted concrete walls and floor. Kariven knew these rooms all too well, having been brought to them many times over the years. In every museum, there were rooms set aside for items that could potentially embarrass the institution. These rooms were usually utilized when the antiquity in question was thought to have been stolen, because a scandal was the last thing desired by any museum. In this case, that seemed probable, based on the nervous speech of Fink-Nottle, and the mention of the trustees.

The item in question was hidden beneath a small white sheet, an unnecessary bit of theatricality in Kariven's opinion. But the French archaeologist did manifest his disapproval. Such was the price all academics paid for consulting with institutions such as the British Museum. They needed their little eccentricities when presenting new and potentially interesting exhibits.

Fink-Nottle slid over to the table in which the item in question was placed and grasped the end of the sheet.

"As my friend Bertie is prone to say, 'let's get the thingee on the road so to speak'."

And he gently pulled the sheet aside. A statue stood in the center of the small table, approximately six inches in height. It appeared to have been made of a pale, stone-like substance. The figure was unusual and highly detailed, an apparently ancient creation that had withstood the test of time.

Kariven raised an eyebrow, surprised and impressed despite his usual air of calm disinterest.

"Do you recognize it?" Fink-Nottle asked, noting the spark of interest in the Frenchman.

Kariven nodded and slowly stepped closer. Yes, the sculpture was unusual looking, but also very familiar to anyone who possessed an expertise in the most ancient artifacts of mankind. '

"Yes," he replied. "I helped unearth three similar items some years back."

Fink-Nottle continued to prattle on, but Kariven had stopped paying attention to the man's words. His eyes and attention were focused completely on the artifact, and would not waver unless absolutely necessary. Pulling out a small magnifying glass and a pair of soft silk gloves, he began to examine the statue.

The face of the figurine was inhuman, possessing a short lizard-shaped snout with two tiny holes where the nostrils would be placed. They eyes were long narrow slits that rose to a smooth sloping forehead. Atop the skull was a conical crown or helm without adornments. The figurine's shoulders were broad and the torso was covered in small round nodules. The waist was narrow and the tiny hands appeared to be grasping a pair of rods.

"...more involved in a study of the mating habits of newts, but this statue did impress me. The face is rather like that of a newt, eh?" Fink-Nottle was prattling while Kariven continued to run his magnifying glass over the sculpture.

225

He focused for several seconds on a tiny, almost infinitesimal, brown stain near the feet. before straightening and looking at the curator. Happily, the rotund Englishman quieted immediately and stared at Kariven intently.

"Not a newt, a lizard," said the Frenchman as he began to put away his magnifying glass and strip off his gloves. "The Al Ubaid site has yielded several such statues."

"Sumerian then?" Fink-Nottle asked, his interest apparently waning.

"No," replied Kariven, shaking his head. "The Ubaidian culture is of the same region, but quite apart from Sumer. Both are pre-historic, but quite different in architecture and, apparently, worship. But in this case, the details are academic. This statue…"

The French archaeologist's words were cut off by the door swinging open and crashing into the nearby wall. Three short, squat men dressed in yellow robes strode into the room, their boots causing harsh echoes in the small chamber. The oddity of these men was immediately apparent, even to the most casual observer. Though facially they appeared to be Asians of some type, they all possessed dark gray skin that was completely hairless. Their heads were rounder than humans and each man possessed only four fingers on the ends of their huge hands. They stood only about five feet tall, but their shoulders and heavily muscled arms were of that of a far larger person.

"I say!" Fink-Nottle stated, stepping into the path of all three men. "This is not an area for the public. Kindly return to…"

The leader of these three odd men stepped forward and backhanded the chubby curator aside. Fink-Nottle was propelled across the room and slammed into the concrete wall, stunned. Then, the oddly shaped man turned towards Kariven, swinging a heavy arm at the French archaeologist with surprising speed.

But Kariven was ready, aware that a blow from that massive appendage could be very damaging. Ducking, he shoved the man aside and used the momentum of his attack to send his opponent off-balance. He then kicked the back of his attacker's leg, causing the odd-looking man to crash head first into the wall.

The second intruder stepped up and tried to grab the Frenchman's arms. This forced the archaeologist to step back to avoid being captured. The odd man stepped forward and tried again, forcing Kariven to move back and, unfortunately, stumble over Fink-Nottle's fallen form.

The attacker stood over Kariven for a moment, but then turned and left, following the third man out of the room.

The figurine was, of course, gone, the third intruder having taken it while Kariven was avoiding the others' attacks. But the man the archaeologist had tossed into the wall was still lying face down on the concrete floor, still apparently stunned.

"Are you well, sir?" Kariven asked, helping Fink-Nottle to his feet.

The rotund curator appeared more annoyed than injured, and he dusted off his expensive suit with a pale hand.

"That does it! I am accepting the offer from the American Museum of Natural History! My family can go to the Dickens! My wife Emerald will be delighted to return to America, and I can go back studying my beloved newts!" Fink-Nottle snapped, pulling away and marching out of the room with a determined look on his fish-like face.

"I am too late, it appears," another man stated, stepping into the room after the Englishman left.

He was approximately Kariven's height with pale blond hair, lightly tanned skin and handsome features. He was dressed in a black suit and his eyes were covered by a pair of thick, dark glasses. Kariven sighed and shook his head.

"Polarians again. I should have known. You believe the Al Ubaid lizard figurine to be a Denebian weapon?"

The Polarian nodded once, his movements slightly jerky. Kariven had observed over the years that, though they looked rather like humans, the Polarians were often unable to reproduce common human gestures. Nods or shrugs, even relaxed smiles, were performed as one attempting to act in an unfamiliar way, as if these gestures were odd and unfamiliar. This served as a constant reminder him that, though the Polarians were essentially benevolent, their motives remained alien.

"That statue was one of the Denebians' most terrible creations. It acts as a gateway between worlds, opening the way for their servants, the Yig," the Polarian stated. "We must track it down or this world, and many more, may be lost."

"Then let us question the intruder I disabled," Kariven replied, irritated that yet another horrific weapon from the Polarian-Denebian War was being unearthed and endangering Earth.

Stepping aside, Kariven stepped back and yelled, "*Mon dieu!*"

The reason for his shock was instantly apparent. The gray-skinned man with the four fingers and the round head was not where he fell. Instead, a slowly growing puddle of gray colored liquid was spreading, soaking the discarded yellow robe.

The Polarian appeared unsurprised and stepped forward. Pulling a narrow tube made entirely from a glowing crystal, he thrust the end into the liquid and stared at the lights that appeared along the length of the tube.

"Sontaran / human hybrid, vat-grown but unstable," the Polarian pronounced.

"Can you track these creatures?" Kariven asked, used to the Polarian technology.

"Yes, easily. Follow me," the Polarian replied.

He led Kariven down a corridor and out a back exit. A long black car with no adornments of any type was parked near the curb and the doors opened as they approached. The Polarian placed the crystal tube in a hole in the dashboard and the car leapt into motion. Without touching the steering wheel, the Polarian car shot through traffic, causing the distance to fly by as a blue.

"Are these Sontarans allies of the Denebians?" Kariven asked.

"No, not at all," replied the Polarian, shaking his head, the motions oddly jerky and birdlike. "They're another empire in space, a race of warrior clones. Their main enemy is a hive intelligence known as the Rutan Host. That war has been conducted over 50,000 of your years. Occasionally, their war has drifted into this sector of space, but not in a thousand years I believe. The human using their technology has found a means of creating dangerous, but short-lived, Sontaran / human hybrids. They will be very strong in battle, but I doubt any would last more than a few days."

"So another race is using Earth as an alien dumping ground," Kariven groused as the car pulled up before a small building that appeared abandoned.

The scent of the river was immediately apparent and the Frenchman knew they had covered a vast distance in London in mere moments. He was about to say as much, when two hybrids stepped into view. They entered an unlit doorway, a wrapped item in one of their hands.

"Hurry!" the Polarian exclaimed, running for the door, his crystal tube in hand. "All they require is a small energy surge and the gateway will open!"

Kariven followed, but he appeared less rushed and more amused by the situation. Before he could ask how the Polarian meant to enter what was probably a locked door, the alien warrior raised his gun and a small yellow beam fired out. It struck the door and the wooden structure exploded into tiny slivers.

The Polarian rushed in, his crystal weapon in hand. Kariven stepped into the building mere seconds behind him, spotting the two hybrids as they dutifully handed the figurine to a man. Kariven immediately recognized him—the madman behind this plan, a squat Asian man, bald, dressed as a clergyman, with amber-colored eyes. His name was Ming Tsai Tsou, a.k.a. the Yellow Shadow.

Ming turned their way and smiled, placing the Al Ubaid lizard sculpture on a crowded work bench.

"Good afternoon, gentlemen. You are just in time to witness my triumph." He then nodded their direction and addressed the hybrids. "Kill them both."

The hybrids spun and stepped towards Kariven and the Polarian. The Polarian fired his crystal weapon twice, causing both creatures to fall to the ground with wet sounds.

But that was all the time the Yellow Shadow required. Two wires were connected to the figurine and the Asian mastermind tossed the switch. The Polarian cried out in terror, stepping back and raising his weapon. He bumped into Kariven, who was watching the proceedings with a wide grin.

"Kariven, flee! I will hold them back for a time!" the Polarian yelled, surprised by the smile on the Frenchman's face.

Kariven raised a perfect sculpted eyebrow and asked, still looking very entertained, "Hold who back?"

The Polarian spun back towards Ming, only to stare in shock, an expression echoed on the face of the mad genius. The smell of burnt copper filled the air, but nothing else happened. The stillness was only broken by the breathing of the two humans and the alien.

Kariven stepped past the Polarian and pointed at the tiny statue.

"You did not give me a chance to explain. That figurine? Not from Al Ubaid at all. It was a copy—a forgery if you will. An impressive one, but the artist failed to remove a tiny trace of the solution used to add the appearance of age. After my cursory examination, I believe it was made in Persia in 1920 or so. There was a small market for such items at that time."

The Yellow Shadow listened with unblinking attention. He looked at Kariven for a heartbeat, and then vanished from view behind his workbench.

Both Kariven and the Polarian ran to where the mad scientist had stood, the Polarian's weapon at the ready. But the Yellow Shadow was not visible and no trace of how he vanished was apparent. They searched the workbench and the area surrounding for several minutes before Kariven sighed and picked up the figurine.

"It appears Monsieur Ming's reputation for being a wily foe is well-earned," Kariven sighed.

By then, the Polarian was gone as well. Kariven wrapped the forgery in a cloth and headed for the exit. He hoped the London underground was nearby. He now needed to tell the truth about the "great find" to the British Museum's Director. This would be an interesting discussion!

*Sam Shook's latest tale is all action and mystical threats from an age un-dreamed of, featuring a stalwart crew of heroes fighting against an unspeakably ancient evil menace...*

## Sam Shook: *The Eldritch Stones*

*Rio de Janeiro, 1929*

He couldn't run. His mind screamed, begging his legs to move like the wind, but he knew he couldn't. To run would mean his death. The dark presence was all around, as *they* tailed him. *They* tailed him. He knew not why, but all Sâr Dubnotal knew was that he was, for one of the few times in his long life, afraid.

He who had encountered monsters, demons and Old Ones alike, felt almost helpless. *They* had been after him for two weeks now, ever since he found that ruby from Opar... He figured, no, he knew, that it had something to do with it. Why had *they* not attacked him yet, though? If it was the ruby they were after, why not just try to kill him and take it? True, *they* might be afraid of him; he was the Great Psychagogue, after all, but why then didn't *they* attempt to steal it?

No matter, all he knew was that he was being followed through the crowd-ed streets, and that he might just be overpowered by their numbers, if he could sense how many there were. Some on the beach, some on the streets, and others in the shadows, all moving with utter silence. He saw the Copacabana Palace hotel up ahead; his salvation was nigh. The sun was setting, so it looked like he had made it just in time. A bellhop let him through the door, and, while he knew he wasn't being tailed anymore, he could feel their baleful eyes peering into his very soul.

When at last he made it back to his hotel room (a well decorated room on one of the upper floors), he locked his doors, and placed holy symbols on every possible entrance. Though he wished he could leave the window open on this wonderful autumn night to let the sounds and smells of the ocean soothe his fraying nerves, he knew he couldn't take that chance. Even if he so much as had Annunciata with him, things would be better, but he had given her a leave of ab-sence a few months back. She had served him well, and had more than earned some time off. At least, he could rest assured that she would be safe—hopefully...

He went to his closet and checked inside. The parcel was still there. Good. Clearing his throat and breathing a sigh of relief, he sat at the small table to look at the newspaper which he had neglected to read that morning. The front page read that, apparently, Monsieur Zenith had escaped the clutches of Sexton Blake yet again, and, wouldn't you know it, was hiding out in Rio. The Sâr couldn't help but smile and shake his head; just his luck. The one time he was traveling here with a priceless gemstone.

*No matter*, he thought, *I would rather him than the ones after me.*

At least the article also said Blake was searching for him here. That was comforting. Suddenly, he heard a voice, one that was not his own, in his mind.

*Help! I am reaching out to the mind of the one called Sâr Dubnotal.*

"A powerful psychic," mumbled the Sâr to no one in particular, and responded:

*I am he. Who are you, stranger?*

The voice spoke but one word:

*Chandu.*


### Peru, Cordillera de Vilcanota

Few ordinary men were brave enough to traverse the Willkanuta Mountains alone, but, then again, Hareton Ironcastle was not an ordinary man. When he had received the telegram from his old colleague, Sâr Dubnotal, telling him the situation was dire and asking him to come, even if inconvenient, he had not given it second thought. He had grabbed some weapons and supplies, made contact with a pilot he knew in Rio, and embarked on his next adventure.

The one known as "Chandu" had, evidently, told Dubnotal everything he needed to know; the Sâr had, in turn, dispatched Hareton Ironcastle. Chandu's captors had set up camp near Siwinaqucha Lake. They were armed, but so was Ironcastle.

In his hands was his .577 axite express elephant gun. In his belt he carried two revolvers, one for him and one for whom he was rescuing, and a hunting knife. Over his clothing, he wore one of the spear-and-arrow-proof suits and masks his nephew Sydney Guthrie had brought on their expedition to Gondokoro. The dark color of the long armored coat was useful for helping him blend in with the darkness of the night. Yes, he was ready for whatever, he reassured himself as he marched across the stony ground near the lake.

Ironcastle stopped to hide behind a ridge, and peered over; he could see the fires of his enemies sending up their smoke and sparks. He was very close now. In the light of the fire he could see a sizable camp made up of numerous tents set up near the lake. In the darkness near the edge of the camp was a makeshift wooden cage. There was his man. However, there had to be at least a score of people there; some were men hidden under black robes, others looked like hired guns. Some were from America, some from Mexico, and a good number of native mercenaries were among them as well, armed with primitive weaponry.

Ironcastle heard something, and swiftly ducked behind the ridge. One of the men in a black robe was staggering towards him, obviously drunk. Fortunately, the man in black stopped about two steps away, so the explorer remained undetected. The man removed his robe in order to pass water; Ironcastle saw his chance. Leaping over the ridge, he bludgeoned the man with the butt of his rifle, knocking him unconscious. Donning the man's robes, he headed to the camp, feigning drunkenness to keep up the charade. Keeping in the shadows as best he could, he sneaked toward the cage. Inside was a man, no older than thirty, dressed in a pith helmet and other apparel fitting for a safari. He wore a black moustache above his lip, and his face was marked with several cuts. Ironcastle was surprised; he actually knew who this man was!

"Captain Chandler," he hissed, removing his mask to let this old acquaintance see his face.

The man immediately sat up and grinned, recognizing that man with straw colored hair and sea-green eyes.

"Ironcastle, I have never been happier to see you."

Hareton put a finger over his mouth.

"Not too loudly. Now, how do I get you out of here?"

"Can you pick a lock?" the prisoner asked.

Ironcastle shook his head.

"I can't. I could break it, but I'd need a distraction first."

Chandler cracked his knuckles.

"I think I can help you out with that."

The prisoner pressed the index and middle fingers of his right hand to his temple. Without any warning, there was a great ruckus, with robed men and hired guns alike running towards a mirage of Chandler, who was running towards the mountains. Ironcastle did a double take.

"How did you...?"

Chandler was laughing like a child laughs at a practical joke.

"Just a little trick I picked up in India. Now, break the lock. I need to concentrate."

Ironcastle smashed the lock with his gunstock, and, after three good hits, it broke. He picked up his mask, and then looked in the distance. The duplicate image of Chandler had faded. The men looked back at the camp, and, seeing the real prisoner now freed, began to charge.

"I think we've overstayed our welcome," said Chandler. "Before we retreat, though, I need to grab something."

"Make it quick."

Ironcastle threw off his robes and checked one more time to be sure his rifle was loaded and ready to fire. Chandler sprinted back, carrying something in a small leather satchel.

"All right," he called to his rescuer, "now let's get out of here!"

When Chandler was near, Ironcastle pulled out one of his revolvers.

"You still a good shot?"

"Let's hope we don't have to find out," replied Chandler, taking the weapon,

At the report of a gun, like runners at the Olympics, the two men began to speed away. Bullets began to strike the ground, missing them, but still too close for comfort. When someone got near, Ironcastle would pick them off with his elephant gun. When he needed to reload, Chandler would shoot his own revolver. They stumbled over stones hidden by tall grass in the pitch dark of night, and the cold wind burned their lungs. The sounds of nocturnal predators were drowned out by the yells and chants and gunshots of their pursuers.

"Are you sure you know where we're going?" questioned Chandler.

"Don't worry, this is the right way," Ironcastle puffed back.

As their legs were just starting to feel like giving out, Ironcastle spied a campfire.

"There he is!"

"Who?"

Ironcastle looked over to his companion.

"The pilot!" he replied.

When they were about seventy meters away, Ironcastle exclaimed:

"Get the plane going! We need to get in the air, and fast!"

The pilot, who had been smoking his pipe while trying to see the stars through the clouds, got up and waltzed toward his aircraft. They heard the engine begin to roar as the plane came to life.

Running through the camp, Ironcastle didn't bother retrieving any supplies. The two men climbed into the plane, and immediately they were off, leaving the cries of their infuriated foes beneath them.

After stopping in Bolivia to refuel, they took off again. One long journey later, they could see the city of Rio swiftly approaching.

When they had landed in a field a few miles from the city, they were greeted by Sâr Dubnotal, who, every once in a while, would peer over his shoulder, waiting in an automobile. Ironcastle, no longer in his protective suit, but instead in his safari jacket, jodhpurs, and slouch hat, thanked and paid the pilot, and then walked with Chandler up to the motorcar.

"Good Doctor," he said, referring to the Sâr's more common appellation, "you never told me that 'Chandu' was Frank Chandler."

"In point of fact, I did not know him by that name until now," the Sâr replied with a smile. "I met him once, a while ago, while he was still training in India. How do you know him?"

Ironcastle looked over at Chandler.

"He and I both fought in the Great War; I knew him as 'Captain Chandler' back then. Tell me, Frank, now that we're out of that plane and I can actually hear you, how's your family?"

"They're fine, thank you," Chandler responded cordially before asking, "and how do you feel, being world famous and the like?"

"That might be a bit of an exaggeration," said Ironcastle, laughing, "but thank you, and it feels no different than before."

Before the two acquaintances could revel in the past any longer, Sâr Dubnotal spoke up.

"I hate to interrupt you, gentlemen, but the word is, not long before you arrived, two explorers have been discovered unconscious in a cave in the Tijuca forest. Would you accompany me there?"

The men acquiesced, and, once more, they were traveling, on the open road, this time, instead of through the clouds. Chandler and Ironcastle caught up on the past years they had missed. The explorer spoke of his niece's marriage and of the Gun Club in Baltimore; Chandler talked about his adventures in the Orient, as well as his defeating of a madman named Roxor, but the Sâr remained mostly silent. Something was troubling him, but the men could not figure out what.

"Tell me, Chandu, what happened exactly?" the Sâr eventually inquired. "You're a long way away from the East. How did you wind up in the clutches of those men in Peru?"

Chandler took a drink from his canteen.

"I had come across a strange item in a bazaar in Turkey," he replied.

He then reached into his satchel and retrieved a spectacular object. It was a golden orb, smooth, but marked with strange hieroglyphics.

"The shopkeeper told me that, according to legend, it came from the mythical island of Mu," he continued, "so I was on my way here to investigate. If the legends were true, I would surely find some evidence of the orb's origins, as it is said the people of Mu colonized parts of South America in ancient times. Unfortunately, I ran afoul of some Tsathoggua worshipers here. I guess they wanted the orb too. It was quite lucky they didn't search me too thoroughly. If I didn't have my crystal ball to communicate with you, God knows what would have happened to me. Do you have any insight into why they wanted the orb, Doctor?"

But all Sâr Dubnotal said was, "We've arrived."

*Egypt, 1929*

The Great Sphinx of Giza was a testament to the science of the builders of antiquity. As the setting sun cast long shadows of the two men standing at its secret entrance, Professor William Channing Webb, an American explorer of some note, couldn't help but be enthralled. He had seen it before in his very long existence, but every time he saw it, he just couldn't help but be amazed.

Even the steely, wandering warrior Francis Xavier Gordon, known in those parts as El Borak, meaning "the swift," was impressed. Nonetheless, he didn't let its immensity distract him as he stood with his companion.

Gordon was a rough-looking man, compact, but imposing. A gunslinger hailing from Texas, he was dressed in khakis, but upon his head was a headdress like one would see in the Arabian Peninsula. Over his shoulder was slung a Lee-Enfield rifle; in his belt he had his six gun and a scimitar with a hawk head decorating the pommel. With him, too, was a bag of basic supplies, such as rope, flint, and jerky.

He was the guide to the professor, who was an old man dressed in a white suit and a Panama hat. To be frank, he hadn't aged well. While he might have been tall, he had quite a head of wild white hair, a unibrow, a large nose, and a grand white moustache.

After a long time of not speaking, Webb simply said:

"Well, I suppose we're here. What a fine piece of art, for it is art, El Borak... Anyway, we now must leave the world above behind to enter the land of the dead."

Gordon, without a word, entered first. He was surprised Webb was so quiet when they arrived. He wouldn't shut up on the way there. Gordon was halfway sure the leader of the caravan would shoot Webb just to get some peace.

"Do you think," the professor began while catching up, "that Houdini was telling the truth?"

"What, about mummies coming back from the dead? Bah," Gordon said, "it was probably just fatigue or bad opium."

He then paused to light his torch. The two men descended down the long staircase into the shadows below. Strange hieroglyphics were painted on the stone wall. Some depicted what one would normally find: depictions of Anubis and Osiris, or kings passing on to the next life. Others, however, were of a kind that neither Gordon nor Webb had ever seen: tentacle-covered abominations, hellish beasts, and a dark pharaoh.

"There's no need to worry about the death god, I think," Webb whispered in an affable tone.

"Death god?" asked Gordon.

"Yes," replied Webb, "Houdini claimed there was one down here. From my own research, however, I have concluded that it was the avatar of a certain 'Crawling Chaos,' which, according to several accounts is elsewhere, and..."

"It's quite alright, professor," Gordon interrupted, "you can spare me the details. You wanted to go on this expedition to see if Houdini was telling the truth about his imprisonment with the pharaohs, right? Well, as for me, while I doubt his tale, if it is true, I assure you I'm more than ready."

"I suppose I was saying it more so for my own sake than yours," chuckled the professor. "I do get nervous, don't I? I remember, once, when I was in..."

"Hush!" Gordon loudly whispered.

He raised his hand and listened.

"Apologies," Gordon said, "I thought I heard something."

They continued on, but Gordon was bothered by that fact. He had never had problems with hearing things. His ears, like his hands, had never betrayed him. He went on, though, trying to push that thought away.

When they reached the bottom, they found the sizable room they had entered was surrounded by sarcophagi. Surprisingly, there were fires lit. Even if El Borak did not believe in the undead, he certainly believed in grave robbers. He went on high alert. Webb, on the other hand, noticed a black, spherical stone with markings in an unknown language in the center of the room.

Gordon looked at it for a moment, and then continued to scan the walls for traps. There were none he could see. Furthermore, when he looked at the ground for any sign of life, he saw fresh footprints, but they were barely human. Perhaps some robbers had already been here and ran off? Why didn't they take the stone?

While Gordon contemplated this, Webb walked to the center of the room and took it.

Suddenly Gordon heard movement again. This time he saw something he had missed before. One of the sarcophagi was open. Then, out of the shadows behind Webb, came the shambling corpse of some sort of man. Its head, though, was that of a crocodile, and its gaping maw opened to devour the professor.

"Watch out!" Gordon cried, his hand already having raised his rifle to fire. Too late, though, as the professor struck the beast, killing it! He was amazed at the man's strength, but he supposed one couldn't be an adventurer and not be in good health. Be that as it may, the man was in his late nineties...

Gordon didn't have time to dwell on this anymore. The other sarcophagi came open, and more corpses of human-animal hybrids poured out. He raised his rifle, and began to gun them down. Neither could have been prepared for what happened next. By some deviltry, the walls by the stairs caved in, blocking their way. They were trapped.

"There's an antechamber!" called Webb, who was pointing to an opening in the northern wall.

"We're going to have to fight our way out!" Gordon yelled, his voice resonating over the blasphemous dialect of the mummies.

His rifle was empty, and the undead were closing in fast as he charged to help Webb get out alive. He crushed the skull of one with a swing of his Lee-Enfield, and then slung it back over his shoulder. Their way was blocked, but Gordon was not called "the swift" for nothing. He pulled leather, and fired six shots in a flash, his revolver becoming the very scythe of Death in his hand. Six shots he fired, and six mummies fell.

Holstering his gun, he unsheathed his scimitar, and hacked his way through the rest of the foul creatures. A skull split here, an arm severed there; all of this was so surreal. No one would ever believe it. He wasn't even entirely sure if *he* believed it was happening.

"The path's as clear as it's going to get. Make haste!"

Webb obeyed, moving expediently for a man of his age. Gordon followed. At the end of the empty antechamber was a stone door. They raced towards it, leaving the undead beasts behind.

When they got into the dark room, they looked for something with which to barricade the door. There were several peculiar statues of unearthly creatures lining the walls, one of which was by the door. The two men pushed it over, blocking the mummies' way in. Now that they could finally have a breather, they looked around for an exit.

As they did, they found what looked like the remains of some sort of camp. It was ancient, but there was something wrong with it. There were the carcasses of machines that looked nothing like either of them had ever seen. Stranger yet was what Gordon nearly stepped on.

"What in blazes is that…" he mumbled.

It looked like the husk of some insect, but there was more. Old bones lay scattered underneath it. They looked almost like wings of some sort.

"Gordon," the professor whispered, "come over here, I want to see this in better light."

Gordon complied. This room also had a pedestal, but it was different than the one in the other room. The pedestal here was made of a sort of metal which Gordon didn't recognize, with thick copper filaments extending from the sides connected to several glowing rocks. On the top of it was an indention for something round.

Webb looked at the black stone in his hands.

"It would be a perfect fit."

He placed it in the indention, and suddenly, after a blinding burst of light, the two saw no more.

### Brazil, the Tijuca Forest

After a short jaunt through the forest, Ironcastle, Chandler, and Sâr Dubnotal found what they were looking for. Underneath the giant trees, near a small flowing brook which sang a calming melody, they saw a hole.

"This is it. We're going to have to crawl," the Sâr informed them, looking behind himself one last time. He could feel only one dark presence behind him now; it was a woman watching from the shade of the trees.

They did as he said, and when they each had squeezed through the small opening, and the Sâr turned on his electric torch, they were greeted by a bizarre sight. It looked like the ruins of an outpost, but not of human make. It was built with metal and basalt, and some of the structural vestiges were non-Euclidean in design. A few broken canisters, most rusted to the floor of the cave, littered the dark corners. None of this, however, caught the attention of the three adventurers. What they did notice was, to them at least, stranger.

On the floor beside a pedestal with a black stone on top, were two men. A gruff-looking one with a scimitar in one hand and an extinguished torch in the other, and next to him was a very old man, dressed in a white suit and Panama hat. The man with the scimitar was stirring, and Ironcastle knelt by him.

"Sir? Are you hurt?"

Like a flash, the man shot up, grabbing the explorer by the lapel and bringing the sword to his throat.

"Where am I, you dog? Speak! Or never speak again," punctuating the last phrase by pushing the scimitar closer to the man's neck.

"Calm yourself," Dubnotal commanded as he looked into the peculiar man's eyes.

The stranger slowly put the sword down and let Ironcastle go, but he reiterated his query.

"Where am I?"

"You're in Brazil," said Chandler.

"Brazil?" the man grunted, "What day is it?"

Dubnotal raised an eyebrow.

"It's November third, about four o'clock in the afternoon."

"That's impossible," the old man said, finally waking up. "Gordon and I were in Egypt only an hour ago... unless of course, that pedestal is some sort of transport... Gordon and I will tell you all about it, but first, help an old man out of here..."

He got up and, turning to his cohort, said:

"If you please, Mr. Gordon, will you fetch the stone?"

Gordon knocked the black stone off with his scimitar, and then retrieved his Lee-Enfield.

"I would guess by your clothing and weapon that you, Gordon, are Francis Xavier Gordon, the famed El Borak?" said Chandler to the man with the sword.

"That's my name," replied Gordon, "and this gentleman with me is Professor William Channing Webb. Whom do I have the pleasure of addressing?"

"I'm Hareton Ironcastle," said the explorer. "This is Frank Chandler, who you might know as Chandu, and this is Sâr Dubnotal."

Gordon nodded respectfully at each of them, while Webb shook each of their hands.

"A pleasure," said Web. "Now, shall we depart? We will tell you everything."

*Rio de Janeiro, The Copacabana Palace*

The hotel had anything a man could want; crystal glasses and electric chandeliers, fine food and drink, beautiful women, and lovely beaches. To Monsieur Zenith, though, it was all so... boring.

238

He sat at the table in the ornately furnished hotel restaurant with its polished floors, nice Pol Roger champagne in his glass and a small platter of caviar in front of him. He was an albino with snow-white skin and hair, and eyes like rubies. As usual, he was clad in an impeccably tailored evening suit, and in the breast pocket was his cigarette case, which held his unique opium cigarettes, one of which he was smoking at that moment. It must be understood that opium and brushes with death were the only two things that excited him. Neither money, nor power, nor sex, nor love held any thrill for him. To him, danger was not only his favorite vice (besides opium), but his way of life. A Romanian prince once, he was now the most wanted man in Europe, constantly hounded by that detective, Sexton Blake.

He sat, trying to let the opium work its magic, when he saw five men enter the restaurant. They all looked like explorers, save for one dressed in a black frock and a white turban, who sported a somewhat impressive beard. Zenith recognized him; it was the occult detective Sâr Dubnotal.

*He's probably here for a séance or some other such business,* thought Zenith.

The man with Dubnotal, though, immediately filled Zenith with indignation. He never forgot a face. It was t Hareton Ironcastle. The man who, a few years ago, had thwarted his attempt to rob the Gun Club of one if its priceless old pistols, and there he was, standing only a few meters away. It looked like they were searching for a table, but the dining room was crowded tonight. They changed their minds and left. With his food untouched, Zenith put his money on the table, grabbed his ebony sword cane and top hat, and followed. Retribution would be his.

When the company of five reached the Sâr's room, the Psychagogue performed his ritual of locking and marking every entrance with holy symbols, as well as examining the closet to see if the package was still in place. He then had each of them place their weapons inside, though Gordon tossed his gun belt on the bed, just to have it ready.

Once everything was in order, Dubnotal turned off the lights, save for one large fragrant candle in the middle of the small table. The Psychagogue had managed to shake his pursuers today, but he wanted to be sure they didn't know he was in this room, especially as he suspected he had been followed by other interested parties. Between the outlandish droning noises he heard while they traveled, and the two men outside who stole a few too many glances as they entered the hotel, Dubnotal knew he couldn't be too careful.

"So, this is all a bit odd," noted Chandler. "It seems both the professor and Gordon have a stone, just like Hareton and I."

Then, observing the table, Chandler beheld the largest ruby he had ever seen, and it too appeared to have markings.

"It seems you have one too, Sâr."

"I do," Dubnotal responded, "and that is what troubles me."

He sat each of them down at the table and began his tale.

"Each of us arrived here in Brazil, each with a stone. While this might seem like dumb luck—and perhaps it is—I think there's something more to it. Destiny? No, it is not that, but something deeper is happening than what appears on the surface..."

Taking up and quickly scrutinizing each stone, he continued:

"Chandu, the shopkeeper was correct in saying that your gold orb is from Mu. Professor Webb, the hieroglyphics carved into your stone are characteristic of those from Yuggoth. It once belonged to the Mi-Go. I will warn you that, despite the short time it has been in your possession, the Mi-Go will still be after you. They already know you have it, and as long as you do, they will pursue you. Chandu and Hareton, you will likely be in danger, too. The cult of Tsathoggua will have contacts in this city. In fact, I believe the men watching us outside the hotel are assassins."

"Why do they want the orb in the first place?" asked Ironcastle. "Is it for its value, or does it serve some greater purpose? From my own research, I know Tsathoggua was worshiped in Hyperborea, not Mu. Why would they want a Muvian stone?"

"For the same reason they wanted Chandu," replied the Sâr. "They needed to find the place the stones lead to, and only a psychic could lead them there with the help of one of the stones. Let's look at these strange coincidences that brought us together, shall we? Why did I choose to go to Brazil in the first place? Could my mind have been influenced by my stone? Were you, too, Chandu, influenced by your stone to come here? Legends say the Muvians fled to other places besides South America, why not go somewhere else? And then, Professor Webb and Gordon show up with a stone of their own. All of this is too much for there not to be greater powers at work. There is but one terrifying conclusion: the stones want to be reunited. It all lines up with the legend."

"What legend?" questioned Gordon.

The Psychagogue began to set the scene with his words:

"In times immemorial, after Mu sank, there were refugees who fled to South America, to the Amazon rainforest. Among them were humans, whose decedents make up some of the local tribes, and ape-men, called Maricoxi. Together, they established a marvelous city of gold with pyramids, monuments, and palaces..."

"The City of Z," added Hareton.

"What?" Dubnotal said, taken a bit off guard.

"Four years ago," Hareton began, "a British adventurer named Percy Fawcett led a small party in an expedition to a lost city in the Amazon. They were never seen again. Also, during one of his earlier adventures, he claimed he had encountered some of these Maricoxi."

Dubnotal rubbed his fingers through his beard.

"Yet another piece in this puzzle... Moving on, the Muvians made some unlikely allies with the Mi-Go, who shared in their misery, as they had colonies on Mu and lost them. After some exploring, they encountered an indigenous tribe of worshipers of Hastur. Soon, they shared trade, tools, and technology, and lived in peace for a long time. One day, though, the enmity between the Hastur worshipers and the Mi-Go began. When a rather zealous shaman of Hastur believed the Mi-Go were abominations to be destroyed, the Mi-Go called for reinforcements from another colony in Stygia—what we now call Egypt—which is why they set up that teleportation device that brought you, Professor and Mr. Gordon, here. A bitter war started and, eventually, the Muvian colony was dragged into it. It was a short fight, but it ended when a greater threat emerged in the form of a war party from Khokarsa across the sea..."

The Sâr then passed each of them a small phial of liquid.

"This is an elixir of my own making, distilled from the plant *taduki*. Drink it, then join hands with me. It will allow me to show you a picture of the past with my mind."

The others all drank, but Chandler hesitated. One skill he had learned was to hear a "yogi bell," a ringing in his head when he was in danger. He had heard it just as he put the elixir to his lips. Danger was all around, though it couldn't be anything he didn't already know.

*You're worrying too much*, he thought, and pushed it to the back of his mind.

Drinking the blue potion and all joining hands, each of the men were transported to days gone by...

The young soldier clad in cloth armor and holding a wooden club stood in horror as he watched his comrades butchered by the forces from the other side of the world. The lush jungle was burning with some kind of fire which water could not quench. The enemy warriors—he thought he had heard them called *numatenu*—were charging with swords made of a strange metal. He and his fellows had to hold the line.

He watched the Mi-Go, who had taught several Muvians the magic of Tsathoggua through the *Book of Eibon*, fly towards their enemies, only to get cut down. The men who had been taught to become wizards approached. They looked hideous, but the soldier supposed that learning secrets man should never know came at a price.

The magic-men raised their hands and formed mystic signs. They caused the very roots of the jungle trees to rise from the ground and impale their foes. The ape-men and the Hastur followers hurled their obsidian javelins. Some men fell, but most missiles missed their mark. The young soldier was too distracted to see a *numatenu* come up and lift his sword to decapitate him.

The vision suddenly changed.

Now there were men and Mi-Go gathered around a table, building some machine from gold, basalt, and wood. It looked like a veritable monolith, with large gears whirring and fires burning in basalt furnaces. When it was complete, some men decorated with body paint and feathers, holding rods marked with unusual runes, said some unintelligible phrases, and the machine came to life. The sky suddenly grew dark, to the point of looking like the void. The moon was there in place of the sun, but only a tiny sliver.

The vision then took them to the Khokarsan camp. The men were starving, their supplies in ashes. Some lay dead, poisoned arrows riddling their bodies. They saw one man nursing a bite from a poisonous insect. He wasn't going to last for more than an hour. There was a scream. A *numatenu* was dragged by a wild cat into the darkness. He shouldn't have strayed from the camp. Two men who looked like generals were talking about launching a full-scale assault on the enemy city.

The vision then showed them the *numatenu* charging, then time sped up, and they were retreating, at least, what was left of them were retreating. The machine stopped. Daylight returned. But there was no celebration. The city was in ruins, crops were destroyed, and corpses littered the streets. There was unusual snowfall everywhere. They then saw men in robes carving glyphs into three different stones.

Then they woke up.

Each of the men sat in stunned silence. They all had so many questions. What could they say after something like that?

"What you have just witnessed," the Sâr finally said, "was the creation of the three stones we now possess. They haven't been together for thousands of years, and yet, here they are now. When the fighting grew too fierce, the humans and ape-men from Mu, the Mi-Go, and Hastur worshipers, formed a triple alliance. When that failed, they created a machine to drown the world in eternal night. Understand, as extreme as it seems, it was quite a strategic advantage, for the Maricoxi as the Mi-Go could see in the dark. Not only that, but the jungle is a terrifying place to be at night time.

"After the triple alliance won a pyrrhic victory, they saw that their crops and livestock had died, and many of their people had succumbed to the unnatural winter. The elders decided to lock away the machine, only to be used in dire emergencies. To do so, they took a gold orb their ancestors had brought from Mu, the Mi-Go's teleportation stone, and an Opar ruby which they had taken as spoil of war, and turned them all into a key, to seal the device in their treasure room."

"And then the civilization fell?" Webb presumed.

"Correct. Most of the Mi-Go went to colonize elsewhere, hence the reason you found their outposts in the state you did. The Hastur worshiping tribe divided, and, through oral tradition, the name Khokarsa turned into the name of their mythical city, Carcosa. The Muvians abandoned their colony, some going to form a Tsathoggua cult, and their City of Z, as you called it, disappeared into myth and legend. You understand now why it is urgent that we protect the stones. Imagine if someone found the city, and used them to get to the machine. What if it fell into the wrong hands? The damage could be catastrophic! I've been hunted by children of the night for many days now. I know what they will do with them if they can get them. The stones must be kept safe at all c..."

To Sâr's great horror, when he looked down to the spot where the three stones were, he saw that the gold orb was gone! The others saw it too. Dubnotal ran to the door and found it was open. Someone had picked the lock. Ironcastle ran to the window. Below was a pale-skinned man in an evening suit, admiring the stone. A limousine was approaching, and the explorer didn't find it too hard to believe it was his escape.

"Zenith!" growled Ironcastle.

"Who?" Gordon questioned.

"One of the most dangerous criminals alive," Ironcastle explained.

The Sâr heard him, and cursed himself.

"I should not have been so careless with the elixir; he must have robbed us while we were under its effects."

"If he only has one stone, we don't have to worry, though, do we?" Chandler said. "I doubt he knows what it can be used for, and even if he did, he can't open the door with just one."

"No," said Webb, shaking his head. "The stones will find each other again, just as they did today. We cannot take that chance. We must protect them, not trust them to a villain such as he."

"We need to act," said Dubnotal running to the window. "Call the police!"

"No time," said Ironcastle. "By the time they get here, he'll be long gone. We must go after him."

Gordon had already tied on his gun belt and was holding a great length of rope from his supplies.

"Leave that to me," he said.

Without detailing his plan to the others, he went to the balcony. Hooking his rope through the railing, he took one end in each hand, and leapt to the next balcony below, startling two newlyweds sharing a romantic moment. Then, living up to his name, he tied a quick but sturdy knot around their balcony's railing, and began to propel down. It wasn't long enough to reach the street, but enough for him to fall without injury.

He let go of the rope, and dropped to the street below just as the limousine was pulling up.

"Face me, coward!" he called to Zenith, who turned to look at Gordon.

The gunslinger went for his revolver, but found his holster empty. He beheld the albino, cane under his arm, holding the orb in one hand, and, in the other, raising Gordon's own pistol.

Zenith smiled sardonically.

"The legendary El Borak, I presume. I see you noticed your side arm is missing. I took the liberty of borrowing it, for, at the time, it seemed I could use it more than you. It is a pity, I don't wish to kill you, but as you have insulted my honor by calling me coward, you've left me with little choice."

Gordon glared defiantly. He heard Zenith cock back the hammer. He was determined to die facing his foe. Suddenly, there was a gunshot, but not from the albino. The people on the streets were now running in terror. The two men in trench coats and hats, who had been eying Dubnotal and company as they entered the hotel, now appeared, each armed with a Luger.

The short one on the left said in a Portuguese accent:

"Hand over the stone! We've got a goodly sum waiting for us if we bring it back."

"I would like to see you try to stop me," Zenith said, laughing. He entered the vehicle and instructed: "Antonio, drive, I'm afraid my honor will have to be avenged another day."

The cultists fired a volley of bullets, several of which shattered the windshield and tore apart Zenith's driver. Annoyed, the albino got out, and casually put a bullet between each of their eyes. He was just about to enter the driver's seat, when Gordon tackled him. The two assassins had provided just the distraction he needed. As the revolver flew from Zenith's hand, Gordon struck him in the face. The albino retaliated with a knee to the ribcage.

The brawl was violent, as the two men rolled, punched, elbowed, and choked the other. Both were equally matched; blood ran from Zenith's mouth, and from Gordon's nose. They rolled over again, now with Gordon on top once more; he went to club his foe with his fists. Zenith blocked him, and with his free hand reached for the discarded gun. Gordon saw what he was doing, and tried to grab his arm. But his opponent was too fast. With one hand he socked Gordon, and with the other he got the gun.

He put it to the Texan's head.

"Goodbye, El Borak."

Gordon closed his eyes and prepared for the end.

"Stop!" cried a voice.

Zenith looked up.

Chandler, with two fingers pressed to his temple, was walking towards them. He looked Zenith in the eyes, and suddenly, it felt to the albino as if his very being was becoming molded like clay by some astral hand created by this interloper.

Chandler's eyes burned.

"Your will is no longer your own. You will put down the gun."

Zenith's mind was strong, but he could not resist this man's influence. He couldn't do anything but obey, and with a stiff movement he threw the weapon.

Chandler continued, "Now you will give the orb..."

The droning noise was back, louder than ever. It interrupted Chandler's thoughts, and, when he turned to see what the cause of the sound was, he was met with a horrifying sight.

There was a beast, not quite insect or crustacean or dragon, but some profane amalgam of the three. It was a Mi-Go! Just as the Sâr had predicted, it was after them for taking the black stone. It swooped down at Chandler, but he dodged just in time. He saw more were coming. He sighed; just what he needed.

He got his gun ready and shot two of his assailants, but they were resilient. One finally surrendered to its wounds and collapsed, dead, but the other three still came at him.

Just as one of them raised its claws to spear Chandler, it and another's torso exploded into gore as the sound of two gunshots echoed through the air.

As they collapsed, Chandler saw Hareton Ironcastle with a smoking elephant gun in his hands. The surviving Mi-Go turned to look at the one who killed its compatriots, giving Chandler the time he needed to load one round into the chamber, and shoot the beast point blank.

While this was transpiring, Zenith had retrieved his cane and drew the rapier blade from it. Gordon was at a loss. He really wished he had his own sword. Just before the fight could commence, a look of shock came over the albino's face.

"What the devil is that?"

Gordon turned around to see two Mi-Go. One grabbed him and threw him. Gordon struck the pavement, landing a good ten feet away. He groaned in pain, but then looked up from his daze. One Mi-Go was busy with Zenith, who was dancing around it and stabbing it with his sword while keeping hold of the orb in his off hand. The other was making its way over to Gordon. He got to his feet. If he was to fight this creature hand to hand, so be it.

"Gordon!" Ironcastle's voice called to him. "You're going to need this."

He heard metal sliding on pavement. He turned around to see his scimitar lying at his feet.

He didn't have time to thank the explorer; he picked it up and, with a hacking motion, cleaved the Mi-Go's skull (if it could be called that) just as it reached him. Looking up, he saw Zenith finish his attacker with a stab to the neck.

Chandler and Ironcastle had reloaded their weapons and were going to help their friend deal with the albino, when two bullets whizzed by them. They went for cover behind a palm tree, and the explorer looked up to see the origin of the shots. The "newlyweds" on the balcony, where Gordon had landed earlier, were now armed with Winchester rifles and shooting at them!

"Assassins, it seems," the explorer noted cynically.

Chandler pondered for a moment.

"I believe I can do something about that."

The two assassins on the balcony were readying their rifles, when a voice called:

"Wait! We'll give up the stone, don't shoot!"

A mustachioed man in khakis stepped out from behind a tree, putting his revolver on the ground. He looked into each of their eyes, and waved his hand. They were about to point their rifles at him, but instead of rifles in their hands, they each held a viper. The man and woman's eyes grew wide. They shrieked in abject horror, dropped the serpents, and retreated into their room. From Ironcastle's perspective, he saw two sane people look at their guns, scream, and run.

Chandu swaggered up to him and was about to speak.

"Let me guess," Ironcastle spoke for him, "a little trick you learned in India?"

Chandler laughed and then bowed like a magician who had just received a standing ovation.

Gordon and Zenith were still squaring off. It was as if there was nothing else around, only the two of them, ready to do battle. Zenith saluted his foe; Gordon twirled his scimitar. Gordon charged. It was a flurry of steel, as the most dangerous man in the West and the most dangerous man in the East crossed swords. As they fought, they got further and further away, until they were easily ten meters from where the duel began, then twenty, then thirty; their blades clashing the entire time. Gordon went for a wide slash, Zenith parried and then lunged. They were locked in *corps-a-corps*, the battle of wits and finesse turning into a contest of strength.

"Can you get a shot, Hareton?" Chandler asked hurriedly.

"I can't," the explorer replied. "I'd risk hitting Gordon. Quick man! Go over and hypnotize Zenith!"

"I'm afraid I can't help, either. I've done it once on him, so he'll know what to expect this time."

Gordon was in fantastic shape, but he wasn't as young as he once was. Zenith had youth, and, somehow, greater strength on his side. He forced Gordon down, and then went to run him through. The rapier blade stuck Gordon in his thigh (it would have pierced his heart had he not tried to roll away).

Gordon's comrades saw their chance, and raised their guns to shoot. Zenith noticed this, and decided that sometimes discretion *is* the greater side of valor. He dashed across the pavement away from the action, retrieving the shaft of his cane along the way. Bullets sped by him, but none hit their mark.

The albino laughed in triumph, still holding on to the orb. None could ever best Monsieur Zenith! He was so busy admiring the gold orb in self-satisfaction, that he realized only too late that his way was blocked by an automobile.

Zenith came to an abrupt stop. A man stepped out of the car, brandishing a snub-nose pistol. No, it couldn't possibly be...

"Halt, Zenith, in the name of the law!" spoke Sexton Blake firmly.

246

The albino knew this was the end of the line.

Later, while Hareton Ironcastle and Chandler took Gordon back to the hotel room to wait for a physician to tend to his wounded leg, Professor Webb and Sâr Dubnotal met with Blake at a small cafe. The streets were empty, and the waiter was forcing a polite smile, though Webb could tell the man was wishing they'd leave. He didn't have to worry, though; they would be gone soon enough.

"It was fortunate," Blake said while lighting his briar, "that your companions were able to distract Zenith as they did. I fear what might have happened had the three of them not been there. You might not have had time to call the police, who, in turn, would not have been able to alert me."

"Glad they could be of assistance," said the Sâr, smiling. "Are you sure the police won't have them arrested for disturbing the peace?"

Blake puffed out some smoke.

"I think catching an international criminal is good enough justification."

"Do you have the orb?" Webb asked with a tinge of desperation in his voice.

Blake produced it, and it thunked against the wooden table as he set it down.

Webb exhaled, relieved.

"Thank you. Well, now that we have this, I must be off. I promised to show my findings from Egypt back at Princeton as soon as possible. I will be sure they are kept safe in an archive somewhere."

Dubnotal looked over at the Professor.

"I'm afraid not," he said. "They cannot be kept together. I will trust the other two to some of my colleagues. As for me, I will keep one in a safe, and bury it somewhere where only I can find it. The world cannot have access to these."

"Well," Webb sighed, "that is disappointing. Can we at least get photographs of them, to be kept in the archives? We will tell them they were destroyed, but not before we could get a picture of them, just for history's sake?"

Dubnotal thought about it for a moment.

"Very well, only if I am allowed to accompany you. It's not that I do not trust you, but I cannot leave anything to chance."

"Splendid, we shall leave immediately. As my luggage is in Egypt, I have nothing to pack. I had already sent for a driver for myself to take me to the train station, and there should be room for you."

"What about the stones? Are they not still at the hotel?" asked the Sâr.

Webb reached under the table and took out a leather briefcase with a lock on it.

"Since you went to the liberty of putting them in here during the commotion with Zenith, I decided to grab it before we left, so you could put the last one here once we got it. Do you mind?"

Dubnotal hesitantly unlocked the briefcase, picked up the orb, put it in, then closed and locked it up.

"Splendid," Webb said, flashing a wide, toothy smile to the Great Psychagogue. "Now we should be off."

The physician had done a good job. Having finished quickly, he left the men in the hotel room to their own devices. They were all sitting around, sharing a bottle of twenty year-old scotch Hareton Ironcastle had bought for each of them. It was nice to have a *legal* drink again.

"Blasted Volstead Act," the explorer grumbled at the very thought of Prohibition.

Moonlight shone in through the windows, and the smell of the ocean was strong. As Chandler was going for his second scotch, in his mind he heard an ethereal ringing. His yogi bell again! He reached for his crystal ball. Inside, he saw the interior of a nice automobile (the back seat it seemed), but it was through someone else's eyes. The view changed. Through these eyes, he saw Professor William Channing Webb. Except, it couldn't be Webb, he looked like he had become slightly younger... No. He was transforming. He was getting younger with every second...

*Chandu,* a voice in Chandler's head spoke; *it is I, Sâr Dubnotal. I don't have much time. Webb is not what he seems.*

*Who is he?* Chandu responded telepathically.

Dubnotal answered Chandler's question.

His face paled; he dropped the crystal ball.

"Chandler?" Ironcastle asked. "What's wrong?"

"I should have known it was you from the beginning," the Sâr growled.

The man who was not Professor Webb laughed.

"Well, I don't blame you for not figuring it out. Your successes have dulled your skills, *El Tebib*, but I also put a good amount of work into this performance. I think it was a success, even if I do say so myself."

As he spoke, his accent changed from American to that of an English aristocrat.

"Your underlings did well following me," Dubnotal glared. "Why did they never attack me? How did they know my every move?"

"To answer your first question," the other man grinned, "I needed all the stones together. Though my minions are loyal, I didn't want to risk anything, such as one of them letting his greed surpass his loyalty. I had to retrieve your ruby myself, but I needed spies so you couldn't escape. You see, I knew the legend too, and had planned my little expedition to try to find one stone in hopes of finding the rest. As luck would have it, they all came together for me! To your second question, I will say what the Americans say: Always have an ace in the hole..."

The lady in the passenger's seat turned to look at the men in the back. Dubnotal immediately recognized her. He covered his mouth with his hand.

"Annunciata…"

"You would have been proud of her, *El Tebib*, the way she stood up against my children. They gnawed and groped and cut, but she fought back. I was even a little impressed. But, like all, she eventually fell to my dark kiss. I drank her blood, and she drank mine. Think of it, *El Tebib*, your loyal disciple, now my lovely bride."

The Sâr went to strike the fiend, but, with inhuman speed, it was he who grabbed Dubnotal's wrist. With little effort, he crushed it. There was a crack, and pain shot through the Psychagogue's entire arm.

It was broken.

"Now that the stones are mine, all that is left is to find the city, and then the machine. The world will never see light again, and I, Count Dracula, will be a god among men!"

"Son of a… I don't believe it," Gordon groaned, running his hand over his forehead. "Webb played us… the dog played us…"

"How is Dracula still alive?" Chandler asked the others, ignoring what Gordon had said.

"I didn't even think vampires were real," Gordon continued, "but I suppose I've seen even stranger things just today."

"It doesn't matter," Ironcastle said. "All that does matter now is that we stop Dracula before he reaches the machine. Chandler, what did the Sâr instruct us to do?"

"All he said was that he would give us further instruction on where they were after we looked in the box."

Ironcastle headed toward the closet.

"We know they're going to the City of Z; we'll just have to trust the Sâr to lead us there. Now, let's see what's in the package…"

The explorer opened the door, took out the long box, and undid the string holding it closed. He opened it. The others gathered around.

Gordon stared in awe.

"Is that…?"

"Yes. It's the Staff of King Solomon," replied Ironcastle with all the wonder of a child, "the weapon of the hero Solomon Kane. It is the bane of evil. If Dracula fears anything…" he stopped to look at the staff. It was the length of a sword, covered in arcane markings, and with the head of a cat carved on top. He finished, "…it's this staff."

With renewed vigor, he looked at his companions.

"Gentlemen, let us be off! We're going to find the lost City of Z."

*In 1902, Gustave le Rouge and Gustave Guitton, the authors of* La Conspiration des Billionaires *(translated and published by Black Coat Press as* The Dominion of the World*) published* Le Sous-Marin Jules Verne [The Submarine Jules Verne], *a deliberate homage to* Twenty Thousand Leagues Under the Sea. *Dominion was about American billionaire William Boltyn's insane scheme to bring Old Europe to its knees. The storyline of* Submarine Jules Verne *is briefly summarized in the story that follows. Michel Stephan decided to turn the tables and create a "Submarine Le Rouge" in this tale that pays homage to both Le Rouge and H.G. Wells...*

## Michel Stéphan: *The Submarine "Le Rouge"*

*Off the Coast of Spain, 1901*

Jacinto was not a simpleton and wondered sometimes, with a mix of amusement and bitterness, why people on the mainland kept thinking he was.

Jacinto lived on a tiny island off the Spanish coast. Fishing was his work, his trade; let's say that it was enough to make a living. From time to time, he could even afford the luxury of going down to Alicante to visit Madame Florence, who ran the best brothel in the city. Her girls were very beautiful and never rude, which was a great pleasure to the fisherman and a nice change from all the well-dressed people who normally came to his island and addressed him like the village idiot.

"Well, my good Jacinto, did the monster come back last night?"

"Well, Jacinto, did you see the devil dancing in the moonlight in the cemetery?"

What condescendence in the voices of these important and so-called learned people! It was the end of the 19th century, the dawn of the 20th, and yet, the Inquisition was not far off. Penitents still rambled through Spain, which was struggling to come out of the Middle Ages, and Jacinto played the game that passed him off for an idiot, but he knew more than these people from the capital who pretended to come to his island for vacation, but in reality wanted, above all, to see the monster, the abominable sea monster that wandered off the Spanish coast and had sunk at least two boats during the last three months. He took the attitude of a good, superstitious fisherman and gave them the well-calculated phrases that the fools loved to hear. But these pompous peacocks would never know the truth.

"The fabulous animal, gentlemen, that you consider a monster, is in reality a very complex machine, an extraordinary submarine invented by a man who is no longer alive. As for the old cemetery on the island, if no more human remains

250

are buried there, it's not because of the devil dancing in the moonlight like everyone say, but simply because it serves as a meeting point for Captain Fowler and his crew. But I don't think your learned brains are ready to accept this kind of thing. You need a few more years yet. So, I just play my role and tell you about demons and monsters since that's what you want to hear."

It always happened like that. However, for some time, the island had felt restless. Jacinto acted as go-between. He told the submarine about the coast guard patrols so they could come ashore without being spotted. He also advised the "guests," those who came for the iron vessel. The information never changed.

"You go to the cemetery at the end of the island. There, you'll see a huge ditch dug out of the ground and lit from the inside. It's an old pauper's grave that's been flooded for years. Don't be scared of the snakes: they look frightening, but they're not dangerous. You can go down by the rope ladder and you won't have to wait long for them to meet you."

In exchange, Jacinto always got a substantial sum of money and felt a certain pride in being part of such a special crew. Even if he stayed on land, he always carried a big responsibility.

Tonight, someone had come to the fisherman while he was getting ready to sit down for dinner. The night had fallen an hour before and Jacinto knew that he had to take him halfway to the cemetery, so that he would not take a bad fall in the dark. He also gave him the usual instructions to find the common grave. When his nocturnal visitor answered, Jacinto realized that, despite his impeccable Spanish, he was French. He was sure that he had seen his smiling beard before. His face was familiar. Then, the fisherman remembered where he had seen the broad-shouldered man, because he was educated and a voracious reader.

On returning home, he rushed up to the attic where he kept his trunks of books and, in no time, he found the photo of the stranger. He was none other than the astronomer Camille Flammarion, who was paying a visit to Captain Fowler on this hot night of May 1901.

A few years earlier, Tony Fowler had been the unlucky loser of a bold competition organized by Norwegian billionaire Ursen Ströem. Its goal was to build a submarine to prove the scientific usefulness of submersible vessels beyond their military function. Fowler, confident in his skills and the power of his father's wealth, had entered the competition sure that he would win. But faced with the passion and courage of his rivals, he quickly had become disenchanted and his twisted mind eventually planned to win by stealing a competitor's invention, the fabulous submarine *Jules Verne* created by French inventor, Gaël Mondax. Mondax had been caught off-guard but later, had spent all his strength and energy to build a second submarine, the *Jules Verne II*.

A fierce race had then taken place between the two submersibles, that had ended up with the *Jules Verne*'s destruction. Fowler escaped, but the explosion had not left him unharmed. He was sent back to the United States, where his father, with an insanity plea, managed to save him from justice. However, his punishment was already dreadful enough. because the blast from the *Jules Verne* had left him limbless and his face destroyed, without nose or lips.

Thanks to one of his father's friend, billionaire William Boltyn, Fowler had gotten some of dignity back with the help of metal prostheses, but now, he looked more like a machine than a man. Once a brilliant engineer, he had not given up on his submarine project.

While Boltyn was preparing a final attack on Old Europe by installing long stretches of rail underwater to facilitate the invasion of the continent by robot-soldiers, Fowler had finished building a third submarine, equipped with sophisticated weapons. It was an exact replica of the *Jules Verne* but Fowler, because of the bitterness he felt towards France, had decided to name it after a famous pirate from his family tree, Jack Rackham, nicknamed Red Rackham—hence, the submarine *Le Rouge*.

Camille Flammarion had come of his own free will, answering the invitation that Fowler had sent him. Knowing the American by reputation, and the hatred that Fowler harbored for the French, it was curiosity only that motivated the scientist to meet the submarine captain.

It had been a week now since the astronomer had boarded the submarine *Le Rouge* and he was starting to get impatient. Nothing was happening as planned. He felt he deserved a frank explanation from Fowler, or else he would demand to be taken back to dry land.

There had been other guests aboard, something which he was not happy about. First, there was billionaire William Boltyn, whom Flammarion knew by reputation. The embodiment of dollars and crime, his hatred of the Old World could be easily read on his puffed up face. The second guest was a man nobody liked: Dr. Moreau. The French astronomer had never heard of him, but listening to his theories on evolution had convinced him Moreau was at best a charlatan and at worst a madman, lacking any humor and table manners.

It was, in fact, during one of their evening meals in front of the huge sea bay window that Fowler had come out and explained the reason for his invitations and apologized for the delay. The sight of the engineer was always awkward, if not horrifying. Even though his clothes, impeccably tailored, hid his half-metallic body, his face—missing lips and nose on the right side—made one believe that his brain, as potent as it was, was forever twisted. His steely gaze, reflecting his unbearable loneliness gave the French astronomer goose bumps.

"Gentlemen, first of all I thank you for your patience," Fowler said. "Although a voyage on board this marvelous machine of mine should be pleasant enough, I cannot leave you waiting any longer. I'm going to tell you about some extraordinary events of late, as well as the reason why you're here. Several months ago, off the Spanish coast, around the continental shelf, at the exact point where it sinks into the depths of the Ocean, I found a spherical machine containing three strange beings, which I assumed came up from the bowels of our planet. These three voyagers were completely exhausted, to the point that one of them was dead already. The other two are with us on this vessel right now, and I will introduce you to them soon. They are not mollusks, even if they look a little like them. They need oxygen and are not amphibian."

"Are they like us—I mean physically?" Dr. Moreau asked.

"No. They're quite hideous," Fowler replied. "You'll see for yourselves. They have no limbs like ours, but tentacles of a sort, and pretty handy, I must say. They're small, especially compared to a human. But after studying their craft,. I have no doubt that we're dealing with a technologically advanced race."

"Are they hostile?" the astronomer asked.

"Not at all. They're despondent, like laboratory animals after being captured. Listen, gentlemen, now I'm going to reveal to you my project and why we've been slightly delayed by my good friend, Mr. Boltyn."

Their eyes turned toward the American billionaire who pretended not to notice.

"A few weeks ago, Mr. Boltyn, who is my financial backer, and to whom I reported my discovery, decided to help me again by providing the necessary funds to meet these creatures beyond the continental shelf. This, of course, meant perfecting my submarine so it can descend even deeper into the abyss. There's no doubt in my mind that these creatures are the vanguard of a whole race that is trying to come up to the surface of the Earth. As I said, they are not mollusks. We may be in the presence of mutated Atlanteans... But there's a problem. Mr. Boltyn has declared war on the Old World, and this has delayed my plans and makes it impossible for you to return home, at least for the moment. But don't worry, the war will be a lightning attack and we will soon be able to resume our project."

"You mean to say that the Old World is in flames?" Moreau asked.

"The Old World will soon cease to exist," Boltyn said. "I've been preparing this war for years. I have to tell you, Monsieur Flammarion, with all due respect, that, right now, your precious Paris observatory is probably gone, along with your beautiful Montmartre district. But worthy men like you will always find a secure position amongst your conquerors."

"Is this true?" Flammarion asked Fowler.

"We will surface soon and you can see for yourself. Andalusia is in flames and the sky is blood-red."

"Is there no way to stop this massacre?"

"I can't contact America from this submarine," Boltyn replied. "Anyway, I wouldn't want to do it. I promised Fowler this: if he lets me destroy the Old World, then I'll help him with his work. Give and take. Knowing how our dear captain feels about Europeans, you can imagine how easily he agreed to my terms."

"Is this true?" the French astronomer asked again.

"Two hundred years ago, the Valladolid Debate took place nearby, in the city of that name. It was about proving that the natives of the Americas were human beings. When this war will be over, we'll do the same. My submarine will sail up the Guadalquivir to Seville, we'll find the city's religious authorities and show them the two beings I have found. When everyone sees that a superior race lives at the center of the Earth, with testimonies by you, Dr. Moreau, and you, Monsieur Flammarion, we will ask this religious authority to verify whether these creatures also have a soul. Then, I think that a new era will begin and I, Tony Fowler, will finally be given the recognition I truly deserve!"

The French astronomer was no longer listening. He was thinking of his family and friends, everyone he loved and whom he had probably already lost. And he struggled not to lose his mind.

Nothing happened as planned. The two Atlanteans—they called them this out of convenience—looked too different to bestow upon them a human conscience. Tentacled arms, a kind of duck's beak, as ugly as could be imagined, enough to make the bravest of men shiver... Everything about them was too different. Moreover, the two creatures were clearly not in good health. Their long journey up from the bowels of the globe had weakened their vital system, and it did not seem like they would recover.

The night after his first encounter with the Atlanteans was a troubled one for the French astronomer. He slept very, preferring to stay awake rather than suffer the horror of sleep that plunged his unconscious mind into dark places of his soul which he had been careful not to explore.

However, he had to admit that something was changing in him. An obvious change that all the crew would notice. According to Fowler, and the information from Boltyn, the war was about to end and they could then surface without danger into the Guadalquivir river and proceed onto Seville. It had been a week of waiting. Flammarion gradually came out of his silence and went to find the Captain in his cabin.

"I see you're doing better," Fowler said. "I'm delighted because you're a man I respect."

"I need to talk to you."

"I think I know what you have to say. I've been watching you. I noticed that something was happening between you and the female creature, our new Eve from Atlantis. Am I right? Did you experience a telepathic contact with the creature? Tell me, Monsieur Flammarion. It would be wonderful news for all of us, and for the world in general."

"You're not wrong. But it's not like that. Truthfully, I don't really know how to explain it..."

"Try anyway. Did you or did you not communicate with the creature?"

"It's simpler than that. I think I'm in love."

To the astronomer's great surprise, Fowler exploded in laughter.

"What do you mean, *in love*?"

"Well, I mean something quite simple. We don't have to go looking for a complicated communication, some connection between two worlds. It's just an emotion between two beings separated more than you can imagine."

"I think it must be mutual," Fowler said. "She's doing a lot better since you saw her. It's damn surprising." He kept smiling. "And how do you see the future? Are you thinking of some project with this being?"

"That would be hard. No, I just feel an inner well-being. Beyond the physical, beyond appearances. It happens to a lot of people on Earth. I'm just happy like a child."

"That's absolutely baffling, but it confirms my theory. I want you to see her every day, and you'll be part of the expedition that will contact the religious authorities. If everything hasn't been destroyed, we'll start a Second Debate in Seville or Valladolid. We've never been so close to the future!"

The submarine *Le Rouge* cruised slowly up the Guadalquivir before rising cautiously out of the water. Fowler was the first to get out, followed by Boltyn and Flammarion. Standing on the deck, the three men looked around. The banks of the river were equal distance apart; they were a good hundred yards from the shore. And the sight was the same everywhere: desolation and silence.

A few people, however, appeared on one bank of the river.

"Look, Boltyn," Fowler said. "The survivors should have no idea that the man responsible for their suffering is right in front of them. Do you think you wiped out all trace of life in Europe?"

The billionaire did not answer, stunned as he was by the desolation before his eyes.

"We'll go ashore," Fowler continued. "The dams and bridges have collapsed and my submarine can't go any farther. Monsieur Flammarion, take our Atlantean with you. I had her placed on a special stretcher that you can drag over land. I hope it won't be too hard to get to Seville, which is about twenty miles from here."

The astronomer nodded. After some preparations, a small group of two crewmembers, along with Fowler and Flammarion, and the creature lying on the makeshift stretcher, started out down the towpath along the Guadalquivir.

After a few hours, it became obvious that the destructive madness of the Americans had spared little of Old Europe. Spain looked like a cemetery. But there was something even more worrisome... Flammarion glanced anxiously at the stretcher. The creature looked more and more agitated. At one time, one of her tentacles gently touched his shoulder, then shot back as if it had felt a sudden shock of electricity.

"Hurry!" Flammarion shouted. "I don't think she's coping well with this voyage."

"Bear up," Fowler said. "We're almost there."

"And where's that? A country hospital? Everything in this ravaged world has been destroyed by man's madness!'

"No, look! There's a town over there that doesn't look as bad as that. We still have a chance."

Urged on by a new hope, the group resumed its march with more enthusiasm. Flammarion noticed a huge steel machine smashed on the ground to their right. A war machine, no doubt, and truly enormous. The creature's tentacles grazed him less and less. All of a sudden, he felt them stiffen up.

"She's dying," he screamed. "Hurry up!"

The group ran to the town. At least half of the place was still standing. In the center of town, a few haggard men wandered around like zombies among the ruins.

"Stay here," Fowler ordered. "I speak Spanish."

The astronomer held back saying that he, too, spoke the language fluently. Instead, he gazed at the creature who looked worse and worse. He had never before felt so helpless. The war seemed really secondary compared to the Atlantean's death.

One of the Spaniards to whom Fowler had talked lumbered over to their small group. Upon seeing the creature on the stretcher, he screamed loudly and ran away. Flammarion did not react. He watched Fowler walk back towards them like a robot. His features were drawn, his shoulders slumped; now, he looked like the other survivors.

"We were wrong. We were fooled," he announced.

"Wrong about what? Fooled by whom?" the astronomer asked.

"The war between America and Europe never took place. Martians are the cause of this disaster! About a month ago, some meteorites fell out of the sky on all the continents, launching a war of worlds that we, apparently, barely escaped unharmed."

"What?"

"I don't know anything else right now. But some of these meteorites crashed into the sea. Hence our confusion. What I took for people from Atlantis or the Center of the Earth were actually Martians."

Incredulous, Camille Flammarion listened to the rest of the captain's story. In the meantime, around his wrist, the little creature slowly released her grip, defeated forever by the Earth-bound germs.

*Translation by Michael Shreve*

*Mephista is the female embodiment of evil created for a series of horror films starring the beautiful actress, Edwige Hossegor. But she acquires an unholy life, independently of Edwige, and embarks on a murderous spree. Mephista is usually associated with the private detective, Teddy Verano. Both were created by the prolific French writer Maurice Limat. An omnibus volume of three Mephista novels has just been translated and released by Black Coat Press. Since the beginning of time, two supernatural entities known only as HE WHO CONTROLS LISA and HE WHO CONTROLS LEONOX battle each other on Earth. Lisa is a beautiful woman with inky-dark eyes. Leonox is a man with a crooked smile. Neither can truly die and they assume different guises at different times. Both enlist human agents to assist them in their conflict. Lisa's ally is journalist Francis Dalvant. A recurring character in the series is the meek Mr. Mower, the incarnation of Death, who obeys neither power. Like Mephista, the Leonox series, created by writer Paul Bera, was published by the "Angoisse" imprint of Editions Fleuve Noir from 1971 to 1974.*

## Artikel Unbekannt : *Leonox Meets Mephista*

*Paris, the 1970s*

*To Paul Béra & Maurice Limat*

A faint rumble grew slowly louder in the back of the catacombs. With their heads bowed forward in reverence, fifty hooded individuals repeatedly mumbled obscure incantations before a huge purple curtain. Two torches in the shape of human arms, planted ten feet off the ground on either side of the wall hanging, made the shadows of the cabal dance and tainted the walls with their tiny, distorted figures. As if hypnotized by this tentative stuttering, a colony of brown rats, crouched along the walls, gazed in awe at the private expressionist screening, although no member of the mysterious gathering paid them any attention. The real show was still to come and, sensing that they were not welcome guests, the rodents scattered when the heavy folds of the curtain spread open.

A cloud of dust mixed with smoke from the incense concealed the scene for a few seconds, then it dissipated and revealed a platform that looked like a theater stage. A crude altar, made of a black marble slab lying on roughly hewn stones, stood in the center. Out of nowhere, a figure draped in a red cloak suddenly appeared. Turning its back to the audience, it placed a small, wrapped object on the primitive structure. Infant cries rose out of the thick layer of swaddling clothes and echoed off the walls of the crypt.

As if to cover the squawking, a husky, sensual voice immediately started in on a strange chant. A woman's voice. While reciting her haunting chant, the priestess pulled a knife with a curved blade out of her tunic.

A shiver ran through the ranks of disciples. The woman cursed them in a foreign tongue and, to give even more importance to her litany, she whirled around, in a graceful, animal movement, to face them. With her face mostly hidden by a black mask that intensified the ferocity of her eyes, she held high the dagger and climaxed her ritual with a profession of faith that sounded like a death sentence:

"I am hatred. I am evil. I am..."

All of a sudden, just as the masked woman was about to plunge her weapon into the newborn's heart, her arm froze, and she broke off her monologue.

After a moment of hesitation, during which she looked troubled and confused, she finally spoke again, but her voice had changed in a strange way.

"Leave... What you are waiting for cannot happen... Leave... Or else you will suffer the law of HE WHO CONTROLS LEONOX... Flee... Don't come back... If you stay... I see his hideous grin... Torrents of lava... Flayed bodies... Dismembered corpses... Yours! This is not what you want... Get out of here!"

Although frightened by her change of attitude, and her threatening speech, some of the cabal nevertheless tried to protest, but the priestess did something that none of them were expecting. Dropping the knife, she ripped off her scarlet cloak and offered the assembly the superb sight of her naked body. Then, staring at her disciples with eerie, inky-dark eyes that they had never seen before, she removed her mask.

The hooded figures ran for the exit of the catacombs howling in fright.

Edwige Hossegor woke up screaming.

"Her! No, it's not possible!"

The young woman's entire body was trembling. Completely disoriented, she fumbled for the switch on her bedside lamp, but, in her haste, she knocked over the table, which crashed to the floor.

Feeling both nerve-racked and strangely lethargic, she spent the following hours curled up in bed, unable to fall back asleep.

Early in the morning, exhausted, she got up and took a long, pleasurable bath. Although the warm water relaxed her statuesque body, it did not dissipate the anxiety from the night before.

After a frugal breakfast, the actress felt an irresistible urge to share her terrible vision. Two telephone calls and forty-five minutes later two men stood in her living-room. The first was a seductive, middle-aged playboy, Baron Tragny, her official fiancé, but Edwige was more interested in talking to the other, a well-built man in his forties, looking self-confident and determined.

"Teddy Verano," she said, "you know that I don't make it a habit to bother you for nothing. Besides, it's been months since you've heard from me, except what you read in the press. You know that I've started acting again since you got rid of Mephista, who was poisoning my life. Or at least I thought you had... until last night!" Here, the young woman's voice broke into sobs. "Because Mephista has returned! I don't know how, but she's back!"

The detective offered her a handkerchief

"You were right to call me, Edwige," he said in a soothing voice. "If you can manage it, can you tell me exactly how she manifested herself?"

"At first, I thought it was a dream, but I was wrong. The scene was so real, so frightfully real, Teddy! A child,--a baby was on an altar and this woman, this monster who looked so much like me, was about to kill it in front of a coven of cultists, when, suddenly, she stopped. I can't tell you why she changed her mind, because that's when I woke up."

"Where did it take place? Do you remember?"

"How could I forget? I've never seen a more creepy place than the catacombs. I'm not very surprised that such evil creatures would choose to meet there."

Teddy Verano kept silent for a minute. Mephista! At first, she was just a simple role played by Edwige Hossegor. Then, a shadowy phantasm that turned real in a gruesome way...

The detective was puzzled. He knew Edwige's tormented personality, but he also knew by experience that her "visions" were never wrong. The actress seemed to have a mysterious psychic link with her frightful alter ego.

"Can I make a phone call?" he asked.

"By all means."

His friends in the police told Verano that a baby boy, barely one year old, had been found that very morning near the entrance to the catacombs by a milkman making his rounds. Wrapped in a thick red cloak, the infant looked in fine health. They had brought him immediately to a doctor who had examined the child thoroughly. He was relieved to conclude that the baby was in perfect health, to the great delight of his mother, a recently retired dancer who had rushed over to pick him up.

There was still the question of the kidnapping, and two plausible sources provided pointed to the catacombs. After making sure that Baron Tragny would keep an eye on Edwige while he was gone, Teddy Verano left, promising to give them news as soon as possible.

Meanwhile, on the other side of town, two men were talking in a small, run-down apartment.

"Dalvant, I'm not authorized to tell you what happened," said Mr. Mower, trying in vain to clean his fingernails with a nail-clipper. "Believe it or not, even

I am not sure I understand it myself. But you should know that Lisa returned in the guise of a woman who is of great interest to our common friend, Leonox."

"Leonox? Our common friend? I don't appreciate your sense of humor, Mower. Besides, you know very well that HE WHO CONTROLS LEONOX has no power over Lisa!"

"Yes, under normal circumstances, certainly. But as it happens, this new, er, body is not, er, neutral. Lisa is forced to fight against it constantly, and Leonox is trying to use this to his own advantage, trying to push the envelope as it were. My masters even think that the choice of Lisa's new body may have been 'guided.' In some way or another, someone 'up there' has abused their privilege. I'm here to put things back into balance."

"Are you telling me you came to 'reap' Lisa? Then, you're going to be disappointed! Not only do I know that your position forbid you to reap her, because that might tilt the balance, but I am determined to protect her!"

"Oh dear, no, that's not what I meant at all, Dalvant. I've already seen you at work. I know what you're capable of. I wouldn't dream of fighting you. But will you be strong enough to protect Lisa against herself?"

I turned to Lisa, who had sat silently, slumped in a chair. during the whole argument.

I, Lacana, the criminal who had become Francis Dalvant after turned by Leonox, was no tenderfoot when it came to the Powers who controlled us, but a strange shiver ran down my spine when I saw the young woman's eyes. Oh, she certainly had her usual, inky-dark eyes, but now, I saw a flame dancing in them that I had never seen before, staring back at me with unearthly intensity...

Leonox and Lisa, although they each served two opposing Powers, were not without some points in common. Above all, they shared the ability to change their appearance, or rather their earthly incarnation. Leonox was always betrayed by that awful grin that twisted half his mouth every time he tried to smile, and Lisa fell into trances that transformed her eyes into black pearls.

This characteristic allowed me to identify them without fail, no matter what new body they wore. I had "lost" Lisa for a long time, and I wasn't about to let Mower ruin my joy at having found her again. Mower stared at me, absent-mindedly while continuing to pick at his dirty fingernails. He was the one who had told me about Lisa's return and Leonox's interference. Mower now claimed that Lisa was not herself. Might she once again be lost to me?

Without worrying any more about this, I went to the young woman still slumped in the chair and took her in my arms. That was when, for the first time since her return, I heard her voice, hesitant, gentle, fragile, so much so that it kept breaking up.

"Francis, I don't understand... what happened... to me... I don't know... how I got here... how I found you... I feel... my personality... is not stable..."

"Well, your condition seems quite normal," I replied, aware of the stupidity of my response. "Your reincarnations don't always go smoothly... You've gone through those disturbing stages before... And there's the emotion caused by seeing each other together again... But now, you're here and that's all that matters. How about starting by taking off this gruesome mask?"

I reached out toward her face to remove the mask that was still hiding it.

"No!"

In the grip of some irrational terror, Lisa had howled like a wolf. Her voice had become hoarse and created a chill wind into the room. Seeing that I was stunned, she pushed me away and ran to the front door. Mower did not interfere and let her rush into the hallway. Paradoxically, his passive attitude reassured me, because it meant that Lisa was not in any immediate danger. I, however, decided to run after her.

The clicking of her heels echoed through the stairway. I hurtled down in pursuit. Although I took the stairs two by two, I did not catch up to her by the time I reached the lobby. I barely had time to see her run outside the building as the dumbstruck concierge looked on.

She was thirty feet ahead of me. My heart was pounding. I pushed open the glass door and saw Lisa on the street, getting farther away, her slender shape a shadow among the shadows. I called out, but my cry got lost in the depths of the night. Without losing hope I resumed my frantic pursuit.

Dalvant had been a good athlete and I, using his mortal coil, should be able to catch her sooner or later. So, I sped up and managed to gain some ground.

Lisa was almost in arm's reach when, all of a sudden, a man jumped out of an alley right in front of me. I tried to avoid him but, surprised by the suddenness of the apparition, I could not do it. I crashed into him and fell.

In spite of the violent collision, I leaped up right away, as if doped up on the adrenaline flowing through me since I'd left the apartment. The man had not moved and Lisa had disappeared. Furious and desperate, I was about to take it out on the evening stroller when I recognized the hateful little grin that half-twisted his mouth... It was Leonox!

A bitter, metallic taste tickled my taste buds. I forgot the pact that had sealed my destiny and all my old mistakes. I emptied my mind of all the fleeting images that had been the identities of Lisa and Leonox. ... Nothing mattered anymore. I was Lacana again, the blood-thirsty, merciless criminal, ready to do anything to make Leoneox's crooked smile disappear. I was seeing red; the blood in my mouth was boiling like the blood in my veins, pulsing in my head. I felt a ball of molten hatred grow bigger and my hands, my murderous hands, grabbed the throat of the grinning monster.

Without trying to break my hold Leonox stared straight into my eyes. I squeezed harder until my knuckles turned white. I wanted him to fight while I threw all my rage into him; I wanted him to feel his sick, monstrous life leave his rented body, but I only saw his smile grow bigger. And it grew bigger like... like a wound... a scar... like the mark on my chest!

A terrible pain spread through my chest. I felt as if someone was carving it with a knife... a signature... a tattoo? No, I refused to know what was being done to me. I did not want to remember! But the awful, unbearable pain spread through me like the germs of some sudden disease and, in spite of myself, almost without realizing it, I let go of my grip to feel my chest. It was soaked in blood; I hurt so much. I fell to my knees before Leonox, before this vile creature who mocked me as if nothing had happened.

"Did you forget that you can't hurt me, Dalvant? Did you forget that you bear, on your chest, the mark of HE WHO CONTROLS ME?"

Paralyzed by pain, I did not answer. The cadaver-thief walked off into the night after throwing a last sarcastic glance at me. Little by little, as his silhouette faded away, I felt the pain vanish, even though my head was still spinning. Gathering all my strength, I tried to stand up.

Suddenly, out of nowhere, a hand reached down to me. A helping hand in this dark, empty city? Yes, but a hand with dirty, black fingernails. A hand that it would be better not to touch... Mower's hand!

I recoiled in disgust, instinctively.

"As you please, Dalvant. But maybe you'll be interested in what I have to tell you... Especially if, as I believe, you want to find Lisa as soon as possible."

Teddy Verano absent-mindedly watched the first drops of rain forming thin streams down the dusty hood of his car. The sky could no longer hold back the storm clouds that had been threatening since early in the evening. With no clues about Mephista's trail, the detective had decided to stake out the entrance to the part of the catacombs where the black mass had been held, even though he supposed that the members of the sect would not come back so soon to the site of their aborted crime, but he had to have faith in the mysterious bond that connected Edwige Hossegor to her evil twin.

Before falling victim to another cataleptic fit, the actress had experienced another vision in which Mephista again had the starring role. Although Edwige had been unable to describe the various players in the macabre scene, she had given him a precise location.

"She's going to go back to the catacombs," she had said. "But this time, she won't be the executioner. The Dark's mouth has opened and ready to swallow her."

Anyone but Verano would have paid no attention to these obscure prophecies, but what made him the celebrated "ghost detective" also made him trust Edwige. The actress had already proved her talents by helping to resolve several similar cases in the past, and once again, her weird premonitions were blurring the line between dream and reality.

The storm broke out at the twelfth stroke of midnight. As if waiting for this moment to leave its mysterious hiding place, a slender but ominous masked form suddenly appeared out of the shadows of the dimly lit buildings.

It was an apparition straight out of horror movies, Verano thought, even if its performance seems a little too mechanical.

Indeed, Olga Mervil—Mephista's other instrument—was acting like a sleepwalker or someone who has been hypnotized. She walked jerkily and looked like she did not know what direction to take. Finally, after a few awkward, hesitating movements, the young woman entered a dark alley. She fell out of sight immediately, absorbed by one of the many shadows that the night had cast over the neighborhood.

Without wasting a minute, Teddy Verano jumped out of his car and ran after her. The alley turned out to be a dead end, but the detective glimpsed Olga enter the arched doorway of a rundown hovel. After sprinting two hundred yards, he opened the age-worn door that led directly down a flight of stairs.

Verano descended cautiously and came to a cellar where a thin ray of light filtered through the back. He slowly approached the dim light, then ran into an iron gate, which opened easily. Realizing that he had just come into the basement of a clothes shop, the detective held back a cry of surprise in discovering what was being stored there...

Mannequins! Mannequins everywhere, with their empty eyes staring into nothingness, cold, plastic dolls lined up neatly, bare or dressed artistically from head to toe. There were dozens of them, delicate robots waiting for a trendsetter, a miracle-worker to breathe a spark of life into them.

Right before Verano's stunned gaze, Olga took her place among the mannequins, as if it was the most natural thing in the world to do. He watched her silently, like a shy spectator invited to a forbidden show. The young woman froze, in a display of slow motion, and she faded into the background until she had become part of the decor, a supple statue masked in lifeless elegance.

All of a sudden, a creaking sound broke the dark spell of this strange scene. The detective saw a hidden door, hitherto unseen, open in the opposite wall. He immediately slipped into the nearest changing room. Feeling his way behind the curtain, he figured it was better to wait in hiding to see what would happen since he did not know how many cultists he might be dealing with. And he congratulated himself on his decision when he heard a cynical voice boom out as the rusted hinges whined a second time.

"You again, Dalvant? How did you know?" There was a pause as the door creaked again. "Oh, I see! It was that dear Mr. Mower who wanted to see us all gathered together, no doubt hoping to get us to do his job. Well, it doesn't matter now. You're going to be very disappointed, my friend."

A deadly silence followed this ominous declaration. Then the voice continued.

"Lisa's latest reincarnation was a mistake, Dalvant, not some kind of ploy. The woman in which she reincarnated—and for whom we've come looking here—has too strong a will. She cannot be controlled because she is already under the influence of other powers, which neither my Master nor Lisa's can afford to upset. Lisa, therefore, must 'disappear' again, but as a token of good will to those who control her 'vehicle,' her new body will be preserved. He who controls me has forbidden me to harm her. As for Mower, he's come here for nothing!"

At that instant, a mannequin collapsed to the floor. But it was a doll of flesh and blood, her face hidden behind a mask...

I could not hold back a cry. I did not recognize my voice (was it Lacana's or Dalvant's?) because it was distorted by fear.

Lisa was my double, my soul mate. Bu now, she was unconscious on the floor, a few feet away from me. I took her in my arms and caressed her hair. Her eyes were closed, but my heart started beating again when I felt a pulse in her neck.

I looked up, searching for Leonox to heap insults on him but the monster had disappeared. Mower had also gone. Realizing that his presence was no longer necessary he had vanished, probably in search of easier prey.

I did not really care because Lisa was all that mattered to me. But I had lost her again. The woman whom I held was no longer Lisa. She had only served as her incarnation briefly, in a vague, confused and conflicted manner, because she had had to share that body with another entity... I knew by her dazed look when she opened her eyes that she had no memory of anything that had occurred during the last few days.

"You should leave, Monsieur Dalvant. There's nothing left for you to do here."

I jumped. Pulling myself together, I swung around to confront the person who had just spoken to me. He was a man of around forty who had just emerged out of a changing room and was walking towards me with confidence. I know how to judge a person and it was clear that this guy was tough.

"Who are you?" I asked bluntly, clenching my fists.

"I'm here for this young woman, just like you came for another. You did the best you could, but now it's my turn to take over. Besides, the police will soon be here and, even if you've done nothing wrong, I don't think you want to talk to them, do you?"

I wanted to answer but the words got caught in my throat. In utter despair, I had to admit the stranger was right. Lisa was gone and, like a tired, bleary-eyed boxer at the end of his match, I left that mannequin of flesh and blood rest on her plastic pillows and staggered to the door.

I felt empty and useless. I knew that Lisa would not return soon, but I could not resist glancing at every woman I met in the street, in case one of them would return my stare with that inky black gaze that I had come to love so much...

A few hours later, Teddy Verano returned to Edwige Hossegor's apartment. Dressed in an elegant, black satin negligee, the actress received him warmly.

"In spite of all the harm Olga caused," said Verano after recounting the events of the night, "I can't help feeling sorry for her. This time, I'm sure that she had nothing to do with what happened in the catacombs. She was manipulated by another entity."

"I feel you're right," said Edwige, sensuously blowing out smoke from the cigarette that Verano had offered her. "She was just a receptacle. But her personality, even though confused, was still a magnet for evil. And I felt that in my flesh and in my soul, because, in spite of myself, I am still connected to this terrible creature whom I was the first to incarnate. But tell me, Teddy, these men you heard, who were they?"

"To tell you the truth, I only really saw one man. He was sad, grieving, the victim of dark fantasies. Regarding the other two, I think we can be glad we had nothing to do with them. One of them was probably responsible for Mephista's return. I don't know how or why he did it, but it was obviously for nothing good. As for the second, I didn't hear his voice. They referred to him by a weird name, but I'm pretty sure that it's better not to know anyone called 'Mr. Mower.'"

The young woman shivered.

"Now that the evil aura of Mephista is gone, we can hope they won't show up again… What do you think? Is it over for good?"

"Over? Concerning Olga Mervil, yes, possibly. She is back at her hospital and they'll keep her safe there. As for her other personality, however, I don't know. This strange adventure has proven to us once again that there are nefarious powers that don't hesitate to use her as a catalyst. Evil has many faces and who can say that one of its aspects won't summon Mephista again?"

*Translation by Michael Shreve*

*A* Tales of the Shadowmen *would not be complete without a story featuring that wonderful rogue, Arsène Lupin. The following tale takes place after Lupin has managed to outwit Sherlock Holmes in "The Blonde Phantom," and is traveling abroad—North Africa, South America, the Far East—under the alias of Duc de Charmerace...*

## David L. Vineyard: *The White Star of Atlantis*

*Tangiers, 1905*

Tangier was one of those cities where a man might sit at his breakfast late and expect the world would eventually pass before him. On this morning, that was exactly the mood the Duc de Charmerace was in; a mood to idly sit with his coffee and watch the world on parade.

Lighting a thin black cigarillo, the Duc looked up in time to see a tall, fair-haired man with the features of a Greek god and the eyes of a lost soul walking towards him. On the voyage from South America, the tall, fair Englishman, a dark black Irish-American named O'Rourke, and the Duc had become bosom companions, a company of adventurers, a band of brothers of sorts, each sailing to or from some unspoken adventure.

Over cards and brandy, the three had spoken, at first guardedly, and then with greater openness, of their wide travels and experiences; the world-weary Englishman, the French aristocrat, and the American soldier of fortune finding more in common than a casual observer could have imagined.

The Englishman and the Irish American both stood in contrast to the slender French aristocrat, whose average height belied a whipcord physique. Any one of the trio would have been a fit companion for adventure; the three together were a formidable force.

The Duc began to rise and was waved back to his seat by the Englishman as he arrived at the table:

"You haven't seen our friend O'Rourke about this morning, have you?" the Englishman asked with a hint of concern in his voice.

"Not since last night," the Duc said as the Englishman sat.

A waiter appeared, as if by magic, to take the newcomer's order.

"He seemed rather taken with our mystery woman," added the Duc, "and I assumed he was off to an early start. He doesn't strike me as the type to sit around yearning. I would say he was a man of action above all."

The Englishman with the haunted eyes nodded. He had been the first to note the mystery woman, somewhat surprisingly as the Duc had an eye for beauty in all its forms, and the striking mystery woman had that in no short supply.

266

Stately, exotic, with pale alabaster skin and kohl-lined dark eyes, she wore a white gown trimmed with pearls and a hooded white cloak that hid her tightly braided dark hair. Her was face veiled, but almost transparently so. Gold bracelets twined around her wrists and ankles; her sandals were so delicate they barely seemed to exist, and she walked with the grace of a queen. She was preceded by a spotted leopard on a thin metal leash and followed by a large Tuareg whose white garments identified him as a slave.

She had only paused for a minute in the marketplace, but her eyes had made contact with O'Rourke's and frozen him in his tracks. Both the Englishman and the Duc reacted as well, the former with a curious recognition though he obviously had never seen the woman before, and the Duc captured not only by her beauty, but by the jeweled broach that acted as clasp for her cloak at her throat, an impossibly large white diamond that gleamed as if it were part of a fallen star and no mere crystal dug up from the ground.

All three men has an eye for the fair sex, but Terence O'Rourke, Colonel Terence O'Rourke, the O'Rourke, late of a certain South American revolution, and currently with neither commission nor prospect, seemed particularly stricken by her beauty and poise.

"Good lord, gentlemen," O'Rourke had said after the woman and her entourage had passed, "I have never seen a woman like her in all my life. She's like a queen from an ancient tale of the Arabian Nights. I could swear I heard some strange music when she passed, like chimes of some queer bell."

The Duc had been about to voice the same opinion when the Englishman had spoken up in a harsher tone than seemed necessary.

"She's not for you, O'Rourke. Trust me on this one. Some mysteries are better left unsolved, and I sense hers runs deeper than any of us dare kin."

"Tosh," O'Rourke had said. "The O'Rourke isn't one to be put off by a slip of a lass, however formidable her escort. In any case, I caught the look in the lady's eyes, and queen or serving girl, that look is universal."

The Duc had said nothing. His mind was on more than the lady's beauty or romantic proclivities for the moment.

They had returned to the hotel and dined, but after eating, the American had failed to join them for brandy and cards, a fact that had disturbed the Englishman more than seemed normal in the Duc's opinion. The Englishman now seemed even more concerned in the cold light of morning.

"Our friend O'Rourke can take care of himself with the fair sex, my friend," the Duc said as the waiter brought a menu. "I'm sure he's a match for any woman."

"Not that lady," the Englishman replied.

He seemed older than his years at times like these, and it struck the Duc that the full story behind this sad eyed man might be just as exotic as the woman they had spotted earlier in the marketplace.

But the subject was dropped and the two men ate quietly and parted ways when they had finished.

The Duc, dressed in whites beneath the Moroccan sun and wearing a Panama hat, walked around the city, chatting with shopkeepers and eyeing their goods, but as evening neared, he rented a donkey cart and rode up into the hills above the city where it was cooler and many of the more prosperous citizens had villas.

He went with a purpose, though, and straight for one villa in particular. Finding it after having it described to him was an easy enough task, though beyond directions, the shopkeepers had divulged nothing of its resident. Indeed, they had seemed almost afraid to even speak of *her*. It had cost considerable *baksheesh* to pry her location from a Levantine rug seller.

Like most of the villas in the area, it was a mixture of Spanish and Moorish influences, the main house surrounded by a high white wall with a simple iron gate in front and a heavy wooden door in the rear, through which deliveries were made. A few date trees lined the wall, and from the small grove of date trees where he sat in semi concealment, the Duc was deciding whether to shimmy up one of them for a look in the courtyard when he recognized he was not alone.

He heard voices. Both European, one most certainly French, and after a moment, he spied two men dressed in native garb cloaked in the shadows on the side of the villa. The smaller man was no doubt the French voice he had heard, but the taller figure could be no one else but his English friend.

Dismounting the donkey cart, the Duc cautiously approached the two men, and was startled when the Englishman turned toward him and spoke:

"I'm glad you are here, my friend. I'm afraid as I predicted our friend O'Rourke has gotten in over his head."

That the Englishman had detected his approach was shocking enough. When the Duc did not wish to be heard, few men heard him.

The man beside the Englishman had turned when his companion had spoken. Now the Duc saw a man, who, though still youthful in years, had the hollow eyes and translucent skin of a drug addict, perhaps a *hashishin*. He seemed brittle as if a puff of wind would turn him to dust.

"You'll pardon my manners," the Englishman said. "Monsieur le Duc de Charmerace, this is Lieutenant. André de Saint-Avit, late of the *Légion étrangère*."

Lt. de Saint-Avit did not extend a hand, but nodded. Again, the Duc noted the somewhat archaic style of the Englishman's speech and formality of manner. He could not have been much past thirty in age, but he seemed strangely older, out of time.

"You say our friend O'Rourke is in trouble, *mon ami*," he said. "There are many kinds of trouble where women are involved, and with a woman such as this, and a man such as O'Rourke... I have to wonder how dangerous such trouble could be, short of a jealous husband or a protective father."

"Forgive me, Monsieur," Saint-Avit said before the Englishman could respond, "but the lady in question has had many lovers and we are all jealous unto death, but no outside force poses a threat to your friend. Even her entourage of Tuareg slaves is a lesser threat than she. She is more savage than that leopard she keeps as a pet, more deadly than any scorpion or asp. You cannot imagine how dangerous her affections are, Monsieur. Your friend's life is not only at stake, his very soul is in the balance."

The Duc weighed the words. Once, he might have found such a statement melodramatic, but he too had known such a woman. Her name was Josephine Balsamo...

"I'm afraid you will have to explain the danger to me then. I can't be expected to help if I don't know the nature of the threat that our mystery woman poses."

The Englishman looked closely at Lt. de Saint-Avit.

"Tell him," he said. "Tell him the whole story. We have time; it is still too light to act. We will have to count on our friend O'Rourke's strength for now."

Saint-Avit seemed to draw from a nearly empty well of strength but finally spoke:

"When I was with the Third Spahis, I was stationed here in Morocco, and on a mission into the Atlas mountains with my fellow officer, Morhange, we encountered and saved a strange white-robed Tuareg who called himself Eg-Antouen, a Kel-Tahal, serf of the Kel-Rheka tribe one of the oldest and most noble tribes of the Hoggar. At first he seemed a life saver, and it was he who led us through the mountains and savage tribes to her—to Antinea..."

He paused as if to again draw strength.

"Deep in those mountains lies a city lost in time, the remnants of lost Atlantis, and it was there we were brought to worship at the feet of the most beautiful woman I have ever seen, a Grecian goddess brought to life, beautiful, and cold and cruel, utterly sensual and erotic and utterly without heart or soul. Such is Antinea, queen of lost Atlantis.

"Her passions are real enough, intoxicating as absinthe, and like the green *jinn* in the bottle, as demanding and as deadly. She takes young men for lovers, for toys, and when she tires of them, they linger for a time, wasting away until they die for lack of her love and are entombed beside their predecessors encased in Orichalcum, a strange Atlantean metal that preserves their beauty in a great hall where she can walk, immortal and untouchable, among the legions of her lovers.

"I was one of her lovers. Mad with passion and jealousy, I murdered my best friend who resisted her. Perhaps that was why I was able to escape, at least for a time. But I was drawn back and she sent her Tuareg to draw me there again. I followed, oh, I followed, but a storm caught me and I nearly died in the desert. I was found by natives, and they nursed me to health, and though her spell was not broken, it was weakened. Since then, I have haunted her footsteps waiting, and now she has left her stronghold, there is perhaps a chance; a chance to strike at the heart of her, if she has one; a chance to end the evil that is the beautiful devil Antinea. She is as cold as the great diamond from King Solomon's mines that lies on her breast."

All the time, the Duc had watched the Englishman, and noted the strange far-away look in his eyes as he listened.

"You believe this to be true?" the Duc asked.

The Englishman sounded much older than his years when he answered:

"Many years ago, I made a similar journey. I met a fate as singular, and found and lost a love as savage, only to find her again and lose her again. I came here seeking this Antinea, hoping that she would be my lost love, but she is not. Thank God, for whatever Ayesha's flaws, and they were many and murderous, she was not this Orichalcum princess of death.

"We must spare our friend O'Rourke if we can. We must breach these walls and save his body and soul. Are you game, my friend?"

"There is always a way," the Duc said matter of factly. "How many of these Tuareg do we have to worry about."

"Lt. de Saint-Avit can tell us that; I'm more concerned with that cat of hers."

"Oh, I wouldn't worry about him," said the Duc., smiling. "I have a way with cats."

The Englishman accepted him at his word

"She won't have forgotten me," Saint-Avit said. "If I present myself at the gate, they will let me in, and until she summons me, I will be free to roam. She is sure of her hold. I'll have the freedom of the place and can answer all your questions when I let you in through the rear entrance."

"From what you say, she will be with O'Rourke," the Duc said. "Still, once in, we will need a diversion."

"I can provide that as well, but you must be swift. You can still save your friend, but soon..."

"We will strike swiftly, but what of you?" the Englishman asked.

Saint-Avit smiled, a sad distant smile that spoke volumes of his suffering. His teeth were yellowed and missing, his face collapsed in on itself, but there was still something of youth and courage in him.

It was growing dark when Saint-Avit left the two and made for the gate.

"I fear for him," the Englishman said.

"As do I. He is on his last frayed and taut nerve, but he will hold. He must, or I fear, if what he says is true, O'Rourke is lost."

Terence O'Rourke paced the small room where he was waiting like a caged cat, though not perhaps the lady's leopard who seemed far less perturbed than O'Rourke under the circumstances.

"Well me boyo," O'Rourke said to himself, "you haven't half gotten yourself in it this time have you?"

He had a nose for trouble at the best of times, and this time it looked as if it was going to get chopped off. He could have listened to the Englishman last night, or sought out the Frenchman's advice. He was in a foreign country where he did not know the language or customs, and one noted for its savagery and strangeness, but wisdom had a way of bypassing the O'Rourke whenever a beautiful woman's smile beckoned.

When he left his friends the evening before, he had returned to the Arab quarter retracing his steps from the afternoon before. He knew he would not find the lady herself, she was not some *nautch* girl waiting in the shadows, but he did have hope someone who had seen her would know her name.

No luck there.

Whenever he spoke of the lady with the leopard, even the most garrulous of the locals dried up. They seemed almost frightened, which intrigued him even more. Still, that explained how a woman dripping with fine jewels and gold could pass unharmed through the Arab quarter unassaulted, with only a great cat and a single servant, however fierce either was. Something more than the cat and the Tuareg had frightened the locals.

He was on the verge of giving up and calling it an evening when the Tuareg suddenly appeared at his elbow as if out of the night itself.

O'Rourke knew something about the Tuareg from his reading in *National Geographic*. They were a tribe of nomadic warriors whose men concealed their faces and dressed in blue garments. Those who wore white like this one were slaves. They were savage warriors, often given to feuds and internecine warfare in their strongholds in the Atlas mountains, not unlike the Native Americans of the Great Plains.

A Tuareg in a city, servant to a beautiful woman, any woman, was not something often seen.

"Effendi," the big Tuareg began, greeting him. "You are looking perhaps for the white-robed lady, who spied you earlier this afternoon?"

Question or not, it was clear the Tuareg knew the answer.

"And if I am?" O'Rourke bristled.

Something about the man and his manner got his Irish up. He had been in danger often enough in his relatively young life; he was a military man through and through, and he had an instinct for the dangerous individual, and this one was dangerous as they came.

"You are the fine gentleman my mistress spied earlier today, sir," the Tuareg continued ignoring O'Rourke's tone. "You and your two companions perhaps noticed my lady?"

"Perhaps," O'Rourke answered, aware that he must seem a bit juvenile and foolish to this experienced rogue, something that did not improve his temper for the night.

"My mistress was quite taken with you as well, effendi. She sent me to look for you in hopes you were seeking her. If the effendi wishes, I shall escort him to her quarters, her villa. She hopes you will excuse her haste, but she departs in yet another day on a long and arduous journey home, and there is only the present.

"I think, perhaps, effendi, my mistress needs a strong fine young man such as yourself. She does not confide in this servant, but perhaps there is trouble which she would seek some council or advice about from such a man."

A lady in distress, mystery, O'Rourke to the rescue on a white horse, however gray he appeared in the dark, he could no more resist that than a whole harem of beauties. He was the O'Rourke and forever charging into heavily fortified positions alone with nothing but a saber, courage, and the token of a beautiful woman's affection. Galahad and Lancelot had nothing on the O'Rourke, he wryly reminded himself. She could not have hooked him better with a harpoon.

And certain as he was born of the gentle rolling green hills of Ireland, the Tuareg led him to the villa in the foothills above the city, through the finely latticed gates, past an elegant courtyard out of Scheherazade by way of Omar Khayyam, past heavy doors and other white-robed, sullen-eyed Tuaregs into the interior and a delicate fountain.

The Tuareg left him. He noted his surroundings, almost unconsciously counting the servants, estimating how many were lurking but unseen, planning his escape by sheer bravado and the skin of his knuckles if need be, laying Tuareg and the handful of Nubians he spotted to the way side if the chance came his way... But the Tuareg returned and no desperate fight for survival broke out, mores the pity.

"My mistress is most pleased you have come, effendi. Business keeps her for the moment, but she has prepared a room for you, should you be so kind as to wait upon her. There are brandied dates, sweetmeats, and scented wines for your pleasure, or coffee if the effendi prefers, and there will be sweet music as well, and great comfort."

Feeling ever more like a lamb led to slaughter, and guilty because his hostess had been nothing but gracious, he followed the Tuareg to a Damascus curtained salon where low couches, Persian carpets a man could get lost for two weeks in, and low tables laid out with exotic treats awaited him. Even the music was dancing through the perfumed air, though no musicians were present, and O'Rourke had entertained visions of gossamer-clad women with lyres on satin, silk, and velvet pillows.

"Be at home, effendi," the Tuareg said, bowing behind O'Rourke as he entered.

Then the great door to the salon slammed shut and O'Rourke heard the bolt thrown.

He flung himself against the door. His shoulder smashed into wood as hard as iron and no more giving. Cursing, he turned to the heavily curtained windows, only to find only solid wall behind each concealment.

It was a prison, satin-lined, and laid out for a prince, but still a prison.

*You've done it this time*, O'Rourke chided himself.

So he paced and fumed, swore a blue streak in English, Spanish, French, and Portuguese, damned blue and white-robed Tuaregs, mysterious beauties, mystery, Allah and his prophet, and every son and daughter of every camel trader from the Pillars of Hercules to the far side of Suez, and when he was done, cursed them again in no uncertain Anglo-Saxon terms capable of making Chaucer blush.

All this time, his quick brain was working. If it came to it, he would set the place ablaze and see what happened.

Then, through a passageway behind a curtain, *she* entered, and he knew nothing more.

He had known beautiful women. Cool-eyed Boston Brahmins and hot eyed senoritas, tall Yankee lasses with blonde locks, Southern belles supple as willows, barefoot gypsies lit by campfires, but *this* woman. *This* woman.

Her beauty of face, he had already noted in the marketplace. Now he could see her divine form, somehow concealed and revealed at once in a metallic dress that flowed like liquid metal over every contour and curve.

One dare not stare too long at the sun, he thought unable to wrench his eyes away.

"Welcome to my home, Colonel O'Rourke," a voice supple as fine whiskey chimed with hypnotic effect. "I am Antinea."

She sat on a low divan, rather she folded into it so gracefully he was mesmerized. A simple wave of a finger drew him to her side, and he fought the urge to throw himself at her feet.

When he did sit beside her, she reached for his hand and lifted his fingers bringing them to her breast.

"You can't know how long I have waited, Terence O'Rourke," she almost whispered, her eyes as hypnotic as an asp.

This was what Caesar and Antony must have seen when they looked in Cleopatra's eye. Samson had seen it in Delilah's, and surely David in Bathsheba's. Odysseus had found this in the eyes of Calypso and poor doomed Holofernes in those of Judith.

*Terence O'Rourke, my fine lad, you are lost*, he thought.

After that ,his fragile hold on free will and thought flew apart at the touch of her lips.

"He's taking his time," the Englishman whispered.

The Duc said nothing. Patience was not always his greatest virtue, but in action, he was cool and utterly without nerves.

273

Beside him the Englishman grasped a .45 Webly Fosbury he obviously knew how to use. The Duc was unarmed. The mere presence of firearms meant they were more likely to be employed, and while he had no hesitation about defending himself, he found violence to be a mark of failure, save when needed. Cruelty and ruthlessness were a disease for the man of action. He recalled how it had undone Josephine.

He was not easily put at unease, and yet, now he was, in his own way, as impatient for action as his English friend. He had no use for spirits or for the uncanny, but there was something about this woman, about the mad Legionnaire's tale of lost Atlantis, some hint of truth among the fancies, that he could not deny. Josephine had claimed herself to be the daughter of Joseph Balsamo, Cagliostro, and like him, immortal, and there were times he had believed her, or at least that she believed it herself.

Despite his logical and even clinical mind a certain Gallic romanticism had touched his soul when he saw this woman in the marketplace. It was something hypnotic and lovely, and like all great beauty unredeemed by soul, cruel and even malignant.

He had lived long enough, and seen more than enough, to know evil when he was in its presence, and this evil was older even than the Atlas Mountains Saint-Avit babbled on about. He knew also that the Englishman, too, had known the embrace of a woman like this Antinea, and that their friend was surely ...

*Lost*, O'Rourke thought.

Her embrace was as fiery as a volcano and cold as the ice fields of the far north. Her touch burned; her kisses snatched at his reason.

There was no real sense of time with her. With his head in her lap, he might have passed hours, days, centuries. The world was swept away like the wind-swept sand of the Sahara, while all around him a mirage wavered and shimmered, lost in her touch and kiss. Her curiously accented words were powerful drugs injected beneath his skin, and all about him colors became tactile and sounds drugs pouring into his soul.

When she left him, he became desolate. Anger, fear, even self destructive thoughts crowded his addled brain. His soul cried out, bitter and in pain.

But he was as yet Terence O'Rourke, soldier, adventurer, and above all man, and soldier bred, soldier-born; the blood of the great captains ran with his. Surrender was not in him, not even to a woman, not even to *this* woman.

So he fought, fought like an addict fights opiates, fought the intoxicant of her perfume, maddening as the lotus, fought her visceral soft caress, fought her lyrical voice, fought her protestations of love and his own in return. He fought for Terence O'Rourke's immortal soul, or whatever was left of it, and gradually, as the hours passed and the day waned, he began to win, even as he knew each hour closer to darkness would mean her return and a renewed, and ultimately hopeless, battle.

It was at that dark moment, when his soul was at its lowest ebb, that he heard the scream.

The Duc stood in the shadows pressed flat to a wall. As the white-robed Tuareg passed, he could almost smell the fellow. Beside him the Englishman was coiled like a lion about to spring.

Saint-Avit had unlatched the rear door and let them in only minutes before. "I was delayed," he whispered.

Time near his precious Queen had done him no favors. He seemed on his last razor thin nerve.

"The Tuareg is suspicious, but I think I have convinced him for now. You must move quickly and quietly though. We have little time..."

He explained the layout of the villa, both to Antinea's quarters and the salon where O'Rourke was held, and he assured them the latter was held against his will—for now.

"He may not welcome you. Antinea's spell is powerful, though he has only spent a short time beneath it. You must be strong for him. Stronger than I was.

"You will know when to act. I assure you, you will know..."

His face was feverish, his eyes wild.

Several minutes passed. The Duc and the Englishman stood waiting in the shadows across from the bolted salon door. It was not guarded, but every few minutes, a Nubian or Tuareg passed to check it. Saint-Avit had assured them the leopard would stay at its mistress's side and she would withdraw at the first sign of trouble, but neither man fancied dealing with the beast. According to Saint-Avit, her chambers were beyond the salon, entered only by a secret passage.

The inhuman scream shocked both men into action.

They leaped forward, but no sooner had they broken cover than two white-robed Tuaregs appeared, as if out of the walls. The Webly barked and a red flower blossomed on the chest of one of the Tuareg slaves. True to his vow of silence, the man made not a sound.

The shot gave the game away.

The Duc was struggling with the other Tuareg, but called out:

"O'Rourke! Get O'Rourke!"

The Englishman stepped over the fallen slave and threw the bolt.

O'Rourke was struggling to rise from a low divan. He was unsteady, feverish, but both men were relieved when he spoke.

"And here I thought you lads had lost your invitation to this shindig."

The grim Englishman caught O'Rourke as he took a stumbling step forward.

"Sorry," O'Rourke said, "I'm a bit light headed." He looked enviously at the Webly. "Don't suppose you brought one of those for me?"

Smiling, the Englishman withdrew a wicked looking Bulldog revolver from his jacket and pressed it in the American's hand.

"It was all I could find."

"'Tis a fine specimen at that, it's the man after all, and not the weapon."

Already O'Rourke sounded stronger.

"We must go, they will be swarming soon..." the Englishman began.

"Where did the Duc go?" O'Rourke asked.

The Tuareg the Frenchman had grappled with lay on the floor deathly still now.

"Damned if I know," the Englishman swore, "but the Devil take him, he's on his own if he is sightseeing. Come on, man!"

They encountered no more servants. On the floor, by the delicate fountain, they found the big Tuareg with a Legionnaire's saber broken off in his bloodied chest, and beside him Saint-Avit gravely wounded.

Strong as he was, the Englishman could not possibly carry both men out, and was cursing the Frenchman when the Duc suddenly appeared grabbing up the mortally wounded Saint-Avit.

"Where the Devil...?" the Englishman began.

"Not now, *mon ami*, we must go."

The Duc hefted the wounded Frenchman with surprising ease for his size.

"Hurry! Time is short!"

The Englishman had brought horses reigned near the grove of date trees. The four men mounted, the Duc carrying the wounded Saint-Avit, and they spurred the animals on.

They rode up into the foothills, beyond the edge of the city, a ragtag group of wild eyes animals and wilder men, and only towards light did they slow, when they had reached a high clear point where they could determine no avenging army of Tuaregs had followed them.

They placed the Legionnaire gently on the ground in the shadow of another date tree. He had lost too much blood, and his hold on life had not been strong to begin with.

The Englishman kneeled by him. It was as if they shared some uncommon bond. It was he who heard the man's dying words.

"What did he say?" O'Rourke asked, still ignorant of the whole story of his rescue.

"He thanked us," the Englishman replied. "He thanked us for his soul and his honor, and he asked a question."

Neither the Duc or O'Rourke spoke.

"He asked my real name," the Englishman said. "Not the one I gave him, or you."

There was silence.

"It will mean nothing to you. It would mean nothing to him, but I owe him that at least."

He seemed to hesitate.

"Once, a long time ago, my name was Leo Vincey," he said.

They buried the Legionnaire under the date tree with no marker so no one could steal his body or encase it in a strange metal.

"He's free," the Duc said. "Free of her, and her curse. At least, he shall not stand with her army of lovers in tribute to her cruel passions."

"God help him," O'Rourke said. "I think I know a little of what he suffered. Such madness..."

"Madness indeed," Leo Vincey said. "Divine madness."

They returned to Tangier where the American and the Englishman slept like the dead, but the Duc stayed vigilant.

The next night, they returned with Lee Enfield rifles to the villa only to find it deserted and no sign of the supposed Queen of Atlantis or her loyal Tuaregs, alive or dead.

The three men parted company a day or two later, O'Rourke bound for Marseilles and then Paris, the Duc for points East, and Leo Vincey, well, who could say where his journey would take him.

But that is not quite the end of the story...

For, if you travel to France, you will find standing off the Normandy coast a remarkable feature, sometimes known as the Needle, and while experts will assure you it is a solid rock, a bit of lucky exploration might reveal another truth, and should you penetrate its secrets, there, in its center you will find a treasure room with few rivals in the world.

The treasure of the kings of France lie there, and many more, and among them, in no small place of honor, is a great white diamond that once adorned the bosom of a beautiful and evil woman and which, like her, has seen worlds rise and fall, and like her, is cold and heartless, a stone predating Babylon and ancient Egypt, Solomon and his diamond mines, and countless empires since—a white star of distant Atlantis, wrenched from the breast of the queen of that fabled land.

But don't be tempted to liberate it again.

Arsène Lupin is jealous of his treasures.

*We end this year's collection of Shadowmen stories with a slightly spicier story by Jared Welch. The lesbian affair between Eugenie Danglars and Louise d'Armilly, her piano teacher, who elope together at the end of The Count of Monte-Cristo has been the subject of a number of articles and scholarly studies. Here, Jared shows them drawn into the criminal web of intrigue of the Black Coats, one night, by the beautiful Bay of Naples...*

## Jared Welch: *The Piano Maidens*

*Naples, 1839*

Eugenie Danglars was preparing for her performance.

"I'm very nervous" she confessed to her companion.

"You'll be fantastic just like you always are," replied the radiant, blond Louise d'Armilly.

"This is the largest audience we've ever performed for."

"That's true, but it doesn't matter; you still have the most beautiful voice in all of Europe."

Eugenie smiled, feeling reassured.

"And you have very talented fingers," she said, with a wink, to her former piano instructor, causing her to blush.

"You're on, Mademoiselle Danglars," a voice said, indicating it was time for their performance to begin.

At the end of the show they received a hearty round of applause. They then went to a party hosted by the distinguished Count Corbucci.

Eugenie Danglars wore a dark blue dress that complemented her short black hair well. Louise d'Armilly, with her long, golden blond hair and blue eyes, wore white.

"I'm delighted you decided to join us," the Count said, welcoming them both. "Mademoiselle Danglars, you have the most captivating voice I have heard in ages, and your partner played the piano masterfully. And, may I add, you both look positively stunning."

"Why, thank you, Count," Eugenie replied.

"We are both honored to perform in this beautiful and ancient city," Louise added "I have wanted to see Naples since I was a little girl."

"Allow me to introduce you to some of my distinguished guests," the Count said, as he led them into the gathering.

"This is my dearest and most trusted friend, Vicomte Annibal Gioja, des marquis Pallante..."

Eugenie could not help feeling that Gioja had a mean look in his eyes.

278

"Nice to meet you, Vicomte," she said, curtsying.

"And it is a pleasure meeting you, Mademoiselle."

"Also," the Count added, "this is Signor DiLaurentis..." The Count paused, realizing that the next guest was, in fact, not there.

"I'm afraid he's late," Gioja interjected.

"Typical," remarked the Count, "you can never trust a DiLaurentis to arrive when expected."

"Don't worry about it, we can wait," Eugenie assured him.

"And this," the Count continued, "is a visiting associate of mine, Gian-Paolo de Felipone."

"So these are the musicians who positively mesmerized us earlier?" Gian-Paolo said. "How fortunate that I brought my visiting cousin from Paris, Paolo de Felipone,"

Another Sicilian approached

"You didn't bring your son?" the Count asked, addressing his friend's cousin.

"I'm afraid Andrea is not very sociable these days," Felipone replied, then turning to the two ladies, "Paris hasn't been the same since the daughter of Baron Danglars and her lovely piano instructor disappeared."

"I'm afraid I only vaguely remember ever meeting you," Eugenie said apologetically.

"That is all right; I am quite unremarkable," Felipone replied.

"Paris... That reminds me," the Count interjected, "I must introduce you both to my favorite Parisian..."

He directed them towards a well-dressed, elderly gentleman, no younger then eighty.

"My oldest and most distinguished friend, Colonel Bozzo-Corona."

"You flatter me too much, my dear Count," said the Colonel politely. "But I am quite grateful that you have introduced me to these beautiful guests."

"The Colonel, I remember quite well," Eugenie said. "My father courted you as a client quite frequently."

"Yes, he did," the Colonel confirmed. "I appreciated his offers, but I remain quite confident in my current banker, Monsieur Jean-Baptiste Schwartz."

"So, this is what became of the mysterious Eugenie Danglars?" said a young girl with long, raven-colored hair, of about Eugenie's age.

"This is my grand-daughter, Comtesse Francesca Corona," said the Colonel, introducing her, "affectionately called by her friends and family Fanchette."

"You've grown since I last saw you," Eugenie observed.

"As have you. And this must be the pretty piano instructor I heard so much about," Fanchette said, gazing intently at Louise d'Armilly.

"It is a pleasure to meet you," the blond girl replied.

"You are more beautiful then I imagined," Fanchette said, smiling coyly.

Eugenie now stared at Fanchette with a hint of jealously in her eyes.

"Is it true that the Count of Monte-Cristo himself assisted you in your flight from Paris?" the Colonel inquired.

"Yes, but I realize now that he had ulterior motives. Still, I did appreciate his help."

"Other motives aside, he seemed to be a remarkable fellow, and quite observant, too. I bet that he suspected the nature of your, er, relationship with Mademoiselle d'Armilly."

Count Corbucci and his other associates had now left the two girls alone with the Colonel and his grandchild. Eugenie was taken aback by the older man's words.

"I'm... unsure of what you mean?" she replied

Louise, too, looked nervous now.

"No need to pretend with me, I'm quite open minded. I know an Iphis and a Ianthe when I see one."

"Who?" Louise asked

"He's referencing Ovid," Eugenie explained, "and that analogy is quite flawed," she continued, responding directly at the Colonel.

"I suppose it is," he said. "You also remind me of Oscar Francois de Jarjayes, whom I had the pleasure of meeting when I visited Versailles before the Revolution."

"A better analogy," said Eugenie, "would be Sappho of Lesbos, or Damophyle of Pamphilia."

"Or Artemis and Britomartis," Louise added.

"Or Mary Crawford and Fanny Price," Fanchette interrupted, "or my favorite Emma."

Eugenie and Louise were puzzled for a moment.

"My granddaughter is rare among the French," explained the Colonel, "in she is a devoted reader of that British 'Lady,' Jane Austen, although I'm afraid she has an interpretation of some of her characters that is hardly conventional."

"Most French women haven't been able to read them in English," Fanchette responded.

"It's a shame Iamblichus of Syria's epic *Babyloniaca* has not survived for modern readers to enjoy, with its account of Berenice and Mesopotamia," the Colonel lamented, as if he had read it.

"It was rumored that Queen Marie-Antoinette also enjoyed the company of women," Fanchette said.

"I heard those rumors too," said Eugenie.

"I had the pleasure of meeting her as well," said the Colonel. "The Duchesse de Polignac and the Princesse de Lamballe were indeed very close to the Queen. But Mademoiselle Jeanne de Valois was certainly making up her stories."

"Well, I have some other friends I must catch up with," Fanchette said. "Do feel free to say *bonjour* later."

She smiled at Louise and walked away. Eugenie glared at her.

"I apologize for my granddaughter's flirtatious nature," the Colonel said. Sadly, she is quite unhappy in her marriage. It was my daughter who insisted on marrying her to our talentless Cousin, just because he's a Count, back in Corsica."

"So, she is like us then?" Eugenie inquired.

"She has shown occasional interest in people of various types, but the great love of her life is a man whom she believes she once brought back from the dead."

Eugenie raised her eyebrow in confusion.

"It's a long story," the Colonel replied.

"It just occurred to me," Louise said suddenly. "Doesn't Colonel Bozzo-Corona resemble that older man we saw in that painting in Rome?"

"Yes," Eugenie answered. "I thought of him at the time but didn't put much thought into it".

"Ah, *The Brigand's Painting*," said the Colonel. "I get that a lot. I suspect some unknown relative of mine might have modeled for it. It is based on a Corsican folk-tale."

"Perhaps you could tell it to us?" asked Louise.

"Another time perhaps, but I, too, have some pressing matters to attend. I think this may well be my last affair," the Colonel said, before leaving them.

Eugenie and Louise continued to mingle amongst the guests as a few hours went by.

"This has been fun," Eugenie aid to her partner.

"Indeed, it has, but I think I'm about read to return to our rooms," Louise replied, with a knowing smile.

"Soon we shall," Eugenie responded, squeezing her hand.

Suddenly, a priest approached them.

"I was quite charmed by your performance. Allow me to introduce myself, I am Father Rodin."

"It is a pleasure to meet you, *mon père*," said Eugenie.

"That name sounds familiar?" Louise said.

"Most likely you heard it slandered by that vulgarian, Eugene Sue," Rodin replied with contempt.

"Ah, yes," Eugenie said. "I enjoyed that novel; it was quite absurdly melo-dramatic."

"Yes, he does have a modicum of talent," Father Rodin said.

"It was certainly a work of fiction, having immortal Jews and all."

"It was, er, loosely based on some actual events I had a hand in back in 1832," admitted Father Rodin after a pause. "And they did involve a couple who claimed to be the Wandering Jew and his sister."

"Well, in Paris," Eugenie said, "I knew a man who was suspected of being everything from Lord Ruthven to Cagliostro to the Comte de Saint-Germain."

281

Ah, yes, I, too, heard of the Count of Monte-Cristo, quite possibly the only man whose wealth could rival the fabled Treasure of *Il Padre d'Ogni*," Father Rodin said.

"Don't bore our beautiful guests with more of your conspiratorial nonsense, Rodin," said another male voice approaching them. "Corbucci only invited you as a courtesy."

"And I only accepted," replied Rodin, "because I suspected I might see things here to confirm my suspicions of his ties to the Camorra and the Carbonari. Which I have."

"Allow me to introduce myself," the newcomer said to Eugenie and Louise. "I am Signor Ricardo DiLaurentis."

"Ah, yes! Count Corbucci wanted to introduce us to you earlier," Eugenie said.

"I apologize, but I am a busy man."

"I understand," Eugenie said, not understanding.

In the meanwhile, Father Rodin wandered off.

"Rodin is obsessed with conspiracies—the Freemasons, the Illuminati and the *Alta Vendita*. He believes Filippo Buonarroti was the elusive Nubius."

"It sounds more logical then the other theories I heard," said Louise. "About him being Napoleon and still alive somehow."

"I grow annoyed with these conspiracies spread by Catholic Royalists. Rodin, I suspect, is a Jesuit."

Eugenie chose not to comment on the obvious hypocrisy.

"Buonarroti died rather mysteriously, didn't he?" observed Louise.

"So did Nubius, apparently," DiLaurentis replied. "As the Comtesse de Clare once told me, 'Two can keep a secret, if one of them is dead.'"

"She was quoting Benjamin Franklin," said Fanchette, approaching. "And she changed it, too. It was originally, 'Three can keep a secret, if two of them are dead.'"

"I think I like her version better," said DiLaurentis, before departing.

"You two know each other?" Eugenie asked.

"Yes, he's very close to Lecoq, who has always made my flesh crawl," Fanchette answered. "I once overheard Lecoq saying to him, '*Nos Animadvert Totus.*'"

"What does it mean?" Louise inquired

"It's Latin," Eugenie said. "It means, 'We See All.'"

"When I was young," reflected Fanchette, "I once met the notorious Countess Cagliostro, who claimed to be the daughter of Cagliostro and the future Empress Josephine. My grandfather, however, said her mother was Jeanne de Valois... He didn't comment on her paternity."

"You and your grandfather seem to have a lot of stories to tell," Eugenie observed.

"Very interesting ones," added Louise.

"My grandfather has a lot of connections," Fanchette explained, explaining nothing..

The three conversed on various subjects for a while, then Fanchette asked:

"Have you two been enjoying yourselves?"

"Yes, it has been a wonderful evening, but I think we are ready to retire now," said Eugenie.

"Well, I hope we can meet again sometime," Fanchette said. Then, she took Louise' hand, and added, "Especially you, beautiful."

She kissed it gently and walked away.

After saying their farewells, Eugenie and Louise returned to their suite.

"Well, that was an interesting evening," Louise said.

"Certainly not boring," Eugenie responded.

"That Fanchette was an interesting girl—and very pretty".

"I don't like the way she kept flirting with you".

"Jealous?" Louise asked, playfully.

"Not at all!"

Eugenie then took Louise' head in her hand, pulled her in closer, and pressed her lips against her. Louise wrapped her arms around Eugenie as she kissed her back. Eugenie switched to hold Louise with her left arm, and with her right hand, reached under Louise's dress.

"Oooh," Louise moaned as Eugenie ran kisses down her neck.

They two former Parisians continued to make out as they retired to their bedroom. And then they made sweet passionate love until sunrise.

# Credits

## Ardan at the Pole

| Starring: | Created by: |
|---|---|
| Doc Ardan | Guy d'Armen |
| | and Lester Dent |
| Hareton Ironcastle | J.-H. Rosny Aîné |
| The Inutos | H.P. Lovecraft |
| The Lomarians | H.P. Lovecraft |
| Jean-Louis de Venasque | Charles Derennes |
| The People of the Pole | Charles Derennes |
| **Co-Starring:** | |
| Michel Ardan | Jules Verne |
| Louis Valenton | Charles Derennes |
| Jacques Ceintras | Charles Derennes |
| Tsathoggua | Clark Ashton Smith |
| **And:** | |
| The Gun Club | Jules Verne |
| The God Slayer | Robert E. Howard |

**Jason AIKEN** is a fantasy and horror author. He enjoys penning weird fiction and sword & sorcery tales. Jason chronicles the adventures of his red-haired swordswoman, Nuja of Lomar, in a sword & mythos setting in various fantasy and horror anthologies. As a Brobdingnagian fan of Philip José Farmer and his Wold Newton Family concept, writing a short story in the Farmer-style has been a dream come true. Jason can be found online at www.jasonscottaiken.com and he's @jasonscottaiken on Twitter. This is his first contribution to *Tales of the Shadowmen*.

## The Lament of the Duke and the King

| Starring: | Created by: |
|---|---|
| Duke of Bridgewater | Mark Twain |
| The King of France | Mark Twain |
| Doctor Omega | Arnould Galopin |
| Miki Saegusa | Shinichiro Kobayashi |
| Steel General | Roger Zelazny |
| **Co-Starring:** | |
| Madame La Farge | Charles Dickens |

| | |
|---|---|
| Chevalier de Maison-Rouge | Alexandre Dumas |
| Florence de La Salle | Raphael Sabatini |
| André-Louis Moreau | Raphael Sabatini |
| Dr. Moreau | H.G. Wells |
| Marguerite St. Just | Baroness Emma Orczy |
| Sir Percy Blakeney | Baroness Emma Orczy |
| Edmund Blackadder | Richard Curtis & Ben Elton |
| Joseph Balsamo | Alexandre Dumas |
| The Scarecrow | Russell Thorndike |
| Natty Bumppo | James Fenimore Cooper |
| Dr. Campos | Fernando Osés |
| | & Enrique Zambrano |
| Kukulcan | Russell Bates & David Wise |
| Godzilla | Tomoyuki Tanaka, Ishirō Honda |
| | & Eiji Tsubaraya |

**Also Starring:**
Jean, Baron de Batz
Anton Mesmer
General Antonio López de
Santa Anna
**And:**

| | |
|---|---|
| Hynerian Empire | Rockne S. O'Bannon |
| *Don Juan Triumphant* | Gaston Leroux |

**Matthew BAUGH** lives and works in Albuquerque, NM. He is the pastor of a small church and an editor for Permuted Press. He is also the author of *The Vampire Count of Monte-Cristo*, a mash-up of the classic story of adventure and revenge with vampires, ghosts and Faustian bargains, the co-author, with Win Scott Eckert, of *A Girl and Her Cat*, which continues the adventures of classic TV heroes, Honey West and T.H.E. Cat, and a regular contributor to *Tales of the Shadowmen.*

## The Revelation of the Yeti

| **Starring:** | **Created by:** |
|---|---|
| Barton Werper | Peter Scott & Peggy Scott |
| Doctor Omega | Arnould Galopin |
| Ki-Gor | John Peter Drummond |
| Nora | Félicien Champsaur |
| The Mi-Go | H.P. Lovecraft |
| Dr. Karswell | Montague Rhodes James |
| Madame Palmyre | Renée Dunan |
| The Master | Hal P. Warren |

| | |
|---|---|
| Cristaldi | Miguel M. Delgado & Alfredo Salazar |
| **Co-Starring:** | |
| Tarzan | Edgar Rice Burroughs |
| Mowgli | Rudyard Kipling |
| John-Gor | Robert Moore Williams |
| Lt. Werper | Edgar Rice Burroughs |
| Paula Dupree | Ted Fithian, Neil P. Varnick, Griffin Jay & Henry Sucher |
| Felifax | Paul Féval, *fils* |
| Helene Kilgore | John Peter Drummond |
| Solomon Kane | Robert E. Howard |
| Cthulhu | H.P. Lovecraft |
| Azathoth | H.P. Lovecraft |
| Dagon | H.P. Lovecraft |
| Tcho-Tcho | H.P. Lovecraft |
| The Jermyns | H.P. Lovecraft |
| Yog-Sothoth | H.P. Lovecraft |
| Baal | Renée Dunan |
| Dracula | Bram Stoker |
| Manos | Hal P. Warren |
| **And:** | |
| Planet Vulcan | Urbain Le Verrier, Gene Roddenberry, David Whitaker |
| Memphre | John Peter Drummond |
| Karkosa | Ambrose Bierce, Robert W. Chambers, Philip José Farmer |
| Opar | Edgar Rice Burroughs |
| Kor | H. Rider Haggard |
| Mexican Gorilla City | XXX |
| Plateau of Leng | H.P. Lovecraft |
| Aklo Language | Arthur Machen |

**Adam Mudman BEZECNY** has been writing even before a race of ancient inner-earth aliens gave him the name of Mudman, which is his creed and sacred drive alike. Since then he has been a Multiversal witness in worlds of fiction both his own and of the cosmos of pulp stories and awful movies. He is currently looking for a publisher for several novels of original fiction set in his Multiverse, and recently graduated with a BA in English from the University of Minnesota Morris. This is his first contribution to *Tales of the Shadowmen*.

## The Evil Among Us

| Starring: | Created by: |
|---|---|
| Dr. John H. Watson | Arthur Conan Doyle |
| Jules Maigret | Georges Simenon |
| Mocata | Denis Wheatley |
| Abbé Jules Dervelle | Octave Mirbeau |
| Father Brown | G.K. Chesterton |
| Comte de Saint-Germain | Claude Farrère |

**Nicholas BOVING** lives in Toronto. He was formerly a mining engineer and traveled the world widely. He also worked from time to time as a docker, fruit inspector and forester. His books and screenplays draw on these experiences to provide characters, backgrounds and scenes. He is the author and publisher of the *Maxim Gunn* series of action/adventure books. He has also written some fifteen other novels and screenplays which follow the central character to countries and places where the forces of nature as much as people provide the conflict. He is a regular contributor to *Tales of the Shadowmen.*

## The House of El Hombre Loco

| Starring: | Created by: |
|---|---|
| Waldemar Daninsky | Jacinto Molina |
| | & Paul Naschy |
| Pete Dumond | Herman Cohen |
| | & Aben Kandel |
| Dr. Génessier | Jean Redon |
| Guido Anselmi | Federico Fellini |
| | & Ennio Flaiano |
| **The Fake Monsters:** | |
| Gourroull (Frankenstein Monster) | Mary Shelley |
| | & Jean-Claude Carrière |
| Princess Dala | Maurice Richlin |
| | & Blake Edwards |
| Eva | Jean Rollin |
| Blood Beast | Martin Varno |
| Metaluna Mutant | Raymond F. Jones |
| | Franklin Coen |
| | & Edward O'Callaghan |
| Knights from the East | Armando de Ossorio |
| **Co-Starring:** | |
| Christiane Génessier | Jean Redon |

**Nathan CABANISS** is a writer from Atlanta, GA who is slowly cultivating a career at this whole "writing" thing. His stories have appeared in *Voluted Tales, Cranial Leakage, Vol. 1, The Writer's Arena, The Vampire Almanac* (also from Black Coat Press), and *Fictionvale Magazine*. When not writing, he's usually reading whatever he can get his hands on or slowly whittling through his Netflix queue. He is a regular contributor to *Tales of the Shadowmen*.

## *Of Beasts and Men*

| Starring: | Created by: |
|---|---|
| Dr. Moreau | H.G. Wells |
| Felifax | Paul Féval, *fils* |
| Captain Silver | Guy d'Armen |
| **Co-Starring:** | |
| Dr. Cornelius Kramm | Gustave Le Rouge |
| Sir Eric Palmer | Paul Féval, *fils* |

**Christophe COLIN** is an accountant by day and a warrior of the imagination by night. He is 44-years-old and lives in Paris, France. He has written articles and fiction for the magazine *Présence d'Esprits*, and comics scripts for the Association Ganesha. He is also a member of Gallifrance, the French fan-club of *Doctor Who*. This is his first contribution to *Tales of the Shadowmen*.

## *Turning Point*

| Starring: | Created by: |
|---|---|
| Sergeant Bertrand Caillet (The Werewolf of Paris) | Guy Endore |
| Selene | Len Wiseman, Kevin Grevioux, Danny McBride |
| Sâr Dubnotal | *Anonymous* |
| Michael Corvin | Len Wiseman, Kevin Grevioux, Danny McBride |
| **Co-Starring:** | |
| Lucian | Len Wiseman, Kevin Grevioux, Danny McBride |

**Matthew DENNION** lives in South Jersey with his beautiful wife and daughters. He currently works as a teacher of students with autism at a Special Services School. Matthew writes giant monster stories for *G-Fan* magazine and he has recently published three giant monster novels, *Chimera: Scourge of the*

*Gods, Operation R.O.C.: A Kaiju Thriller* and *Atomic Rex*. Matthew is a regular contributor to *Tales of the Shadowmen*.

## *A Bond BetweenGentlemen*

| Starring: | Created by: |
|---|---|
| Arsène Lupin (Rostat) | Maurice Leblanc |
| A.J. Raffles | E. W. Hornung |
| Harry "Bunny" Manders | E. W. Hornung |
| All Others | Peter Gabbani |

**Peter GABBANI** lives in Sacramento, California with his wife, a 2nd grade teacher, and one-year-old son, Wolf. As a community college librarian, he has an MLIS and is completing an M.Ed. He also taught English in Korea for a couple years and then married his Korean co-teacher. He enjoys late-evening walks, Mountain Dew, and collecting books that his son will hopefully read one day. This is his first contribution to *Tales of the Shadowmen*.

## *The Stake and the Sickle*

| Starring: | Created by: |
|---|---|
| Boris Liatoukine | Marie Nizet |
| Von Bork | Arthur Conan Doyle |
| Polly Bird | Paul Féval |
| Kostaki | Alexandre Dumas |
| **Co-Starring:** | |
| Sherlock Holmes | Arthur Conan Doyle |
| Baron Vordenberg | based on Sheridan Le Fanu |
| Countess Marcian Grigoryi | Paul Féval |
| **Also Starring:** | |
| Raymond Collishaw | |
| General Denikin | |
| Baron Wrangel | |
| **And:** | |
| Selene, the Sepulchre | Paul Féval |

**Brian GALLAGHER** has a BA in Politics and Society and lives in London. He works in the media and for many years has written on the politics, economics and many other aspects of Croatia and has been quoted in Croatian and international media. In relation to that he has written extensively on Croatian-related cases at the International Criminal Tribunal for the Former Yugoslavia. He has always been interested in science fiction, classic horror, comics and is proud to be a lifelong *Doctor Who* fan. He is a regular contributor to *Tales of the Shadowmen*.

## *Rouletabille on Mysterious Island*

| Starring: | Created by: |
|---|---|
| Joseph Rouletabille | Gaston Leroux |
| Cyrus West/Cyrus Smith | Jules Verne & John Willard |
| Missy-Lou Pleasant | John Willard |
| James Worth | Martin Gately |
| Ian Hassett | Martin Gately |
| Dr. Grierson | Martin Gately |
| Neb Jr. (Nezzar) | based on Jules Verne |
| Hell-Cat Maggie | Martin Gately |
| Captain Englehorn | Merian C. Cooper |
| | & Edgar Wallace |
| | |
| **Co-Starring:** | |
| Hugo Danner | Philip Wylie |
| Anthony "Buck" Rogers | Philip Francis Nowlan |
| Captain Nemo | Jules Verne |
| Adam Worth/Captain Shard | Historical / |
| | George H. Plympton, |
| | Lewis Clay & Royal K. Cole |
| Rulu | George H. Plympton, |
| | Lewis Clay & Royal K. Cole |
| Kapitan Mors | *Anonymous* |
| The Lloigor | August Derleth |
| | & Mark Schorer |
| Sherlock Holmes | Arthur Conan Doyle |
| James West | Michael Garrison |
| Thunderbirds | Gerry & Sylvia Anderson |
| Predator | Jim & John Thomas |
| **And:** | |
| The Mysterious Island | Jules Verne |
| The Maracot Deep | Arthur Conan Doyle |

**Martin GATELY** is the author of the official prequel to Philip José Farmer's first novel – The Green Odyssey (*Samdroo and the Grassman* in *The Worlds of Philip José Farmer 4 – Voyages to Strange Days*). His writing career commenced in 1988 when he wrote for D C Thomson's legendary STARBLAZER comic book. He is also a contributor to the UK's journal of strange phenomena *Fortean Times.* For Black Coat Press, he has provided stories for the following anthologies: *Night of the Nyctalope, Harry Dickson Vs. The Spider* and *The*

*Vampire Almanac* Vol. 1 – as well as the Rouletabille *Nemo-Cycle* for *Tales of the Shadowmen*. His previously dilapidated mansion in Nottingham is now undergoing extensive refurbishment. Hallelujah.

## *The Case of the Curious Cadaver*

| Starring: | Created by: |
|---|---|
| Etienne Camparol | André Laurie |
| Doctor Omega | Arnould Galopin |
| Stella Astarte | Alfred Driou |
| Spiridon | André Laurie |
| Noel/Dara Luc | Travis Hiltz |
| | based on Bram Stoker |
| Inspector Ganimard | Maurice Leblanc |
| Janos Skorzeny | Jeff Rice |
| Abraham Van Helsing | Bram Stoker |
| The Giles Family | Joss Whedon |
| Doctor Seward | Bram Stoker |
| **Co-Starring:** | |
| The Red Leech | Arthur Conan Doyle |
| Antoine Gerpré | Alfred Driou |
| Arsène Lupin | Maurice Leblanc |
| C. Auguste Dupin | Edgar Allan Poe |
| Fantômas | P. Souvestre & M. Allain |

**Travis HILTZ** started making up stories at a young age. Years later, he began writing them down. In high school, he discovered that some writers actually got paid and decided to give it a try. He has since gathered a modest collection of rejection letters and had a one-act play produced. Travis lives in the wilds of New Hampshire with his very loving and tolerant wife, two above average children and a staggering amount of comic books and *Doctor Who* novels. He is a regular contributor to *Tales of the Shadowmen*.

## *The Tomb of the Veiled Prophet*

| Starring: | Created by: |
|---|---|
| Hadji Abdu (El Hichmakani) | Gaston Leroux |
| (Daroga) | & Richard Francis Burton |
| Erik | Gaston Leroux |
| Mokanna | Thomas Moore |
| | & Sax Rohmer |
| Shirin | Rick Lai |

**Co-Starring:**

| | |
|---|---|
| Abd Dhulma | G.G. Pendarves |
| Yog-Sothoth | H.P. Lovecraft |
| | & E. Hoffmann Price |
| Nug | H.P. Lovecraft |
| Yeb | H.P. Lovecraft |
| Great Old Ones | H.P. Lovecraft |
| Erlik | Robert W. Chambers |
| Yolgan | Robert E. Howard |
| Thulsa Doom | Robert E. Howard |
| Kathulos | Robert E. Howard |
| Rotah | Robert E. Howard |
| Mardanax | Lin Carter |
| Descales | David C. Smith |
| Attluma | David C. Smith |
| Maharani of Pankot | George Lucas |

**Also Starring:**
Anis-ed-Dowleh
Nasir-ed-Din
Richard Francis Burton

**And:**

| | |
|---|---|
| Black Litany | Joseph S. Pulver Sr. |
| Moon of Yian | Robert W. Chambers |

**Rick LAI** is an authority on pulp fiction and the Wold Newton Universe concepts of Philip José Farmer. His speculative articles have been collected in *Rick Lai's Secret Histories: Daring Adventurers*, *Rick Lai's Secret Histories: Criminal Masterminds*, *Chronology of Shadows: A Timeline of The Shadow's Exploits* and *The Revised Complete Chronology of Bronze*. Rick's fiction has been collected in *Shadows of the Opera*, *Shadows of the Opera: Retribution in Blood* and *Sisters of the Shadows: The Cagliostro Curse* (the last two titles are available from Black Coat Press). He has also translated Arthur Bernède's *Judex* and *The Return of Judex* into English for Black Coat Press. Rick resides in Bethpage, New York, with his wife and children. He is a regular contributor to *Tales of the Shadowmen*.

## The Adventure of the Orcival Rain

| **Starring:** | **Created by:** |
|---|---|
| Sherlock Holmes | Arthur Conan Doyle |
| John H. Watson | Arthur Conan Doyle |
| Jean Saint-Clair | Jean de La Hire |
| Lecoq | Emile Gaboriau |

293

Gouroull                          Jean-Claude Carrière
                                  based on Mary Shelley

**Nigel MALCOLM** lives in Kent, England. He works as a teacher of English as a Foreign Language. He is a long-term *Doctor Who, Star Trek* and *Prisoner* fan—long before all the new-fangled versions came along. He is still working on that elusive steampunk novel and various short stories. He is a regular contributor to *Tales of the Shadowmen.*

## *Behind the Mask of the Ripper*

| Starring: | Created by: |
|---|---|
| Sherlock Holmes | Arthur Conan Doyle |
| John H. Watson | Arthur Conan Doyle |
| Lestrade | Arthur Conan Doyle |
| Gregson | Arthur Conan Doyle |
| Patterson | Arthur Conan Doyle |
| Harry Dickson | *Anonymous* |
| Tom Wills | *Anonymous* |
| **Co-Starring:** | |
| Dr. Drum | *Anonymous* |
| Count Dragomin | *Anonymous* |
| **Also Starring:** | |
| George Bernard Shaw | |
| Charles Warren | |

**Jean-Marc MOUILLER** lives a quiet and discreet life in a small village in Southern France, between his 800 books and his family, including two children adopted in Colombia. His favorite authors are Fredric Brown, Ambrose Bierce, Robert Sheckley, Poul Anderson, Jack Vance, Terry Pratchett and the often much underestimared Jack Ritchie. This is his first contribution to *Tales of the Shadowmen.*

## *Justice and the Beast*

| Starring: | Created by: |
|---|---|
| Dr. Cornelius Kramm | Gustave Le Rouge |
| Professor Tornada | André Couvreur |
| Felanthus | Christofer Nigro |
| | based on Paul Féval, *fils* |
| Judex | A. Bernède & L. Feuillade |
| Cocantin/Licorice Kid | A. Bernède & L. Feuillade |
| Mole People | Laszlo Gorog |

| | |
|---|---|
| Triffids | John Wyndham |
| Octaman | Harry Essex |
| Zinj apes | Michael Crichton |
| Colonel Bozzo-Corona | Paul Féval |
| **Co-Starring:** | |
| Fritz Kramm | Gustave Le Rouge |
| Deep Ones | H.P. Lovecraft |
| Dr. Alex Zorka | Wyllis Cooper |
| | & George H. Plympton |
| Dr. Nolter | Edward Mann |
| | & Robert D. Weinbach |
| Gouroull | Jean-Claude Carrière |
| | & Mary Shelley |
| Felifax | Paul Féval, *fils* |
| Preda-plants | Aben Kandel & Herman Cohen |
| Black Orchid | Don Rico |
| Black Swamp Flower | Don Rico |
| Phantom of the Opera | Gaston Leroux |
| Kongoid apes | Merian C. Cooper, |
| | Edgar Wallace, Leon Gordon, |
| | James Ashmore Creelman |
| | & Ruth Rose |
| **And:** | |
| Incandescent silicate | Laszlo Gorog |
| Subterranean Sumeria | Laszlo Gorog |
| Kingdom of Zinj | Michael Crichton |
| Mangani | Edgar Rice Burroughs |
| Lemuria / Atlantis | Concepts from Mark Brown |

**Christofer NIGRO** is a writer of both fiction and non-fiction with a strong interest in pulps, comic books and fantastic cinema, and a regular contributor to *Tales of the Shadowmen*. He may be known to some by his websites *The Godzilla Saga* and *The Warrenverse*, as he is an authority on the subject of *dai kaiju eiga* (the sub-genre of cinema specializing in giant monsters), and the characters featured in the comic magazines published by Warren. He has recently revived and expanded Chuck Loridans' classic site MONSTAAH, and has since been published in the anthologies *Aliens Among Us* and *Carnage: After the Fall*.

## *The Inn of the First Voyage*

| **Starring:** | **Created by:** |
|---|---|
| Long John Silver | Robert Louis Stevenson |

**Also Starring:**
Surcouf

**Pierrick RIVAL** lives in Nantes, France, where he teaches French in a secondary school. In his spare time, he is a proof-reader, an oboe player for the rock band Cherche-Lune, as well as a member of a teaching union. He's passionate about reading and role-playing games. His bookshelves are filled with French and English authors, with a marked preference for fantasy, supernatural, science fiction and adventure literature. This is his first contribution to *Tales of the Shadowmen*.

## Ancient Space Lizards and Other Visitors

| Starring: | Created by: |
|---|---|
| Jean Kariven | Jimmy Guieu |
| Gussie Fink-Nottle | P.G. Wodehouse |
| The Sontarans | Roberty Holmes |
| The Polarians | Jimmy Guieu |
| M. Ming | Henri Vernes |
| **Co-Starring:** | |
| Duke of Denver | Dorthy L. Sayers |
| Bertie Wooster | P.G. Wodehouse |
| The Denebians | Jimmy Guieu |
| The Rutan Host | Robert Holmes |
| | & Terrance Dicks |

**Frank SCHILDINER** has been a pulp fan since a friend gave him a gift of Phillip Jose Farmer's *Tarzan Alive*. Since that time, he has written his first novel, *The Quest of Frankenstein*, for Black Coat Press. He has had stories published in *The New Adventures of Thunder Jim Wade*, *Secret Agent X* Volumes 3 And 4 and *Ravenwood, Stepson of Mystery*, *The Black Bat Mystery*, *The New Adventures of Richard Knight* and *The Avenger: The Justice Files*. He is a Senior Probation Officer in New Jersey and a martial arts instructor at Amorosi's Mixed Martial Arts. Frank resides in New Jersey with his wife Gail who is his top supporter. He is a regular contributor to *Tales of the Shadowmen*.

## The Eldritch Stones

| Starring: | Created by: |
|---|---|
| Sâr Dubnotal | *Anonymous* |
| Frank Chandler (Chandu) | Harry Earnshaw, |
| | & R. R. Morgan |
| | & Vera Oldham |

| | |
|---|---|
| Hareton Ironcastle | J.-H. Rosny *Aîné* |
| Prof. William Channing Webb | H.P. Lovecraft |
| Francis Xavier Gordon (El Borak) | Robert E. Howard |
| Zenith | Anthony Skene |
| The Mi-Go | H.P. Lovecraft |
| Sexton Blake | Harry Blyth |
| Dracula | Bram Stoker |
| Annunciata Gianetti | *Anonymous* |
| **Co-Starring:** | |
| Sydney Guthrie | J.-H. Rosny *Aîné* |
| Roxor | Harry Earnshaw, |
| | & R. R. Morgan |
| | & Vera Oldham |
| Tsathoggua | Clark Ashton Smith |
| Hastur | Ambrose Bierce |
| **And:** | |
| The Gun Club | Jules Verne |
| Khokarsa | Philip José Farmer |
| Opar | Edgar Rice Burroughs |
| Carcosa | Ambrose Bierce |
| Yuggoth | H.P. Lovecraft |
| *The Book of Eibon* | Clark Ashton Smith |
| Taduki | H. Rider Haggard |
| The Staff of Solomon | Robert E. Howard |
| Solomon Kane | H. Rider Haggard |

**Sam SHOOK** is a 20-year-old university student majoring in history, and he would not be caught dead without a nice outfit and a hat. An actor, fencer, singer, and panpipe player, he has always been a bit different from the rest of his friends in Oklahoma. While most of them like things such as hunting or cars, he has always enjoyed reading and writing. He has been creating stories from a young age for the entertainment of himself and others. Through those simple tales he honed his skills, and he decided to make a career out of it. He is a regular contributor to *Tales of the Shadowmen*.

## The Submarine "Le Rouge"

| **Starring:** | **Created by:** |
|---|---|
| Tony Fowler | Gustave Le Rouge |
| William Boltyn | Gustave Le Rouge |
| Doctor Moreau | H. G. Wells |
| The Martians | H. G. Wells |

**Also Starring:**
Camille Flammarion

**Michel STEPHAN** was born and lives in Brittany with his wife and two children. He has been a fan of science fiction, fantasy and horror since age 10. He loves Universal monster movies (especially the *Frankenstein* series), sci-fi serials and collects Aurora model kits. He has recently written a new *Madame Atomos* novel for Black Coat Press's French sister imprint, Rivière Blanche, and is a regular contributor to *Tales of the Shadowmen*.

## *Leonox Meets Mephista*

| Starring: | Created by: |
|---|---|
| Edwige Hossegor | Maurice Limat |
| Baron Tragny | Maurice Limat |
| Teddy Verano | Maurice Limat |
| Mephista | Maurice Limat |
| Olga Mervil | Maurice Limat |
| Francis Dalvant (Lacana) | Paul Béra |
| Lisa | Paul Béra |
| Mr. Mower | Paul Béra |
| Leonox | Paul Béra |

**Artikel UNBEKANNT** (not his real name!) lives in western France and is the author of several short stories published by Black Coat Press' sister imprint, Rivière Blanche, as well as a horror novel, *Bloodfist*, released in 2013.

## *The White Star of Atlantis*

| Starring: | Created by: |
|---|---|
| Arsène Lupin (Duc de Charmerace) | Maurice Leblanc |
| Leo Vincey | H. Rider Haggard |
| Terence O'Rourke | Joeph Louis Vance |
| Antinea | Pierre Benoit |
| Lt. de Saint-Avit | Pierre Benoit |
| **Co-Starring:** | |
| Joséphine Balsamo | Maurice Leblanc |
| Morhange | Pierre Benoit |
| Eg-Anteouen | Pierre Benoit |
| Ayesha | H. Rider Haggard |

**David L. VINEYARD** is a fifth generation Texan (named for his gunfighter/Texas Ranger great grand-father) currently living in Oklahoma City, OK, where the tornadoes come sweeping down the plains. He has useless degrees in history, politics, and economics, and is the author of several tales about Buenos Aires private eye Johnny Sleep, two novels, several short stories, some journalism, and various non-fiction. He is currently working on several ideas while battling with a three month old kitten for household dominance and the keyboard of his PC. He is a regular contributor to *Tales of the Shadowmen*.

## *The Piano Maidens*

| Starring: | Created by: |
|---|---|
| Eugenie Danglars | Alexandre Dumas |
| Louise d'Armilly | Alexandre Dumas |
| Count Corbucci | E. W. Hornung |
| Annibal Gioja | Paul Féval |
| The de Felipones | P.-A. Ponson du Terrail |
| Colonel Bozzo-Corona | Paul Féval |
| Fanchette | Paul Féval |
| Père Rodin | Eugène Sue |
| Ricardo DiLaurentis | based on Sara Shepard |
| **Co-Starring:** | |
| Baron Danglars | Alexandre Dumas |
| Comte de Monte-Cristo | Alexandre Dumas |
| Jean-Baptiste Schwartz | Paul Féval |
| Lecoq | Paul Féval |
| Lord Ruthven | J.W. Polidori |
| Comtesse Cagliostro | Maurice Leblanc |

**Jared WELCH** lives in Racine, WI. He is a fan of *Pretty Little Liars*, DC Comics, Paul Féval, Alexandre Dumas, *Annie On My Mind* and *Good Moon Rising* by Nancy Garden, The Animes *Pokemon, Sailor Moon, Noir, Madlax, Code Geass, Death Note, Revolutionary Girl Utena, Rose of Versailles*, and the *Star Wars* prequels. He is currently working on a few plays, novels and has blogs online where he discusses various topics under the name JaredMithrandir. He is a regular contributor to *Tales of the Shadowmen*.

Lightning Source UK Ltd.
Milton Keynes UK
UKOW02f1913251116

288584UK00001B/204/P